Three Pa...

PHOTO CREDIT Kajri A

SHAILAJA BAJPAI works as a journalist. She is currently with *The Indian Express*. She has been involved in media research and is co-author of the book *The Impact of Television Advertising on Children*.

THREE PARTS DESIRE

SHAILAJA BAJPAI

HarperCollins *Publishers* India
a joint venture with
THE INDIA TODAY GROUP
New Delhi

First published in India in 2011 by
HarperCollins *Publishers* India
a joint venture with
The India Today Group

Copyright © Shailaja Bajpai 2011

ISBN: 978-81-7223-820-9

2 4 6 8 10 9 7 5 3 1

Shailaja Bajpai asserts the moral right
to be identified as the author of this work.

This is a work of fiction and all characters and events described in it
are the product of the author's imagination. Any resemblance to actual persons,
living or dead, is entirely coincidental.

All rights reserved. No part of this publication may be reproduced,
stored in a retrieval system, or transmitted, in any form or by any means,
electronic, mechanical, photocopying, recording or otherwise,
without the prior permission of the publishers.

HarperCollins *Publishers*
A-53, Sector 57, Noida 201301, India
77-85 Fulham Palace Road, London W6 8JB, United Kingdom
Hazelton Lanes, 55 Avenue Road, Suite 2900, Toronto, Ontario M5R 3L2
and 1995 Markham Road, Scarborough, Ontario M1B 5M8, Canada
25 Ryde Road, Pymble, Sydney, NSW 2073, Australia
31 View Road, Glenfield, Auckland 10, New Zealand
10 East 53rd Street, New York NY 10022, USA

Typeset in 11/14 Bembo
InoSoft Systems

Printed and bound at
Thomson Press (India) Ltd.

In memory of my parents, Kamala and Uma Bajpai

The sound of laughter. Smoked. Like a cigarette just extinguished.
Then the voice.
'You are mistaken. I don't owe you, you owe me …' In her right hand, she dangled the bill between her long, bony fingers. With her left, she plied back her thick hair so that it fanned out against her neck. Her pallu slid slowly down her arm and with practised ease, she swept it across her shoulder at the precise moment it threatened to slip down the slope of her bosom. She stared straight at the young, slick-haired shop assistant, mocking him a challenge.

The assistant was concave, imli-chutney brown with a charcoal smudge moustache and an Adam's apple straining out of his neck. He wore a black shirt and black trousers with a thick brown leather belt around the waist. He stood behind the counter, and Kartik noticed how he sought to unnerve the customer by piercing her breasts with his gaze.

She heaved, waited, her body arched, a bow strung tightly for release. The assistant's head snapped back and he looked into her eyes. What he saw stimulated an erection so taut, the zip of his skin-tight trousers started down. Kartik wanted to laugh out aloud.

Instead, he observed the assistant go limp and hand her back the change that she snatched at in triumph. He stood there immobile, between the stall of historical books and the magazine rack, watching the shop assistant meekly reduce his discomfiture in a corner of the shop with hands groping at his trousers' fly.

Something clutched at his heart. Was it a part of the past that refused to release him?

The sound of her voice, the breeze of her hair. The twenty-year-old girl he had once known.

'Will you always love me?' she had demanded then, her eyes wild in the reflection of his. The glass panes of the single window in his room were arms flung open to welcome the nightlight as the moon projected the steel bars of the grill across their bodies, strapping them together on the bed.

'Will you?' she had repeated like a threat, banging his head on the pillow.

'Always,' he had agreed.

In that instance, he would have pledged to her his ancestral property, his name (which she didn't ask for), and his pounding heart. He was overwhelmed by her: by her hair on his tickled nipples, by the curving line of her lips, which he could erase with a rub of his thumb, by the glow of her eyes, shining as if polished with a yellow felt cloth.

Kartik inhaled the memory of her.

Dark glasses protected his eyes from the brightness of hers, blazing with her victory over the shop assistant. 'Like …' she began, then halted. 'The Indian male is a raw …' she stuffed the money back into her black bag, '… egg: firm on the outside, pil-pilla inside.'

'Hard but soft,' agreed Kartik, automatically.

'Would you help me carry these?' she asked, nodding at the pile of books, 'or are we going to stand here exchanging clever remarks?'

Her eyes were sunny but didn't quite acknowledge him. He stood aside. She shrugged and walked away with her purchases. The shop assistant, back from his massage, smiled nastily. Kartik stood his ground, beginning a mental count of how long he should wait before going in search of her.

'Fifty-one,' he called out, 'and your fly is open.'

He discovered her at the dry-cleaners.

'Shall we go?' He blew boldly on the exposed skin of her back. He thought he felt her indecision rise with the fine strands of hair along her nape.

'Thank you. I have a cab waiting.'

He reached to take her arm. She jerked it off. He held out his hands for her parcels.

'I don't like the indecisive type,' she remarked, walking away.

He suddenly realized that this was a game she was playing and decided to go along. They had reached her taxi.

'Would you mind giving me a ride?' he inquired, with exaggerated politeness. 'It's not like you don't know me.'

She turned, very slowly.

'Oh, I know you,' she said, tracing her upper lip with her tongue, 'only too well.'

She gave him her fingers; he clasped her hand. Soft, the lines on her palm, a map of her life. As he thumbed them, she withdrew her hand. Then she climbed into the back seat and slammed the door of the Ambassador. He fell back. The taxi trembled into first gear. As it began to move away, she reached across and flung open the other door.

Kartik climbed in, smiled at her haughty expression.

The taxi clattered into motion. He leaned back, saw her turn away from him to face the open window, and thought, wistfully, that the bookshop had been witness to significant moments in their relationship. This is where they had reunited a year earlier; this is where she had proposed to him one July when they had hurried into Bahri Sons, steamed by the heat of a monsoon evening.

KARTIK
1976

Steamed by the heat of a monsoon evening, the sky was a translucent liquid grey with the sliver of the moon an eyelash on the back of the hand, ready to be blown away by a wish. A lozenge sun streaked peach across the mercury sky.

Kartik stood outside Frank Antony School, a few minutes' walk away from her college, LSR. Lady Shri Ram. 'Be there under the lovers' lampost,' Baby had instructed, giggling at the description of the tube lit street. Under its milky, neon glaze, Kartik noticed his companion. Young men, men in love, frequently stood here expecting a girl from LSR to join them. Dressed in a tomato-red shirt and brown bell-bottom trousers, this young man regarded his pointed and polished black shoes intently. Occasionally, he flashed a hand across his right buttock, whipped out a small, black comb and fanned it through his hair.

Is he me, am I he? Kartik cupped the match flame to his cigarette and contemplated the gathering clouds.

His companion hid his head (and real intentions) in Sartre's *Iron in the Soul*. Kartik was astonished at the choice: the guy didn't look Jean Paul's type at all. Mr Bell-bottoms did not glance at Kartik even once. In fact, at no point while they stood together beneath the steely blaze did either acknowledge the other's presence – a tacit, unstated understanding between men waiting for their girls.

Twenty minutes later, Kartik recognized the white chikan kurta with its generous cleavage. The red-and-yellow tie-and-dye chunni she wore fell to the left and her hair trailed behind, never catching up, as she ran towards him. His pink-and-white floral shirt was moist. So were his armpits.

Kartik scowled at her as she approached. Baby smiled, apologized. She danced her eyes over to his male companion.

'You have much better taste in women.' She grazed his ear, bit the lobe.

He heard an appreciative whistle and saw Mr Bell-bottoms wink at him.

'Why, you …' Kartik turned to rebuke him but Baby grabbed him by the arm so urgently, his reluctant body followed.

Before he knew it, they were seated in a three-wheeler, streaking down towards Moolchand. Clutching his arm to her like a closely guarded secret, Baby turned her head outward to the warm and heavy wet air. Kartik eyed her glumly: his irritation with Baby and Mr Bell-bottoms could not rise above the snore of the scooter, so he sat there envious of her ability to give a part of herself to him through the physical touch of her hand, her body lining his, while her mind and emotions were scattered elsewhere by the wind against her face. Kartik felt jealous, possessive, hot with ill usage.

He didn't much like the smell of himself.

Red light at Def. Col. A navel appeared level with Baby's nose. It belonged to a blackened male torso, naked, and with an orange-and-green checked lungi tied at the waist. The man held out an empty aluminium cheese tin in his right hand. His left arm was the spindle of a rolling pin.

'Baby-ji, Baby-ji, give the poor some money.' The words sprang out of thick lips in the young, unlined face, eyes bright, not supplicant. 'Baby-ji, Baby-ji, your child will live a long and prosperous life,' the man repeated, and when Baby still didn't reply, he offered a final inducement: 'Baby-ji, your pappu will live to be a hundred!'

Baby jutted out her face, close to the man's.

'But I'm not even married.' She drew back in merriment.

The man was nonplussed.

'Never mind, it will happen,' he promised hastily, rattling the tin. But time had run out for him: the air suddenly became thick with the fumes of engines; the signal turned green. The three-wheeler rattled into action, leaving the man stranded in the moving traffic, and raced away.

They seemed to fly till Lodhi Hotel but near the Oberoi, the scooter spluttered, staggered and came to a halt. The driver couldn't revive it; so Baby and Kartik alighted and tried to hail passing autos. Each one refused. At the hotel's entrance they found a scooter stand, with half a dozen vehicles. But none of the drivers agreed to take them on the short journey to Khan Market.

'I'll take down your numbers and report you all to the police, bloody ...' Kartik warned, ignoring Baby's restraining 'no, no'.

The scooterwallahs smirked.

'What are you laughing at, you, you spider?' spat Kartik, seizing a sniggering man by the shirt collar.

'Oh, please. Don't.' Baby pleaded and pulled at his hand. 'Do you want to see me murdered or raped, here and now?'

The vein dividing her forehead protruded as Baby tried to make her tense mouth stretch into a smile.

Kartik couldn't think. Certainly, his response was disproportionate to the incident but all he wanted was to stay, fight, crash his white-knuckled fists into each one of those insolent faces. Baby swivelled and marched away.

A moment later, the evening was rent by a painful howl: the scooter-driver had bitten Kartik's thumb.

Kartik released his shirt, sucked at the bleeding thumb and spat on the road. I am not about to swallow his spit, Kartik told himself worriedly, better get a tetanus shot. God knows where his mouth has been. The scooter-drivers watched him, hands twitching inside their trouser pockets, fingers snaking up their nostrils with the same pleasure as an act of penetration.

'Ja, ja ...' they dismissed him.

Kartik stumbled backwards, right, left, right, left ... Their surly faces blurred in the intensity of his emotions. He lifted his middle finger and buggered them.

Then he turned and ran after Baby. His throat ached, his skin felt like the damp earth after a sudden downpour, moist with the rising warm odour of his body. Baby's kurta was translucent with the sweat on the small of her back. Kartik passed her, halted a few feet ahead and hung out his thumb.

'What?' she asked.

'He bit me,' he replied.

She sprayed him with her laughter. He fisted his hands into his pockets and strode ahead, her mirth echoing in his ears. They continued the rest of the walk in silence: hers amused, his mortified. They reached Khan Market twenty minutes after turning down Cornwallis Road. As they reached its front of shops, Baby and Kartik plunged into the one straight ahead. Bahri Sons.

'Why did you tell that beggar you weren't married?' Kartik demanded as they moved towards the stationery counter.

'Well, I'm not, am I?'

Baby turned to the bookshelves.

'Yes, but why did you have to tell him that?'

He was behind her, so close his words disturbed her hair. She pulled out a heavy book and turned its pages mechanically.

'It's not as if he was really interested,' Kartik added, hot, angry saliva collecting in the well of his mouth.

'And you are?' she replied, her body stiff and alert. 'Is this then a proposal of marriage?'

She turned to face him, her eyes unblinking as the old man's in the photograph on the cover of the book in her hands.

He ought to have remembered then: remembered how she took the most important decisions of her life at random, unmindful of consequences, moved only by the moment. And he should have answered, 'Yes, it is, and will you?'

Instead, he replied flippantly, 'Sure. Shall we make a bonfire of these books and dance around it seven times?'

Baby glared, then pushed past him.

Kartik lurched back into the present as the driver braked the taxi abruptly at the red light after Khan Market to avoid a collision with a bullock.

He watched Lodhi Gardens glide past as they picked up speed.

'It was here that you told me you preferred New York to me,' he remarked, 'just like that.' He snapped his fingers. 'I can picture the exact spot above the bridge where you stood. I remember throwing pebbles up into the air and watching them fall into the canal without causing a ripple – it was dry. I felt as ineffectual …'

He remembered it all with the sharpness of a pinprick and a pain no less acute in its memory. Like a bruise, he thought, you press and the wound reappears. She gave him her eyes.

He looked away. She still had the power to enrapture him just as she had the first time they had met.

They had been truants then, two teenagers on the run: Kartik from being the dutiful son his father wanted him to be, Baby from the mother she didn't want.

Didi.

'You know,' remarked Kartik suddenly, thinking aloud, 'but for your mother, we would not be together today.'

Baby replied without turning, 'She has a lot to answer for.'

'Well, but she's satisfied you now,' he remonstrated.

Baby slid across and rested her head against his outstretched arm. Then she laughed: that smoky, thick laughter which always vibrated in the pit of his stomach.

'With Amma you never know. I wouldn't be surprised if there's something she's still hoarding. She's always so secretive. Okay,' she added briskly, 'let's concentrate on what we have to do now that you are out of jail.'

He listened to her but without hearing a word. Once again, he thought wryly, she had with great deftness steered the conversation away from Didi.

She complained that her mother was evasive. Kartik disagreed. The first time he had met her, Didi had been uncommonly frank – to a fault – and willing to answer all his questions.

That's where this story had begun.

One early morning with a lean brown dog.

KARTIK
1978

A lean brown dog pushed his wet black nose directly into the divide of his trousers.

'Om bhur bhuvasvah,' Kartik began in whispered anxiety as his body coiled into stiffness. 'Om tat ...'

'He won't bite; dogs smell to identify people.'

Kartik swivelled around so abruptly, the dog's snout swerved off the edge of his knee. After a dismissive shake of its body, it retreated to the comfort of the shaded veranda and closed its eyes.

Kartik stared at the figure in front of him: straight, graying hair parted to the right, reaching the nape. The startling pink of the scalp beneath the thinning hair. Eyes a clear dark brown, nose straight and proud as an ancient monument, lips full with a thin line scarring the top left corner as though an artist had run a sharpened nail through wet paint. And the skin, unblemished, unlined. Kartik's eyes travelled down. The feet were shrouded in double-knit black socks and thrust carelessly into a pair of chappals.

'I feel cold,' she said.

Kartik licked his dry, half-open mouth. His palms were sweaty; he rubbed them against the side of his trousers, did a namaste and then offered her his right hand.

'I'm Kartik.'

'You know I know that.'

'I suppose Baby mentioned me.'

'Talked of, wrote about, photographed and framed.'

'Oh.' A foolish giggle escaped him.

'So.' She stood holding one frame of the door open. 'Why are you here?'

'Hey bhagvan, this Didi of mine never had any manners.'

The voice preceded its owner's appearance in the doorway. Kartik smiled in recognition. Sita. She carried a silver tray and brushed past the woman who stood in her way. 'Even as a child, she was so rude.'

'I merely asked him what he is doing here.'

'At least let him brakefaast before you start,' retorted Sita. 'Sit, beta, sit. What would you like to eat? Egg-omelette or Sita's special stuffed parathas?'

'Who's invited him to stay?'

Kartik asked if he might use the toilet. She nodded him inside without giving directions. Kartik entered the house, then shivered and sprang back in alarm. The sun's beam had lit up a leopard's head that dangled from the wall facing him: its pelt had been nailed to the ceiling. He hastened down the cool corridor to an empty bedroom and found his way to the bathroom. At the basin, he slapped water on his face and into his eyes till the whites reddened in response. Glaring at his reflection, he recalled that on his first and only visit two years earlier, his eyes had been equally bloodshot.

On that occasion, Baby and he had travelled up by train without a reservation. It was the first week of October, the Dusshera holidays; and Baby had said she had to eat home-cooked food, or else. Kartik had been reluctant to accompany her, wishing to avoid a meeting with the mother she spoke of so distantly, as if they did not share the closest relationship in the world. But Baby dismissed his scruples, saying her mother was away.

With no berths available, they had sat up all night in the open doorway of the coach, the air blowing cigarette smoke back into their faces.

Next morning, upon arrival at the house, he had encountered Sita in the veranda. She was small, round of face, rotund of figure, with a large gold nose ring and shining black eyes.

'Baby! Oh my Baby!' Sita had stumbled forward, clapping her creased hands and pressing their warmth to her cheeks. Seeing Kartik, she had looked from Baby to him, then put out an open palm and slapped it over her mouth in mock horror.

Kartik apologized for arriving 'just like that'.

She patted him on the back.

'What would you like to eat? Omelette-egg or Sita's special parathas?'

The next two days had been spent in the warmth of a strong sun, with aimless conversation, chilled Rosy Pelican beer and Sita's comfort food: omelette-eggs, stuffed parathas, pakoras and chutney.

On the morning of their departure for Delhi, Kartik had sat out in the veranda, straight and stiff in the easy chair. Baby came and flopped down beside him. A bullock sauntered up to the gate, stopped and peered in at the two of them, then plodded on with a dismissive twitch of his tail. Kartik breathed in the cool air, eyes steadfast on the gate.

'So? What will it be this morning – are we going to fight, not speak to each other, or …' Baby blew him a kiss.

He turned away, reached for the Wills Navy Cut packet and lit a cigarette.

'Don't you know how to behave even in your own house?' he asked. The night before, their lofty, idealistic discussion on the state of the nation had descended into petty recriminations about their relationship. Now, he was in no mood for her.

She stole the cigarette from his fingers, reached for his untouched cup of tea.

'Is this going to be the pattern of our relationship?' she asked. 'You playing the hurt one and me doing all the making up?'
She tugged at a lock of his hair.
'Baby, stop troubling him,' Sita ordered from the doorway.
Baby turned.
'This spoilt boy, Sita, is sulking.'
Sita looked fondly at the Sulk.
'Only because of you, Baby.'
'Oh, Sita, I cannot always be responsible for him.'
'But that is your duty,' replied Sita, curling Baby's thick hair about her ears. 'Every wife must look after her husband.'
'I'm not his wife,' Baby replied, taking Sita's fat hands and chafing them against hers.
'You will be, you will be.'

Kartik wiped his soggy features on his shirtsleeve and studied himself in the bathroom mirror. Baby had been right about that, she hadn't married him.
He returned to the veranda, irresolute, when he felt a cool breath on the nape of his neck. Didi walked past him into the garden. She bent to remove wilting leaves from a potted plant. Kartik went to stand behind her. She smelt of warmed mustard oil.
'May I stay?'
She laughed. Baby's laugh.
'What would you do if I said "no"?'
'I'd go into town, eat at a restaurant, sleep on a bench at the station and catch the night train back to Delhi.'
She turned.
'Maybe that is why Baby left you. You are impetuous, too quick to feel a slight,' she observed, starting up the veranda steps, 'too sensitive to stand out in the strong sun.'
The next morning, Kartik was awakened by the complete absence of sound. It had rained all night, and even in those intervals when day and night meet. It came down in a flurry before it eased into a

steady rhythm. He had become so accustomed to the tap-tapping, he awoke the instant it stopped.

A sunbeam broke through the thick foliage of mango trees and fell on the gravel path leading up to the house. Nothing stirred but raindrops. Standing outside, Kartik breathed gently, not wanting to disturb the morning with his breath. A solitary grey-black bird sailed gracefully across the blue expanse, a dinghy on a calm sea. Tiny insects and bigger buzzards floated sluggishly, as though on the surface of water. Dahlias drooped from the relentless drenching. Golden showers fell like wet ringlets from hanging planters; red fireballs, yellow dahlias, orange nasturtiums and pink roses lined the steps of the house.

Suddenly, there was a commotion.

Kartik heard the squawking of parrots: Sita had strewn grains on the patio and the lime-green birds were snapping up the seeds. The gardener's young son came around the corner of the cottage and in one twirl, the birds pirouetted into the trees.

'You should see them when the litchies are in fruit,' said the boy, 'then they are eating and eating – they never completely finish one. They're very greedy.' He laughed, picking up a few pebbles and juggling them from hand to hand. 'They take a bite here and then one there.'

'At night you won't be able to sleep,' added Sita, from behind Kartik, 'the fruit bats are on the prowl and the litchi gatherers sit under the trees beating drums, singing and making awful sounds from their throats, to frighten them away.'

'How long does this go on?' Kartik inquired, alarmed.

'Oh, about a month,' replied Sita, examining a strand of her hair.

He was an obedient guest at Didi's. He stayed out of the sun. He sat in the veranda, drinking Sita's ginger tea or rum, the Old Monk rum he had purchased from a nearby market. At night, Didi would join him. Diplomat whisky. She would measure it out in tablespoons and add just enough water to fill half of the crystal tumbler. She circulated each mouthful before swallowing. When her glass was drained, she'd pour herself another. She seldom touched a third.

'I drink because I enjoy the taste, not because I want to move something inside.' She stared at Kartik hunched over his rum. 'Not because I wish to forget. My memories are the only things I'll take with me when I go.'

She coughed. Kartik asked why she didn't take a syrup.

'An allergy, that's all,' she answered. The second night, when the cough was a constant reminder of her wakefulness, he heard a sleepy Sita react.

'Why don't you take mixture and let Sita sleep?'

'What else do you do apart from sleeping?'

'Hai hai, Mem, only listen to this ungrateful tongue,' retorted Sita.

'Go to sleep, Sita.'

'Who can sleep with you?'

'Then don't sleep with me. Go away.'

'You have the biggest fan here and you want me to go under the small one?'

'Go buy yourself a big one, then. You have saved enough money to buy one made of gold. But will you spend a paisa? No, not you, not Sita. You will live off me until I die.'

'And *after* that too!' exclaimed Sita. 'May Bhagvan grant me forgiveness for saying that.'

'Not likely, but He may grant me some peace and quiet if only you would go away.'

A door slammed.

Outside, Kartik raised his glass to the squabbling women, then returned to his contemplation of the black-etched leaves, motionless against the still night. He wondered whether trees slept. When the wind shook them up, when a heavy downpour battered them, did they experience pain? Like he did since Baby had left him?

He heard a bed complain. 'It's nearly three.'

He turned to see a pale sari in the doorway.

'Can't sleep.'

She came out and sat down beside him.

'Didi, Didi,' he recited. 'Don't you have names in your family?' Before she could reply, he added, 'Mem, Didi, Baby – who is Mem?'

'My mother,' said Didi, 'short for Memsahib. Everyone called her that. Even Father.'

'And you, Didi? What's your real name?'

'Real name? Would it make any difference to who I am?' She squinted at him in the dark. 'It's the only name I've had since I was born.'

'That's funny.'

'What else can you expect from Sita?'

Sita had named her Didi. Sita, who came to Mem's house, the ten-year-old daughter of driver Biru's dead sister.

'Mem, please keep this orphan with you.' Biru stood in front of his mistress with folded hands. There was Sita in a satin ochre blouse that was loose and too long, and a purple lehenga, scraping one ankle against the other, chewing the end of the yellow dupatta that covered her head. She looked at Mem with bright appreciation in her black pupils.

'Nahin, Biru, what will I do with a little girl?'

Biru aimed his hands at Mem's feet.

'Please, memsahib,' he entreated. 'What will I do with her? If she is bad, you can throw her away.'

'Hai Ram, Biru!' Mem exclaimed. 'You have not given birth, or you would not talk so. No woman could say that,' added Mem, who had lost two sons in premature deliveries.

So Sita stayed.

When Mem gave birth to a girl, it became one of Sita's duties to rock the child's cot. Sita liked to sing and wanted to sing to the baby.

'But Mamaji,' she asked her uncle during a visit to his quarter, 'what shall I call her? She is like a little doll! Shall I call her Gudiya?'

'You show some respect, otherwise Mem will throw you away,' warned Mami. 'Your uncle has given pe-misshun.'

'No, she won't,' wailed Sita. 'Mem is not like you.'

'Chup, chudail.' Biru clamped his hand on her mouth.

Sita pulled away from her uncle and stuck out her tongue at Mami's bent-over bottom.

'Didi,' she announced in defiance of the bottom. 'Mem's daughter is the Didi of the house, no?'

'Didi means older sister, idiot-girl,' Mami's bottom replied, 'and you are eleven years older than the child.'

'Didi, Didi,' trilled Sita as she ran back to the main house.

Kartik laughed at the story.

'Mystery solved. But why is Baby called Baby?' he asked.

Didi knuckled her nose.

'All little girls are called Baby until they marry. Besides, I couldn't think of a name that would suit her. So Baby she was. Now,' added Didi rising, 'it's time to lie down and stare at the ceiling if you can't sleep. Let the veranda enjoy what remains of the night in its usual solitude.'

The next morning, Kartik was heavy with a cold. He stayed in bed, underneath a blanket. Sita fussed over him. She placed a rod-heater in the bedroom and brought him a series of hot liquids – ginger tea, clear lentil soup, egg flip. She even gave him a large rum with honey and warm water.

Didi did not visit him. He heard her say in the corridor, 'Better tell the dhoodhwallah to give us plenty more milk. It seems we are going to entertain him longer than I thought.'

'This Didi of mine,' he heard Sita reply, 'is becoming more and more kanjoos each year. Soon, I will get no milk in my tea!'

'If you don't get any milk in your tea, it is because you drink most of it with five Marie biscuits every morning!' came Didi's instant reply.

'See how she talks? Five Marie biscuits – one for each finger! Who can eat so many?'

'Sita, you know as well as I do that you eat five Marie biscuits every morning with a large glass of milk. What is the point of pretending after all these years?'

'I will not listen to any more …'

Kartik fell asleep, comforted by their quarrelling.

On the fourth day, he felt robust enough to eat lunch at the dining table. Didi passed him the food without enquiring about the state of his health. He slept all afternoon in the weak exhaustion of recovery; it was late evening when he awoke. The sky was black and a cool breeze announced a drop in temperature with a flutter of the curtains.

Kartik found Didi in the drawing room, behind a newspaper. Reluctant to disturb her, he went across to the mantlepiece and admired the photographs.

'Why did you cut it?' he blurted out. 'You had such beautiful long hair.'

'It gave me a headache.'

'What non—'

'What do you know? Ever had long hair?'

She had made the discovery quite by chance, she told him. It had been a hot, humid afternoon. Her scalp ran to sweat, the long hair dragged her head down. She felt an intense pain, one she recognized well after years of suffering. She tugged at a few strands of hair and felt the pain increase. She repeated the gesture. It struck her then that her hair was too much of a burden for her head to carry. She had risen tempestuously, found the scissors and chopped her hair to just below the nape of her neck before she had time to reconsider her actions.

'Sita almost fainted at the sight of my hair lying on the floor.' The newspaper shook with Didi's chuckles. 'She gathered it up in a paper and cried over it until I told her it was crawling with lice. The same afternoon, she burnt it!'

'Sounds like you wanted to be a different you,' said Kartik and added hastily when he noticed her lower the newspaper and frown at him, 'I mean, maybe subconsciously ...' He trailed off, wondering if he had gone too far.

She observed him over the edge of a page. 'Acute,' she replied and returned to her newspaper.

Accustomed to her abrupt manner, her curious style of conversation by then, Kartik suddenly experienced a strong physical attraction. He wondered how she would react if he were to gently, very gently run the tips of his fingernails along the ripples of her neck. Would she flinch, would she maintain her regal imperturbability? He sensed it was a very long time since she had been touched.

'My problem,' she said distantly, 'is that I continually bang into myself. I hurt myself, I hurt others. I made some poor choices and faced the consequences.' She rolled the newspaper into a tube and tapped it gently against her nose.

'Everything was fine,' she added, 'until that final year in New York.'

There was a shuffling behind them and Sita appeared.

'Dinner.'

Didi shooed her away with an impatient wave of the newspaper.

'Never did listen to me,' grumbled Sita as she disappeared inside, 'never listened to anyone.'

A snort from Didi.

'She's right. Never did listen to anyone. Always wanted my own way. Got it too. Poor Mem could never say "no" to her only child.'

MEM
1932

Poor Mem could never say 'no' to her only child. After two miscarriages robbed her of two sons, Mem treated her daughter as a rare possession to be handled with utmost care and indulged in every way. Didi grew up as an over-protected child whose life from the day of her birth was governed by Mem's vast collection of superstitions.

Mem did not name the girl in the belief that nameless, she would evade the attention of evil spirits. She refused to feed her anything but mother's milk until she was three years old. She would not allow Didi to go out further than the courtyard of the house till she was four (unless, of course, Father came and took her off in his Buick). She would not let the cook, the driver or anyone else come closer than five feet of Didi, fearful of infections. Didi was her rani-beti. She had to be protected. Only Sita (whose hygiene Mem personally supervised), Father and Mem were allowed to touch Didi.

Throughout Didi's childhood, Mem did what she could to ensure the well-being of her only child. Every morning at seven, after her monologue to the gods in the puja room, Mem would see-saw towards the kitchen, muttering verses from the Gita under the sari pallu which covered her head and shaded her face. She would pick out a heavy black iron ladle, pour ghee into its cup, add a red chilli, mustard seeds and sometimes a pinch of salt for extra-special auspicious effects. She would hold the ladle firm over the burning orange-grey coals of the fire until its contents turned as black as the ladle, the mustard seeds popped and the smoke rose, a snake responding to the charms of her incantations.

Still chanting, Mem would leave the kitchen as quickly as her legs would carry her, down the long, open corridor which linked the kitchen to the rest of the house and from the side-door, enter her bedroom, where Didi lay in her cot. She would turn the ladle clockwise many times over the girl's head.

The ritual of frightening away evil from the environs of her daughter's mahogany cot continued unchallenged, despite Father's scepticism. Who could, who dared, accost a woman who had lost two sons and was now determined to save her daughter?

The ritual didn't stop of Mem's own volition. What happened was this: one morning, Didi was lying on Mem's bed, fast asleep, her arms flung out above her head in complete surrender. Mem entered the room. Her hair was freshly washed; it was a Wednesday, good for a 'head bath' because it fell between Tuesday when she had fasted all day and Thursday which was the worst possible day for washing or cutting hair on account of the adverse effects it could have on one's husband. Or so she had been told by her mother.

So there was Mem, in perfect harmony with her gods and the stars, approaching her daughter. Her footfall disturbed Didi's sleep and she opened her eyes. Seeing Mem trailing grey smoke in a white cotton sari with a grey border, her pallu slipping over her damp black hair which fell over her chest like a shroud, Didi screamed, 'Witch, it's a witch! Sita!'

From the dining room, Sita came racing to the rescue, urged on by the high-pitched voice. Determined to save her Didi, she barged into the room. Something solid arrested her progress. She tripped over her big right toe, buckled under the impact of the collision, and fell hard. But her landing was soft.

'Get off me! Get off me, you …' squealed an agonized Mem under her.

Didi was clapping her little pinks palms.

'Sita has won! Ravana is dead, Ravana is dead,' she screamed in delight. She giggled, she laughed. She had never looked prettier or happier.

In the evening, Mem remembered the ladle. Her nose had been broken by the fall and she was lying in bed, her nose throbbing under a white beak – the doctor's efforts at repairing the damage. Sita stood by, fanning Mem's face with her dupatta, farting in misery.

'Sita, haven't you had an opening this morning?'

Mem breathed in deeply and then clutched at her nostrils, which caused her to nearly faint with excruciating pain.

'Sita,' repeated Mem, wiping the tears from her eyes, 'find my spoon. Tomorrow morning you take Biru and the big car and go to the banks of the Jamuna. Throw this ladle as far as you can.'

The story of the ladle was often recounted by Father. It was one of the child's particular favourites, not least because she had played a significant if minor role in the accident. Father named the incident Sita's Folly.

Mem's superstitions interfered with Didi's education. She did not attend school till she was seven years old; Mem believed her child would be kidnapped, run over, lost or otherwise assaulted. Father bore these fears with patience and understanding until Didi's seventh birthday. The next morning, he drove her to the convent school in his car and sat outside the classroom till it was time to go home.

A month of Father's persistence, and Mem relented: Didi attended school but with Sita waiting for her outside in the Buick. The result was that Didi finished school when she was almost nineteen, two years later than most girls of her age.

A solitary child, Didi made few friends. Father's government job took them to a different city every three or four years. But the pattern of her days remained the same wherever they lived: every morning Didi went to school, every afternoon she learnt music and dance, every weekend Mem and she went to a matinee film show, escorted by Sita. Each summer, the family travelled to the hills with her cousin, Mahendra.

By the time Didi turned fourteen, Father was senior enough to remain in Delhi. The Bharatanatyam dance and Indian classical music classes continued despite Didi's obvious lack of talent or interest in either. Then, into her fifteenth year, Didi rebelled. She got rid of her teachers by sprinkling a tablespoon of red chilli powder in their paan.

This display of character and wilfulness in a young girl of good breeding alarmed Mem, amused Father. He was an indulgent parent and husband, pliable to his daughter's whims, favourably inclined towards Mem's superstitions.

There was only one topic that made him rigid and unbending. 'Do your family duty' was a phrase Didi heard constantly during childhood, sometimes directed at Mem (when she was reluctant to visit his parents for anything more than a week), and otherwise at her.

'The family is something you wear at all times, like your skin,' he would tell Didi when she played a prank or crossed the line of his tolerance. 'Remember, it is on display, always. Never do anything that could bring on a blush.'

This was difficult for Didi on two counts: first, she was very pale and her colour heightened at the slightest exertion; second, she liked to have her own way. Since the age of four, she had argued with Father. She would stand in front of him, clutching her doll, her lip protruding in opposition to his decisions.

'I am not listening to you,' she would announce and turn away with a flounce.

Frequently, she used Mem and Sita, or Mahendra, as her decoys. If she wished to go to a matinee during the week, she made Mem ask Father – he could never say 'no' to his wife. If it was a shopping trip, she had Sita complain about the state of her underwear – Father was particular about clean linen and lingerie. If she wanted to have chicken sandwiches at the Delhi Gymkhana Club, she would tell Mahendra to challenge Father to a game of tennis. On these occasions, Father subsided without much demur because, as he confided to Mem, 'Didi is my minx.'

'Do your family duty' came up rather more frequently in Father's conversations as she grew older, but Didi filed it away in the corner of her mind where other noble thoughts preached by Father – ' Do a good turn every day', 'Waste not, want not' – resided in forgetfulness. It was a mistake, as Didi was soon to learn.

Didi was in her teens when she decided she wanted to attend a political rally addressed by Congress leaders. Father forbade it.

'My daughter will not be seen at a public rally.'

'I want to go. I support the fight for Indian independence.'

'No.'

'I do.'

'The answer is still "no".'

Father bought her Nehru's *Glimpses of World History* and recommended she read it carefully.

'I want to be part of history,' Didi sulked. 'What's the point of this,' she waved the heavy book from side to side, 'when Dada and you plan to marry me off to the first man you can find when I finish school?'

Father studied her gravely from behind his round spectacles.

'Your grandfather is old and ailing. He wishes to see his only grandchild, you, married while he is alive. And that,' Father added, removing his glasses and wiping them with his cream silk handkerchief, 'is what he shall do once he finds a boy who suits our spoilt little girl.'

'What if I don't like his choice?'

Father neatly folded his handkerchief, placed it in his trouser pocket, then slowly replaced the spectacles on his nose before looking Didi straight in the eye.

'When the time comes, Didi, you will do as you are told. We have to do our duty by the family.' He rose and came across to her, pinched her lightly on the cheek. 'Remember: don't do anything that will make us blush.'

On the day of the Congress rally, Didi remained in her room the entire day as a mark of protest against Father's refusal to let her attend it.

This had an unexpected consequence for Didi: Father employed one Mrs O'Hare as her governess.

'Teach her to waltz, lay a table properly, and Shakespeare – but above all, to mind her manners, Mrs O'Hare,' were Father's instructions to the wife of an Irish civil engineer posted in Delhi.

And so Didi learnt to be what Mrs O'Hare called 'a lady in waiting'. She read the English classics, learnt how to cook and serve, and how to waltz. There was just one problem: she was not allowed to dance with anyone except her father or Mrs O'Hare. The men she could meet were restricted to family or close acquaintances.

'Keep your head down and don't look out of the car window,' Father ordered whenever Didi went out. 'You never know when a boy is looking in.' Biru, the Buick and Sita were her constant shields against any male intruder. Friends were encouraged to come home. She seldom visited theirs. Father offered what was, from his point of view, a perfectly reasonable explanation.

'Friends have brothers, brothers-in-law, cousins, uncles.'

Thus, Didi grew up deprived of male companionship besides that of her father, her cousin Mahendra during the summer holidays, and of Dada who came on annual visits every summer and winter for a month at a time. Dada, a retired lawyer, lived by himself – at his own insistence and despite Father's many entreaties – ever since his wife had died. He devoted himself to his garden and to the task of looking for a man fit enough to marry his granddaughter.

In this honourable quest, Dada was assisted by an enthusiastic Mem. They searched their entire community for a boy of the same social standing. Each one was subsequently crossed off Dada's notepad for one shortcoming or another.

He's shorter than she is.
Darker than Sarojini Naidu.
He's too spoilt.
Too old.
He doesn't hold a job.

Doesn't let go of his mother.

By the time Didi finished school, the search had become frantic. Father told Dada to let him know when he tick-marked a boy on the list. Meanwhile, he sent his daughter to college. It was during Didi's first year at Indraprastha (IP) College in Delhi that Father was offered an assignment with the United Nations in New York. Identified as a 'colonial' after Independence, he had been overlooked for top administrative posts in Delhi. So when the UN offer came, he accepted it with alacrity. He decided to take Mem and Didi with him.

'Travel will broaden Didi's mind,' he told Dada, when he had objected. 'Besides, who should I leave her with here? You're too old to look after a young woman.'

Thus, at the age of twenty-two, with an interrupted English Honours degree, Didi set sail for New York. Dada was at the Bombay dockyard to wave them goodbye. Didi stood on the ship's deck with her parents and Sita, who wanted to know how a ship could stand on the surface of the water. Didi told her to be quiet and waved frantically to Dada. This, she said to herself as she blew him kisses, was when life began.

NEW YORK
1954

Life began with a stutter. Didi's dreams of a life in the fast lane were continually stalled by Father's set of rules and regulations. According to him, Didi could go out only during the day, accompanied by Mem, or with the daughters of his colleagues whom he approved of. She could visit the public library alone, provided the chauffeur waited for her outside. On Fridays she was allowed to spend the night at a friend's home. Saturdays, she dined out with her parents; Father and she would dance, Didi with the acute self-consciousness of dancing with a much older man, that too her father.

All around her, young couples waltzed on the smooth parquet ballroom floor where chandeliers glinted like clustered diamond earrings. They sat on high stools at the dimly-lit bar, sipping cocktails the barman invented. They held hands, they kissed – they looked divine to Didi. Father would command her to keep her eyes on her plate and relish the exotic dishes he ordered for her.

'Acquire taste, that's important in life.'

Didi wanted to taste life, not chicken a la Kiev. She sat in glum acquiescence and watched Father and Mem enjoy their meal.

Friday nights saved Didi from everlasting boredom. At her friends' homes she listened in awe to the stories told by the girls, incredulous at their lives: how gallant men kissed their fingers and begged to kiss their painted lips; how they received chocolates in the morning and corsages in the evening, from aspiring beaus. How they went out for breakfast, brunch, lunch, tea, high tea, cocktails, supper, after supper parties, the theatre, films, symphonies, the ballet, skating, American football, and drank martinis until they swayed to the music in their heads. And oh, those intimacies in the dark, hidden recesses where love was a hasty fumble against a wall …

Didi, emerging from the protective fold of her parents' embrace, desired nothing more than to be like these girls. Their stories evoked in her feelings she had never experienced before. Alone in her bed, she longed to open the front door and run wildly, aimlessly into the unknown.

Didi had grown into an attractive, striking young woman. She was firm, and so pink and white, Father called her his 'little sausage'. This upset Mem visibly and deeply. A strict vegetarian, Mem found terms of affection related to animal flesh revolting to her soul, a deliberate and wilful challenge to her gods.

Didi didn't quite like being a sausage either, but since Father said it with such gentleness, she accepted it as one of the peculiarities children must tolerate in their parents.

'My side of the family,' boasted Father.

'How does it matter?' Didi would ask Mem, who insisted that Didi's light skin came from her side of the family.

'Achcha, you bite your own nails,' Mem would reply, 'this is between me and your father.'

'Your father and I,' corrected Didi.

Didi knew the colour of her skin was irrelevant. With her long dark hair, her small black bindi, the delicate kajal grazing her eyelids, she made a striking statement of her identity.

Mem insisted Didi wear saris.

'No daughter of mine shows her legs in public.'

Didi wore blouses collared at the neck, puffed at the shoulders, long in the sleeve – blouses which reached down to cover her navel.

'No daughter of mine is going to show the goras her baby hole,' Mem ordered.

The primness of her blouses was undermined by the way Didi draped her sari the moment she escaped Mem's watchful eyes. She would stretch the cloth around her waist and buttocks, for the fullness of the latter to curve out; she would pull the pallu tight across her bosom and toss it lightly over her shoulder. (Mem would ensure that Didi's pallu was so long, it reached her knees, and safety pin it to the shoulder of her blouse.) When she bent ever so slightly, or turned ever so suddenly, the pallu would glide down her arm or fall forward, exposing the curvature of her breasts. With her plait reaching her waist, a tiny scar at the left corner of her mouth from a childhood fall, her full lips breaking into a slight smile, she was almost voluptuous and expectant of pleasure.

Yet, what pleasure could there be when she had to stay home all week and go to bed by ten?

Did any twenty-two-year-old girl, throbbing with the yearnings of her youth, go to bed at ten in the US of A? It was unfair, inhuman. Relentlessly and with tears glistening in her eyes, Didi complained to Mem that it was 'IMPOSSIBLE' to meet such unreasonable conditions as Father's.

Didi began to realize that tears alone would not win her any concessions. For that she needed a plan. At night, underneath the bedclothes, she devised extraordinary strategies to change Father's mind, only to dismiss them as too feeble to dent his strict code of conduct. Unless, of course, she worked on Mem …

She began to spend the afternoons in her mother's room. She would massage the knotted veins on her mother's legs, the arthritis in her bones. She used bubbling sarson ka tel, cooked with ten garlic cloves till the cloves were as brittle as her mother's bones and almost as black as the kajal in her eyes. She would carry the katori of oil up to her mother's bedroom, draw the curtains tight, and climb onto the feathered double-poster bed. Seated cross-legged, Didi would be ready to attack Mem's thighs. She would hoist up her mother's sari petticoat; Mem would protest by slapping at her hands, slap not so much in prevention as in playfulness. Didi would pour the oil onto her mother's flab, watch the muscles twitch in anticipatory pleasure and then bring down her hands, alternately, as though thumping a tabla. This would continue for five minutes. After this, more oil would be applied and the ritual repeated.

Didi pinched, knuckled, squeezed while Mem expelled a series of responses, not always intelligible. She would burp, pass wind (never pungent because the girls in her family never had smelly ones); she muttered prayers for her husband, for Didi, her future son-in-law and their children. She wheezed. Sometimes she would begin to sneeze and the sneezing would continue for a couple of minutes. Somewhere between wheezing and sneezing, relaxation would set in.

It was then that her dutiful daughter would strike. How absurd of Father not to allow her to go out with other girls in the evenings. All his Indian colleagues allowed their daughters to go out in a group to the movies, the theatre, supper, even a party. Mem had to see that this was completely 'an impossibly unfair situation'.

And if she, Mem, could not make Father see sense, then she, their daughter, would simply stay at home. Forever.

'In which case,' she added, giving Mem's thigh an extra hard slap, 'in which case, you might as well have left me behind in India with Dada. Why bring me to New York?'

Mem, who loved and lived to fulfil Didi's every wish, listened to the same arguments, the same questions, week in, week out. Didi added more ammunition: she threatened not to accompany Mem to the Saturday matinee show she so loved until she persuaded Father to change the rules. While Mem procrastinated, Didi carried out her threat: one Saturday, she refused to accompany Mem to the matinee.

That did it. Mem rose to the occasion. She pestered her husband in private and demanded answers from him. Why had they brought Didi to New York? So she could sit at home and practise laying the table the way Mrs O'Hare had taught her?

A querulous wife and a persistent daughter eventually succeeded: Father capitulated.

In addition to her Fridays, Didi was permitted to go out alone during the day thrice a week, to a party once a week, and for Sunday afternoon drives into the countryside. With two riders: Father must approve of her companions and Sita must accompany Didi. To this, Sita took strong objection.

'I am not sitting in the car outside alone, Father Sahib. What if some man steal me?'

Father laughed heartily at the thought of *some man* wanting to kidnap Sita. He, however, agreed to let Didi go alone on the condition that she be home by 11 p.m. Oh well, midnight.

Eight months after she had gained Father's permission to attend parties, Didi returned home one night, exhausted by her revelries.

'Too sleepy,' she claimed.

'Too many drinks,' replied Sita with a sniff.

Sita helped her into bed, then proceeded immediately to Mem's room and pummeled Mem's expectant flesh with unnecessary force.

'Father Sahib is strict but you, Mem, you allow Didi too much,' Sita said in disgust. 'You know she drink? And eat meat?' Sita's tone clearly indicated that these habits were only second and third behind everlasting perdition. 'Were I in your place, I would give her two-two tight ones.'

'Achcha,' replied Mem, tart and tired of hearing this particular opinion, 'only I am in my place, so manage your tongue.'

'Well, I would,' insisted Sita, 'on her bottom. Hai hai, Mem, will any man marry her if he knows she be drinking bhiskee – and cigarettes also? And doing,' added Sita, relishing this speech of doom, 'who knows what-not.'

'What?' asked Mem, turning abruptly so that Sita, balanced on her knees, toppled backwards. 'What *what-not?*'

'You don't know? As if …' replied Sita, sitting up.

In the dark, Mem sought Sita's hand and held it fast.

'As if what?' repeated Mem.

'As if you don't know.'

'Don't know what?'

'About Jafferi,' said Sita.

'Jafferi?'

'Oho,' exclaimed Sita, annoyed by Mem's stupidity. 'You know, Jafferi.'

Mem rapidly scanned her memory for all the Muslim men of her acquaintance in New York. Since there weren't any, it didn't take long.

'Who Jafferi?' she demanded, straightening out.

'You know – our Jafferi Sahib. Pata nahin kya,' added Sita, 'what-not he is doing to our rani-beti?'

Mem was becoming increasingly alarmed with each of Sita's utterances. Her child, her Didi, her one and only daughter, was secretly seeing a cow-eating Muslim with who knows how many wives! Hey bhagvan, and then, too, he was doing 'what-not' to her?

'Press,' Mem ordered Sita and fell back on the bed, beset by horrifying images of a long and greasy beard entangled in her daughter's glistening hair. 'At once, you tell me about this Jafferi. Arre, let the sun rise and see if I don't send you both packing on the next ship back to Hindustan.'

'And what,' Mem added, snapping up like a twig that has been stepped upon, 'were you doing while this Muslim goat was chasing my daughter?'

'Muslim goat?' Sita's hands stilled in mid-air. 'Now there's a Muslim goat after our Didi, too?'

'Too who?' shrieked Mem, sinking back again, in complete bewilderment and dread. Mem never did listen carefully to Sita's conversation, which normally consisted of salacious gossip about the maids' private affairs or pitiful warnings about the tragic consequences of displeasing the gods and living in countries where they ate meat to celebrate festivals.

'Sita, are you telling me that this Jafferi is a Muslim, or are you not?'

Sita beat a palm on her forehead.

'Hai hai, Mem, what are you saying? Jafferi and Muslim? With those green eyes and hair like ivory?'

Then did Mem understand: Jafferi was Jeffrey, Jeffrey James Wilby Jr. Jeff, the army cadet, son of Father's old classmate at Oxford, Wilby Sr. Jeff, with his superb physique, his biceps that bulged in repose, his white, sand-blond hair. Jeff, on study leave, who came to their home for dinner with his parents and was always present when Father, Mem and Didi dined at theirs. Jeff, who took to accompanying Mem and Didi on their Saturday matinees with Mrs Wilby. Jeff, who took them on shopping expeditions during the sale season. That Jeff was doing what-not with Mem's Didi?

That night, Mem did not sleep or even close her eyes. Each time she did, she saw Jeff with Didi's hair wrapped around his neck. For the first time in her life, gentle Mem had a violent urge: to strangulate Jeffrey James Wilby Jr.

The next morning, without a word to either Father or Didi, Mem wrote a letter to her father-in-law.

Didi, ignorant of what had passed between Mem and Sita, continued her 'secret' life. She had begun to 'see' Jeff before Father lifted his curfew. She knew him from the family dinners. She thought him good-looking in an obvious American way: tall, blond, tanned, with a swimming champion's taut body. She found him always attentive – he listened to her opinions with more deference than they often deserved and laughed at all her jokes, even if they deserved no more than a smile.

There was nothing more to it until a series of seemingly chance encounters at the public library. Didi went there every day as much for the books she brought home as for the privacy of the place where she could pretend to be one of the girls seated at the tables, either taking notes or exchanging them with the boy seated opposite. In the last week of August, she'd gone to exchange books and found Jeff amongst the shelves. She had been startled by his presence and naive enough to believe it was by accident. The second time she suspected a design, the third time confirmed it. Later, he admitted that he had deliberately followed her to the library and arranged these accidents with his 'hot little Indian summer'.

The library meetings, with their whispered conversations, created a quiet intimacy between Didi and Jeff. She began to read more voluminously than ever, sometimes, forsaking outings so that she could spend more time at the library. Father was proud and pleased by the manner in which she cultivated her mind; Mem remained unimpressed.

'Who does she think she is going to be? Mrs O'Hare?'

Two months after the first library 'date', Jeff had reached for her hand and drawn a circle in it. This was something the girls of her acquaintance had described, but none could explain the feeling that made her ask Jeff to rotate his finger on her palm, until she thought she would collapse in a puddle at his feet.

Suddenly, Didi was dangerously close to breaking bounds.

When it happened, it was simple; nothing contrived. The Wilbys invited them for a weekend at their country house. Didi accompanied her parents and Sita, who could not be left alone at home. On their first afternoon there, Father received a message that he was needed in New York for an unexpected consultation and made plans to leave the same evening. Mrs Wilby pleaded that the women be left behind; so Mem, Didi and Sita stayed on.

Jeff arrived next morning but Didi was out by the lake and met him only at lunch, when he was careful to keep his distance. In the warm afternoon somnolence, Didi pressed Mem's legs with extra vigour and expertise; she was rewarded with regular snores within half an hour. It was then that Providence intervened: Mrs Wilby's maid had taken a great fancy to Sita's sparkling eyes and vigorous nods. She took her home for tea.

Alone and free, Didi found Jeff in the garage, tinkering with his red sports car. He led Didi up to his childhood room and locked the door behind them.

When she rose from the browning stain on the white sheet, Didi didn't immediately identify it with anything she had done. She stared at the coffee mark, more in wonder than in fear. Was this the colour of her blood? Could she bleed on and on? Would Mem and Father discover her just so, inert on the bed, her death spread out beneath her like a rug?

Didi sat with her arms clasped about her knees, watching the stain as though it were alive and might move. Jeff dozed. She wished he would awaken. She got up noisily, examining the floor beneath her, expecting it to turn crimson; there was a soreness between her legs and she walked bow-legged.

'Hey, where are you going?' Jeff Jr. asked.

'Pee.'

'Yeah, women always do.'

'Do what?'

'Pee,' he replied.

'There's blood – everywhere,' she exaggerated, feeling important.

'Oh yeah?' he inquired. 'Oh, that,' he added dismissively when she pointed to the stain, as if he found bloodstains on bed sheets commonplace. Then he saw her face, the smeared black bindi, the smudged kohl in her eyes, the trembling mouth.

'It's nothing – it happens. The first time.'

'Will there be more?' she wanted to know.

'No,' he reassured her.

'Then I'll go and pee.'

'Do.'

They exchanged no more conversation. Didi left the same evening with Mem and Sita. Mem hugged Mrs Wilby and thanked her for a wonderful weekend, Sita embraced the maid warmly and invited her to New York. Didi thought Jeff winked at her but refused to look at him.

That night, he rang her.

'I didn't hurt you, did I?' he asked.

Didi thought of deceit but practised honesty.

'A little.'

'Not much?' he sought reassurance.

'More than I thought,' she said.

'Oh yeah!' he exclaimed.

'Doesn't matter,' she consoled, 'I rather liked the pain.'

She told him she had to go; Sita was always listening in on any conversation that crossed two minutes. He hastily advised her to use some cold cream 'down there'. She replied by disconnecting the line. Cold cream, indeed. She, who didn't quite rightly know what was 'down there' was now supposed to find it, cream it and no doubt, pat it to sleep! Silly idiot.

If Sita noticed anything that night, she remained inscrutable. When Didi locked herself in the bathroom, Sita stood outside the bathroom door, regaling her with details of tea with Mrs Wilby's maid. Didi opened the jar of cold cream, scooped out a dollop and, seated on the toilet seat, lathered it 'down there'.

The following night, while Didi sat on her bed applying cream to her face, Sita stood folding her clothes.

'Why was there an oily stain on your panties?' she demanded.

'Why does anyone apply cream anywhere? Because it felt dry, itchy, that's why.'

'Better now?' queried Sita.

'Yes, Sita, thank you very much. So much better.'

'Really?'

'Want to look?'

Sita dropped the clothes on the bed and rushed out, crying, 'Hai hai, Mem, just listen to her.'

After that red-stained day in Jeff's childhood room, they met, whenever Didi could get away, at his friend Ed's studio apartment in the city, where the afternoon sun strained in, a searchlight seeking out their bodies on the bed. She'd feel its rays straighten the tiny strands of hair on her nape just as she felt his fingers goosepimple her arms.

Didi did not stop to consider whether the relationship had any future beyond the immediate. The enormity of what had happened, what continued to happen, was obscured by her immediate delight in it. Within a few short months, she had slipped out of the cocoon of the past and into the present, one that was warm, exciting and smelt of Jeff.

New York and Jeff had momentarily released, if not liberated, Didi from the life her parents had chosen for her. She had finally broken free, got away. Away from Father's strict supervision, away from Mem's arthritic bones and groans, her perpetual lecture on the behaviour of 'good Indian girls', away from Sita who followed her everywhere, if not physically, then with her eyes; Sita who opened her letters but couldn't read them, who sniffed the envelopes, the paper used in the letter and claimed she recognized the author by the smell; Sita who told Didi categorically, one particularly late night, that no Indian man would marry an Indian woman whose hair perpetually smelt of yesterday's cigarette ash, whose mouth tasted of yesterday's 'bhiskee'.

All the years of being a dutiful daughter and her strict observance of Father's rules helped Didi flout them now. She would say she was visiting a girl friend for the afternoon and join Jeff at Café Alfresco opposite Ed's apartment.

On the first few occasions, she had been shy, unaccustomed to sharing the sight of her body with anyone but Mem and Sita. She would climb into bed still dressed in her blouse and petticoat. Then she took to hanging her blouse and sari. She'd strip off the petticoat quickly, after she'd changed the bed sheets. She couldn't lie in someone else's smell, she explained to Jeff.

At some stage, Sita discovered them. Not in physical fact but in spirit. Didi never got to know how. On the days she met Jeff, she was careful not to wear any underwear. On her return home, she went straight for a bath. So her body hadn't betrayed them. She seldom spoke of Jeff, never clearly described where she went or what she did.

One evening, while she was fighting the knots in her long hair, Sita walked in and began to fold her discarded clothes.

'You can sit combing your hair all your life but you won't be able to straighten out the mess you have made.'

'What?' Didi replied, crossed-eyed and preoccupied with a particularly stubborn knot.

'You know what.'

'What?'

'What you've done.'

'And what am I supposed to have done?' Didi demanded, sweeping the hair off her face.

'Ask yourself.'

'I am asking you.'

'Ask your Jafferi Sahib then.'

'You ask him – and it's not Jafferi, it is Jeffrey. How many times must I tell you?'

'It's wrong, that's what it is – wrong.'

'Leave me alone,' shouted Didi, throwing the comb in Sita's direction.

Sita went about her work. She drew the curtains, closing out the light on their dark secret. Didi had admitted to nothing. Yet, at the mention of Jeff's name, or whenever he accompanied his parents to Didi's, her eyes would magnetically fix upon Sita's. Just one brief, locked look before she blinked: an involuntary admission of a shared confidence.

Sita's strictures did not have the desired effect on Didi. She continued to meet Jeff. And when he circled her palm with his forefinger or tongue, she felt her blouse tighten around her chest and her nipples pinpoint her desire. She took to pulling her pallu around her, afraid people would notice. It was all so effortless, so pleasurable and fulfilling. Until the evening the letter arrived from India.

Didi picked it up from the silver platter embossed with her father's initials, tapped it lightly against one hand, her mind pleasantly preoccupied with a major concern: should she wash her hair this evening or oil it now and shampoo in the morning?

She entered Mem's room without knocking.

'Letter from Dada,' she called out to the darkness.

Switching on a light, she found her mother seated on a stool by the dressing table, with the Bhagvad Gita in her hands, her eyes closed, turning the pages sightlessly and reciting the words by heart. Didi deposited the letter on the bed and waved goodbye to her mother's reflection in the dressing-table mirror.

'Where are you going?' demanded Mem, interrupting her recitation.

'Right now I am going to the toilet. After that I think I'll have a head bath. Then, I might go look in the mirror and confirm that I'm as beautiful as I think I am.'

'Don't be rude to your only mother,' replied Mem, turning a page.

'Sorry, sorry, very sorry,' said Didi, coming up behind Mem and encircling her shoulders with her arms to place her pink cheek against Mem's pale white one.

'Shall we go to the movies tomorrow?' offered Didi.

'Which one?' asked Mem who loved movies.

'*Little Caesar*,' replied her daughter. 'A wicked drama about a gangster and his moll.'

'You mean doll,' said Mem, glad to be able to correct her daughter's English.

'No, I mean moll,' replied her daughter haughtily. 'Don't you know the difference?' she teased, pulling Mem's ears this way and that.

'How must I know?' complained Mem. 'Does anybody speak to me in English? Your father thinks I don't know ABC and you only speak to me in English when you don't want Sita to understand what you're saying.'

'There, there,' Didi stroked her hair.

'Where?' asked Mem, looking around in some puzzlement.

In public, Mem marvelled at Didi's fluency; in private, she couldn't understand half of what she said. She switched to Hindustani.

'Achcha, go from here – let me finish my reading.'

'Asking God for a handsome husband for your lovely little me?' queried Didi, sliding out of the room.

'Thinks too much of herself,' Mem told the pages of the Gita.

Didi had bathed and was humming to herself in front of the mirror when she heard the sound of deep breathing outside the bathroom door.

'How many times have I told you to call out my name instead of standing there making strange noises!' she demanded.

'I've got the cold,' retorted Sita.

'You've always got a cold,' protested Didi.

'Mem's calling,' sniffed Sita.

The house was warm and quiet. Didi, attired in a pale blue woolen dressing gown with pink flowers and a matching towel knotted around her head, went to the kitchen. She found Mem cooking moong ki khichdi.

'Awful,' complained Didi, looking at the yellow, glutinous substance. Mem stirred the contents of the vessel.

'Your father eats too many greasy meats and puddings – not good for his heart,' Mem said, reaching out for the katori of ghee. 'This will keep him warm, strengthen his bones.' She added zeera, two dry red chillies, powdered heeng and haldi to the heating fat. 'Ghee—' she continued.

'Chhi,' interrupted her daughter.

'I'll chhi-chhi you just now,' threatened Mem, raising the stainless steel ladle in her left hand and making as if to strike her daughter who had darted to the other side of the kitchen table. Mem would have chased her around it, just as she did when Didi was a little girl, but Thelma, the dour but diligent maid, was watching this scene with disapproval as thick as the khichdi. Mem tersely requested Didi to behave and continued with her cooking.

Five minutes later, she followed Didi into the study. Didi was unravelling her wet hair and massaging her scalp with the towel. Mem removed an envelope from its safe-keeping inside her blouse.

'From your Dada.'

'I gave you the letter, remember?' replied Didi.

'Don't be cheeky – I can slap you harder with the palm of my hand than with the bottom of the spoon,' promised Mem, rustling the sheets.

'Violent …'

'Achcha,' Mem silenced her, holding up a hand. 'Dada is quite ill,' she said as she read the letter. 'Hey bhagvan,' she added, 'he's found him!'

Mem collapsed on the sofa. She stared at the letter. 'He wants us to go home. To meet the boy and his family. Solemnize the union. Wedding can take place in April.'

Mem folded the papers. She placed her left hand on the protrusion of her bust, patted it for comfort. The letter had relieved her mind of a tremendous anxiety. Ever since Sita had told her about 'Jafferi Sahib', Mem had been waiting for her father-in-law's response to her urgent missive, pleading with him to renew his efforts to find Didi a groom. Now, Dada had found this alliance, admittedly not the best, he said, but under the circumstances, it was as good as he could find. Mem saw no reason to read that portion of the letter out to Didi. Just let her go home and get married, God, and I will ask for nothing more, she prayed.

She rose with the ladle in her hand and looked out of the window, bracing herself for the challenges ahead.

It was then that she heard Didi's silence and looked down at the girl towelling her hair.

'You said something?' she asked.

'I said, did you just say Dada had found a groom for me?'

'That's what.'

'And you expect me to marry this first man Dada approves of?'

'Then you'll marry the tenth? The eleventh? Or what?'

Didi twisted her hair round and round and glared stubbornly at her mother.

'Who do you think you are, memsahib?' asked Mem, clutching the ladle to her bust. 'What did you think? I, Nando Rani, am going to tell your Dada that his granddaughter, my daughter, can't attend her own wedding because she won't marry the first man he liked?'

Mem's blink had become a tick. This happened to her in moments of tremendous stress.

'Mem, please, you can't expect me to go through with this?' Didi clutched at her mother's swollen calves.

Mem gazed into her daughter's startled eyes; her heart thumped like a mother's heart will when she must oppose her own child.

'I don't understand anything, but. Why you are saying "no"? You are now twenty-four, Didi. Already too old for most eligible men in our community. In fact,' added Mem, seeing them disappear before her eyes, 'you have missed the best already. Remember that Agra boy? So handsome.'

'So gora, you mean,' corrected Didi.

'Achcha, he was fair but good-looking,' Mem insisted. 'I was telling your father then, you should have married him, but he wouldn't listen. "Let her learn, Mem",' she mimicked her husband's tone. 'See where it has got us, this learning.'

Didi didn't reply.

'And then there was that Ramesh, so promising, but he failed his bar exam and your father said that if he fails his bar exam, he would fail in other trials of life. Hai hai, is there any sense in what he says?'

'That's because,' explained Didi, 'Sita told him she had noticed how Ramesh kept his hands close to his fly throughout their meeting.'

'Achcha,' exclaimed Mem, dismissing the image of Ramesh with his hands in the wrong place. 'And then there was my own bhabhi's nephew. His hands were never … In business too. I told your father to write and he promised – "tomorrow, tomorrow". By the time your father's tomorrow came, he had become engaged.'

Mem swallowed the saliva in her mouth along with her disappointments.

'Too many girls in your generation in our community,' complained Mem, settling down on the sofa again. 'I produced only one, but your father's cousin Iravati? Five.'

Didi clenched her right hand into a fist and thumped it on her left palm. 'Why are we talking about Iravati Aunty, when my life is at stake here?' she yelled.

Mem ignored her.

'It is settled,' she insisted. 'This boy's family is the only one left of the same rank as ours.'

Didi got up, threw the towel on the floor and stamped on it.

'Who is this man?'

Mem retrieved the letter from its hiding place and read aloud: 'Purushottam. Purush for short.'

'Where does he live?'

'With his father, mother and older brother.'

'What does he do?'

'Lawyer by training. Highly qualified.'

'Pah,' exclaimed Didi and flung herself next to Mem on the sofa. 'I won't! I won't marry him, I won't, I won't.'

She heaved silently but with tremendous force, and burst into tears. Mem swallowed hard at the sight of Didi's evident unhappiness and began to stroke her head. For one moment, she was tempted to give in to her whims as she had so often in the past. But the thought of losing one more potential bridegroom and 'Jafferi Sahib' carrying away her beloved daughter held her back.

'Na-na,' she consoled, 'marriage is not so sad.'

Didi awoke to a hand against her left cheek. Cold. Father's. As a little girl, Didi used to fold her tongue as a waiter does a napkin, tuck it inside her mouth, and then place Father's cool hands against her cheek. It was deliciously reassuring.

'Father,' she whispered.

'Upsie.'

He withdrew his hand, placed both under her armpits, straightened her up like a rag doll. She held her fingers where his had been.

'Oh, Father,' she gulped, 'Mem is making me very unhappy.'

'And the khichdi, I can tell you, the way she is stirring it. What's the matter?'

He braided his fingers with hers.

'Mem says I must marry the man Dada has found.'

'I take it you are not against marriage?'

'No.'

'And you have nothing personal against this particular specimen?'

'How can I? I don't know him.'

'Then let's say we are sending you back to become acquainted.'

Didi clung to his hand.

'Please say I don't have to marry him.'

Father lifted her chin.

'We all did what you are about to do and we didn't do too badly. Look at Mem and me.'

Didi rushed to her feet.

'You can't compare!' she protested. 'Did Mem go to school? College? Did she have an English governess who forced her to read Jane Austen and Sir Walter Scott? Did … did Mem wear Egyptian cotton frocks? Mem never went out to parties, never danced till—'

Father held up his hand.

'Enough. Don't throw your good fortune in Mem's face. Mem ceaselessly thinks of ways to please you.'

Didi hid her head in her father's lapel.

'She has been shopping for your wedding since your fifth birthday. Packed away the clothes with neem leaves and wrapped them in muslin cloth to preserve them for the day you get married. And though she will never admit it, she hopes that even though you will see us very rarely after you begin your new life, you will be surrounded by so many of the things she has bought and given you that we will always be there with you.'

There was a tear in his voice, the way old cloth suddenly gives way. He cleared his throat. Water dribbled out of Didi's nose.

'Didi, Didi. You knew you were to marry. It was just a matter of your Dada finding the right match.'

That, Didi wanted to say, was before New York, before Jeff. She observed her father's unyielding features and sank down on the carpeted floor, instead.

'You should not have brought me to New York, Father, if you were going to send me back to the mohallas your father came from.'

Father spoke quietly.

'I cannot oppose Dada's wishes. And,' he added, 'marriage has no foundation in the mind.'

He flicked the lapels of his charcoal grey double-breasted coat.

'Nor is it a geography lesson. It doesn't matter where you are and where he has been. What is important is that you share the same background.'

Didi flung her arms around his legs. She felt the muscles harden against her.

'I must do as my father expects me to, Didi. I expect you to do the same. Now be a good girl, go wash your face and join me for a delicious bowl of khichdi.'

With that he left the room.

Didi did not join him for dinner. She remained upstairs in her room, listening to Sita's stories of all the wickedness the women in her family had endured after marriage.

For the next few days, Didi stayed in her room. When Father left for work, she had Sita summon Mem to her. Alone with her mother, she cajoled, she entreated, she implored. She tried tears, she tried reason, she tried threats – she gave Mem the best massages ever. Much to her astonishment, she realized that Mem outflanked her with her own tactics: when Mem sobbed, it was so loud that Thelma came to inquire the cause; when she begged her daughter not to shame her, it was with folded, wringing hands and a reminder that the women in her family never lived long; if she beseeched Didi to keep the family honour intact, it was with an offer to die.

'Hey bhagvan, take me into your care, rather than leaving me to see my girl remain unwed!'

This flair for the melodramatic was a new aspect to Mem and Didi found her own histrionic talents wilt before Mem's superior performance. So when she said that if Mem truly, truly loved her one and only daughter she would not foist this man on her, Mem replied that if Didi had any concern for Dada's failing health, her father's spotless reputation, the family name and her mother (in that order), she would know where her duty lay.

Didi was nonplussed. When she weighed her desires against the combined wishes of the two people she loved most and Dada's ailments, the scales weighed heavily against her.

As Didi lay on her eiderdown and thought about what to do, it came to her that Jeff had not been primary to her concerns. This was more about her, not the two of them. In all honesty, she had not thought of Jeff and herself as *us*. If she didn't want to marry the man of Dada's choice, it was because she could not accept marriage to a man she had not met before and not because she had considered marrying

Jeff, always supposing Jeff wanted to marry her. Did she wish to marry him? At the cost of her parents? Didi, normally so firmly grounded in her resolve and sure of what she wanted, faltered.

She began to avoid Jeff and his telephone calls. She put Sita on the job, who in turn instructed Thelma. Whenever Jeff rang, Thelma told him in a monotone, 'Miss is not well and is not taking any calls. Thank you.'

A week after Dada's letter had arrived, there was a knock on Didi's door.

'Enter!'

Didi lay inert on her bed, her arms and legs flung out like someone about to be crucified. She could smell aftershave. Father. She felt the mattress sag.

'I have noted your absence from the dining table in the last few days. I also gathered from Sita that your meals have followed you upstairs. So are you quite well?'

'Yes, Father.'

'Good. I hope you have had enough time to overcome the suddenness of the marriage plans and will now oblige me by getting up and helping Mem to make whatever preparations are necessary.'

Didi turned on her side, grabbed her father's hand where it lay on the eiderdown.

'I can't, can't you see?'

'All I see is a very disobedient girl who hasn't combed her hair, washed her face or changed her clothes in days. Now get up, bathe, get dressed and come downstairs. Stop this foolishness.'

He rose but Didi tugged at his hand.

'Father.'

His back did not respond.

'Father, please.'

Father spoke in a terse voice.

'You have enjoyed a wonderful time in New York, Didi. I have allowed you more freedom than any girl from our community ever had. You've gone to parties, spent the night …' he paused, as though arrested by a sudden thought and turned to look at her. 'I hope there is nothing you are hiding from us?'

This was Didi's moment. Blurt it out and be done with it. *Yes, Father, I have been with Jeff.* She pushed her hair out of her face, stood up, her eyes meeting his.

'No, Father.' Didi blushed.

'Mem and I love you dearly, but the time has come, Didi, for us to let you go. We would fail in our duty to you as parents, otherwise, and that I will never allow.'

He patted her on the head before he left the room. Didi stamped her feet on the floor and flung herself back on the bed.

Later, she joined her parents for lunch and ate heartily. Anxiety had not diminished her appetite. Returning to her bedroom after the meal, she lay curled into a question mark.

For the first time in her life, Didi was scared. If she followed Father's orders, how would she explain the absence of a bloodstained bed sheet on her wedding night to the husband she didn't know? And how would she explain the marriage to Jeff? Suddenly, her life had taken an irrevocable turn and those afternoons in Ed's studio loft seemed to have no long-term connection with the rest of her life.

The next day, Didi met Jeff at Café Alfresco. When he tried to take her hand, she withdrew it.

She ordered a large martini.

Jeff raised his right eyebrow.

'I am to be married I have a headache I am going back to India Jeff.'

Didi spoke without pausing, as though each sentence was a continuation of the idea expressed in the one before it.

'What?'

'I am to be married I am going back to India Jeff.'

Jeff's cheeks reddened.

'How come?'

In staccato sentences, Didi explained.

'Shall we drive away and get married?' he asked, meeting her eyes with the shine of his own.

The proposal was as unexpected as a hiccup and Didi gulped. Then she tapped the tip of his nose.

'I can see you asking my father!' she said, shuddering.

'I'd like to.'

'And I'd like another martini. Don't be absurd,' she added in a voice that would have wavered had she not strained the muscles in her throat to steady it.

'I'm serious …'

'And I'm Doris Day!'

'But I care, Didi, and I think we should—'

'Where I come from, marriage has nothing to do with feelings or thoughts. Or the mind,' she mimicked her father. She swallowed her drink. 'I think I am already married to a future without you. And anyway,' she added, summoning the waitress for another drink, 'we don't really want to marry, do we?'

'I am ready to.'

'You say that because I have just announced that I am getting married. Counter offers are never genuine.'

Jeff crushed her hand and took a gulp of his drink.

'I can't believe it. You're simply vanishing. Why did we—'

Didi placed a cool hand on his mouth.

'I know. I can't explain it either. But when you are in the middle of something,' she said in a distant voice as though she was already far away, 'you don't think how it will end.' She patted his hand. 'I suppose I knew I was to be married, but I never thought it would be now. It was always in the future, like a receding horizon.'

He took her for a long walk through Central Park, where he asked her, once again, to marry him. She thanked him. She was grateful.

'It's honourable of you, but I just don't see how. What will happen to Mem and Father and Dada? Suppose it kills the old man? And suppose we are terribly unhappy together? Then I will have killed him for nothing and made us very unhappy too.'

Jeff halted.

'I think it is better than marrying someone you don't know.'

'That's not what I asked you.'

'But I am asking you.'

'It's the custom, Jeff, not unusual.' Didi explained arranged marriages and her grandfather's quest for the appropriate husband. She spoke of Father's sense of 'family duty' and Mem collecting her trousseau since she was a child.

'Sounds scary, yeah,' Jeff remarked, 'I'd want to run away from all of that.'

'But how can I?' she responded. 'I know you would marry me, but I don't know if that is what I want or should want.'

With that, she told him to walk her home without any more discussion. She was drunk.

Once there, she went upstairs, took a bath and lay down on the white eiderdown. She felt a pain in her temples. It was the first of her famous headaches.

In tired wakefulness, she considered Jeff's gallant offer and what might happen if she ran off and married him and had his children. They would have his green eyes and her black hair and perhaps Mem's pert nose. Mem. Hey bhagvan, Didi shuddered. She suddenly felt sick and rushed to the bathroom, where she threw up. Oh, why had she been so wilful; why had she allowed Jeff an intimacy reserved for her husband? She summoned Mem's gods to forgive her.

Over the next few weeks, Jeff battered at her resolve with phone calls, flowers, chocolates and entreaties. She ordered him to stop: if her parents came to suspect … It was not something Didi could bear to contemplate.

She met him at Alfresco's over martinis (she had begun to drink regularly). During those meetings, Didi tried to explain her dilemma to Jeff and to herself. Of course she liked him very much, but could she disappoint her parents? At the same time, she couldn't just marry a man she had never set eyes on. But then again, how could she marry Jeff? What would Mem say?

'She never intended that I marry a whitey like you.'

'Then why …?'

'I don't know why myself. It just happened, didn't it?'

Jeff rose from the table and walked away. Didi remained with her martini and a strong desire to cry or run after him. She did neither.

While Mem completed her plans for their departure, Didi watched in detached silence. Each day, she saw the morning rise from her bedroom window with flakes of snow. Winter still lingered. A harsh, stinging wind mowed down people in its passage, the air screeched like a car rounding a sharp street corner at high speed. Didi wished it would carry her far away from Mem's preparations for her wedding.

She accompanied Mem on her shopping excursions because Father had ordered her to, but she did not indicate any preferences or desires. She accepted no dinner invitations, her overnight visits to her friends' homes stopped. She remained aloof, listless. Mem tried to cheer her up, transmit some of her own joy to her daughter. But as she became increasingly preoccupied with the arrangements, she did not pay much attention to Didi's passive resistance, believing it would pass once they returned to India.

One evening, Didi took a long, aimless walk through the city; something she often did during those sombre weeks in New York. She wandered down streets, entered shops, stared at window mannequins, studied the latest sale offers, halted at a corner, purposeless, oblivious to the rush around her. There came a moment when, in the middle of a sidewalk, she cried into her hands till they sagged with her unhappiness.

She wept for Jeff, for herself and the period she had just missed.

She sat in an outdoor café, shivering. How would she explain the missed period to Mem? She did not want to even think about it.

What became clear to her as she drank the coffee was that she would not tell Jeff. It would be unfair to both of them, more to him than to her: he would be forced to marry her. That was worse than her being forced into marriage with the man Dada had found for her. When she returned home, she was startled to hear from Sita that Jeff and his parents were in the drawing room. Sita said they had dropped by for 'pot'. Didi entered the drawing room and went to sit by the glow of the fireplace. Father had opened a bottle of champagne and was passing around the glasses. Jeff stood warming his hands.

Everyone raised a glass.

'Didi, I've been telling our dear friends the good news, but I thought they should hear it from you too.'

Father smiled warmly at her.

In the complete stillness that followed, Didi could hear herself say, *Ladies and gentlemen, I have just missed my period.*

She placed her champagne glass on the carpet and got to her feet. Jeff was looking straight at her. She met his gaze without blinking.

'Didi?' he asked.

Didi glanced at Father, who beamed at Jeff's parents. She looked at Mem, who gazed at her with such softness in her eyes. She smiled at her mother and saw Mem's eyes dissolve in tears. She took a deep breath, held out her hand to Jeff.

'Yes, I am going back to India to be married.'

Jeff crushed her fingers in his hand's embrace.

After they left, Father accompanied Didi to her bedroom, one protective arm about her shoulder.

'Fine young man, that Jeff. Terribly young, though. You know what he said before you came in? That he wished he could marry a girl like you.'

Father guffawed and clasped Didi to him.

'I told him he was too late, you were already spoken for!'

'What if I wasn't?'

Father put an arm's distance between them, chuffed her chin.

'What if I wasn't?' Didi repeated.

'Didi, I said it so as not to offend him; his father is such an old friend. You can't marry a man outside your community, let alone a foreigner!'

Didi filed the memory of Jeff into a small folder of her mind and labelled it – The End.

Everything that happened thereafter happened to a person Didi wasn't sure she knew or recognized. After marriage, she would often stare into the stained dressing-table mirror which was chipped at the top right hand corner but which had never been repaired because Purush said changing mirrors brought bad luck.

Bad luck? she would ask herself. What could be a greater misfortune than this?

She would stare at her reflection, the woman would stare back. A woman who was a complete stranger to her, stranger than if they had only just met.

Your face, she would tell herself, always catches up with your past.

HILL STATION
1978

Your face, she told herself, always catches up with your past. Didi observed in the bathroom mirror, the deepening lines around her mouth, the heaviness of her eyes, the downward tug of her mouth. She looked like a woman who had misplaced sleep a long time ago. She returned to her room and peered at the clock. It was 3.47 a.m. Another night spent gliding on the surface of slumber without ever sinking in.

She walked down the corridor to the other bedroom door. Kartik was snoring. She went back to her bedroom and read *Pride and Prejudice*. On the first page of the book, she had pencilled in 23 behind 22. That was how many times she had read the novel.

She felt her left palm itch and rubbed her hands furiously. She had creamed them before going to bed, just as she had creamed 'down there' as Jeff had advised her to, all those years ago. It was a ritual she had followed ever since. She couldn't say why. Perhaps to remember him by.

The supple skin on her arms was still smooth. There was a dry, burnt patch on the forearm – the day before, she'd fallen asleep in the hot midday sun. She picked at the dead skin the way she picked at her food: indifferently, mechanically. She removed as much skin as would peel off, chafed her hands and placed their warmth on her eyes as though the heat would revive inert memories. That was the handicap with memories: you seldom recalled the feelings behind the events.

Didi remembered the touch of Jeff Jr. but not the texture of his skin; she recalled his murmured 'I adore you, my hot Indian summer' but couldn't hear the emotion. She pictured the roses he bought at the florist around the corner from the apartment, she could see herself stuffing them into an empty green wine bottle at Ed's, but couldn't breathe in their scent. Like the air, you can put your hand through the past without displacing anything.

All those years ago, with Jeff, in Ed's room, never had she imagined that life would end up here in a small, cool house on the outskirts of a hill station, with Sita and stray dogs for company.

The dogs never entered the house even when she left the door invitingly open. They knew their place in life. 'Like good Hindus,' she would tell Sita. She fed them, clothed them with coats and covered them with blankets in winter; she made sure they took a rabies injection every year and that the maali bathed them once a fortnight. Sita refused to touch the dogs, being as finicky about animal flesh as Mem had been. The dogs ignored her and returned Didi's dutiful caring with their barks. The moment anyone other than the maali neared her gate, they were up and flying towards its bars. She was safe. Protected.

'As though I live in solitary confinement,' she told herself.

No, Didi had never imagined it would be like this. She had immersed herself in the immediate. She had been a deep-sea diver exulting in wondrous, exotic, hidden pleasures, forgetting that she must eventually come up for breath. If at all she had thought of herself in the future tense, it was in the form of a question mark on a blank page.

Just as well, Didi whispered to herself. What's the use of a future if you know it already?

She sat on the edge of her bed, staring out of the window. It had rained all day, all night, and twenty-four hours later the rain was still falling gently, like a ghost tapping on a keyboard. It aggravated Didi's mood.

'A pest,' she thought out aloud, 'you are a pest.'

The pest responded by falling more heavily and Didi acknowledged her lack of power over the elements.

'Why just them,' she said to the rain, 'my life, Baby, everything.' With her index finger she knuckled the bridge of her nose.

Six hours later, she grumpily refused Sita's breakfast. Instead, she sat outside in the veranda drinking tea while Sita see-sawed before her eyes with unaccustomed swiftness.

'Hai Ram, hai Mem, but see what he is doing?' she slapped at her breasts which wobbled obligingly.

Kartik appeared in the frame of the doorway, smiling.

'I tucked some money into her blouse, that's all.'

'That's all?' asked Didi tiredly.

Didi took out the crumpled remains of a cigarette from inside her bra and smoothened out its creases. Kartik shook his head at the two women and said he would go buy a pack.

'He is a sincere boy and would make our Baby a bilkul very good husband,' remarked Sita, watching Kartik walk out of the gate. 'You talk to Baby. Tell her to return.'

Didi placed her hands on her lap and studied them. 'Baby stopped listening to me long ago.'

Sita paused in the doorway.

'If only Mem were alive, she would have made Baby understand.'

'Well, she's not and I am. Now go get me a matchbox so I can smoke my cigarette in peace.'

'Shanti, shanti,' muttered Sita down the hallway, 'that's all we ever have around here – for years and years.'

'Oh, why don't you go to the toilet and have an opening,' advised Didi. 'That will certainly disturb the peace.'

Sita offered no reply and Didi was left to contemplate the idea of Kartik. Lean, fine-boned, the long, unruly curls on his head disturbing the neat picture he otherwise presented – that was the unconventional about him, thought Didi, what Baby must have found appealing. Poor boy. Didi felt a surge of sympathy and a moment's regret. Baby ought to have married him. But who was he?

'Who are you?' she asked when Kartik returned.

'You really want to know?' he asked, his voice eager.

'Would I have asked otherwise?'

Immediately, he sat down cross-legged at her feet.

'Begin,' Didi commanded with a wiggle of her toes, 'at the beginning. Begin with Baby. How did you meet that beautiful but self-willed daughter of mine?'

Kartik arched his back, stretched out his arms as though to gather his memories. 'It was 1975. The Emergency.'

DELHI
1975

The Emergency. August. At a clandestine meeting of students. Fifteen or twenty of them under umbrellas, clutching bundled papers and blue gum bottles. In the sleet rain of a monsoon night, beneath an old amaltas tree.

'So what if it's raining?' she had shouted. 'Like I said, we can paste these posters along the walls, just as we planned. There's nobody about.'

They were here on Independence Day, full of themselves and their idealism. They would protest against Mrs Gandhi's Emergency. They would fight it with all their might. They were midnight's children too, born after 1947. They would preserve the democracy their forefathers had won; they would squash her dictatorial, imperious nose. Yes.

But paste posters in the rain?

'They won't stick, yaar,' argued one girl.

'Some will,' Baby insisted. 'Many walls have thick borders on top. You can stick the posters beneath them, in the space that remains dry despite the rain. What have we got to lose?'

'The posters, if they get wet, and a lot of needless effort,' replied a young man with a Lenin beard.

'Scared of a little rain? There won't be a better opportunity,' Baby pleaded. 'Look, we've waited five nights for this. Every night there have been police patrols. Tonight is the night. The first time we haven't seen a police car in the last half hour.'

'She's right, of course,' agreed a man in a white kurta.

'Arre, we will get soaked; and with the glue, it will all be so messy,' complained a short, stout girl in parallel jeans.

'And suppose the posters don't stick?' asked Lenin's beard.

'Or suppose we are raided by the police in that state?' asked a tall, curly haired girl. 'Wet and sticky – we'd never make it.'

'We could, but only as far as Tihar Jail,' smirked Lenin's beard.

'Are you just flesh hanging onto bones or have you any guts?' Baby cried out. 'Are you human beings or cows?'

'Eh bhai,' protested a slim boy in a black kurta with a gold chain around his neck, 'cows have guts.'

'Literally,' laughed Lenin's beard.

'And in our land,' continued the boy, 'the cow is more precious than human life. So don't say that.'

'Do they have an afterlife like us?' the girl in parallel jeans wanted to know.

'What's that got to do with anything?' Baby yelled.

'If you're so brave, why don't you just go ahead and do it all by yourself?' asked Lenin's beard, turning sarcastic.

Baby peered through the rain.

'You? I don't remember seeing you before. Who are you? A jhola-wallah Commie comrade with pickled onions for balls? A man or a pyjama?'

'She make him a compliment or,' asked the curly topped girl of the girl in parallel jeans, 'an insult?'

'I'm not sure,' replied the girl in parallel jeans, 'but I think it has to do with sex.'

'All I am saying is, why do it on a rainy night? Why not wait another day?' Lenin's beard demanded.

Baby regarded his trousers.

'Definitely pickled onions,' she observed. He lunged out and caught her plait.

'I will pull this from the roots of your scalp,' he shouted, 'if you don't apologize right now.'

Her laughter was the thickness of glue.

'Apologize? To *you*? A guy with bits of meat stuck in his teeth?'

Angrily, his tongue located a piece of chicken wedged in the gap of his top incisors. He swallowed. Yanked her plait. Hard. Her face strained in the dim glow of a distant neon light and the Morse code rain. Nobody moved.

He pulled her plait once more, had the pleasure of seeing her eyes clench in pain. Then he let go.

She screwed up her mouth like she was sucking upon a toffee and spat in his face.

The saliva landed on his nose and trickled down towards his mouth.

It was their first kiss: warm and tasteless, like the monsoon rain.

The rain spluttered to a halt; the posters were pasted. At one point, the girl in the parallel jeans took out a camera from her bag.

'Say cheez to the freedom fighters of 1975!'

Unlike many Delhi University students, Baby, Kartik and their friends were not young radicals with an interest in politics. Perhaps that's why they were friends. They had come from smaller towns to study in Delhi for more personal reasons: the boys to advance their education, the girls to improve their marriage prospects. When they joined the protests against the Emergency, it was from a breathless expectancy for a new experience, a momentary diversion from the routine, rather than any ideological conviction. There was a delicious thrill to the clandestine meetings, in the torchlight processions through the university evenings, in the posters they plastered on the university walls. Yes, they did what they could, brash with youthful idealism. Couldn't they stare down a middle-aged woman with a streak of white hair? For sure. Did they hate Mrs Gandhi? Not all of them. Some of Kartik's college friends thought she had style: she dressed tastefully, that white peak lent her distinction – and arre, wait on, man, hadn't she won a war for India?

'More than Nehru did, yaar,' said Ajay.

'More than all the other political parties together have done,' added Prakash.

'But now we have more Bangladeshi refugees and less food for our own starved people because she wanted to play Durga devi,' protested Vinay.

'You have to say, not bad for a woman, but,' declared Abhijeet.
'She's sexy,' felt Ajay, 'sexier than ... Sadhana.'
'Sexier than Zeenie-baby?' inquired Prakash.
'No, fuller, but,' judged Abhijeet.

'But what? You guys can't speak the English language and you presume to talk about the prime minister of India like she's some bimbo? Is this the level of political discourse you're capable of? You're losers, man – boozer-loozers,' exclaimed Kartik.

Vinay clapped and the others joined in:
Kartik/vartik
Limp as a wick
Used a broomstick
Instead of his dick
Girls thought it sick
A lousy trick
From such a hick
As Kartik/vartik

Baby's friends quite liked the Emergency. Quite liked it a lot.

'Like it?' repeated Kartik. 'How can you girls talk about a dictatorship as if it were a new nail polish? Don't you care about politics at all?'

It had been their first time alone. Together. Why had he invited her to watch *The Odessa File*? Was it because of her insulting manner? Or what he imagined was hidden beneath the loose shirts, tight trousers and black boots?

She stared at him with eyes that bore holes into his.

'Care about politics? Do men care about women when they *are* interested in politics? It always boils down to their bodies, no matter what interests them. The next time a man looks at my breasts like he wants to suckle, I will sock him,' she replied. 'Is that politics?'

'No, that,' Kartik continued, 'is absurd.'

'No, it's not.'

They were seated on the steps of Yashwant Place shopping arcade, near Chanakya Cinema, sipping tea in chipped white ceramic cups.

It was a typical Delhi winter afternoon when the face was hot in the sun and the back cold in the shadows.

'Like I said, you can ideologically oppose the Emergency because you are a man,' explained Baby. 'But personally, as young women in this city, it has given us back our freedom, our bodies.'

'Like how?'

'Like, we can walk the streets alone, after seven, catch a bus after nine – without any fear of the locals. I can wear a skivvy …'

'Why don't you?'

'What?'

'Why don't you?'

'Would you stop interrupting when I am talking? This is what is wrong with you guys.' Baby splashed the chai on her thighs as she rose. 'You don't really want to know what I think about the Emergency.' She forked her fingers through her thick hair. 'Let's go and watch the film. It's so much easier that way.'

He pulled her down next to him.

'That night when I met you, you were so passionate about the Emergency …'

Baby glanced at him, her eyes suddenly honey and striped.

'That's because I am bored of Mrs Sircar's lectures on the "mammaries" of Keats and Shelley, sick of Mrs Kumar's twenty-year-old notes on the industrialization of England and tired of the girls talking about their favourite Hindi film star during the Shakespeare tute. The Emergency was just something to do. Different.'

Baby took a loud slurp of tea.

'So you'll tire of the protests soon?'

'Probably,' replied Baby, staring dully at her cup.

'Why do girls like you come and study subjects like English literature when all you want is to have fun?' he demanded, clutching her hand.

Baby gave him her eyes, but this time they were intense and dark brown.

'To meet boys like you, marry and settle down. Why else?'

Later, seated outside the university library, eating monkey nuts, shelling them and littering the steps with their discarded coats, Kartik and Baby exchanged their thoughts. Mostly, he spoke and she listened. The longer he spoke, the more his mouth pursed in excitement, his straight, sharp nose twitched, and his curly hair curled even more, tightened by the excitement of intellectual puzzles. She had made him shave off his Lenin beard – 'You look like a Commie jhola type when you're just a good farmer boy!' – so he would scratch his chin in contemplation.

'If I had to commit suicide, I would lock the room, dim the lights and slit my wrists,' he proclaimed once.

'Messy,' she replied, clasping her knees.

'But life is messy,' he had pronounced with the self-importance of a young man on the brink of adulthood, 'so too must death be.'

'So unnecessary.' She looked at his wrists, wide where the fine bones stood out.

'I wonder what it would feel like.' He was persistent. 'The blood, warm and sticky, pouring out as you grow increasingly weak, spreading like a carpet under you. You know you are dying and you know you can't stop dying – isn't that just terrifyingly beautiful?'

'No,' she added, 'it's just messy.'

'Seriously, to cause your own death is the ultimate statement of life.'

She reached out to touch his left knee ever so lightly. He shivered.

In that touch, Kartik made contact with the rest of his life.

She was his future, but like the future, she remained elusive. Over the next two years, as she completed a B.A. Honours in English and he an M.A. in history, there were many instances when he thought he had finally comprehended her, only to realize she was a language he didn't understand.

She took him by shock and by surprise. She would hitch a ride wherever she went, not to save money, but because there was the delicious thrill of the uncertain: would the driver stop? If it was a man, would he try to grope her? What if he didn't stop where she wanted him to? Would he try to kidnap her?

Kartik warned her not to take such risks but she only mocked his concern.

'Scared?'

'For you.'

'Then come along for the ride.'

She would stand by the roadside and make him hide partially behind a tree or lamppost, something he did willingly enough since it allowed him to watch over her.

Once she had thumbed a lift, she seated herself on the bike or in the car and just before they began to move, she'd shout out, 'C'mon Kartik, hurry up, man – this guy doesn't have all day!' Mostly, the duped driver would refuse to give them a ride and they would end up on the curb, Kartik annoyed by her wilfulness, Baby entertained by his discomfiture.

If they got a ride, Kartik would immediately try to roll down the car windows, check to see if the handles were in place and that the doors could be opened.

'You're such a baby,' Baby would sneer.

'And you're foolish. The least you can do is make sure you can yell out or get out in case there's a prob.'

Baby was scornful of such precautions. She always took a chance.

One August evening, the intense humidity of the monsoon broke suddenly into a downpour as Baby, Kartik and Ajay stepped out of Kamani Auditorium. They had gone to watch a play but walked out during the interval. The plan was to eat pizzas at the Cellar. They had fifty rupees between them, just enough for two cheese pizzas and three colas.

Baby saw a white Fiat with dark panes drive towards them on the Mandi House roundabout. She hailed it. It stopped.

'CP?' asked Baby, leaning into the open car window. Before the man behind the steering wheel could refuse, she yanked open the door and sat beside him. She beckoned to the boys. The middle-aged driver, in a white safari suit and a gold knuckle duster ring on his forefinger, his straight black hair swept off his forehead and held there by oil, frowned; but seeing their soggy, sagging clothes, allowed them to climb in. They had barely travelled a kilometre when the Fiat began to stall near the Tolstoy Marg crossing. Water had collected in its engine. The man halted at the curb, tried to rev the engine and when it did not respond after several attempts, switched off the ignition.

'Sorry, ma'am,' he addressed Baby, 'but we'll have to wait here till the rain slows down.'

Baby shrugged.

'We're in no hurry. Just going to Regal Building, the Cellar,' said Ajay.

The man nodded but did not turn. He was staring at Baby.

'You should go to Nirula's Chinese. Best chop suey with the fried egg wet on top.'

Ajay laughed.

'Too expensive.'

The man laughed too and met his eyes in the rear view mirror.

'No problem, I'll take you. Why not now? We can take a bite there and then we can go to Lido.' He winked at Ajay. 'Pretty dancing ... Arre, ma'am, what are you doing?'

Baby had jerked open the car door and jumped out into the rain.

'It's pouring!' protested Ajay as Baby crooked a forefinger at him. Seeing Kartik climb out, he shrugged and followed.

'Arre, I will drop you to your destination!'

Baby took a hairbrush with a wooden handle out of her satchel, and without a moment's hesitation, hit the man repeatedly on the head.

'Pig, what do you think of yourself?'

The man tried the ignition with one hand and to snatch the brush with the other. The engine gurgled to life and he drove away, even as Baby jerked back and out of the car, splashing them with puddle water, the passenger door open, the brush flying through the rain.

'What's your problem?' Kartik demanded of Baby.

'Bloody dog! He had opened his zip and was ...' she completed the sentence with a gesture.

'Oh please!' Ajay shuddered, spitting out his disgust. 'What a bloody local!'

Kartik laughed, for once finding the predicament Baby had placed them in amusing.

Back at his barsati, dressed only in his white kurta and a towel turban on her wet hair, sipping rum and Coke, she raved about what Delhi did to men.

'They're like ants. They're always ready to scurry over women with their measly eyes which cling like the pinpricks of an ant's bite. I want to hit them each time a man travels over my body with that particular look of lust and loathing. I want to stamp on their hands, the fingers that roam through their nostrils before settling on the zips of their trousers.'

'You're hysterical,' Kartik protested. She glared at him, leapt up on his bed and began to yell out:

'An Ode to Delhi'
The mosquitoes of sleepless nights
The power cuts of stale sweat
The water shortage of unwashed clothes
The clogged sewage pipes of rotting smells
The grey fumes of car farts

> *The sticky flies of rubbish dumps*
> *The paan-stained hundred rupee*
> *Note of corruption*
> *The men*
> *Like cockroaches.*

She flopped down on the bed, exhausted by her theatrics, and said, 'You wanted to know why I liked the Emergency? That's why.'

He turned his back on her.

'You're drunk.'

She poked him in the buttocks with her foot.

'You want to?'

Baby and Kartik: like flints they rubbed against each other, sparks flew, igniting fires that consumed them.

They made an unlikely pair: he was shorter by an inch and a half, wore plain khadi kurtas or shirts and jeans or trousers, his spectacles square – a picture of earnestness, indistinguishable from the thousands of other boys who came from all parts of India to study at DU.

She, on the other hand, was as provocative as a rude question: straight, thick hair the colour of sand, a tall, big-boned frame, eyes hooded in dark shadow and highlighted by black mascara, full lips always bright with lipstick. Baby wore clothes from Janpath that would have turned the head of a statue. Tight trousers in different colours were often pressed inside black boots that went halfway up her calves. Loose men's shirts, thick belts around the waist, beads strung about the neck. She painted her nails purple, orange or white and wore silver rings and silver bracelets bought from Cottage Industries. Everything about her made a clear statement of intent: look at me.

Although Kartik liked looking at her, he suspected he saw only what she projected. If he probed deeper, he saw the liquid honey of her eyes freeze into opacity. When he pressed her to tell him about herself, she would offer him an anecdote about Budhoo, the family dog, instead. Rarely did she refer to Didi or the rest of her family, switching the topic to the present or the future: 'Shall we go tomorrow to Gurjari and buy you some jootis?' or 'Let's go to the Icon for cold coffee and buy pastries?'

He noticed how she always avoided the subject of her father as though he was an open manhole she might fall into if she didn't tiptoe around it. 'Like I said, we lived with his family till I was six, then Amma and I went with Sita to live in the hills – it was better for Amma's health.'

Kartik noted how she had said 'his family'.

'But what's he like, your father?' he'd persist after such unsatisfactory replies.

'Oh, he was there.' And she'd recount an incident from her childhood that never included him. Occasionally, she spoke of her grandmother Som Devi or her Bhai Chacha, but only in passing.

'Don't you visit them, ever?'

'Told you, my mother likes the hills.'

When he complained that he couldn't get a 'fix' on her, she'd draw her eyes back deep into their sockets, small hard pebbles on the expanse of her smooth, expressionless face. In time, he learnt that with Baby you could not step back into the past or update to the present.

This combination of boldness and withdrawal fascinated Kartik, distracting him from the main purpose of his M.A. degree: the IAS exams.

It had all been decided between them. He would be an IAS officer, she the collector's wife. For the next thirty-five years, he would rise from one position to another until they occupied that white bungalow in the heart of New Delhi she so longed for.

All Kartik had to do was study.

'Like I said, it's your job,' Baby reminded him, 'for the next year.'

In order to devote himself entirely to his 'job', she made him leave the college hostel and found him a small barsati in D Block, Def. Col.

'Otherwise, you'll be loafing on the campus,' she said, 'and getting involved in the Emergency stuff. I don't want you mixed up in all that. You could be arrested.'

Kartik began to protest but she stopped him.

'I know, I know, you're very idealistic and want to save the country. But, there are other ways of doing that. I don't want you in jail. You can't join the IAS with a police record. See, I am really serious about this: I've promised myself that I will only marry a man who is a collector.'

'What about a secretary?' he teased.

'That will happen too, so make sure you get in. Otherwise …'

'Otherwise?'

Baby shrugged and slit her throat with her hand.

Kartik was left to wonder what kind of man she wanted him to be. He asked her once, after she had covered his body with hers and was rubbing her nose along his jawline.

'I want you to be the man who wants me! *Bas.*'

And so, Kartik turned away from the world outside his barsati. Baby had become his ambition. Wanting her, wanting to be with her became his purpose.

She visited him every day, or every other day, and so they fell into a companionable routine.

Alone, he would study through the day and Baby would arrive just when the sun had tipped over into the late afternoon. She'd stay till 7.30 p.m. and return to her college hostel in time for the 8 p.m. deadline. She spent Saturday nights with him. Before she left, she tidied up his papers, set out the books he had to study the next week and took away any notes that he needed to copy. It was a joint exercise, and Kartik felt she was dedicating herself to it with more zeal than him.

On a particular afternoon, he was seated outside in the veranda, when he heard the expected sound: the thup-thup of her kolhapuri chappals on the stairs. Then she was upon him, her shadow cooling him before he shivered from her fingers on his nape.

He smacked at them. Missed. She laughed. Throaty, smoky, pleased.

'Swat your books instead!' she counselled, reaching for the cigarette pack.

She picked out two and lit one up with the lighter from her bag. She sucked in till the tip flared into an orange. Like a dart, she aimed the cigarette into his mouth. Then she placed the unlit one between her Vaseline lips and bent to light it with the tip of his, her hands balancing her body on his arms. He wanted to ... but her eyes stopped short of accepting the invitation in his.

Kartik sat, legs stretched out on a cane stool, books piled up on either side as tables. On the right hand pile rested a white mug with a sip of coffee left for a fly to drown in. It floated in the middle, on its belly. Kartik had almost swallowed it, his eyes on the turning pages of the book on his knee. The fly wriggled, a novice in the deep end of a swimming pool, flapping desperately to stay alive. He watched it fail; he had wished to save it but suppose in picking it out, he squeezed the life out of it?

On afternoons like this, Kartik would regard his notes and occasionally sigh deeply, hoping Baby would pay him more attention. She chose to ignore him. She would stray in and out of his room, casually empty an ashtray, blowing the ash in the face of the air, remove his empty mug and replace it with a fresh, steaming one of tea.

Sometimes she would rearrange his cupboard, so that when he had a hot bath later to remove the tiredness from his mind and muscles, when he searched for his khadi kurta-pyjamas, he'd never find the right combination. Or else, she'd change the bed sheets and collapse on the fresh ones. She changed them frequently before she lay down ('Don't know which of your friends has been on them').

He'd watch her, flat on her stomach, left leg bent at the knee, arms outstretched above her head, fingers bunched into half fists. And he knew that when he turned in, when the words on the page were blurred by the exhaustion of his eyes and brain, when he finally stretched out on the bed, he would reach out for the feel of her and wrap himself around it.

He felt embarrassed, sometimes, by his romantic, sentimental attachment that was not always adequately reciprocated.

'The fact that I am here with you should be enough of a statement,' she'd say when he pressed her for more.

Was this the girl who had once lain in his arms, searing him with the pressure of her fingers and pleading, 'Will you always love me?' Had that been just one year earlier? Had their relationship become a routine she followed like a college timetable?

He wondered why she had chosen him.

'Like I said, you're going to be an IAS officer and I the collector's wife. That's something to be.'

In the evening, they would stroll down to Gulshan ka Bhandar, the tea-biscuit stall around the corner; blow smoke rings with the cold air; buy chocolates, which he loved, or cigarettes, which she couldn't live without. Baby would light her cigarette with the burning string hanging from a nail on the wall. That annoyed him.

'Must you do that? What is it you're trying to prove?'

He would stare stubbornly at the main road to avoid the scene she was creating. She would wave the cigarette in his face.

'Do you want to?'

On days when Baby did not visit him, Kartik would try to study and end up with daydreams about her, them and their future. When those had distracted him sufficiently from his preparations, he would go down to 'Uncle', the landlord on the ground floor, to make a telephone call. It cost him 25 paise per call. He'd ring Ajay, who had moved to his girlfriend Avantika's uncle's house in GK-I. He was taking the exams too, and attending special IAS tuition classes. He had urged Kartik to sign up for the tuitions but it was expensive and Kartik didn't think his father, who had vehemently opposed his studying in Delhi, would agree to fund it.

'I'll share my tute notes with you, yaar,' Ajay told him, 'now chal, let's go for a spare.'

They would just drive around aimlessly, stopping at India Gate for an ice-cream cup or Keventers in CP for a softee ice-cream before driving to the university. Sometimes they halted outside the hostel gate at Miranda House and watched the girls come out.

'Loaded, man.'

'Mumtaz's hips, Marilyn Monroe's bust and Meena Kumari's eyes.'

'Three-in-one cassata ice-cream!'

They'd meet up with the 'gang' in the university: Prakash, Abhijeet, Vinay and Rakesh. They'd pool resources and go to Sheila for the latest English movie or, if they were feeling rich, eat tandoori chicken at Khyber restaurant. Later, there was always paan and cigarettes at Prince Paan in Daryaganj.

Towards the end of the month, low on funds, they went around the campus from class to class with an empty Kraft tin can asking for chavannis.

'Just 10 p, man, for a good cause.'

On the occasions when this did not yield generous donations, they would abandon the attempt halfway and settle for tea-cigarettes and a game of bridge or teen patta in Vinay's hostel room.

Baby did not join Kartik on these occasions.

'All you boys do is eat, drink, smoke and gup-maaro. Boring.'

Kartik's friends found Baby equally unattractive: she was abrupt, outrageous, even unstable. Ajay in particular disapproved of Baby, thinking her childish, and, as he put it, 'showoffie'.

'There are hajaar girls around, why do you have to choose one who wears the clothes she does, those boots? What's she, a cowboy?'

'So off-putting,' agreed Avantika.

They wondered why Kartik did not find someone 'more like us'. Kartik would grin, shrug it off with a casual 'Don't talk nonsense' and forget about it. But that didn't stop them.

Avantika would pester him to meet other girls, ones she thought were more suitable. She specialized in early morning 'emergency' telephone calls and he would race down to Uncle's, apologetic about the early morning disturbance.

'Sweets, Rinky's father is in the army – a colonel posted in Ambala. Neetu's father is an artist whose paintings are selling like hot cakes. And Shalini's father deals in tea – he's near this weirdly named place.' She giggled. 'Arsensol – imagine—'

'Asansol,' corrected Kartik automatically.
'Brilliant! Now why don't you meet her for lunch?'
'Avantika, why do you bother?' he'd ask.
'Because I know I can rid you of that witch.'
'Just to prove that you can?'
'No, sweets, I want that we can be a loving foursome.'
'That sounds scary.'
'Oh, Kartik, you're so cute. What I love about you is your shyness.'

After frequent and persistent requests, and perhaps to put an end to the morning calls that saw Uncle frown upon him, Kartik agreed to meet the girls Avantika pressed upon him. The first was Shalini; he didn't like her hooked nose. Rinky didn't talk about anything but Hindi films and imitated Rajesh Khanna in *Aradhana*; Kartik felt himself too superior to even admit he had watched the film, although he had with his family. Neetu, in an exaggerated English accent, spoke of her famous artist father and how she hated him for deserting her mother and her.

Alarmed, Kartik told Avantika that he didn't wish to meet any more girls. 'They're too silly.' She pleaded with him to meet one more girl, 'a serious type' he would really like.

Which is how he found himself at Aka Saka Chinese restaurant in Defence Colony market one afternoon.

In the dimly lit, long, narrow room, the air was filled with piped music, the smell of soya sauce and the whirr of the fans.

Her name was Nikki. She was very pretty. Twenty-one, dressed in a pale blue kameez with a white embroidered dupatta that had small white beads at the edges. She wore a turquoise nose ring and turquoise earrings. Her long hair was tied with a blue string. Even the ring on her finger was blue: sapphire. She wore silver bangles halfway up her forearm.

Nikki was studying history, just like Kartik, which was why Avantika must have thought they would suit each other. She sat opposite Kartik with a smile of expectation.

He felt obliged to ask her what she wanted to do after college.

'You see, I always wanted to be a journalist,' she said.

'Unusual.'

'You see, I just luuuvve writing.' She spread out the words like dosa batter on a hot pan.

'Oh really? And what do you like writing?' Kartik asked.

'Words,' Nikki expelled.

'Yes, no, I mean, what do you like writing about?'

'The middles in newspapers. Shall we have some wonton starters?'

He hailed the waiter and ordered a plate of chicken wonton for her and talumein soup for himself.

'Yes, you see, you can write about anything, like my pet dog or my last summer holiday in the hills, or even the population problem.'

When he didn't reply, she continued, 'I had a choice between Eng. lit. and history. I wanted lit. because I thought it would help my language, but my father said journalism was too risky. But I like risks.' Her eyes protruded daringly as if he was one she was prepared to take.

'I hold many strong opinions,' she added, tightening her fingers into fists as if opinions were something you held in your hands. 'My father taught me that. He says you have to be bold and strong in the world of journalism.'

'Which, of course, you are not?' Kartik asked before he could stop himself, and saw her blush. 'Well, I love history myself,' he added in haste, not knowing what to say. 'Shall we order the other dishes?'

They ordered vegetable chowmein, vegetable fried rice, sweet and sour chicken and chilli pork.

Nikki excused herself and when she returned he could smell the fresh scent of her – he recognized it: Charlie.

Their lunch arrived.

'What did you think of the '71 war?' she asked, serving herself chowmein and drowning it in vinegar and soya sauce.

'Why?'

'I am thinking of writing an article on it.'

'Well, I am glad it ended quickly,' replied Kartik, reaching for the chicken.

'I think we should have taken Lahore,' Nikki replied. 'That would have settled Pakistan's hash forever, don't you think? We should have taken over Pakistan. We could use some more space; see how fast we are multiplying.' She swept one hand around the crowded restaurant.

'You don't really mean that?' asked Kartik.

She giggled.

'Exactly, I mean it. That way we would be as big as China, bigger.'

Kartik swallowed a piece of chicken without chewing it.

'And we could have avenged 1965.' Nikki paused for breath.

Kartik wiped his mouth with the napkin.

'What if I told you,' Kartik offered her the sweet and sour chicken, 'that thousands would have died in a terrible war between the two countries?'

'I'd say I am very sorry for them, but all the better to get rid of them and reduce our population problem,' she returned immediately, laughing heartily.

That evening, Uncle rang the bell twice for him. It was Avantika on the telephone.

'Well?'

'So?'

'Stop it and tell me at once what you thought of Nikki. She said you were a bit on the slim side but like bread, she liked her men thin.'

Kartik replied that Nikki was really pretty.

'See, didn't I tell you?'

'... really pretty sharp. That is a quality I appreciate in a knife, not a wife.'

'You're just another MCP.'

So ended Avantika's attempts at finding a girl for Kartik.

Kartik had sat for the main papers in the UPSC exams and felt confident of getting through. Baby was so sure of him, she made him begin preparations for the interview. He spent the afternoons at the university library, reading newspapers and magazines, or academic publications like *Economic and Political Review* and *Seminar*. The latter invariably put him to sleep. Baby was right: he passed the written examination and was selected for the interview.

The monotony of Kartik's routine did not change even though the seasons did. While friends like Vinay and Prakash openly campaigned against the Congress after Mrs Gandhi called elections in January 1977, Kartik suppressed his desire to join them. He studied for the interview. Only on the day of polling in Delhi did he drive around the city with Ajay on his motorcycle, checking out the polling stations. There were crowds everywhere.

'Not looking good, yaar,' observed Ajay, 'hajaar people are voting for her.'

On the evening of the vote count, Baby arrived at the barsati, nonchalant as ever. Kartik kept a transistor by his side and listened to BBC World Service for news of the results. Baby switched it off, saying his listening would have no bearing on the election results but a good night's sleep would definitely improve *his* concentration the next day.

'So go to sleep.'

He fell asleep next to Baby, cradling the transistor. He woke up to a knock on the door. He opened it. His landlord, 'Uncleji' Paramjeet Singh, stood there holding out a box of laddoos and beaming at him.

'She has lost! Lost! Mrs Gandhi has lost!' he said, and broke into an impromptu bhangra. Kartik had barely stuffed two laddoos into his mouth when Baby called out for him and after hastily thanking Uncle, he went back to bed.

He switched on the transistor, volume low. All he could hear was a faint crackle. He tried to move, detach himself from Baby and tune the transistor, but she stirred and flung out a restraining arm across his body.

'Stay.'

Winter had yielded to spring, officially over by late January – Lohri, Makar Sankranti. But climactic changes hadn't obeyed the festival calendar. Holi was so chilly, it was played with dry colours instead of water.

Clearly, Nature was mixed up. A few trees had shed all their leaves at the end of April when the loo, searing, parched, brittle as the dry leaves, swept through the city, swirling the fumes from vehicles and the dust from construction sites. Travelling in the 'university special' buses, Kartik would wrap his face in his handkerchief as they sped down the Outer Ring Road where the ash became a fugue and midday vehicles had their lights on to tunnel through its opacity.

By early May, lime buds, evergreens and rusted leaves mingled on the ground. Naked brown trees stood sheltered by fresh bloomers on either side. The evenings were acid-washed in pale colours and new shades of bougainvillea appeared, unexpectedly, around every corner: mauve, purple, brilliant magenta or orange.

This city, beautiful and bare, thought Kartik. It crackled and spat like the dry red chillies his mother used to cook in hot oil. Thirty-nine degrees in the sun, but at night Kartik curled up under a light shawl. Nothing made sense to him.

Was it surprising, then, that inexplicable things began to happen? His small refrigerator droned but didn't cool; the fans whirred but churned out only hot air.

On a May morning that intermittently blew a hot wind, Kartik's telephone rang. It was Ajay: the results were up on the board at the UPSC building. How fast could Kartik make it?

'Very fast,' he laughed in relief.

He dialled Baby's hostel.

'Who are you?' answered Maya, the hostel ayah.

'You hear my voice every day and you still don't know who I am?' Kartik yelled.

'You give your own name only,' Maya insisted.

He slammed the phone down.

Ought he to wait for Baby or rush off? Kartik was undecided. His stomach settled it for him with a growl. Lunch. Ram Singh, from Uncleji's, came in each morning to cook Kartik's meals. This morning he'd produced Kartik's favourite: full green bhindi, fat with brown masala stuffing, steaming pale yellow kadhi with pakoras, and boiled rice. He began to eat in nervous anticipation.

A shadow reached out across the white tablecloth.

'So hungry, had to,' he mumbled, 'eat.'

Baby sat down, right leg over left, ran her fingers through her satchel, found the cigarette pack, threw back her head so that her long hair fought her shoulders for space.

'The results,' he told her, helping himself to more food, 'they're out.'

She puffed out smoke rings, one inside the other.

'Want a bite before we go?'

She shrugged.

He frowned.

She blew smoke from the corner of her mouth into his face.

'Not funny.'

'I know.'

'Then why did you do it?'

'For fun.'

She was wearing a white sleeveless blouse, a white handloom sari with a black embroidered border. As she reached for the ladle in the bowl, he smelt the sweat in her armpit. It aroused and repelled him simultaneously.

'Clearly, your mind is not on the food – or the results,' she said, snatching at his eyes with hers.

'They can wait,' he said, smiling.

Later, he remembered an extra tenderness in Baby that afternoon. Her hand stopped on its journey through his hair as if in blessing; her normal tautness was more fluid, her aggressiveness gentler with an unusual passivity. Everything about her suggested, no, not surrender, but resignation. When she lifted the bed sheet and draped it over them, Kartik thought nobody would be able to distinguish where he started and she began.

Afterwards, he leapt out of bed and into his clothes, shoved his feet into shoes, ran his hand through his curls, thought them too unruly, wet his hair and put it through a comb. He patted aftershave on his cheeks, splattered some on his shirt, smirked in the mirror and came charging at her with open arms.

'Aren't I the most desirable man ever?'

She stared at his pleased, polished face, went up on her knees and bit his earlobe. Then she put the pieces of her wardrobe together as carefully as a watchmaker assembles a dial. He raced down to Uncleji on the ground floor and requested him for the loan of his black Ambassador.

'The results, Uncleji.'

'Bring news to sweeten our mouths.'

Kartik and Baby drove out in silence.

'Why didn't you turn?' she asked as he went towards Khan Market, instead of turning right for the UPSC building.

'Look up God first.'

He stopped at the corner of the market. He opened the door for her but she declined. At the steps to the mandir, he touched the brass bell above his head and entered. There was the pandit, dozing next to Lord Shiva. Hands folded, Kartik recited the Gayatri mantra and bent down. The pandit rose with a start, and seeing Kartik about to give himself a teeka, remonstrated with a loud ejaculation.

'Wait, I will do it properly ...' He straightened up, picked up the rice and ground it into Kartik's forehead.

Baby carved out the doorway with her form.

'Cover your head, beti,' recommended the pandit.

'I'm not married,' she replied.

'Never mind, you are in the presence of God,' explained the pandit, his teeth red with betel juice.

'Hindu gods don't believe in rituals,' Baby replied. 'You people force your rules upon us and make us bow to them. You ...'

'Oh god,' Kartik exclaimed, moving swiftly towards her.

He pushed her stiff back out of the doorway. Stumbling, she grabbed a fistful of marigolds.

'Don't throw them at him!'

Baby glanced over her shoulder.

'Don't be ridiculous.'

She marched out, clutching the flowers, forgetting her chappals. Kartik heard a few titters from the locals standing by the paan shop at the corner of the street. Any other time, he would have thrust out his neck and charged at them. But there were the results, the rest of their lives to think of.

She sat in the car. He held out the chappals. She snapped her fingers in his face and grabbed the chappals.

Outside the UPSC building, the street was lined with trees and vehicles on either side.

'Wait.'

'It's okay,' he reassured her, 'it's fine.'

'Of course.'

'Look, I'll go in, you stay here.'

Baby formed a fist and knuckled the bridge of her nose.

When he scanned the typed numbers on the sheet of paper pinned to the notice board, he felt he didn't exist except as part of the heavy breathing crowd around him. This is how it must have felt to be a Jew at the concentration camps, Kartik thought: no name, age or sex. Just a number.

People jostled for space, shoved others aside, surged forward. Kartik mopped his face.

'You're missing.'

He felt the touch of her coolness on his nape. In one swift motion, he pivoted on his right heel and raised his hand to slap her. Just before he could, hands grabbed him from behind, pinned him to the nearest wall. Someone spat on his cheek.

'It's men like you,' began a beautiful tall sardarni, her thick black plait tight and straight like a baton, 'who make women like me want to join the police force.' She raised her arm but Baby grabbed it.

'Please, go away. This is personal.'

She was leaning against the door of the Ambassador when Kartik emerged into the scorched afternoon. He couldn't speak.

He drove straight down Shah Jahan Road to the circle of India Gate and went round and round until he began to feel dizzy with the repeated circular motion. Then, abruptly, he stopped. The lawns on either side of the avenue were deserted. A handful of tourists in shorts and T-shirts posed for photographs while an air-conditioned bus stood in wait for them.

Kartik switched off the car's engine.

'You know what? What I can't take is your lying. Yes, lying,' repeated Kartik as Baby shook her head. 'There next to me with your hand in my hair, knowing what had happened. Tell me …' his fingers pressed into her arm as his mouth spat out the words, 'what kind of obscene pleasure did it give you to do that?'

She looked down.

'The final fornication before the guy's sentenced?' He tightened the sari pallu around her neck.

'Don't let's be crude,' she whispered, loosening his stranglehold.

'Oooh, sensitive, too.'

Baby stared at his long, knuckled fingers. She removed the pallu from his grasp and flicked it in his face. Kartik caught it.

'I know every little bit of you.' He forced his nose into her cheek, wrenched the hair around her temples. 'Every mole …'

'Oh, please.' She snapped her fingers to her nostrils like a clip.

'… your every little thought.'

'Then, tell me – tell me what I'm thinking right now!'

'You're thinking, why did I ever waste my time on a failure like this,' he replied without hesitation.

'Not bad.' She opened the car door and slammed it on his outrage.

'I was actually thinking that after the way you behaved just now, I don't have to want you any longer.'

He was still wiping the spit trickling down the right side of his mouth and mingling with the sweat accumulated in the slight folds of his neck when she ran across the road, threw the marigold flowers in the air, and spluttered away in a three-wheeler. Her pallu flew out into the open space, a wave of farewell.

HILL STATION
1978

'A wave of farewell and she was gone.'
It was evening in the hill station. Everything looked like a shadow of itself. Still. As though waiting for something to disturb the peace that had settled for the night upon the inhabitants.

Kartik was seated by Didi's feet, his legs stretched out and his back resting on the chair beside hers. Looking down, he noticed the payal on top of her socks and thought it rather touching: it suggested she was very particular about the way she looked. He noticed the emerald-and-diamond ring on the second finger of her right hand: it was oval, with the diamonds clustered around the emerald as though in protection. He wondered if it was her wedding ring.

'Why?' he said, remembering where he had left the conversation.

Didi glanced at Kartik and hugged herself.

'Why what?'

'Why did Baby leave like that? First said she had to go home and disappeared for months, and when she returned, nothing was the same. Next thing I knew, she had bought a ticket to New York. Why did you let her go?'

'Could I have stopped her? She said she wanted to go away. To New York, just as I had when I was about her age. You know Baby. She chases you round and round like you're her tail, until she catches you and makes you do what she wants.'

Kartik nodded. How he had pleaded with her to stay, promised to appear for the exams again, study harder, longer and with greater diligence. She would not listen. Said she had to go, and was gone. On board an Air India flight to New York.

Arms raised above his head, Kartik implored the sky: 'What happened to make her leave like that? It can't be just because of the exams.'

Didi remained with her eyes closed.

'She must have told you,' she remarked.

'Obviously, not enough.'

'As much as she wished you to know.'
'That's not enough.'
'As much as she wished to tell you.'
'That's not enough,' he repeated his protest, 'to understand this absurd need to distance herself.'

Didi strummed her fingers on her nose in a gesture that reminded him of Baby.

'Why would she leave me without the promise of a future?'
'You've come to me because you think the answer lies in her past?'
'Nothing else can explain it.'

He bit the flesh at the joint of his thumb till it started to bleed.

'You're not answering.'

Didi arched her toes.

'What is it that you want to hear? That she had an unhappy childhood? Maybe. That I never gave her the advantages she deserved? Definitely. That she cannot stay loyal to one man because I couldn't?'

Kartik shivered, taken aback by her honesty.

'Tell me what happened when she came home to see you after my results.'

Didi turned her face away.

'Not mine to tell.'

'But I want to understand.'

'Then you'll be a first. Explanations explain nothing. The more you probe, the more you discover, the less you understand. Every new discovery leads to fresh uncertainties.'

Didi licked her flaky lips.

'People do what they do at a moment's notice, then spend a lifetime with the consequences.'

There was in her voice enough to make Kartik reach out to touch her face.

Her withdrawal was as instinctive as a blink.

'There was a time when I ached for the feel of a man,' she said, biting her lower lip. 'But it was never the answer. There aren't any. Answers.' She rose and turned towards the house.

He left three days later. Had to return, he said, to the rest of his life. Didi watched him lope towards the gate, his shoes scuffing the gravel, his curls bouncing to the rhythm of his footfall. At the gate, he stopped to turn and wave. She didn't respond.

As he joined the gates in farewell, Didi wanted to call out – come back. She liked him, this boy who loved Baby. She had learnt to like him. Each evening, they had sat in the veranda, she in her wicker chair, he leaning against the veranda column, opposite the dozing dogs. Didi plied him with liquor, allowing him to drink her Diplomat whisky when he ran out of rum, and prised out details of his life from before Baby had barged in and taken over.

He said he was a young man from a small town who came to the big city in search of his future, only to lose himself.

'Big cities do that to you,' he began, 'they possess you, but you never really belong.'

Delhi was a city that existed as a memory. A place he remembered having lived in rather than living in. Kartik had come to Delhi with dreams as tall as the Qutab Minar but those dreams disintegrated, the way cigarette ash does when disturbed. He failed the exams and a disappointed Baby failed him. His life had been abruptly disconnected like a telephone line with an unpaid bill. He felt he was no longer in touch with the boy who had grown up on a large farm, in the small, secluded world of his family.

His family had lived for longer than anyone could remember in the same old house on the outskirts of the town, at the intersection where the town merged with the village, where the paddy fields took over from the tarmac roads leading into the big town.

'Over a hundred years, can you believe it?' Kartik's father would ask his son, in awe. 'That's how long our family has lived here!'

'Yes, Pitaji,' Kartik would reply automatically.

Pitaji's attachment to the property was more sentimental than accurate. The land originally belonged to Chachaji's family. Pitaji's forefathers had lived in the town, where they had been grain traders. After the mutiny of 1857, Pitaji's paternal ancestor decided he would not do commerce with the colonialists. Instead, he joined Chachaji's great-great grandfather, a cousin three times removed on his mother's side, on the farmland they occupied now. Together, they started a transport business. There was an unwritten agreement between the two: the transport business and the land would belong jointly to both the families, with one condition: the eldest son of either family would always remain on the land.

Together, the two families lived and prospered. Once the British left, they were shrewd enough to realize that India without the British presented newer opportunities, more exciting possibilities than wheat and bajra. They branched out: they grew flowers and sent them to the towns which encircled their own small one. They bought a fleet of trucks that they named 'KissMe' because they had seen the word painted on other trucks.

'Don't know how to spell,' complained Kartik's Chachaji, who fancied his own command over the English language. 'Why would anyone ask for a kiss on the back of a truck? It should have been Kismet – Fate. No?'

They opened the first idli-dosa restaurant in the nearby town, four kilometres down the road, and called it 'Tirupati' because Kartik's parents had visited the holy site just before his birth. They made ice cream at home in aluminium containers placed inside wooden casks, with a wheel to rotate the crushed ice. They sent it out in little cycle carts with the banner: 'English Ice Queen' because they believed people were more likely to buy it if they thought it had British ingredients.

'And let me tell you, no ice cream tastes as creamy as English Ice Queen,' Kartik was to tell his Delhi friends.

The restaurant was a success; the flowers and ice cream sold well. The family felt modern, progressive. However, they never forgot the land, their land. Kartik's father refused to move to the town; he was older than Chachaji – he would stay back. Chachaji went to the big town, reluctantly and alone, to manage the transport business.

'If we all move to the big town, your brother will eat up all the land,' Chachiji warned him. 'We will become landless. Isn't it?'

In Chachiji's opinion – which echoed Pitaji's – to be without land was only slightly better than to be childless and worse than being penniless. Every fortnight, on the days when the local mandis in the nearby town were closed, Chachaji came home.

Kartik and his two cousins went to school in the five-day boys' boarding school, seven kilometres from home. On Friday evenings, they returned to the farm for the weekend.

For twelve years, Kartik caught the 8 a.m. Saturday bus to the town where Mrs Bijoylata Chatterjee, 'Batty Chatty', as Kartik called her, a teacher of English in the missionary day school, gave him extra special classes.

'I want my son to be king of Queen's English,' Kartik's father told him when he complained about studying on a holiday.

Kartik's sister Lata and Chachiji's daughter Rukmini attended the local girls' school three kilometres from their home. Lata was eleven months younger than Kartik. Their mother had conceived soon after Kartik's birth because their parents had wanted to repeat their success of producing a son.

'If you have one child soon after another, they will be same-to-same,' Kartik's mother assured Chachiji. Kartik's mother experienced great difficulties during the pregnancy and a girl was born in the sixth month. Lata was sickly and thin. The local doctor told Kartik's father to leave Kartik's mother alone.

'She is weak.'

Kartik's father waited two months. Then he called his wife in from her evening cooking, just before the sun set over the wheat fields. He believed it was a propitious time for the conception of a boy.

Young Kartik used to sit and watch his mother cook. He felt close to her and enjoyed the smell of the preparations he so yearned for after five days of oily school food. His mother would abandon the food when his father called, the dal in the copper vessel burbling, the vegetables in a gentle sizzle. He never touched a thing – his mother had forbidden it. Occasionally, he would run to the room which had its door slightly ajar, and yell, 'Pitaji, tell my mother something's burning.' He would hear the abrupt creak of the bed, the agitation of the glass bangles around his mother's wrists, the haste of the silver payals on her feet.

Over the next four years, Kartik's mother had three miscarriages. The big town doctor said, 'She cannot bear children any more.'

Kartik's father refused to believe him.

'She comes of good, strong stock,' he would insist. 'Her grandmother bore eight children – only one died. Her mother had nine children and all of them lived.'

Later, Kartik would blame his mother's illness on those miscarriages. And his father's persistence in the room with its door always slightly ajar. When he left home to study history at Delhi University, his mother was still abandoning dinner for his father. Nothing but pleasure, if that, came of it. There were no more children after Lata.

'Just as well,' Kartik confided to Baby, 'Lata barely survived long enough to get married and become her husband's problem.'

Except, it hadn't happened quite that way. What Kartik never told Baby was that the sickly Lata had been sent home the first time she was pregnant. She was eighteen years old.

'Tell your mother she can return to us when she is strong enough,' Lata's mother-in-law told Kartik when he went to fetch his sister.

Lata managed to give birth to a child, a girl, Gudiya, but she was almost bedridden with the effort. For months thereafter, she could barely stand.

'Girls always take more out of a mother,' reflected Pitaji. 'That's why your poor mother never had another child after Lata.'

Lata's husband, Vishnu, would visit her frequently, but his reluctance to take her home kept his head down and his eyes averted. Eventually, a deal was struck. Vishnu came to live with Lata. Pitaji felt the need for a young man about the premises since Kartik had left for Delhi and his cousins stayed in the big town with Chachaji. Lata's husband seemed a sound investment. Kartik's father promised him a piece of the land and a share in the transport business. Only Chachiji lamented the arrival of the son-in-law: she saw him as a piece of land she had lost.

'Don't say that,' chided Kartik's mother. 'When our children marry, everything will become alright.'

★

But it didn't become 'alright'. Just a year later, Pitaji ordered Kartik never to return home, 'out of anger and pride'.

Anger and pride. They would ruin the summer Kartik went home from college. Eleven days after he arrived from Delhi, Pitaji summoned him one mid-morning. Chachiji and his mother were seated on the settee in the visiting room. The women were wrapping paan and arranging them in a damp red cloth inside an engraved silver casket. Chachaji was at the desk, looking through some papers, while Kartik's father occupied the large, wooden engraved chair near the window. Looks like it's been here for a hundred years too, thought Kartik as he approached to touch his father's feet.

Pitaji waved him away with a hand.

'Kartik, we have spoken of your future.'

His fingers hovered about his belly button, occasionally tapping his stomach as though to remind himself it was there.

'Pitaji?'

'Why don't we fix your engagement this time, and when you come next, we can have the wedding?'

'Wedding?'

'Yes, are you not old enough to marry?'

'Yes, Pitaji.'

'Perfect!' exclaimed his father, crossing his hands over his stomach.

'But, Pitaji, I don't wish to marry so early.'

'Why, may I ask, not?'

'I wish to continue studying.'

'For what?'

Kartik drew a very deep breath.

'I like studying.'

'Like-shike is all very well, but what will we do with your studies?'

Kartik gulped.

'I thought I would sit for the IAS.'

'And what of our land, our business?' asked Pitaji, raising a hand to silence Chachiji, whose mouth was hanging open, heavy with words ready to spill out.

'You and Chachaji …'

'Why, are we to live forever?'

'You are strong and healthy, Pitaji. You could live to be hundred.'

'And will we be shaking our bones with work till then?'

'There are my cousins, Ranu and Tarkesh.'

'Yes, but you are the head of the family in the next generation.'

'I will resign gladly, Pitaji.'

'No, ji, you will do what has to be done. Now. Sit. Your Chachaji's very own daughter Rukmini is ready. We will celebrate your engagement. And plan the wedding for next June. What do you say, Kartik, let's do our duty? Let's finally make this family one.'

'Ji, ji, it will be just right,' approved Kartik's mother.

'So long since we had a wedding in the family, isn't it?' contributed Chachiji.

'I want to study,' Kartik repeated quietly, 'and how can I marry Rukmini who I think of as a sister?'

'Simple. Change the way you think,' ordered Pitaji. 'Isn't that why we have educated you? So that you can think and unthink what you thought?'

'That much they must be teaching you in the big college?' added Chachiji.

Chachaji came across and placed a companionable arm around Kartik's waist.

'She is no sister of yours. The blood between our families ran very thin, generations ago – that too on the maternal side. I have treated you like a son because I have been waiting for the day you would truly become my son. By marrying Rukmini to you, we will cement what our ancestors tried to build: one joint family. No?'

Kartik bent to touch Chachaji's feet.

'I think of Rukmini as my sister.'

'Think,' yelled his father, florid in the face. 'Who asks you to think? Do – that is what I demand.' He stood tall, Kartik's shoulders sagged.

'Do as your Pitaji wishes, Beta, otherwise there will be much trouble,' appealed his mother.

'But I cannot, Mummu. I just cannot marry Rukmini and live the rest of my life here.'

'Oh-so, and what is wrong with *here*?'

'Pitaji, I told you I wish to join government service.'

'One hundred years our families have lived here. Can you believe it?'

'Yes, Pitaji.'

'Go.' His father pointed to the half-closed door. 'Go.'

Kartik left without a word.

'Why is it no good for you?' Chachiji asked him, tearful with incomprehension, later that afternoon in his bedroom.

'Because Chachiji, she is like my sister.'

'But not?'

'No, I grant you that. Thank god. In same-blood marriages, there can be problems.'

'Such as?' asked Chachiji, always easily diverted.

'Like … two thumbs in one hand,' replied Kartik, unable to immediately think of anything else.

'But that is very lucky,' said Chachiji, confused.

'But not how God intended, otherwise we would all have four thumbs, would we not?' pleaded Kartik, pressing her legs in a conciliatory gesture.

'I never heard of such a thing. Yes,' replied Chachiji, 'your Dadiji did not have a little toe, but that is because it fell off.'

'Chachiji …' Kartik pinched her calf.

'Well, it did,' insisted Chachiji, 'because she cut herself on a nail and did not tell anyone. The toe was infected, and though it was wrapped in neem leaves thrice a day, it became *that* big and filled with water. One day, when the bandage was removed, it was missing.'

'Where could it have gone?' asked Kartik, perplexed.

'Strange, isn't it?'

And they both laughed.

★

A week before Kartik was to leave for Delhi, Pitaji spoke to him. He had repeated his command but in the language he reserved for requests. Kartik had reiterated his position.

'You educated me, Pitaji. Educated persons cannot blindly follow family traditions,' he argued.

'I need my son to stay and look after the family land,' replied his father.

His mother made one last entreaty the day before his departure for Delhi. Kartik told her that Batty Chatty had taught him plenty besides English.

'Mummu, she says you must serve the country – like your mother serves you food – with love. I want to go out there, Mummu …' Kartik sat on the bed, beside her. He picked up her hand and erased the veins which bulged out. 'The IAS – that's all they talk about in the university. And all my friends are sitting for the exam. I will feel like such a fool saying I have come for a college education to go home and till the land. I want to join the IAS – be someone.'

'Pitaji is going to be very angry' was all she said, withdrawing her hand but not before holding on to his as though she could not bear to let it go.

Kartik returned to Delhi. That was when he met Baby. She would become the source of his distraction and of his happiness when he felt alone and abandoned. She was there, close to him, when his family had withdrawn. Kartik told her about the fight with his family over the IAS, but suppressed the bit about marrying Rukmini. He felt uncomfortable confiding to the girl he wished to marry about the girl his family insisted he wed.

Throughout the year, Kartik received letters from Chachaji, but not his father. The letters carried money transfers for his fees and living expenses. Chachaji wrote about the harvests, the poor rose crop, and to demand more information about the machines Kartik had claimed could produce ice cream, better than their homemade English Ice Queen.

Not better ice cream, Kartik had written back, *just quicker and more of it*.

It was towards the end of the year that he received visitors, at nine in the morning.

He was lying in bed, gazing out of the window, when he saw his father alight at the gate from a taxi with Rukmini by his side. 'Oh,' he chided the sky, 'why are you doing this to me?'

'See who I have brought to meet you!' said his father when he opened the door to him.

Kartik dived for his father's feet and felt himself tremble.

He straightened, smiled at Rukmini. Nervously.

'Get dressed,' ordered his father, 'and join us in the taxi.'

'I am dressed, Pitaji,' he protested.

Pitaji gazed at Kartik's khadi kurta-pyjamas and shawl.

'It's very comfortable, Pitaji.'

'Yes, but you should be dressed smartly in full sleeve shirt-pant. As if you belong to the city.'

'I don't need clothes to do that, Pitaji.'

Kartik loped away to the bathroom. He returned in a white shirt with full sleeves and brown bell-bottoms paired with a green sweater. His father studied him in silence.

'You said to dress like they do in Delhi, Pitaji.'

Rukmini laughed. They climbed into the Ambassador taxi and Pitaji gave the driver an address.

They went to Sharma's Guest In-House, South Extension Part II, where Kartik had stayed when he first arrived in Delhi. It was run by a family from their village; so they got a twenty per cent discount and free meals. In the room, Pitaji wrapped a towel around his kurta and headed towards the bathroom. At the door, he turned.

'You talk,' he ordered Rukmini and Kartik.

'As though we need his permission,' whispered Kartik to Rukmini.

Her eyes shone black.

'Tell me about Delhi, Dada, they say it is bigger than some countries.'

Kartik told Rukmini about the shops, the restaurants, the five-star hotels, the cinema halls, the university, and CP, where he went for a 'spare'.

'Why do you call it a spare?' she asked, perplexed.

'Because it's what you do when you have spare time, silly.'

He promised to take her to watch a Hindi movie at Odeon, a well-known hall, and for Chinese food afterwards at Ginza on the outer circle of CP. They could go round and round CP, down Janpath, or visit Chandni Chowk for the best sweets and buy some cloth for her and Lata from Karol Bagh.

'Sandals,' Rukmini insisted. 'I want white sandals with fat platform heels *this* big, pink nail polish and red lipstick.'

'But you never wear any of those,' protested Kartik.

Rukmini shook her head, shyly.

'You have been away too long,' she replied.

They spent the rest of the day together. Pitaji was impatient with their shopping plans. Instead, he wanted to visit the historical monuments because he said Rukmini must know history.

'Girls' education is very important, right Kartik?'

'Yes, Pitaji.'

They visited the Qutab Minar where Rukmini began to cry because she was not allowed to climb up to the top. They proceeded to Teen Murti House. Rukmini admired the place, especially Nehru's bed, which she said looked very, very big. They stopped near the prime minister's residence at 1, Safdarjang Road, but Pitaji said this was 'bakwaas' because they could not even see Mrs Gandhi.

Rukmini was delighted by Delhi. She said it was like a 'merry-go-round' since it had so many roundabouts.

They wandered around CP and then Janpath. Rukmini stopped at every small shop with knick-knacks: hair clips, bands, silver jewellery ... Kartik's father was exasperated by her constant halts and frequently spat paan on the road. Then Kartik forced them to drink cold coffee at Depaul's.

'It is the most famous cold coffee in all of Delhi,' he explained as they were handed the small glass bottles with silver foil caps. 'People come from everywhere just to drink it.'

'Thhu,' tasted his father. 'We make better at home with our own milk. And to think people crowd to drink this at *this* time of the year!'

Rukmini winked at Kartik.

They ate club sandwiches at Bankura restaurant, outside Cottage Industries.

'We make better ...' began Pitaji, but seeing the wide, expectant grins on their faces, he clamped his teeth on the bread.

In the shade of a disappearing sun, they walked to India Gate and stared at the outline of Rashtrapati Bhavan in the distance.

'Beautiful,' exclaimed Rukmini, nose pink with candy floss.

'The capital of India, then,' Pitaji informed her with pride.

By the time they returned to the guest house, it was past seven in the evening and Rukmini was exhausted. She had a bath and went straight to bed.

'Those sandwiches were very, very big,' she smiled.

'Like Nehru's bed?' teased Kartik.

After she had disappeared into the adjoining room, Kartik's father closed the door behind her and pulled out a bottle of Red Label whisky from his suitcase. He ordered two plates of seekh kebabs and a tandoori chicken from room service. Kartik drew two armchairs in front of the rod heater. Once the guest-house boy had delivered the snacks, they sat down to some serious drinking.

'Then?' asked his father.

'Pitaji?'

'Have you and Rukmini decided a date?'

Kartik shook his head.

'I simply want to live my own life,' he said. His father picked up a seekh kebab and broke it. He put half into his mouth and offered the remainder to his son.

People smoke peace pipes, we eat kebabs for a compromise, thought Kartik, munching.

'Nonsense!' Kartik's father waved away the thought as he would an irritating fly. 'I have promised your Chachaji and Chachiji that you will marry. Rukmini is growing old. She wishes to marry. You are the best man for her husband's job.'

Kartik began to sweat in his armpits.

'Pitaji, we are not cattle!'

'I do not wish to listen. You will come home!' Pitaji shouted.

Kartik took a kebab, broke it into half, put one piece in his mouth and dropped the other. He kicked it, viciously. Pitaji picked up the kebab from the floor and squeezed it in his right hand.

'Will you not marry Rukmini?' The meat oozed out between his fingers. 'You disobey me and see if I let you see your mother's face.' Kartik bent to touch his father's feet.

'Forgive me, Pitaji.'

'Children are like puppies ...'

Kartik turned away.

'That's the last time you turn your back on me!' screamed his father, pulling him around.

Kartik bit his tongue. His blood tasted bitter.

'If I am a puppy, what does that make you, Pitaji?'

Kartik's father staggered back.

'You called me a dog? Saala-kutta!'

He raised his hand to slap Kartik across the face. Anticipating the blow before he received it, Kartik fell back, but his foot caught in the strands of the durree and his knees buckled. The side of his head glanced off the sharp edge of the wooden table as he fell. Pitaji's hand was arrested mid-air. He thumped his chest, burped twice, grabbed the whisky bottle and strode into the other room, slamming the door behind him.

In the morning, Kartik's father observed the bandage stuck on his son's forehead with a critical eye but without comment. When Rukmini asked him how he had hurt himself, Kartik replied truthfully that he had slipped. They left after breakfast. His father refused to speak to him. Rukmini hugged Kartik.

'Bye, Rukmini,' he whispered. 'I'll buy you a pair of platforms *this* high, with gold buckles, for your birthday.'

'Size four, Dada,' she reminded him.

Kartik held her.

That was the last contact between them. Thereafter, Kartik's letters home returned unopened; Chachaji stopped writing to him. Only the money orders arrived with dutiful regularity each month. Kartik was stunned by his father's stubborn anger. He had never imagined that Pitaji would let the distance between Delhi and home lengthen into years. Or that blood could turn to water so fast.

'How can blood turn to water so fast?' Kartik asked Didi.

'I don't know about blood,' said Didi, gently massaging her knuckles, 'but I do know that relationships can be as brittle as human bones. They snap under pressure. Take my marriage. Over. Snap. Just like that. Even before it had begun. I remember thinking that. On the flight home from New York.'

DIDI
1956

On the flight home from New York, Didi's stomach fell out. She felt sickeningly ill. She wanted to be left alone, but Mem flitted about her like a persistent fly. Didi wanted to swat Mem. Had it been Sita, she most certainly would have. Sita, however, was not fit company for the sick. She sat in the window seat, nose flat against the glass, gaping at the beauty of the changing sky, glad to have left America, relieved to be going home. Her cheeriness revolted Didi, who suffered continuous bouts of nausea.

She also felt genuinely scared. Was this travel sickness? Or something else?

'My life is over,' she murmured over and over again to herself and then loudly, 'OVER.'

'Don't say that,' Mem consoled when she heard the pitiful cries. 'Here, suck on this piece of sugared ginger. It will make you better.'

'I wish I could die.' Didi held the paper bag to her mouth. 'Why don't you call upon your gods to release me?'

'Hai Ram! You do not know what you tell,' exclaimed Mem.

'Say,' corrected Didi.

'Achcha, not too sick to correct your mother's English, I see.'

'I want to die. Hai, Mem's Bhagvan, where are you?'

'Achcha, shanti, shanti …' Mem reached for her Bhagvad Gita which was never far from her troubles, and recited a few verses for her daughter's soul, which was in jeopardy.

As the airplane fell out of the grey clouds over Delhi, Didi threw up the remains of her stomach.

Two days later, she visited her cousin in his office. She had to speak to someone. Someone she trusted. Who better than Mahendra?

Mahendra was Didi's first cousin. His father had died of dysentery when Mahendra was eleven, leaving him to be educated by Didi's father. He lived with his mother in Dehi, but went to boarding school. Every summer, he accompanied Didi and Mem to the hills for the holidays. The two children were close, playful. So playful that when one went to the toilet, the other stood outside, listening. Whoever could 'let go' more often won the game and the loser paid for the ice-cream sticks.

He was seven years older than Didi. When she returned from New York, he was an executive in a British biscuit firm.

That March morning, he sat in his Delhi Gate office with its domed ceiling, the large window ajar. There was an overhead fan but Mahendra liked fresh air, even when it was hot. He wore a white, full-sleeved shirt, buttoned to the wrists, and a grey-and-blue striped tie, both tucked into white cotton trousers. He was plump in a jolly sort of way. His circular face and the balding curvature of his head were spared complete roundness by rectangular black spectacles.

Didi sat before him in a starched blue cotton chikan-work sari and an embroidered white sleeveless blouse, her hair plaited, oiled.

'I don't know, Didi. You are either extremely brave or completely foolhardy.'

If Mahendra was appalled by Didi's account of her affair with Jeff, he did not allow it to interfere with his concern for her. She was his sister. His friend. He liked Didi, if not always what she did.

Didi spoke of the sickness, the missed period.

'Prem's lady doctor is here,' said Mahendra, referring to his wife's gynaecologist. 'I will pay for her cooperation. Understand?'

'Maybe I am just sick over this marriage business, and the tension has frozen my blood.'

'Don't talk like that,' Mahendra scolded. 'You're going to be married, Didi. How will you explain your condition, if there is one, to your husband?'

'I will manage.'

'Stubborn Didi,' he said, pulling her plait. 'You will ruin everything. We are talking of your future. Don't be so carefree with it. Like you were with your body.'

'Ouch.'

'I cannot understand it. How did an educated girl like you do this? That too in America with an American, knowing your future lay here with a husband of your family's choice? How?'

Didi remained silent.

'How could you not think, Didi, of the future?'

Didi went across to the brown leather couch and lay down shading her eyes with her right arm.

'It was New York, I was alone, the wind was hurling through the streets, the lights flickering in the shops. The brown leaves outside my bedroom window, the snow on my hair and the warmth of his body ... He felt so, so there. The future wasn't present then. How could I touch it?'

'Think of your future now.'

'I have thought.'

Didi sat up.

'I will not see Prem's lady doctor, I will not die on some dirty operating table.'

'Didi-Didi.' Mahendra knelt next to her, pinched her cheek. 'No one dies like that on the table. Dr Mukherjee is a famous gynaecologist. You'll be safe.'

'Nobody is safe. Completely. Ever.'

Didi heaved herself up and strode across to the open window.

'It's tension, that's all.'

'Oh, wouldn't I like to just shake you!' exclaimed Mahendra, joining her and tapping her on her head. 'Think. Think of the consequences.'

'I don't care,' cried out Didi, coming back to the sofa. 'I don't care. I'm scared, Mahendra, scared of an operation, scared of what I may have done.'

'Then correct it. See the lady doctor.'

He held out his hand.

'Come.'

'No.'

'Didi ...'

'No.'

When Mahendra drove Didi home that evening, she hugged his arm.

'I will manage.'

In the days before the wedding, Didi contemplated her future without the conviction that she would be able to live up to her bravura claim. Indeed, she considered the future, and Purushottam, with dread. Husband and wife. The very idea made her shudder, distracting her from the activity around her. As Mem bustled about making arrangements, she frequently had to call her daughter to attention.

'All the time dreaming, dreaming. Never here where you are wanted. See here, madam, pay attention – I am putting your heavy saris here. You will have to wear them during the first few days at your in-laws'.'

They were at Dada's house. The wedding was ten days away and Mem was aflutter with anxiety. Had she forgotten anything? She would read her checklist every day and make Sita unpack and repack Didi's trunks. Father hurried out of the house each morning before Mem involved him in her plans, saying he had 'arrangements to see to' for the wedding. In truth, he retired to the Gymkhana Club to read the newspapers.

One afternoon, Mem sat by a big black trunk, checking Didi's packed clothes with Sita. Didi stretched languidly on the bed. Mem explained what Didi must wear the following day when she was to meet her prospective husband for the first time. Didi had resisted meeting Purushottam till now, saying that as long as he did not have two noses and four eyes, she didn't care. But now the ceremonies were to begin, and the time for prevarication was over.

Mem advised Didi against wearing high heels. She was a tall girl. The same height as her future husband.

'Remember to bow your head,' ordered Mem, 'and you'll be the right size for Purushji.'

At the mention of him, Didi was on alert.

'Bow? Never.' She jumped up. 'All my life you have told me I come from the most superior family. If you have not been telling your only child lies, why should I bow my head to one who could be an equal but is quite likely an inferior?'

'Achcha,' pleaded Mem, fingers on lips, 'hey bhagvan, why educate this girl?' She slapped her forehead.

'He didn't, you did,' corrected Didi.

'This is your civil disobedience. You will twist everything into a plait and tie your mother up in its knots,' Mem complained. 'Will you cover your head with your pallu? Will you bow your head in front of your husband and his family? Will you touch their feet?' demanded Mem.

'At the wedding, yes, after that, no.'

'Then you will disgrace our proud name. And I think I shall never speak to you again,' Mem threatened.

'Disgrace? Perfect. Then Dada may relent and call off this marriage,' Didi replied.

'No, he won't. He has too much pride and too little time to live. You will have to be punished,' added Mem in an ominous tone.

'How?' asked her daughter, curious.

'He will hit you,' Mem replied grandiosely, winking at Sita.

'With his silver hair brush,' added Sita, winking back.

When Dada called her into his bedroom, Didi marched in. He was reclining on his bed, reading a book.

'Your mother tells me you refuse to cover your head, bow or touch your prospective mother-in-law's feet after the wedding. Is that a correct summation of the facts?'

'Yes.'

'What is it you wish to achieve by this display of discourtesy?'

'I regard these gestures as displays of inferiority and I don't think I am inferior to anyone.'

Didi played with the ribbon in her plait.

'What if I, your Dada, were to tell you it is not a sign of inferiority, but of respect?'

'But how may I respect people I do not even know?' argued Didi.

'Because I vouch for their respectability?'

'You touch their feet, then,' said Didi without thinking. Dada closed the book and set it aside.

'Your tongue is loose, like your spirit. If I had not been old and infirm, you would have learnt what it means to be insolent and ill-bred.'

'I know how you teach lessons – with the back of your silver brush …' she blurted out without thinking.

Dada's head sank fractionally to the right. Then he straightened up.

'You are ridiculous and rude …'

'I beg your pardon, Dada.' Didi kissed his right cheek.

'Perhaps you would like to translate your repentance into obedience?'

'I'm sorry, but it is against my principles.'

'Leave.'

Dr Rai Bahadur, the family physician, was summoned around 9 p.m. He brought a few leeches with him to suck out Dada's blood and reduce his high pressure.

On the chosen day, Didi did marry the man of her grandfather's choice. And went to live in his father's house.

It was a capacious, high-ceilinged bungalow. There were wooden doors, tall and slim as the trees from which they had been hewn, with long, heavy brocade curtains, dark crimson, blue and emerald green. A central black-and-white diamond-tiled corridor with rooms on each side. A study to the left, a bedroom on the right. The master bedroom adjacent to the study, with a bathroom outside in an elongated veranda where they sat to drink sunlit tea in the morning.

Opposite, the drawing room invited you out into a front garden flooded by the afternoon skylight. At its end, the corridor formed a Y, branching into a bedroom on the right curve and to a dining room on the left. The kitchen was detached, down a rough open stone path which was protected by a tin roof to ensure rain and bird droppings did not fall upon the food or passersby.

Didi's father- and mother-in-law occupied the main bedroom and Purush's elder brother Bhai, the one opposite. Budhoo, the family dog, slept in the corridor near the dining-room door. The married couple was in the bedroom near the dining room. It was square with a fireplace, and a door led out onto the veranda and front lawn. A dressing table and stool hid behind an emerald-green velvet curtain. The sofa of the set Mem had bought for Didi in New York ran along one wall. In the centre, where the cross breeze was the strongest, stood a large bed, guarded by mosquito poles.

Except on very special and rare occasions, the bedroom door remained open. Didi's first night was the most special and rarest of occasions. The door was firmly shut, latched and bolted.

Didi sat on the sofa in a burnished gold sari. She had a backache on account of sitting on the floor all afternoon with her head inclined to one side, a concession to her mother-in-law, while Purush's family and friends inspected and then blessed what they saw.

Purush went behind the curtain and returned in white pyjamas and a mal-mal kurta.

He asked, 'Change?'

'Yes.'

She rubbed the small of her back. Then she rose and disappeared behind the green curtain. She returned in a long, pink cotton nightdress and a matching pink dressing gown.

Purush asked, 'What's that?'

Staring.

'My new nightdress. Like it?'

Purush circled his wife.

'You are going to wear this, tonight?'
'I would look very strange wearing it during the day.'
Purush massaged his neck with his right hand.
'The women in this family do not.'
He paced up and down.
'They wear saris.'
'Well, I have always worn a nightdress at night,' Didi reasoned. 'I wouldn't be able to sleep in a sari. Imagine being wrapped up in six yards of cloth all night. How would you like it?'
Didi sat down on the bed. Purush joined her.
'I have never thought about it.'
Again, Purush ran a hand across the back of his neck.
'I think you must change.' He gripped the edge of the bed.
'Why?'
'I just told you why.'
There was in Purush's voice all the helplessness of his sex and background. Men of his kind did not explain such matters to their wives. Why did a man have to spend his first night alone with his wife, anyway? Why couldn't Ma or Bhai be here to tuck him in, smooth out the problems?
'What will happen if I sleep in my nightdress?'
'I do not know.'
The edge in Purush's voice said she had no business doing this to him.
'Well, I will sleep in my nightdress tonight and if the sun still rises tomorrow morning, we'll know that I have not transgressed the laws of nature.'
Didi climbed into bed, tucked the mosquito net in on all sides, and stretched out.
Purush stood undecided. Should he go see Ma? Ask Bhai for advice?
'Please do wear a sari.'
Didi felt trapped like a fish within that netting. She sat up.
'If you can give me one good reason, a reason which is not linked to the traditions of women in your family, a reason which is your own, then I might just consider it.'

Purush swallowed hard.

'I always imagined my wife in a sari. I have never thought of her wearing any other garment. When I saw you at your Dada's house, you were wearing a bright yellow sari. At the wedding you wore a sari. Here, too, you came in a sari. Now, in this, like this, you do not look like my wife.'

Purush clenched his fist and gnawed at his knuckles.

Didi stared at him through the fine mesh of the mosquito net, then swung herself off the bed. She went behind the curtain.

She reappeared within minutes in a white sari with a blue border and a white sleeveless blouse. She sat on the bed, cross-legged. Purush walked forward with a firmer stride.

He climbed inside the mosquito net and lay on the left hand side of the bed. Didi remained seated. She took Mem's name eleven times, a mantra for benediction.

His hand reached out for hers but encountered her thigh instead. He felt the muscles tauten to his touch and withdrew guiltily: maybe it was a little too early for that. But he had never been taught the etiquette of the first night. Did such conventions exist, Purush wondered worriedly.

'I need to tell you something now.'

He looked at his wife. Her body was an unlit candle in the dark: straight, white and motionless.

'What is it?'

Didi crossed her toes.

'You know I was in America?'

'That's why you think women wear dresses at night.'

'I had problems. Women's problems.'

She curled her toes tighter. Forgive me, Mem, forgive me, Didi prayed, but I can say no more.

Purush shook his legs, knocking the feet together. He was thoroughly perplexed by these confidences. What did she mean? And why hadn't she confided in Ma?

Meanwhile, it was his wedding night. He slithered his right hand across the bed sheet. He patted her body in search of the waistband of her petticoat where the sari pleats were tucked in. He tugged at them.

Didi imagined Ed's loft. The feel of Jeff's hands where Purush's now struggled with her clothes. Sunshine hair on arms, the ivory head, bluish-green eyes, brown freckles on the nose, the roasted tobacco breath of him.

Purush pushed aside her sari, lowered the petticoat. He balanced himself on his right elbow and began to undo her blouse with both hands. Didi's fingers reached up and automatically opened the hooks. She looked into Purush's face hanging above hers like an overhead lamp, light brown hair, grey eyes speckled blue, his skin milky in colour, cold cream in smoothness. His hands rubber gloves upon her breasts.

Purush swung a leg across her hips.

Mem, Mem, Didi prayed, her hands on Purush's shoulders.

Her legs were apart. She was wet all over. A headache throbbed at her temples. She burped inside her mouth. He lowered himself.

Didi's hands clutched Purush, her mouth open as she rocked forward.

Suddenly, Purush sprung aside.

'Oh, what have you done?' he exclaimed, looking down.

He jumped off the bed and rushed to the dressing room, holding his kurta away from his body.

Didi had vomited.

'And I had just got there …'

A bucket was filled, water crashed against the floor. By the time Didi had removed the bed sheets, Purush had returned in a fresh mal-mal kurta and cotton pyjamas. His hair was dressed back, his face scrubbed to a shine.

'I will go outside,' he announced.

'Yes.'

Didi poured bucket after bucket of water over her head, wondering why she had chosen the wrong moment to vomit.

'I am doing badly. But I'll manage, I will,' she told herself again and again, as she scrubbed herself with a towel. She pulled the pink nightdress over her head and picked up the accompanying gown.

In the bedroom, she found Purush spread out upon her New York sofa.

'What manner of woman vomits on her husband?'

'All that rich food over the last week and the crowds of people …'

Didi flipped the mattress, tucked in new bed sheets taken out from her luggage.

'I just can't believe it.' He clutched his hair.

'Vomit is not something one can control.'

Didi changed the pillow cases. Purush glanced across at her. Suddenly he frowned.

'Why are you in your nightdress?'

'Because I'm feeling sick and want to sleep.'

'But I told you …'

'I know what you told me and now I must tell you something.'

'What? More?'

Purush's voice was startled. He was anxious and angry. What was it now? Why couldn't she save something for tomorrow, for Ma?

'Why don't we wait till tomorrow, when Ma is there?'

'I said I have something to tell *you*. Not your mother. Some things are between a man and a woman.'

'Well,' he replied, turning his back on her and bending his legs so that he fit into the sofa, 'I don't want to talk with you. First you wear that dress. Then you tell me some story about your medical adventures, which you or your mother should have told my mother before the wedding. Then what do you do? Disgusting.'

Didi did not reply. She lay down on the bed and stretched her arms above her head.

'I must speak,' she insisted. 'Without the truth, how can this work?'

Purush pressed the palms of his hands to his ears. With his knees up, he was like a sleeping snail.

Then Didi told Purush about Jeff and the encounter in his parents' country house. She recounted it in the manner of a sudden, unexpected event, like an accident. She said it never happened again. As she said it, Didi asked Jeff and Mem to forgive her – for betraying them.

At the end of her recital, Purush remained with his back to her; still, silent, hands over ears. Didi waited, wondering if he had heard her and how he was going to react, but Purush was inert, unresponsive. Didi lay on her side, staring outside, unable to sleep through her first night at 3, Chor Bagh, despite wearing her nightdress.

She heard Purush rise in the darkness and leave on heavy feet. He hadn't returned by the time the bulbuls and sparrows began a duet to the early morning on the mango tree outside the room. Didi bathed, massaged herself with almond oil, combed and divided her hair into two plaits, fingered kohl into her eyes. With a hairpin, she planted a small black bindi in the middle of her forehead; touched perfume behind her earlobes; wore a bright yellow taffeta blouse and a bottle-green-with-gold-buti-border cotton dhoti; walked barefoot across the floor.

She stepped out of the room and ran back inside. Brushing aside the green curtain, she stood in front of the dressing table and found the sindoor in a small silver casket.

'This is my red signpost,' she said to her reflection. 'It tells everyone who I am.'

She went through the dining room to the kitchen. Her mother-in-law was seated on her haunches, slapping a paratha on the tava. Maharaj, the cook, was slicing potatoes in a steel bowl. Budhoo sat nearby, gazing hungrily at Maharaj who kept up a constant stream of endearments but gave him nothing to eat.

Didi folded her hands.

Som Devi did not acknowledge the greeting. Her long, straight nose flicked to indicate another steel vessel on the fire.

'So. Have tea.'

Didi strained tea into a cup and sat on the steps leading down into the kitchen garden. Budhoo rose slowly and approached her. He sniffed her behind the ear and she shivered at the cool wetness of his nose. She put out a hand which he dutifully licked. Then he collapsed beside her.

The sun beamed straight on them, highlighting the shimmer in Didi's blouse and the brown glints of Budhoo's hair. Bhai appeared before her from a hole in the hedge that divided the kitchen garden from the lawn in front of Som Devi's bedroom. He stumbled on an uneven patch in the vegetable bed because his eyes were where they should not have been.

'You were like an Amrita Sher Gill painting in those rich colours against the smoothness of your skin,' Bhai described later. 'You stared straight at me, but you didn't see me. You sat still, the cup held fast to your lips.'

Bhai was not married. Mem said he had refused to. Nobody knew why.

'Maybe there is something wrong with him,' Didi had offered.

Now she debated whether or not she should rise in his presence.

Bhai's shadow crossed her. He reached down to pat Budhoo on the head.

'What is it you want, Bhai?' his mother called out.

'Food, Ma, food. I am starving.'

'Ask this one to serve you, phir then,' replied his mother.

She has already decided not to like me, Didi told herself. I wonder, is it because I wouldn't cover my head, or has Purush said something to her?

Didi rose, staring at the man in front of her, not seeing him. She followed him out into the front lawn, carrying a silver tray of food for the men.

'The new bahu of the family is a blessing to this house,' commented Didi's father-in-law. 'The food you bring smells delicious.'

Didi noticed Purush's head sink as if he was searching for what he had lost in the blades of grass.

'Mmmmm,' murmured her father-in-law, munching.

'I have not cooked anything,' said Didi, 'it is all his mother's doing.'

'But you are serving us,' responded her father-in-law. 'That increases the taste of the food manifold. Yes, decidedly,' he added, placing paratha and sabzi in his mouth. 'I eat the food your saas cooks every day and it has never tasted quite so delicious!'

Som Devi reached her husband's side.

'Purush, why are you not eating?'

Purush pulled his face out of his neck.

'I will, Ma.'

'Want that your wife serves you?' asked his father, elbowing him in the ribs.

Som Devi covered her head with her pallu, pulled her nose in.

That night, Didi sat against the mango tree. The day had exhausted her desire for company. Relatives, friends and acquaintances had streamed in with the sunlight and left only when it sank beneath the roof of the bungalow next door. They came to examine the 'American bahu', as her father-in-law had teasingly nicknamed Didi. How many teas, coffees and 'something cold' had she served throughout the day? How many female hands had turned her chin this way and that to admire her features?

Black eyes.

Dark brown.

Very much her mother's skin, fair.

The nose is her father's. Bilkul long like his.

Looks proud.

Looks pretty.

Too much American lipstick.

Too full.

Too tall.

Quite pleasant.

Leaning back, Didi arched her neck and stretched out her hands. Her feet were dirty and tender. Oh Mem, she sank her chin upon her knees, you never prepared me for any of this.

She heard the door open and close. Purush. They had barely looked at each other the entire day, hardly exchanged a few sentences.

Didi heard the creak of the almirah. Then a match was struck. Yesterday, he hadn't smoked inside. Men don't smoke on their wedding nights or what, Didi wondered, wiping her face with her pallu. A switch clicked.

When she entered the room, Purush was lying on the bed, straight and still, with his hands placed near his heart. She bathed, changed into a white nightdress and sank down beside him.

'A new nightdress for every night?' Purush asked, his voice hoarse.

'Part of my trousseau.'

'For him you must have worn nothing.'

Didi felt her eyelashes against her skin.

'How many times?'

Didi did not reply.

Purush rose, lit a cigarette.

'It makes me laugh. Everyone in the family is somersaulting with the honour of your coming into our family. We are the envy of the entire community, the city. Why? Because of you. A wife who has been unfaithful to her husband before marriage. Rubbish all.'

'It can't be unfaithful if it was before,' Didi replied.

Purush stared at Didi.

'What does a husband do with a wife who has already been …?'

'I don't know. What does a woman who is forced into marriage do? Continue, I suppose.'

Purush lay down again.

Didi took Mem's name eleven times. She sat in the darkness beside her husband. She removed the dressing gown. With her left hand she reached up and undid the top button of her nightdress. Purush blinked rapidly. Didi undid the second button. Carefully. Then the third. Slowly. Purush went limp.

'You are not my wife – in this.'

Didi considered him, then rose and went behind the emerald curtain. She opened her big black steel trunk, the one with the wedding finery, and shut it with a desperate hardness.

Didi lay down on the bed. Purush turned to her. She was wearing her wedding lehenga. He loosened his pyjamas, thrust up the lehenga. He saw the hooks of her blouse stretched to accommodate her breasts in repose. He fumbled with them. Then he crouched on all fours, astride her body.

'I am twenty-nine. Yesterday was my first …'

He lowered himself like a curtain, plunging her into darkness.

A few minutes later, Purush went to lie down on the sofa. His breathing was ragged. Didi went to the bathroom. She returned damp in her white nightdress. She lay down with her back to Purush; he turned on his left side to stare at her back and clenched his eyes and fists.

She placed a hand over her stomach. Mem, Mem, she whispered to herself.

With each successive day, Didi was to miss her mother in the way she would have missed herself, had she been absent from her own life. She had once looked at her mother's left palm, the one they said predicted a woman's fate, and compared it to her own. She found the lines, their shape, the length, to be alike in a way that startled her: was she her mother's future? Or was her mother a slice of her own past?

For Didi, there was now a painful sense of separation from her family. Father, Mem, Sita: they existed in time; they were missing in space. Her space. She could not run into Mem's bedroom and rest her head on her broad hip, tickle her tummy, cajole her, tease her, stroke her cool, fat arms. The incredible security of her body. She could not yell for Sita to fill her bath water, put out her clothes and massage her hair with sarson ka tel. The sheer comfort of her attendance. She couldn't ask Father for money to buy a new book, a new cardigan, a ticket to an old movie. The absolute indulgence of his wallet. And she could not turn to feel Jeff's closeness to her, the shiver of anticipation and pleasure he aroused each time he reached for her. The gnawing ache of desiring him.

Recollections. They're like dishes of hot food left on a table, Didi thought, the longer they lie untouched, the colder they become. You must constantly warm them up with remembrance.

Didi sensed a still numbness to life at 3, Chor Bagh, save for the undercurrent of feelings that ran through it in subterranean cavities, like electrical wires. She wrote to Mahendra: *It was like eating frozen peas.*

Didi did not know what Purush did or did not say to his mother. However, Som Devi always spoke to Didi in a manner that suggested she wanted no direct contact with her daughter-in-law; so Didi suspected something had passed between them. She was grateful. She wished to avoid intimacy.

It was a wish easily granted. Purush slept next to her but was careful to avoid her touch in public, except accidentally. By the time she rose in the morning, he would have left the bedroom. Periodically during the day, she saw him. But so little did they have to do with each other that it never struck her as odd that he should always be there.

Until one morning at the dining table.

Purush was lingering at the table, eating leisurely, chewing methodically.

'Don't know what he does,' Didi's father-in-law complained, waiting along with Som Devi and Didi for his younger son to finish the meal. 'He eats so slowly, as though eating were a full time occupation.'

Didi stared at her munching husband. Bhai rushed through his meals because he was always late for work. Purush never did any. Yes, he ran errands – bank work, payment of bills – he drove his mother to the market. Otherwise, he was always at home.

Seated at the dining table, watching his mouth work overtime, Didi felt a chill.

The same evening, she went to Bhai's bedroom. A curtain in the doorway, the shade of light reflected on the floor.

'Bhai?' she called out softly. 'Bhai?'

'Oh yes, yes,' came his voice from a distance, 'come in.'

Didi entered his room. There was a bed in the middle, under the ceiling fan, a desk by the open window with piles of books, a large brass lamp with a blue shade, and a cane chair against the wall. Bhai stepped in from the bathroom, wiping his hands and face on a white towel.

'Didi. Come. Please sit.' He pulled out the cane chair.

She sat down and from the window looked out onto the lawn where she saw Purush. He was swaying with a hosepipe.

'I have come to ask,' announced Didi with all the self-importance of a crucial moment, 'you …'

'Oh yes, yes,' Bhai nodded.

'Tell me then, when does Purush go to work?'

Bhai had thrown the towel on the bed and smoothed back his hair. He stopped and locked his hands behind his head.

'When?'

'When?' Didi directed the inquiry at his face.

'It's like this …' His voice fell along with his hands.

'Yes?' encouraged Didi.

'The thing is, he hasn't quite decided. But he's highly educated.' Bhai's smile revealed encouragement.

'But he's twenty-nine years old,' exclaimed Didi. 'He should have decided ages ago.'

'He did try.' Bhai sat down on the bed. 'He started out as a lawyer, you know. He was a public attorney. But he used to frequently fall ill at the chambers. It was very crowded and dirty and suffocatingly hot.' Bhai passed a hand over his mouth. 'Very, very hot.' He eyed Didi with a gentle smoulder.

'See Didi, Purush is the sensitive kind. So Ma told him not to bother with law. He did a B.Ed and taught in the local private school … but the students? They wouldn't listen to him and talked throughout his class. They didn't attend his classes for a whole fortnight, and the principal scolded Purush for not being able to command their respect,' Bhai paused. 'He decided to quit. Actually …' Bhai peered out of the door and then the window, 'actually, he never told anyone that he had left the school. We thought he was on study leave. Then the principal met Papa at the club and asked him what Purush was up to after quitting the school. Papa was furious, so was Ma, because she said there was no other job in the world which gave you four months' paid holiday.'

'Then?' Didi asked, never once taking her eyes off Purush's back.

'Then ...' Bhai spread out his fingers on the bedcover, 'then Papa told him to join our family publishing business. It was decided he would join me at the bookshop, but there wasn't enough work for the two of us. He spent most of the afternoons sleeping in the storeroom. Ma said he might as well come home and lie down.'

'Now Papa wants him to return to law. "Every man must have a profession," he says. And Ma wants him to start his own business if he likes; and since they disagree, he does neither. So he stays at home.'

'And waters the plants.'

'Yes. But he's very well-read, you know,' Bhai added, sitting up. 'He's read Plato and Thucyclides.'

'And you?' She scratched at a pimple on her arm.

'I love poetry and history, especially about the East India Company.'

'Poetry about the East India Company?' she laughed. 'So your brother does no work,' she added without a smile.

Bhai stood up

'Not to worry, Didi. Papa's publishing house does well. We publish educational books; so there is constant demand. And our bookshop is the biggest English bookshop in the town, so ...' he shrugged and smiled a little shyly. 'There's plenty for all of us.'

'Will he ever find himself?' Didi rose, staring at Purush.

'Oh yes. Give him time.'

Watching Purush asleep beside her, curled up on the sofa or masticating with military precision, Didi never gained the impression of a man in search of himself. He possessed the puzzled air of someone who didn't know where he should begin looking. She blamed herself. Had her revelations about Jeff led to his inability in bed? Perhaps, Didi admitted to herself, I could have made a man out of him, but it's too late for that now. My wedding night was the death of our marriage.

Each night for the first seven nights, Purush approached Didi. She wore a new cotton sari on each occasion. She unhooked her blouse, held her breath, murmured Mem's name. He loosened her petticoat, pushed it up and chafed his hands up and down, down and up her legs. He would rise above her, she would pull the drawstring of his pyjamas and squeeze her eyes tight. After the second night, he closed his eyes too. In this way, they could meet as two bodies belonging to other people.

After he abandoned the attempt to unite with her, preferring the roughness of the sofa to the softness of her skin or the cotton sheets, Didi would bathe him off her. She scrubbed her skin with her finger nails. Then she overturned an entire bucket of water on her head, loving the cool night water on her scalded skin.

When she came back to bed, it was in her nightdress, and to the same refrain: It's your fault.

Didi lay on her side. She stared out at the mango tree from between the panes of the French window. There was much she would have liked to say: yes, it's my fault, yes, I was with another. Yes, I am glad of it. No, I cannot bear your loose, mal-mal skin against mine, your dry, cold hands scraping me, your knocking knees ... Jeff, Jeff.

She never said a word. Too much had happened between them already. And to say more than she already had would permit him an intimacy which their bodies had rejected.

During the first few months of marriage, he continued, as a matter of marital routine, to fumble for her in the dark. Not every night, after that first week, but when the moment seized him. Didi did what was expected of her, Mem's name on her lips. She wore a sari. She performed like his marionette.

Tickle my toes.
Rub hot garlic oil on my stomach.
Bathe in your sari and come to bed wet.
Massage me with your body.
The unspoken plea: *Arouse me.*
She complied with these demands without any feeling of humiliation

or resentment. Why did she comply? Was it to atone for Jeff or for telling Purush about him?

There had been a wilfulness to her disclosure that first night with Purush, a perverse need, perhaps, to fail with him and be faithful to the idea of Jeff. She felt she had lost the moral right to desire again. What was it her father had said to her? Marriage was not about the heart and the mind; it was about belonging.

So be it. She would become a part of 3, Chor Bagh. With that resolve, Didi immersed herself in the household's routine. She found that it sharpened her sense of separation from her past.

The demands made of her were ones she had made of others until then. The need to rise from her seat when Som Devi entered a room; the need to rise early and make tea for the men and then help Maharaj with the breakfast; the need to listen to her mother-in-law's poor opinion of her skills.

'What did your Mem teach you to do with the rolling pin?' she sniffed. 'Nowadays, girls have to be taught everything. I am only asking: should not every girl have household skills?'

Well, I can plait my hair, said Didi under her breath, handing over the rolling pin to Som Devi.

Didi learnt to cook food the way her in-laws liked it, but she never developed a taste for it. She never learnt how to care for the gods either. Mem's gods and now Som Devi's. In an alcove of her bedroom, Som Devi had installed them on a high stool where she dressed them in garlands of marigold, honoured them with rose petals at their feet and perfumed them with agarbatti. Every morning and evening, Didi was told to sweep the alcove, wipe the floor, dust down the gods and bring in fresh flowers.

The problem occurred in the seating arrangement. Didi invariably made a mistake: she placed Lakshmi where Shiva had been. Ganeshji too never found a permanent abode: he shared it with whichever combination seized Didi's fancy at the moment of arranging the gods. This game of musical chairs did not endear her to Som Devi.

'Today's girls have no respect – not even for God. Then who will they respect?'

'How does it matter who sits where,' Didi inquired, puzzled by this heavenly etiquette, 'as long as they are present in your heart?'

Som Devi folded her hands.

'Leave,' she entreated. 'You will create trouble in heaven and in the house if you meddle any more.'

So Didi was taken off puja room duty. She was grateful.

She was equally grateful for her afternoons which she spent alone, free of chores and the family's company till tea time. Didi would lie on her bed, looking out at the mango tree, reading a book, or doing needlework. Occasionally, Purush would join her, but get up and leave soon enough. At four, she would leave her room, prepare tea and set it out on the garden table in the front lawn. Then Som Devi and her father-in-law would stroll up and down while Purush studiously watered the plants.

Four evenings a week, Som Devi, her husband and Purushottam went to play cards at the Gymkhana Club. Didi had no interest in cards, so she was allowed to stay alone at home, until Bhai returned from work. Bhai, who read out poetry while Didi helped Maharaj with dinner, and asked if she liked it.

It was time for afternoon tea in the garden. Didi's father- and mother-in-law were seated on garden chairs. Purush sprinkled the flowerbeds as Didi approached the scene with a plate in her hand. The air was filled with the scent of something deep-fried.

She carried out a plate of samosas; they were a shade too brown at the edges.

'Ah, now these I must taste,' said her father-in-law. 'Didi's samosas.'

'So? I taught her how to fry them,' said Som Devi. 'Fried in oil that was too hot,' she added, observing the savoury with a critical eye.

Didi addressed Purush's shoulder blades: 'Do you want a samosa?'

'No.'

'Have no, Purush! They are fresh and spicy.'

'Not hungry, Ma.'

'Never hungry,' complained his mother. 'Ever since he was a child, he hated eating.'

'I eat very well,' said Purush, between petulance and stiffness, 'just not hungry.'

'Now, our Didi,' commented his father, 'our Didi, I am happy to see, has a huge appetite.'

Purush came to sit on the chair between Didi and his father. There was no other vacant spot because Budhoo was sleeping on the chair next to Som Devi. Purush swung his legs, knocking the knees together.

'I feel hungry, so I have to eat,' explained Didi, munching.

'Who could want more in a young daughter-in-law?' asked her father-in-law. 'May your children inherit your hunger.'

Carefully, Didi wiped her oily fingers on her orange cotton dhoti. Purush lunged forward and grasped a samosa, which he consumed in two large bites.

Didi reached out for the last samosa and bent towards her mother-in-law in a whisper.

'So,' murmured her mother-in-law, regarding Didi with sudden appreciation.

'How many times must I tell you, Purush,' exclaimed his father, stretching out his legs, 'that you should stop this bad habit of shaking your legs? You don't know how ugly it is.'

'Nervous, that's what,' explained his mother. 'Newly-wed – just nervous.'

Didi saw the veins in Purush's throat stand out like a highway on a road map. He rose, walked hurriedly out of the garden scene. Budhoo lowered his head into sleep.

'What makes him so upset?' asked Purush's father.

Didi knew that her mother-in-law's eyes were drilling into her.

'Not sleeping too well,' replied Didi truthfully.

'She's keeping him busy, hain?' whispered Purush's father to his wife with a nudge.

An hour later, Purush strode into their bedroom, locked the door and drew the curtains. Didi lay with her eyes deliberately shut. She felt him approach.

'You told Ma you were having a child?'

'I am.'

'Rubbish all.'

'If I am carrying, I am carrying.'

'It's not mine.'

'He or she. A child is not "it".'

'Most certainly it is not mine.'

'Could be.'

'Could it be?' he asked, almost eagerly and then shook his head. 'No, remove it.'

'Is it a stain on some cloth that it can be removed?'

'I insist.'

'How?'

'How?'

'How will you insist?'

'I will take you myself to the doctor who does these things. I will order the doctor. I will tell Ma.'

Didi opened her eyes wide, met his.

'Your mother wants the child. You should have seen the light in her eyes when I told her.'

'She won't when I've told her.'

'Call me when you do; I will fill in any details she might want.'

Didi rose.

Purush pushed her back.

'Rubbish all, you are rubbish all. She will not want a child that is not mine.'

Didi began to rise again.

'Wait till I tell her about, about … America.'

'I will deny it …'

Purush hit the palm of his hand against the side of his head. He walked across to the garden door, parted the curtains.

'It's so easy for you …'

'No, it is never easy to have a child.'
Purush came and twisted Didi's right arm behind her back.
'Remove it.'
He raised her arm higher.
'Remove it, I say.'
'No.'
He increased the pressure.
'Nahin.'
Purush loosened his fingers. He pushed her away with his arms outstretched, his palms straight out as if to protect himself. She glanced off the side of the bed – that lessened the impact of her fall. She rubbed her arm where he had held it.

Purush went to sit on the sofa. His knees knocked.
'I will tell everyone.'
Didi threw back her head and laughed.
'If you utter a word, ever, first I will deny everything, then I will tell the world what kind of man you are at night.' Didi started towards the bathroom. 'Your choice.'

Purush stared blankly after her. Then he stilled his knees with his hands and rose to leave. At dinner, Purush was missing from the table while Som Devi did not look at Didi throughout the meal. But when Didi went back to her bedroom, her mother-in-law followed her.

'You will not go out till the child is born. Nowhere.'
Didi held her stomach in.
'The child will be born in this house, not in the hospital, not in your home. This is our first grandchild. This is our tradition. No one is to come for the birth – not Mem, not Sita. We consider it inauspicious. I have waited a long time for this. Don't ruin it.'

She turned away, stopped by the open bedroom door.
'My son is very gentle. Lacks confidence, that's all. But now he has proved he's a man, has he not?'

Som Devi waited for Didi to reply. When she didn't, she left the room, murmuring, 'Budhoo,' which the dog understood as summons and dutifully followed her. 'Not you – my son, he is a fool!'

Didi took Mem's name eleven times. Som Devil, as she called her, was pleased about the baby.

It was October. The leaves had shed their inhibitions and fell with abandon, forming a carpet on the lawn to be swept up by the maali.

The first twitches of pain came after lunch. Didi went to lie down and massaged the protrusion of her stomach. She felt a kick of protest, laughed, and gave her tummy a smart smack. Don't you start to bully me already.

When Didi joined Som Devi for tea in the veranda outside her bedroom, she was alone. 'I am getting pains,' Didi announced as she reached for the china teacup.

Som Devi replaced hers, gently, upon the saucer.

'How often?' she inquired.

'Every half hour.'

Didi's mother-in-law pressed her own stomach. 'There has been no child in this house for many, many years. Since Purush,' she said in a way that made Didi feel a twinge of sympathy for her.

Som Devi rose abruptly, toppling her teacup, and went inside.

'What's happened?' asked Bhai, appearing round the corner.

Didi drained her teacup and looked up at him. 'Nothing.'

Through his mal-mal kurta, Didi noticed the muscles on his stomach ripple in response, his rib cage strain. Though he was shorter than his younger brother by a hand, his narrow legs and long torso made him look taller. He had a wrinkle-line for a dimple on his left cheek and Purush's eyes: intense grey on a cloudy day, deep blue on a clear winter afternoon. His hair was black, straight and fine, plastered with oil behind his ears.

Bhai sat next to Didi and poured himself some tea. He stared at her sari.

'You look good in that turquoise,' he remarked, 'I like it.'

Any other time, Didi would have been gratified by his appreciation. But the pain was intense and she was in no mood for pleasantries.

She groaned. 'Nobody is going to like me when this child is born. I think I would rather be alone.'

Didi collapsed upon her bed. The ayah, Roopvati, came in and sat down to press her feet. Roopvati had been with the family since Purush's birth. Bhai and Purushottam called her Roop. So did everyone else. She was now old enough for her flesh to hang apart from the bones, skinny enough for the muscle to be stringy and wrinkled. She had big hands that moved lightly over Didi's ankles and calves, leaving no impression.

'Harder, Roop, harder.'

'Arre Didi, more than this, your bones will break.'

'More likely your useless fingers,' breathed Didi. 'Ouch.'

'See? See? What did I say?'

'I am screaming because of the bachcha pain, not your silly little fingers. Oh, Sita, Sita, where are you?'

'Didi does not like my work. I am going.'

Didi's mother-in-law replaced Roop.

'Bhai has spoken with the doctor,' she said in a distant voice. 'The doctor says we must wait till your pain is coming every ten minutes. Then she'll come.'

'Ooooooh,' replied Didi.

'Women have had babies before, you know,' her mother-in-law reproved. 'I am only telling, women must bear pain like memsahibs – it is men who cry when a needle pricks them.'

'Ooooooooohhh,' screamed Didi loudly.

At 8.30 p.m, Roop went into the bedroom with ginger tea.

By then, Didi was flinging her body from side to side, her sari pallu around her ankles, her blouse half open, her groans deep and pitiful.

Three minutes later, Roop emerged from the room, her mouth concealed behind her left hand. She informed memsahib that Didi had forced her to drink the hot tea. Her tongue hurt.

'Drama-baazi,' Som Devi told Purush and Bhai, who looked rather pinched and pale. 'Just acting. To get more attention.'

They were seated around the dining table, eating dinner.

'But if she doesn't want anyone in the room, Ma, who is she seeking attention from?' inquired Bhai.

'You know,' replied his mother, placing another spoonful of vegetable on his plate, 'nothing about women.'

'Yes, you know rubbish all,' added Purush rudely.

By 9.30 p.m., Didi was whimpering. When the lady doctor, Dr Sunita Sharma, arrived with two nurses at 10 p.m., she found her patient half-naked, half off the bed.

'I told you we should have had her in the hospital,' she said to Som Devi.

'Doctor-memsahib, this one must be born in the house,' insisted Purush's mother.

'Oooooooooh, aaaaaaaah,' was Didi's observation.

'Very good,' observed the doctor. 'Push, push the life out of you.' She briskly shoved Som Devi out of the room, as a consequence of which Som Devi stumbled over Budhoo. The dog had decided to position himself outside the door, ready to spring to action if his services were required.

It was seven minutes and twenty-six seconds past 11 p.m. when Baby informed the house of her arrival. Hearing her cries, Budhoo let out a series of welcoming barks and climbed the shut door before rushing into the dining room, tail wagging furiously. Purush's father, Purush and Bhai, still seated there, never heard Baby's announcement because Didi's last scream had filled the house and reverberated in a fearsome echo.

'Is she crying?' demanded Bhai, moving nearer to the bedroom door.

'More likely dying,' replied Purush, hitting the side of his head with his open palm.

'It is called,' explained Purush's father, 'giving birth, and will you stop that?'

'He's nervous, Papa.'

'He knocks his knees and his mother says he is nervous; he slaps himself on the head and you say he is nervous. What are you so nervous about all the time, Purush?'

'Of becoming a father, Papa,' explained Bhai, slapping his brother on the back. 'Well done!'

Purush shrugged him off.

'Rubbish all. What did I have to do with it?'

He locked his fingers and pressed the knuckles against each other.

One afternoon, when she was almost three, Didi's daughter sat on the floor purring at Budhoo, her nose against his, while he slept on, unperturbed.

'Go and play. Run around the garden with Budhoo. I will send Roop to you,' Didi instructed the little girl as she deposited her in the grass. 'I've got the headache.'

Fifteen minutes later, as she lay in bed, Jeff made an unexpected appearance. He lay beside her, a pair of hands around his neck. Purush's hands. He sat astride Jeff's body. 'You got there, didn't you? Didn't you?' The hands tightened, but when Didi looked into the face, it wasn't Jeff's, it was Baby's.

Didi's eyes burst wide open.

Baby had collapsed against the trunk of the mango tree. Like the rag doll in her lap, her head dangled to one side.

'Baby, Baby!'

Nobody heard Didi scream. The words were trapped in the pit of her dream. Didi ran outside. A bee hovered around a sleeping Baby and Budhoo, who was seated on his hind legs with his ears upright, poised for attack. The bee settled on Baby's nose. Didi held Budhoo back. Then she stole up barefoot, breathing imperceptibly. The bee's transparent golden-and-black striped wings were straight. Didi shadowed Baby with her body. She took her pallu between the thumb, index and middle fingers and advanced her hand like a bird's hungry beak. Then she clamped it down.

'Chor, chor,' cried Baby, flaying her limbs.

Her small feet hit out, striking Didi on the calves. Bent forward to pluck at the bee, Didi swayed, straightened, swayed once more.

'Eeeeee-eeeeee. Oooooooo ...'

Didi fell.

Baby clapped.

And Budhoo yelped because Didi had fallen on his tail.

'I caught Amma! I caught Amma!'

That's how Bhai and his mother found them: Baby and Budhoo prancing around Didi, who lay on the grass staring at the bee squashed into the fabric of her pallu.

Bhai offered his hand but as Didi reached out, Som Devi slapped his arm away. Wordlessly, Didi lifted herself, brushed herself off and after pinching Baby's reddening cheek, muttered to herself, 'Som Devil' before returning to her bed and dreams.

A permanent sag had developed in the mattress where Purush used to lie beside her. But there was a thin, invisible barrier between them which he seemed unable to penetrate. His failure and hers lengthened the space between husband and wife and stretched like a sleepless night into futility.

Perversely, each failure increased the frequency of the efforts and their brevity too. Didi never knew when Purush would come to stand behind her and press his flesh into the small of her back. Didi would immediately accompany him to their bedroom. Purush seldom stayed long.

'I am only telling, why must you sleep on the settee?' Purush's mother would demand, within Didi's hearing. 'Don't you have a bed?' Som Devi would glare at Didi.

Often, her eyes would settle upon her daughter-in-law like the bee on Baby's nose had that afternoon: so hard, so intensely bright, Didi felt scorched by their glare. She had never encountered silent watchfulness before. It was as if her mother-in-law was constantly searching for something she could not find.

Didi was unaware of what transpired between mother and son, but from Som Devil's behaviour towards her, she knew Purush must have said something about their relationship. Som Devil knew that Purush preferred to sleep on Didi's New York sofa rather than with his wife on their bed. That much was clear from her cold eyes.

Only Baby managed to bring some warmth to them. The night of her birth, Som Devi had taken the child from Didi's room into the dining room where the men were assembled.

Purush's father gazed upon the girl.

'Arre, so fine Somji, just your likeness,' he exclaimed, squeezing her hand tight.

'You think so?' asked Som Devi, holding the baby fast to her. 'Bilkul same,' he insisted. 'Light hair and eyes, white skin.'

And Som Devi tightened her clasp about the child.

While his mother doted on Baby, Purush went about the house deaf to the child's cries. He brushed past her as one does the air, without any feeling

When Baby was just short of two years, Didi's father-in-law died of a sudden stroke. Som Devi, shocked by the sudden and immense loss, retreated into herself, like a shadow without light, and confined herself to the house. Contact with the world outside was discouraged. 'I am a widow,' she would piously inform Purush if he suggested a visit to the club.

After his father's death, Purush rearranged his life: he moved the New York sofa to the living room, where it stood alongside its companion chairs. It became his domain, the sofa his throne. From here he commandeered, ruled.

Bring me a nimbu pani.

Fetch today's newspaper from Bhai-Dada.

Make me some pakoras.

Sometimes, he fell asleep on the sofa.

'Why don't you go and sleep in your mother's room?' Didi suggested one afternoon when he had slept for five days in the living room. 'She is one woman you have slept with happily.'

So the inmates of 3, Chor Bagh, lived together but remained apart.

Didi would write to Mahendra: *We live in a beautiful house, almost untouched by events beyond its black iron gate.*

The one contact that remained was the weekly telephone call from Father and Mem or Mahendra. That connection was cut off, abruptly, nine months after Som Devi's husband died.

Later, Didi would believe that the holy fires of her wedding had lit funeral pyres around her. As if her marriage had been a blight and the union forced upon her had left behind a curse upon those who had blessed it. Dada had passed away a few months after her wedding, followed by her father-in-law and then, most tragically, one after the other, Father and Mem.

Father's going would haunt Didi the most, not only because of its unusual circumstance but because it drew a line between her and Mem that Didi could not cross; one that left her stranded on this side of the divide between life and death.

It was late one evening when Roopvati sang out, 'Oh Didiji, telephone.'

Mahendra said, 'Didi, Uncle passed away, suddenly.'

'He died seated outside in the garden under a tree with a newspaper on his face. Colonel doctor says it was a massive heart attack. Mem says the gods sent for him.'

Didi wept with dry eyes. She had always steered clear of Mem's gods; she liked things to be logical, straightforward. Like the ruler Mrs O'Hara used to rap her with on the knuckles.

Still, she had read of people going to meet their death the way the sky meets the horizon, and that, she conceded, must be what happened to Father. The way Mem described it to her, no other explanation seemed reasonable.

It was a dry April afternoon, Mem remembered.

It was hot and unusually sticky for April, like sugar dissolving into caramel. Mem entered the drawing room with the tea tray as she did every afternoon. Light Darjeeling tea, the leaves soaked just long enough for the water to turn the colour of autumnal leaves. Two digestive biscuits, but only two. Father soaked them in the tea, let them cling to the roof of his mouth. This was something he had learnt to enjoy from his toothless mother in her old age.

'Tea,' announced Mem.

'Hrrmmphh,' Father had acknowledged, his mouth half open. Mem went to open up the store and take out the provisions for dinner: half a cup of arhar dal, three-quarter cup of Dehra Dun basmati rice, three ladles of ghee, one cup custard powder, quarter-cup castor sugar, one teaspoon vanilla essence. They would eat a favourite dinner: thick, yellow dal; crisp brown sweet potatoes; pumpkin that was sweet, sour and oh so spicy; and boiled rice. And of course, Father's favourite fried bananas with custard sauce. As she pulled the keys from the waistband of her petticoat, Mem thought her freshly-made lemon pickle with ginger and green chillies would be ready for eating. She would test it out and then send some to Didi.

Didi. Mem's longing for her daughter was ceaseless. There had been letters, a few trunk calls; but because of the child, Didi had not come home. Her mother-in-law was insistent that the first child be born at home and attain at least one year before she travelled with Didi.

Didi wrote to her mother: *Says Baby is the rani-beti of the house and utmost care must be exercised. Silly, isn't it?*

Mem did not think it silly at all. Hadn't she thought the same way about Didi? And whoever heard of a mother opposing her daughter's mother-in-law?

For the same reason, Didi did not attend Dada's funeral. Som Devi said it was inauspicious for a bride to be in the presence of death. Just after Baby's first birthday, Purush had developed mumps and then his father had died. So Mem was still waiting to see her granddaughter, yearning to meet Didi, but she wasn't one to complain. No ji.

Mem pressed the keys back against her flesh and considered rejoining her husband, asleep with his mouth half open. But first, she had to hurry to the toilet.

Once there, she decided to bathe. It was hot and she could feel the sweat crawl out of her scalp. After the bath, she returned to the cool darkness of her bedroom, feeling deliciously drowsy, and lay down on the bed. She fell asleep.

When Hari Prasad bugled his tubercular cough outside her door, she awoke with a thumping heart and requested him to go and spit out that ugly sound. At once. Only then enter.

Hari Prasad cleared his throat again.

'Achcha, what is it?'

'Telephone for sahib. I have looked everywhere but sahib is nowhere. Unless ...' He burped delicately.

'And what would he be doing in my room at this time of the evening?' demanded Mem, seething at Hari Prasad's suggestive pause.

'You may have worked with the family for tweny-five years, Hari Prasadji, but that does not give you the right to say such things.'

The fact that Hari Prasad had said nothing did not bother Mem in the least. He knew precisely what she meant, just as she had understood him perfectly.

'He must be somewhere here-there,' said Mem.

'Gone out?'

Mem placed her swollen feet on the floor and started out of the room.

'Achcha? You are an ulloo, Hari Prasadji, bilkul ulloo!'

'In all these years,' continued Mem, 'sahib has never gone out of the house at this time. Never. Go look once more.'

A search yielded the same absence. Mem sent for Ratan, the driver. He arrived in his white, short-sleeved vest and blue-and-grey striped underpants. Clearly, he had not taken sahib anywhere. Mem was genuinely puzzled. She saw that the teacup had been drained and the biscuits consumed. Normally, he read after tea.

She wandered through the entire house, calling out, 'Where are you? You are not visible to us.'

She found Sita peering behind her bedroom almirah.

'Hai bhagvan, and what should sahib be doing there?'

'It's not Father Sahib I search. I am following a mousie – this small.' Sita clenched her eyes by way of measurement.

Mem slapped her head and proceeded down the corridor. The only practical explanation for Father's disappearance was that there had been an emergency and someone had come and taken him away before he could inform Mem. But what could have been so urgent?

Mem went back into her bedroom to oil and comb out her hair. Twenty minutes later, every tight knot had been straightened out. Still no Father.

Mem sat with the Bhagvad Gita and told Hari Prasad to look outside in the garden. Again.

Five minutes later, there was a clatter of shoes. Hari Prasad, panting, asked her to accompany him immediately.

Father was propped up against the old banyan tree, a tree so large and overarching, it looked like a little forest in the clearing of the garden. His head rested to the left, his right leg was stretched out stiffly, his left bent at an angle. In his left hand, he held a newspaper while the right hand lay unclenched upon his thigh as though about to ask a question. Mem felt a pain on the wrong side of her heart. She began to hiccup.

Father had suffered a major cardiac arrest, the impact of which was the equivalent of three average heart attacks.

'Burst like a hand grenade,' said Colonel Rai, the old family physician who had tended to Father's weak heart and Mem's stiff knees for years. 'It went off – phatak – just like that,' he added, clapping his hands together, rather enchanted by his comparison.

'But why did he have to go out there to die?' Mem demanded, her outraged tone suggesting it would have been more appropriate for him to die inside the house.

Did he notice something out there? Did he sense that the pain in his chest was no ordinary pain, but the final one he would experience? And sensing this finality, did he go out there to join Infinity?

Mem could make no sense of it. Or anything else. She asked Mahendra to call Didi.

'This is what she will come to,' she wept. 'Her first visit home since her marriage, she will come to mourn her father.'

With the child in her arms, Didi walked straight into her parents' bedroom to find Mem surrounded by her female relatives. She placed the bundle in Mem's lap and sank her head upon her mother's shoulder. There was a sharp intake of breath. She glanced up to see Sita peering into the child's face.

'Why,' she exclaimed with a hand on her open mouth, 'just bilkul like …'

The warning in Didi's eyes slashed off the rest of her sentence.

'What,' shouted Munni Masi, deaf in one and a half ears, 'says Sita? Just like who?'

Didi signalled Sita's silence and transferred her gaze to Father's photograph, draped in a white garland, the incense blowing in his face. Her eyes clung to his image, the way her arms had when he had hugged her one last time before she climbed into the the car with Purush, the newly-wed couple.

'I should have come,' Didi whispered, 'I should have visited earlier. Why is it that I never do the right thing?'

Mem watched her daughter grieve.

After Father's last rites, after the family members had dispersed, alone in the bedroom, on the bed with the child between them, Mem sat with her face averted.

'Mem?' Didi pulled her around. Mem turned, stared down at the child, then at Didi, and looked away.

Over the next two days, whenever Mem picked up the baby, she avoided the child's eyes. And when hers encountered Didi's, she closed her own. Didi tried to talk to her; Mem replied with the briefest of answers:

Yes.

No.

I don't know.

I know.

How should I know?

Maybe.

Could be.

Perhaps.

Didi pinched her, kissed her, massaged her legs – all those little gestures that, in the past, Mem had been unable to resist. Now, Mem remained motionless, unresponsive. She had turned her back on her beloved daughter, refusing to speak to her unless it was necessary. Even on the last day of her stay, when Didi embraced her, she withheld herself.

'Mem, oh Mem. You must teach me how to bring up Baby just as you brought me up.'

Mem gently pushed her away.

'I will die soon.'

'But Mem, see how pretty she is.'

Didi held out the girl to Mem.

'I want to die soon ...'

Mem retreated to the puja room. Didi heard her say: 'Hey bhagvan, where are you? Take me also, take me.'

Didi visited Mem every two months. Each time without the child. Som Devi was insistent she leave Baby behind, and Didi was almost glad to: each visit saw Mem smaller, quieter and less communicative than before. Didi tried to blot out this Mem who never looked at her daughter, who retreated into a space Didi was unable to reach.

It is better not to remember what is so hard to forget, Didi told herself, trying not to dwell on Mem's rejection of her child. But her visits to Mem became infrequent, unsolicited, and never lasted over a few days. Mem, who had once devoted herself to her daughter, now turned to God. She spent hours in the puja room or in her bedroom, reading the Gita from memory.

It was fitting, then, that when the time came, Mem was on a pilgrimage to Vaishno Devi with Mahendra and his family. She contracted pneumonia and passed away before they could bring her to Delhi for medical treatment. Mahendra told Didi that they would return to Delhi for the funeral and wait for her to join them. Didi asked him to light Mem's pyre up in the mountains.

'Scatter her to her gods, Mahendra, leave her with them – I want to remember Mem in flesh and blood, not ashes.'

Thereafter, Didi lapsed into forgetfulness, with Sita as her sole reminder of the life that had once been. The faithful ayah, inconsolable after Mem's death, came to join Didi in exile from herself.

As soon as Sita arrived at 3, Chor Bagh, Didi deposited Baby in her lap. Sita stared at Baby, would stare at her often and after her at Didi, who would turn away after the merest eye contact. The old retainer knew she had her answer.

Wary of the past, Didi began to live increasingly in the present. When Sita recounted certain anecdotes, she listened with the wonder of a child hearing a story for the first time. Does what we forget cease to exist, she would ask herself. And what we remember possess a life of its own?

Didi couldn't find a satisfactory reply, but in a symbolic effort to distance herself from the past, she gave away her wedding lehenga to Sita.

'Just don't sell it, that's all,' she remarked.

Sita preserved the lehenga in the black trunk Didi had given to her along with other mementos: Mem's pashmina shawl with a hole where the rat in New York had eaten into it; Father's black leather gloves, which Sita wore in winter; the gold necklace Sita received from Mem when Didi married; and a magenta-and-gold Benaras silk sari Didi had sent Sita when Baby was born.

'Baby,' Sita would murmur with love as she held the garment to her face and sniffed it, 'why did you leave me with this old woman of the hills? Baby?'

HILL STATION
1986

Baby. She was nearly thirty and everyone still thought of her as Baby. Perhaps, she told herself as she opened the gate and walked in trailing a bag, that was why she had never grown up.

The compound was deserted. She looked around with curiosity. She had arrived unannounced, wanting her first visit home since she had left for New York to be a surprise for Didi and Sita. She had last spoken to her mother a month earlier.

'Amma ... how are you?'

'How are you?'

'I asked you that.'

'And I asked you that too.'

'Talking to you is impossible.'

'Then don't.'

'You know what the problem is, Amma?'

'It's all my fault?'

'That of course.'

In eight years of long-distance trunk calls, they had spoken at cross purposes. Now that Baby had returned, she was determined to untangle the lines, change the conversation. She walked down the gravel path just as Didi stepped out into the veranda. The dogs appeared from nowhere, barking around her until Didi silenced them.

'What's happened?' Didi stood arms akimbo.

Baby approached her in silence.

'I asked, what's happened – why have you come home? And,' she added, staring at her daughter, 'what is that?'

'Can I have a glass of water, a cup of tea, before we discuss my entire life?'

'Don't discuss it at all. What do I care?'

Didi turned away.

'Sita! Sita! Such a witch: where is that chaudail?'

No sooner did she see her than Sita flapped about Baby like a palpitating bird. She couldn't keep her hands off 'my Baby', touching her face, her hands, her hair. Ten minutes were spent inspecting her this way and that.

'Nice,' she admired.

'Sita,' Didi commanded, 'go get us tea.'

'Hai hai, Mem, who is she to tell me what to do?' demanded Sita, invoking the spirit of her former mistress while stroking Baby's hair.

'Just her mother and the memsahib of this house.'

Baby was bemused: they had all grown older but their relationships hadn't matured.

At dinner.

'Rice?'

'No, thank you.'

'Raita?'

'Yes, please.'

'Nimbu achar?'

'Oh yes, please.'

'Pickle is bad for you throat. Another hot roti?'
'No pickle, and yes, another roti.'
'What's the matter with you? You were never this polite before.'
'I am changed.'
'Aah-ah …'
'What does that mean?'
'Baby, you keep enough room for this sooji ka halwa I've just made,' called out Sita from the kitchen, 'just the way you like, with orange joos.'

Baby clenched her fist about the tablecloth.
'Sita, I can't, I don't feel like it.'
'You always liked it before,' commented Didi, reaching for an apple.
'Well, I don't any longer, I just said so …' Baby was flushed.
'All right, I heard you.'

Didi peeled the fruit like she was carving a sculpture.

After dinner, Baby sat on the first step of the veranda. Didi had gone straight to her room and switched on the radio. Sita joined Baby. She held Baby's left hand. Baby flicked a cigarette with the other.

'You should apply some cold cream, Sita, your hands are coarse.'
'I use sarson ka tel.'
'Cold cream is better.'
'Your mother thought so too. I remember in Noo Ark, she was always applying cold cream to her body,' recounted Sita, 'even … there.'

'What,' laughed Baby, 'nonsense!'
'Arre bhai, I cleaned her panties.'

Baby shook her head in disbelief and blew a smoke ring at Sita. As Sita coughed, Baby rose to go inside.

'Baby?'
'Hmmm?'
'Why is your hair yellow?'

Baby laughed that throaty laugh.
'Some sunshine fell on it.'

'Baby!'

The next morning, Baby saw her mother seated outside, reading the newspaper. Baby strode forward.

'Give me a page,' she said, sinking into the cane chair.

Her mother held out a page. Baby accepted and nosed behind it. She always liked the smell of printed paper.

'Rajiv Gandhi doesn't resemble his mother at all,' she said, staring at a photograph. 'That nose ...'

'What have you come here for?' she heard her mother ask. Baby threw the newspaper on the floor.

'I came here for three reasons: to see my mother, for rest and recreation, and to stop having to look into the mirror and recognize myself.'

'That sounds like me.'

Not surprising since I am your daughter, thought Baby. But she wasn't going to blurt it out. That would lead them astray, as it had so often. She sat up straight. Waited.

'Why is your hair blond? What has happened to your face?' asked Didi, staring.

'Why did we have to leave 3, Chor Bagh? Why didn't we ever go back? When will we have a proper, grown up conversation? See, I can ask questions too.'

'Know?' asked Didi, heading down the veranda stairs, 'does anyone, ever, really know anything?'

'Amma, don't start this rhetorical conversation with yourself,' said Baby. 'It's an old technique of yours.'

Didi waved at her in a dismissive gesture that made Baby's neck tighten. Amma had this unfailing capacity to get her back up, stiffen it. Baby stretched out to release the tension. She wasn't going to let Amma get away with it, not this time.

She saw Didi crouch beside a tree. It had begun to rain.

'Amma?' Baby whispered, creeping up beside her. 'Amma?'

Baby sank down next to Didi who was gently hitting her head against the trunk of the tree.

'Why don't you tell me?' Baby poked Didi in the arm where the flesh was still tender. 'This mania to keep everything to yourself – it's done enough …'

Didi looked Baby straight in the eye.

'Seen Kartik lately?'

Baby forked a hand through her long blond hair.

'Have you?'

Baby chewed her lower lip, then nodded.

'Here and there.' She laughed. 'Sheer coincidence.'

'Don't believe in those.'

Baby shrugged.

'I've made him an offer I hope he won't refuse,' said Baby, pulling out an apple from her trouser pocket and biting into it.

'I am going to try to chew this thirty-two times.'

She began with the left side of her mouth. When she reached a count of sixteen, she transferred the lump to the right side. 'There!'

'Where?' asked Didi, looking around.

'Don't pretend, Amma.'

'Whenever I used to exclaim "there", Mem would ask "where".'

Baby watched Didi run a hand over the bark of the tree. It reminded her of another tree, another house. She dug a small hole in the wet mud and buried the half-eaten apple. Then she sat back against the tree, pulled out a packet of cigarettes and lit one.

'What do you think?' Baby asked.

'Baby, you left him – like that.' Didi snapped her fingers. 'So who can tell with you?'

Baby blew smoke rings one inside the other.

'I always meant to return. It took longer than I had expected, that's all.'

The same evening.

The telephone rang.

'I'll get it,' Baby yelled out.

She skid across the length of the corridor to the phone extension. Five minutes later, she banged the receiver down on its cradle with such force, the plastic cracked.

'This bloody instrument is useless …'

'Who was that funny man you were speaking to? And don't swear like that in my house.'

Baby saw Didi standing at her bedroom doorway.

'I will. Why were you shamelessly eavesdropping?'

Didi massaged her knuckles.

'He's vulgar.'

'His name is Ramaji Rameshwar Rao and I lived with him, slept with …'

Didi shivered with the delicacy of water disturbed by a sudden ripple.

'Learnt to talk like him, too?'

Baby swung away into the drawing room.

'Like I said, I know worse.'

'So I heard …'

'You're shameless to listen in.'

'So you said.'

'You're your best lawyer, I must say.'

'Hasn't done me much good with you.'

Baby's sari smacked from side to side as she strode across to the almirah. She needed something strong. She pulled out a bottle of Johnny Red Label, proceeded to the kitchen and returned with two tumblers, one of which she handed to Didi.

Baby raised her glass.

'Ra-ra.'

'Want to tell me what's up?' Didi asked. 'I am your mother, you know, whether you like it or not.'

Baby held the whisky in her mouth, gargled with it and then swallowed. Throwing herself onto the sofa, she stretched out, her sari riding up her legs.

'Whether you like it or not,' she repeated. 'You make it sound like a marriage vow: for better or for worse.'

With that, Baby closed her eyes. She didn't want to talk about New York. She didn't want to talk at all.

'Want to tell me?' Didi said gently. Baby felt her nose run. That's how she cried, sometimes.

'I have,' Didi went on, 'made mistakes. Many,' she added as Baby opened her eyes wide. 'I think I might help you through yours.'

Baby wanted to laugh: she didn't need help, she needed answers. She humped onto her side.

'Who said I want help? Who said I made a mistake? I just wanted to come home. Why can't you believe that?'

'Because all these years you never thought you had one.'

'Years change thoughts.'

Didi stretched out her toes, wiggled them.

Baby sat up and went to refill her glass.

'You're drinking too much very fast. You'll be sick soon.'

Baby ignored her. She decided she would have just enough to feel as if she was floating up to the fan and rotating with it.

Didi asked,

'This Ramaji you were with. Is it over?'

Baby nodded as she returned to the sofa.

'You're not going back to New York?'

Baby shook her head.

'That was him asking me to, but I can't. Never. You don't know …' She tossed her hair. 'I don't want to talk about him.'

Didi sank back in her chair.

'Sounded horrid. All right.' She put up a hand as Baby opened her mouth.

There followed the kind of silence maintained by people who don't know what to say to one another. Baby let her eyes close.

'I don't know why,' Didi remarked, 'why you didn't stay with Kartik. He would have suited you much better. I liked him. Why didn't you?'

Baby breathed out slowly.

How could it be explained? Where should she begin?

'As you know only too well, Amma, the leaving is easy; it's the staying that is so hard.'

DELHI
1977

The leaving is easy – it's the staying that is so hard.
Baby recalled the moment she realized she must leave.

It was while standing in front of the UPSC candidates' list, alone, searching for Kartik's missing name amongst those who had made it through the exams. She didn't know how many times she scanned the list for his number, knowing it would be there, only her eyes could not find it. She was jostled, pushed, but stood firm. Then came a sudden chill. In that instant Baby knew she would leave Kartik. She had felt acute disappointment, the same terrible feeling she had experienced when Amma had forced them to leave 3, Chor Bagh. She had banked on Kartik to free her from life with Didi. Now he had failed her. She had to change her luck.

By the time she reached his barsati, she already felt miles away. Later, when she dug her fingers into his back as they lay in bed, it was not out of sexual pleasure but from a passionate regret.

She realized she could not wait for him to succeed. Suppose he never did? I am like Amma, she thought, I make a habit of leaving people behind me.

Kartik. He with the sweating palms and blazing eyes and silly goatee beard she had made him remove. The way he looked at her ... Did she love him? Yes, but she didn't have time to wait to find out if love was everlasting, or just a pop song which eventually lost its romance. Oh, why did he fail the exams and her? Wasn't he supposed to have been the collector and she the collector's wife?

The collector's wife. She had seen her many times. She was the one in the silk south Indian sari and clipped purse at Diwali melas and pearl drops in her ears at the school's Founder's Day. She with the convent school accent and gold string sandals, draped in that confident air which comes from being sure of your position.

'Fifteen years from now,' she had informed Amma at an annual day school function, 'my husband will be secretary to the Government of India. And I will be living in one of those beautiful New Delhi bungalows.'

Baby never forgot her remark. Here was a woman who already knew where she would be fifteen years later. She even had an address.

Yes, an IAS officer's wife was something to be.

Seated on the university library steps, late into the night, Kartik had showed her that stellar future. He would speak of nothing else: district magistrate, collector sahib, secretary sir ...

She listened to Kartik with half amusement and half admiration. There was something so sure about his ambition, it gave her confidence. She had breathed in the charm of his certainty, its purity. It was pure. She could tell by the tension in his body, the earnestness of his words, the salt of his sweat. Baby had been aroused. She would pry open the fingers of one of his hands and draw circles in his palm with the wet tip of her tongue.

'Do you want to?' she would ask.

One evening, they had borrowed Ajay's motorcycle and driven through the shaded avenues of New Delhi. Suddenly, Baby screamed, 'Stop!' Through the knitted leaves of ageing peepul and ashoka trees, on the wide avenues of New Delhi, she had snatched a glimpse of the future in the patchwork sunlight. She admired the gates of the government residences, and pointed at the white Ambassador in one driveway.

'That's our car, our bungalow, and if you hand me the binoculars, I am sure I can see you and me, making love on our bed.'

He laughed in that shy way he had.

'At that age?'

'People do at seventy-five!'

'Nonsense!'

Baby stared into his eyes.

'You want to?'

Once, they had found an unoccupied bungalow and crept in through a parting in the hedges, walked through its emptiness. The high ceilings with echoes of past occupants; the skylights with their nesting pigeons; the ancient fireplaces; the long verandas held up by sturdy pillars; the chalky, whitewashed walls; the expansive lawns ... All at once, she knew what it felt like to be the collector's wife, the woman she had met in the hills. They had spent the afternoon inside. Without clothes, stretched out across the cool stone floor where the skylight directed the sun's rays onto their bodies. She called him 'secretary sahib' playfully, and pretended for those few hours that she was his wife.

That was before he failed the exams and she decided to leave him. That was before she discovered how Didi had failed her too. Before was such a long time ago.

Later, she was never quite able to pin down why she decided to go to New York and nowhere else. Maybe that was her predestination. Since childhood, she had heard of New York from Sita who regaled her with stories of her grandparents, her mother and her own adventures in 'Noo Ark'. It was always meant to be.

When she rang and told her mother of her decision, there was complete silence on the line except for the sound of breathing. Then Didi had put down the receiver. The next time Baby called her and repeated her plans, warning Didi not to ask her why she wanted to go, Didi said, 'When do you want to leave?'

'Why don't you go with me?' Baby asked Kartik, again and again, as she prepared to leave for New York. She knew she was being perverse. She was leaving Delhi to get away from him and yet she could not bring herself to let go of him. Maybe their luck would change if they changed cities, countries.

'To do what?'

'I don't know. Get yourself a real education.'

'For what?'

'I don't know, for what!' Baby threw up her arms and grasped the air. 'Why does it have to be for anything? Why can't it just be for the sake of itself? What is it that you want to do here? There's a world outside Delhi, the government, the stupid exams, Kartik.'

'My father won't understand this firangi stuff. He can't even understand why I want the IAS. He'll laugh if I ask for money to pursue "higher education abroad".' Kartik had put on a voice: 'You don't understand what it's like coming from small-town India. The IAS is what boys like me dream of. It's the ultimate. DM sahib. That's what I want to be.'

He had turned and looked at her in bewilderment, an expression Baby would take with her to New York. 'Why can't we continue the way we are? I don't understand anything. You disappear saying you're going home and want to be left alone. You don't call or write or reply to my mails, and here I am wondering what the hell is going on. Then you're here again but you're not here at all. You say you're going to New York. And now you want to take me with you like an accompanying piece of luggage. What's going on? What on earth are you playing at?'

She pressed her hands to her stomach.

'It's all in there. When I was a child, I watched them – my father on the sofa doing nothing, Amma out in the garden staring at nothing. She likes to say I am a secret to myself, well, her life has been a complete mystery to me. I never realized what was happening. I didn't know anything ...' She struck the bridge of her nose. He reached out for her wrist.

'You were young.'

Baby shrugged him off.

'Children know things. I didn't want to know. I wanted 3, Chor Bagh, to remain as it was, see? My little doll's house. Bhai Chacha bought me one: it had pink walls, a green roof and yellow window shutters. All the plastic furniture was striped in blue and white except for the gas range which was white. And the dolls were white too – firang. I loved them so much, I wanted to be like them.'

She shaded her eyes with a palm so he couldn't see them.

'There are gaps inside me which need to be filled ...'

'Baby ...' He stretched out an arm, held a hand. 'Tell me what happened to you?'

'Nothing.'

'You want to run away – it must be from something.'

He slammed his palm against the side of his head. The gesture reminded her of her father. 'Tell me.'

Baby had remained silent. How could she explain the compulsion to rediscover herself, put into words what she couldn't even put thoughts to? How to tell him of the need to revisit the childhood Didi had shortened so abruptly, of a journey that had led her to this juncture in her life where running away was the only way?

No, she couldn't confide in Kartik. She couldn't reveal how, one morning, weeks after she had left him stranded at India Gate, she had, without knowing why but knowing she must, packed a bag and climbed onto a bus.

A State Roadways vehicle.
It was rickety, and very hot.

The windows were without panes in one, two, three, four, five ... and the sixth was splintered. She felt the straws poke her buttocks through the torn green rexine seat covers. Sections of the floor had been worn away. There was a rusty hole at the back of the bus. She smiled: on this, her first visit to 3, Chor Bagh, in fifteen years, she had chosen to travel in style.

Late afternoon. Hot. The sky was the clear blue of her old school tunic. The heat bore into her body. The bus thudded heavily. Most of the other passengers slept. How, she wondered, could anyone sleep with the noise and fumes of its laborious engine?

She heard a 'ssssssssssss' and turned. A woman, her face hidden by the pallu of her sari, was comforting the small boy in her arms. He was snivelling, his eyes and nose running to tears. Baby felt like a cry too. It might ease the tension that stretched across her head like a tight hair band.

The driver stopped for chai at a roadside dhaba. Golden Peacock, it was called. A fading picture of India's national bird hung from its corrugated roof. Baby slurped tea from a kulhar, tasted the salty grain of the earthen vessel, glad for the liquid refreshment. The steam in her face, the mist of this July evening: suddenly, she remembered the smoke from Purushottam's Gold Flake cigarettes. How it rose from the sofa and contorted into ethereal statues.

Purushottam. Rubbish all Purushottam. Sprawled on the New York sofa, the one Mem had bought for Amma, the one Amma spoke about whenever she talked about Purush. The sofa Amma once threw out because it sagged permanently with the shape of him.

'To be in his presence when he is not there – too much!' she would complain.

'Why was it too much, Amma,' Baby would ask, years later. As she grew older, she had pestered her mother with such questions, demanded answers for the years she had lost and Amma had squandered.

'If you knew Purush, you'd know the answer to that,' she replied.

'But you didn't let me get to know him,' Baby had pointed out.

'That is there,' Amma had agreed.

Baby climbed back onto the bus, found her seat by the window. She sat alone: the bus was half empty. She pushed her long, light brown hair off her shoulders and twisted it. The way Amma used to, seated in front of the dressing-table mirror behind the curtain in the bedroom, combing the black hair off her face. With a dancer's mudra, she would coil the hair into a knot.

She'd graze her little finger along the edges of her kajal box and line her eyes. A hairpin twirled in the kajal and screwed into her forehead left a perfect black dot in its centre. When she rose, it was to shake herself so the pleats of her sari fell into place, one behind the other like soldiers in a line. In the last moment before she moved away, she'd reach out for one of the many, variously shaped perfume bottles on the dressing table, and using her forefinger gently dab behind her ears – an artist applying the last flourish to a painting.

Amma always wore perfume. 'I want to smell sweeter than myself,' she told the little girl who sat on the cold floor and watched her mother.

Baby used to play with those perfume bottles. Housie-housie. The tall, oblong one with a black bowler hat? That was the elegant father. The heart-shaped one with feathers in her hair? She was the loving mother. The thin, twisted one with a crown on his head? The joker-brother she didn't have. And the dainty, tiny one? Baby. And the round, squat bottle with the head covered with rose petals? Sita.

Baby had learnt to interpret Amma's moods through scents. When she wore Je Reviens she was joyous, playful. When she had a headache, she wore Cabouchard. When she was angry, worried or in a passion, she hurriedly splashed on the heavy Joy. And if she chose L'Air du Temps, it meant she was thinking of Mem. Sita and Amma often took Mem's name and cried over her.

Baby didn't know, couldn't tell if the choice of perfume was deliberate. What she did know was that something happened to Amma during the afternoons that lingered on into the next morning. Lying beside her mother, she could smell the inner turbulence of her soul.

Gold Flakes. Je Reviens. In the air blowing against her face, in the sand pitting her skin as the state roadways bus hurtled lopsided along the uneven road, there was the smell of Purushottam and the scent of Amma. His cigarettes and her perfumes combined to make an aroma only Baby could recognize.

A hand touched Baby's hair. It was the small boy with runny eyes and nose who withdrew his hand when his mother smacked at it.

'Sorry, didi, sorry,' she apologized. Baby, she wanted to shout at her – my name is Baby. *Baby*, not *Didi*.

They passed by green paddy fields. An odour of dung was suspended in the air, the way clouds appear in an aeroplane window. It reminded Baby of Amma's 'holidays' – the days she wasn't allowed to help about the house at 3, Chor Bagh, or cook the meals. Baby would spy on her then, as she stayed in her room, with her books, her photographs, her thoughts. Baby didn't know why she did it. Spy. All children do on adults, suspecting there's more to them than meets the eye.

Baby hated, had always hated Amma's secrecy, those afternoons in the bookstore, the afternoons in her bedroom. Amma lay curled up on her left side and stared at the mango tree. Her eyes were so still, Baby knew her mind and heart were wandering.

When Baby crossed her third birthday, she was shifted out of Amma's bedroom and moved into the study, which used to be her grandfather's office.

Dada, who died after a stroke felled him in the bathroom. Amma said that while he was in hospital, Dadi would sit on the corner of her bed, shaking her head, muttering verses from the Gita. Purush would pace up and down smoking more than usual and Bhai Chacha refused to take Amma and Baby for an evening drive because everyone had to visit the hospital.

The long corridor in the house was like a hollow tube; it echoed the movement of the hands on the tired clock and Budhoo's deep breathing. Everyone spoke gently as though their words might shatter the silence irreparably.

Amma said it was too depressing. So she would sing lustily in the bathroom just to keep herself company:

Autumn in New York,
Why does it seem so inviting?
Autumn in New York,
It spells the thrill of first-nighting,
Dreamers with empty hands,
They sigh for exotic lands,
It's autumn in New York,
It's good to live it again.

Baby knew the song well. Amma sang it often during her childhood, especially when she was sad.

Mem died the day before or after Dada. Or so it seemed to the child Baby was at the time. The space between the two deaths didn't exist in her memory, as if it had never existed in time. One night, Dada was dying, the next Amma returned home with Sita.

So Dada's study became Baby's bedroom, the bedroom where she slept with Sita. Dadi had put up printed curtains with pink, blue and brown teddy bears, and filled the room with soft toys and dolls and an old rocking horse. Sita and Budhoo stayed with Baby but she still cried a great deal. She felt sleeping apart from Amma, in another room, was a punishment and she would beat her little fists against Dadi's sagging breasts with their huge dappled pink nipples, and pull her hair.

'Why can't I sleep with Amma?'
'All good girls sleep in their own room.'
'But I am bad, a bad girl.'
'No, you are the best ever.'

Dadi would suffocate Baby with her bosom and rock her, tell scary stories to divert the child's attention. Once, when Dadi thought the child had fallen asleep, Baby heard her say in a distant way to Sita: 'I'm only telling, memsahibs must sleep with their sahibs, not their children.'

Next morning Baby had asked Sita why memsahibs 'must' sleep with their sahibs. She replied by tying Baby's hair into a tight ponytail.

'Hai hai, Mem! Your granddaughter is bilkul like your daughter. Sahibs and memsahibs sleep together, my Baby, because their beds are too big for little children.'

It was a stupid reply then; it seemed ridiculous to Baby whenever she recalled it. Sita could have done better.

Sita was a terrible liar.

Amma's lies were so true, they beat Sita's lies.

Evening was falling as the bus neared the outskirts of the city. The road widened and improved on the approach. There were neon streetlights of which alternate ones didn't work. Along the road, yellow bulbs were strung on wires, linking one wooden pole to another, resembling artificial pearls. There were the usual shops you see along highways: motor and cycle repair shops, a row of dhabas interspersed with green fields, an occasional cement or wood supply store and, in the distance, the brick front of a kiln or the aluminium grey of factories. White fumes from their chimneys. A country liquor outlet, an English liquor store – Royal Sag. Baby laughed: the 't' had fallen off Stag.

She felt in need of a drink but she knew the odds of her getting one were the same as Purush rushing forward to welcome her home.

Unless she could sneak some from his bottle. He used to drink rum. He would pour two and a half caps out in a glass, add water and squeeze in lemon. When Dadi asked him what he was drinking in the afternoon sun, he would raise his glass to her.

'Lemon iced tea, Ma. Want some?'

Sometimes, if Amma was within hearing, she would stop and stare at him and he'd glare back at her.

'Go on, tell her,' he would challenge Amma, 'and I will tell her.' He would nod at Baby, standing in the pleats of her mother's sari.

'Tell? What's to tell?' Amma used to turn away. 'If your mother does not know her son drinks more than milk and tea or lassi, then she either has a very weak sense of smell or she's not very intelligent. Which explanation do you prefer?'

'If you say a word more against Ma, I will tell her.'

'Tell.'

Didi stood motionless, with her body flung back, a bow tightly strung, waiting to be released. Purush shook his legs, knocking the knees together.

'That's how men make out alone,' Kartik explained when Baby asked why she often saw Indian men do the same.

She had slapped him. Jumped on him and punched him, shocked to think her father did such a thing in front of his wife and daughter.

Daughter. Father. Baby grew up believing that a father was a destination that receded with approach, like the horizon. Certainly, she never reached him. He never touched her; she couldn't remember the feel of him. His skin. She imagined it to be a freshly ironed cotton shirt: it looked so white and smooth. Sometimes, as a little girl, she would hide behind the sofa and jump up to capture his cigarette smoke in her hands. That was her way of making contact with him.

Over the years, Baby tried very hard to think of Purush as her father, call him Papa, have a conversation with him in her mind. She was nearly six when she left Purush's house. Plenty of time to have had a conversation.

The bus jerked to a halt. They were crossing a state border. A toll payment. The woman in the seat behind hummed. Hummmmm, hum, hummmmmm, hum ...

Baby wondered about the house she hadn't visited in so many years. Would she recognize it? The mango tree and the garden, their bedroom, her own room, yes; but suppose they had renovated and changed the exterior?

3, Chor Bagh. How would she get there? Were there taxis and scooters? At this time of the evening? Baby cursed herself for coming alone. But who should have come with her? Amma? She shook her head. If she knew anything about her parents, it was that to see each other again was the last thing either would want.

Amma would not mind meeting Bhai Chacha though, thought Baby. Baby liked him. He used to stroke Baby, cuddle her, comb her hair and try to plait it. Amma would laugh.

'Bearing babies and making plaits, my dear Bhai, are things only a woman can do.'

Bhai Chacha was dark like his father.

'The colour of my sandalwood soap,' Amma would tease.

When she reached out to touch his hand, he would withdraw it in the instant she extended hers.

Time alters people, memory preserves them: Purush with a glass of rum, cigarette smoke and Amma's sofa; Bhai Chacha in kurta-pyjama, soft voice and eyes, and restless hands; Dadi stretched tight as the bun on her head. Amma called her the wooden cane that beat everyone into shape. Amma and Dadi. They talked to each other through the little girl. They taught Baby something she never forgot: there was something strange about people who never addressed each other.

That's how she knew without being told that though Amma and her father slept like husband and wife in the same bedroom, they shared something else: a sullen bitterness. When they spoke, it was at each other, in stale, acrid words. Like ear wax.

Baby never saw any affection pass between her parents. Sita said that was normal between sahibs and memsahibs.

'Marriage is not pyar. Marriage is work: memsahibs work at home, sahibs work in office.'

Maybe that was the trouble: Purushottam never went to work.

'Lying on the sofa, again? Don't you think you ought to get up and do some work?'

'I would love to get ... up but you keep me down.'

'You should earn some money. It's not fair on Bhai.'

'Maybe he gets what I don't.'

'What?'

'Ma says he makes laddoo eyes at you.'

'You follow me with yours bulging.'

'If only the bulge would travel ...'

'Please, the child.'

'You and your precious America. Thhu on all of you.'

'Spit all you want. It won't solve your problem.'

'Ma says I am fine, it's you, you ...'

'Ma says, Ma says ... *tain, tain ta-tain tain*. Why don't you go and sleep with your mother?'

'Shut up! Shut up! You rubbish all!'

Baby used to close her eyes to keep their voices out: she thought darkness was deaf to sound.

When the bus reached its stop, she waited till everyone else had alighted. The little boy smiled at her, his mother told him to say namaskar, which he did with little folded hands.

Baby found a scooter rickshaw.

'Chor Bagh.'

'Which one?'

'How many are there?'

'Chor Bagh near Record House, Chor Bagh next to Kothiwallah No.1.'

Guesswork time.

'Kothiwallah.'

'Ten rupees.'

'Too much.'

He shrugged.

Baby recognized the house by its iron gate. It was an ordinary gate, no different from many others. But she knew it was the one she must enter to reclaim her past. As the scooter drove up the gravel pathway, Baby could see Amma pace up and down as she did throughout that summer before they had left 3, Chor Bagh. Often, Bhai Chacha walked by her side. Bhai Chacha. She never showed him the respect a sister-in-law showed her older brother-in-law.

'Too familiar,' Dadi would complain. 'These are American ways.'

As Baby climbed down from the three-wheeler, she recalled the sound of Bhai Chacha's cough – his way of announcing his arrival outside Amma's room. She would laugh and call out: 'Come on in, Bookie.'

3, CHOR BAGH
1960

'Come on in, Bookie.'

He walked into the bedroom. Didi stood in front of the dressing-table mirror, combing her hair. The pallu of her sari spilled onto the stool beside her. Bhai stared at her reflected bodice and Didi immediately snatched the pallu and flung it over her shoulder where it joined her long hair.

'You're here,' exclaimed Didi. 'Good. Will you take me to the market?'

'Why can't Purush take you?'

Didi's reflection tilted her upper lip.

In the mirror, Bhai's hands rose to touch Didi's hair, his eyes never leaving her bust.

'Your brother has no time.'

'You must not talk so. Purush is your husband, father to your child, yes,' Bhai said.

Imperceptibly, he had drawn closer, his eyes clinging to the mirror. Didi plaited her hair.

'Some husband.'

'Didi.'

Didi pirouetted so abruptly, her plait slapped Bhai in the chest and wrapped itself around her neck. She tugged at it.

Bhai released the plait from her fingers.

'A red welt has developed right here,' he said.

With a fingernail, he sketched a line across the air of her neck. His fingers trembled.

'You brothers are such cowards,' taunted Didi, moving away to admire herself in the mirror once again.

'How do you mean,' asked Bhai, hands behind his back.

'You know what I mean. There's him on the sofa, with not a day's work behind or ahead of him; here's you, your eyes like laddoos at the sight of a woman's body, your hand fluttering like a piece of paper under a fan, because it might touch your sister-in-law.'

'I don't know what you mean.'

'You Indian men are such hypocrites.'

It had rained all morning. The atmosphere was a pressure cooker on perpetual steam. Hissing, spitting.

Didi sat on her bed, writing to Mahendra. On the chattai beside her bed lay Sita with Baby within the shape of her body.

I was right to keep what was mine and not let you persuade me into doing what I didn't want to, Didi wrote.

Her letters were written in this indirect way because she had learnt that Purush and Som Devi went through her belongings. He, in search of money, she out of curiosity.

In those years of her marriage, Didi would discover her mother-in-law in places where she had no reasonable expectation of her. On several occasions, Som Devi was found in Didi's bathroom or behind the curtain that separated the bedroom from the dressing table. Once, she found Som Devi trying a key in her trunk. Nothing was ever said, but Som Devi met the surprise in Didi's eyes with a clear look, as though it was the right of a mother-in-law to go through her daughter-in-law's belongings.

And then there was the particular night when, unable to sleep in the moist warmth of the room, disturbed by Purush's presence, Didi had opened the door leading out to the garden, seeking the solace of the cool night. She thought she saw her mother-in-law motionless in front of the mango tree. Som Devi's dark sari had heightened the paleness of her skin; her hair was taut in a bun even at that late hour. She appeared thin and brittle, exhausted, as if tired of a vigil that had been long and unfulfilling. Som Devi had stared past Didi to her slumbering son and then glided away. Like a nightmare, I rub my eyes and she's not there, Didi had thought.

Now, Didi's letter went on, *the house is very silent. Occasionally, we go to the market and once a month Sita and I go with Bhai to the movies. Sita insists on coming even when it is an English film. She says otherwise she will lose touch with the language. How I love the silly. I am thinking of taking up gardening. Bhai says filling the garden with flowers is like filling the house with children. Much he knows about such things.*

In the bedroom doorway, a light pink cotton curtain responded in gentle waves to the overhead fan's air currents. Didi thought she saw her mother-in-law's feet, but she couldn't be sure. Recently, she had begun to believe she imagined these apparitions: the afternoon she had seen Bhai standing over her; the time she felt his hand on the soles of her feet, his breath on her hair. By the time she looked again, there was no one. She was scared by the involuntary reactions of her mind.

On this occasion, however, there was no mistaking him. That nervous cough, those feet in brown leather sandals. As Didi watched, his feet stepped forward, faltered, turned towards the dining room. Then they returned, still hesitant. Another cough.

'Come on in, Bookie,' Didi called out, deciding to make up his mind.

'May I come in, Didi?'

'First time any of you has asked,' replied Didi, staying where she was on the bed, biting her pen.

Bhai was fresh in a light blue kurta and white churidar. He came forward.

'Happy birthday, Didi.' He held out an envelope.

'You may also sit down,' Didi said. She opened the envelope and took out slips of pink paper. She counted. Three movie tickets. Evening, 6.30 p.m. show. She looked up at Bhai and her features widened with pleasure.

'*Gone with the Wind?*'

He nodded.

'I don't believe it. All those years ago, my father didn't allow me to watch it with my friends.'

'We can make up for your lost opportunities.'

Suddenly she felt naughty, playful.

'All of them?'

He fidgeted with his glasses, peering down his nose.

'Didi.'

'Bhai?'

He pushed back his spectacles, gazed out into the garden.

'Shall we plant some seeds?' he asked.

Didi burst out laughing.

'Gardenias, nasturtiums …' His arms hung loose by his side, the fingers clenching.

Didi sprang up off the bed and wiggled her sari into place, twisted her hair into a bun.

'We're only planting seeds for flowers?' she continued teasing.

'Didi …'

'What about brinjals, cauliflower and peas?'

She reached out and placed her hand on one of his. Through the transparency of his kurta, she could see the smooth rib cage, the pumping of his stomach. Sweat collected in Bhai's eyebrows.

'It's terribly hot,' he said, wiping his face with a white handkerchief which he folded neatly and slipped into his pocket.

'Your hands are so cool,' Didi remarked, refusing to move out of his way.

'I'll have the car out in the porch at 6 p.m.,' he mumbled and turned.

Didi watched him lope out.

'You brothers are such cowards,' she whispered.

They groped in the dark to their balcony seats and sat down. Didi swallowed hard, suddenly sad at the memory of Father evoked by the film.

When *Gone with the Wind* came to a film hall in Delhi, she had asked to go with her college friends.

'You may see the film. But only in the company of your mother,' ordered Father.

'Who wants to see Clark Gable kiss Vivien Leigh on the lips, in the company of her mother?'

'I like English movies,' replied an injured Mem.

'But you don't understand the dialogues, Mem, and you won't let me listen either.'

Father had refused.

'Then let Rhett and Scarlett remain on the pages of a fat book and in the folds of my imagination. I will not go.'

Father shook his head.

Didi did not go.

So, many years later, Didi watched Rhett kiss Scarlett, seated between Bhai and Sita at the Mayfair Theatre.

Sita cried throughout the film because she thought Rhett looked better with Melanie than with Scarlett. She howled when Bonnie fell from the horse and died. Didi sat quite still, barely breathing. Bhai remained upright, his arms resting on the arms of the seat, his fingers crushing the foam. He appeared to be perpetually on the verge of rising.

Outside the theatre, Didi felt as if she had been skinned and salt sprinkled over her body, which smarted with aroused sensations. In the car, she covered herself with her sari and secured the pallu like a belt into her petticoat.

Later, across the dining table, Didi contemplated Purush, whose head was bent over his thali, and Bhai who never looked up from his. Som Devi sat straight, a watchful eye on her sons. Baby, seated between her grandmother and mother, divided the contents of her plate into small portions and, when neither was looking, she threw them on the floor where Budhoo gratefully gobbled up the food and kept her actions secret.

Didi felt her eyes spark. She wished dinner would end so she could lie down and imagine herself as Scarlett. She would change the story, naturally. In her version, Scarlett would be in love with Rhett, not that namby-pamby Ashley. And she would express her love in passionate physical gestures ... yes, her story would be filled with secret, volcanic emotions.

Returning her attention to the dinner, she found Bhai's eyes upon hers.

'So. Why don't you stare so at the photographs of the girls I have shown you, instead?' Som Devi demanded of him, serving kheer in steel katoris and pushing them towards her sons. 'Then you look away and say, "Not now, Ma". Not now? Phir, when then? There are many pretty young girls in our community. I am only telling, marry before you grow too old and have to be satisfied with whatever is left over.' Som Devi cut Didi a glance. 'What's the point of making round-round eyes at her?'

Didi turned to Baby. She put a hand on her cheek.

'Amma has a headache, Baby. Lying down.'

'Ek do teen, Amma's so mean,' recited Baby automatically.

Som Devi giggled. 'Always the headache,' she observed, passing Baby kheer which she smeared over her lips. 'Your mother,' she added to Baby, seeing Didi rise from her chair, 'should eat this kheer. It is her birthday. I am only telling that in our family, everyone eats kheer on their birthday. It is the custom.'

'Have a spoon at least?' Bhai offered Didi, standing up too. 'Here, Purush, why don't you give Didi a spoon of kheer in her mouth? It will be more auspicious.'

Purush continued to eat.

'Purush?' repeated Bhai.

'I am perfectly capable of eating by myself.'

Didi reached for the katori and ate one spoonful of the sweet.

'Your Dadi cooks excellent kheer,' she said, addressing Baby. 'Now, if only we could all be as sweet.'

She smiled at Bhai, ran a hand through Baby's hair and walked away.

'Sweet?' she heard Purush say, 'When she is as bitter as quinine?'

Som Devi giggled.

Maybe it was *Gone with the Wind*, maybe the echo of Som Devi's giggle, but Didi's eyes remained wide open underneath their lids. She heard the sound of crickets rise and fall, and wondered where they hid.

Purush was asleep in the bed next to her.

Didi went to the bathroom and splashed water on her face, into her eyes. She was wearing her lemon yellow cotton nightgown with embroidered green-and-white flowers around the neck and bodice, but her arms were bare. Stepping outside, she shrugged her hair loose and dragged her feet across the cool squelch of grass. Above her was an invisible sky, obscured by clouds.

A square of light from Bhai's bedroom window beckoned her. Didi neared it. Bhai was in his white pyjamas, the tape dangling between his legs as he stretched up and down in push-ups. He had discarded his pyjama top. Methodically, without pause, he bobbed up and down. Didi could see his body oiled with the sweat of his efforts, his ribs exposed with each intake of breath. Who would have thought he exercises, Didi asked the night. That too, so late?

She approached Bhai's square of light. She knocked upon the glass.

Bhai was halfway through a press-up. He flopped onto the floor. Didi laughed. He looked about in consternation. Didi knocked once more. Bhai raised his head and stared.

'It is I, Didi.'

Bhai rushed to his feet and reached for his pyjama top. He struggled into it and approached the window.

Didi laughed again, smooth as melted ghee, clear as the glass that separated them. He opened the window.

'Your shirt is inside out,' she informed him.

'Oh.' He sounded boyish.

'Why are you exercising in the middle of the night?'

Bhai moved away and reappeared in a moment, his nightsuit the right way round.

'Best time. And I can't always sleep. It helps.'

He clutched the bars of the window.

'Looks as if you are in jail,' Didi remarked. 'I can't sleep either,' she went on. He was breathing deeply from his stomach and Didi felt the faintness of his breath on her shoulders. 'I think it must be the movie. It has made me feel … Oh, what I haven't felt since I came to this house.'

Bhai gulped, dropped his eyes only for them to encounter her bosom and rise in haste.

'Didi,' he said, 'Didi, don't you like being married to Purush?'

'*Like* is not a word I would use for what I feel for him.'

It was Didi's turn to clutch the rails, just below his fingers.

'At all?'

'How can I tell you. You are his older brother. You wouldn't understand.'

'I would, I would.' Bhai grabbed her fingers.

Didi felt his moist fingers. Bhai's Adam's apple raced up and down the stairway of his throat.

'You brothers are such cowards.'

Didi withdrew her hand.

'Can I come with you to the bookshop tomorrow?' she asked archly as she walked away.

The family bookshop was rectangular. At the back was an office and opposite it, shelves of books. One of the shelves had a handle which opened a door leading upto the store where fresh supplies were kept along with with unsold titles. This room had a skylight which, on a clear day, looked like the sun from a distance.

*

There was a knock on the store door.

She was fitting an earring into the hole in her ear lobe and felt the pain of its rejection. In the small mirror of her powder compact placed on the shelf, she saw a drop of blood start out of the hole and dabbed it with her finger. She rammed in the earring once more and the skin gave way, suddenly. Another gentle hammer. 'I'm coming, I'm coming, can't you see?' she whispered, striding forward.

'Who is it?' she inquired of the door.

'It is I.'

Didi opened the door, gingerly. Bhai slipped in.

They used a frayed carpet, five feet by eight. Kashmiri. Heirloom. A Mughal garden floral design in rose pink, midnight blue and khaki green. Later, he would roll it and stand it up against the wall. She lay on her stomach, her chin in her hands. A small piece of tranquillity settled upon her. Jeff had been ages ago, in a geographical space so distant, her body was in a perpetual time lag from her last experience of passion.

Bhai crouched to the left, his hand on the small of her back where he could feel the notches of her vertebrae. Everything about him was unhurried, rhythmic as his sleeping breath. He scratched her skin, she turned.

So long as Baby didn't know, Didi didn't care. Baby.

3, CHOR BAGH
1977

'Baby?' That was Dadi's incredulous question when the boy announced her name.

'Let her come.'

She was ushered in.

Dadi said, 'Call her here.'

Baby pranced down the dim corridor, placing her toes on the black diamonds. A game recalled from childhood. She halted at the end of the hall. The door to the right led into Amma's room. Baby turned left.

They were seated around the oval dining table. Baby stared at the table: in all these years, it had not moved from slightly off centre beneath the overhead fan.

'Baby,' Dadi declared.

Someone dropped cutlery.

Baby stood at attention.

'She's white as mooli,' observed Dadi, looking at her appraisingly. 'Purush, pass her a chair.'

Baby transferred her eyes to Purush. He did not look up from the geography of his thali.

'Purush?'

'I'll get, Mummyji,' said the other woman at the table. 'Let Purush eat.'

'Always eating,' complained a balding cherub by her side.

'You know rubbish all.'

A Purush favourite.

Baby yearned for a shot of brandy.

Instead, she got a chair.

The next few days passed with the stealth and speed of the night while you sleep. Baby awoke one morning to find herself two days ahead of time. That was not the only disjoint: there was this uneasiness around the heart. Maybe, she told herself, massaging her chest, this is how it feels to dislocate it.

She felt a great sense of detachment from the people around her: Dadi, Purush and Bhai Chacha went about their lives without pausing for their guest. No doubt they smiled at her, Dadi and Bhai Chacha, but it was the same old smile, tired, from constant repetition. For Baby, it didn't take in the passage of the years between them.

There were the routine commands:

Baby, come for breakfast.

Baby, your beaten coffee is ready.

Baby, throw your clothes for a wash.

Baby, use some hot sarson ka tel.
Baby, don't sit so long in the sun.
Baby, come and see the rose bushes.
Nobody said, *Baby come here, let me hold you.*
Nobody asked after Amma or Sita.

The first night was spent in Dadi's room; she alternately wheezed and snored. As Baby became accustomed to the rhythm and was about to fall asleep, Dadi sat up and proceeded to read aloud from the Gita. Baby, with eyes clenched, remained awake till dawn.

Without her knowledge, her bag was moved into her old room in the morning. The walls had been whitewashed; no baby blue and pink with brown teddy bear curtains either. Instead, there were the thick old velvet curtains that used to hang in the drawing room. When Baby wandered through the house, the scent of familiarity met her everywhere, so much so that she began to feel 3, Chor Bagh, had not stepped beyond the past.

On that first morning, she had risen late and run out into the garden. The sturdy mango tree was smaller in reality compared to memory. Or maybe she had outgrown it. She sat beneath it and peered into what used to be Amma's bedroom. A curtain obstructed Baby's view. In contrast, the French windows in the front room were wide open. To an outsider, the large room with three pieces of furniture would have appeared strangely incomplete, as if someone was caught between moving in or out. To Baby, it was natural because it was just as she remembered it. An armchair, a long table and Amma's sofa. Walking past, she saw Purush sitting on the sofa which was frayed at the edges, sagging on the sides. Had they not stirred since the day she and Amma had left? The dining table and her father?

She watched him carefully. He walked through the house, his head bent in perpetual preoccupation. It was a wonder he didn't collide with his own thoughts. Or then there was this sunken man on the sofa. Baby had pictured him with his hair neatly combed back, his white cotton full sleeve shirt well pressed, his grey cotton trousers starched and creased. No wrinkles. That memory of him had been smudged by time. Now his hair was oiled and combed back, steely, the face shaded as if permanently deprived of light. The white shirt and grey trousers were still neatly pressed but they must have worn off on each other with time, because the white had grown dull and the grey had paled. That's what absence can do to a man.

Purush was still instantly recognizable. Bhai Chacha was a complete surprise. He, who had been spare and boyish, was now plump. His cheeks were rounded red. And where was his fine black hair that used to dangle about his ear? He had grown bald and had a hedge along the boundary of his head. A few strands had been left to grow long so he could comb them across the scalp. Just like his father.

'How come you lost all your hair, Bhai Chacha?' Baby asked him one day.

'Because I wanted the sun to warm my scalp.' He smiled back.

Along with his hair, Bhai Chacha had discarded the kurtas and churidars of her childhood for shirts, pants and a jacket with a tie. A scarf in the evening. If only Amma could see him now. The thought made Baby chuckle.

Dadi was still young, but greying into old age. Thinner than ever, her eyes were slightly out of focus.

The house was curiously quiet. It disturbed Baby. In her childhood, there had always been Budhoo to dispel it.

She asked Dadi how he had died.

'That bewakoof Budhoo. Too greedy. I am only asking, why eat a piece of meat that had been flung into the compound?'

'I don't follow?'

'The meat had been poisoned, of course.'

Baby was puzzled. 'But who would want to kill our Budhoo?'

'Them.' Dadi pointed her nose in the direction of the world outside her gates. 'Who else?'

'Them?'

'Who but Musalmaans? Phir then. They don't like dogs. They eat meat. They have constipation. They don't bathe every day.'

These statements had no connection except with Dadi's prejudices.

She usually saw people as religions, castes, professions or by their relationships:
Musalmaan.
Kritian.
Brahmin, chamaar, bhangi, baniya.
Doctor sahib, sabziwallah, maali.
Ma, beta, poti.
Poor Budhoo. A dog killed by religion.
That left one other member of the family.
'Go child, go!'
Chachi's favorite expression, delivered with a smile that lit up her dark face with the startling white of her teeth.

Chachi. When she had risen from the dining table to fetch a chair, that first night at 3, Chor Bagh, Baby had guessed who she was because she was aware Bhai Chacha had married. She had overheard Amma tell Sita that Mahendra had written from Australia of the match. When Baby asked who Bhai Chacha had married, Amma replied, 'A woman.'

Baby had imagined Chachi as a short, plump woman with a pleasant face and a kind look, her head covered by her sari pallu. Someone who giggled a lot when Chacha teased her. This Chachi was tall, thin, angular around the hips. She had black hair which she back-combed every morning to give her a puff, and coal eyes. Her lips were crimson, cherries on a chocolate cake on the stem of a white powdered neck. Every morning and evening, she applied talcum powder up to her chin. She wore nylon saris and called Dadi 'Mummyji'. She possessed a voice of such incredible sweetness, Baby thought her teeth must have many cavities.

Miss Lobo. Chacha's assistant at the bookstore.

'I was Miss Rose-Mary Lobo until your uncle converted me into your Chachi. Good joke, no? Sometimes he forgets I am his wife and calls me Miss Lobo, child.' She laughed out aloud at dinner on the second evening. It was a clear sound which tinkled like bells in the mandir.

Dadi's eyes retreated so far into their sockets that Baby stared: you would need a pair of tongs to pull them out. She made a curious clucking sound.

'What's that, Dadi?' Baby asked.

'Her dentures,' replied Lobo Chachi. 'As you grow older, the gums shrink. So Mummyji's dentures have grown too big for her mouth. Poor Mummyji.'

Lobo Chachi beamed at Dadi.

Dadi suspended the fingers of food near her mouth.

'No-sense,' she commented. 'The dentist made the teeth big, too big, to make more money,' she said and deposited the ball of food on her tongue.

Baby wanted to giggle. 'Mummyji' and Rose-Mary Lobo. Dadi seemed to like her second daughter-in-law as little as she had approved of Amma.

Bansi placed a hot phulka on her thali. Bansi: short, light brown curly hair and eyes, cloud grey. The bridge of his nose had been pressed in when it was soft, creating a wedge. He wore shorts and a kurta. He did all the housework, from washing clothes to cooking and polishing shoes. A mere boy, his body was still childlike.

He was responsible for Baby's first collision with the reality of 3, Chor Bagh. It was on the third day of her homecoming.

She had woken to the sound of Dadi scolding Bansi for misplacing her reading glasses. She liked to sit in the veranda, outside her room, and read the morning newspaper.

'Why have you stolen my glasses? So that I cannot see what little work you do? So that I cannot see how much you eat? That I cannot see the small change you give me when you come back from the paanwallah? I am only telling, you are an out and out thief. Worse, you are a work thief.'

Baby stumbled into the sunlight with a large yawn.

'He is a child,' she said.

'A complete villain,' Dadi replied, glaring angrily at him from the doorway as he searched the room for her spectacles.

'You know, child labour is a crime, Dadi. You are exploiting a small child.'

'I give him food, clothes and shelter. What crime?'

'Why not send him to school, instead?' Baby poured tea from the pot on the wicker table. It was tepid.

'School?' Dadi went into her bedroom and returned with the empty spectacle case. 'He will learn to be more villainous, only. You educate this lot and they become worse. You do everything for them, they are still ungrateful. I am telling you. Everything is nothing to them. See again, you useless boy,' she ordered Bansi.

'I said it is a crime to employ children.'

Dadi stepped into the sunlight. Her slight shadow wobbled.

'I am asking, is this what your mother has taught you? To wake up when the sun is straight above our heads, and show disrespect to your grandmother?'

'No disrespect.' Baby swallowed her tea. 'Just the truth.'

'She knows rubbish all, rubbish all.'

Purush's voice streaked across the blue sky. It was delivered like a cold slap on Baby's face by the breeze.

'Just like her mother.'

Baby could see the pink of his eyes between the crimson petals of bougainvillea bushes nearby.

Eventually, Dadi found her spectacles: within the pages of her Gita.

That evening, Baby had found Bansi leaning against the pantry door, shuddering. She asked him what had happened.

'Purush Sahib – he abused me and,' Bansi straightened up and knuckled his eyes, 'my father.'

'Why?'

'I went to ask memsahib if I should give you, Didiji, a hot water bottle in bed at night, like I give her. Sahib shouted.'

'He didn't want me to have a hottie?'

Bansi cringed.

'No, he said if I call you Didiji again, he would see to it that I join my dead father. I will never say again.'

Baby turned away.

When she had asked Didi why they had left home, she gave her the standard adult reply: you are too young to understand. But when Baby grew older and more insistent, Didi came up with a story, strange and bland, she thought, as the papaya soufflé Didi made when she was troubled.

It went like this: Purush and she did not want to marry. They were forced into it. They were too different. She was an educated woman who wanted more in a man 'than a sofa'. He wasn't interested in children, hadn't wanted any. They fought continuously.

Amma said 3, Chor Bagh, was no home for a child to grow up in, no house for a marriage. That was why Bhai Chacha had remained single. She couldn't breathe in this house where the gate was perpetually closed. She felt she would slowly suffocate to death. She longed to run away with Baby and Sita. However, there was the family name to think of. Those days, a woman did not just leave her husband and sasural. Where would she go? She had no family left except Mahendra – and she couldn't live off him.

So she stayed on.

One night, something happened to Bhai Chacha – everyone called it 'the night Bhai went missing' and Amma said she fell very sick. She sat in the wicker chair under the mango tree, staring ahead of her, refusing conversation, food, water.

Baby would jump onto her lap. 'Amma, horsie!' she would command and Didi's legs would move in automatic response.

They visited Mahendra Uncle in Delhi. But Mahendra Uncle said nobody could diagnose the problem. She felt an absence, Amma had explained, as though she had misplaced a part of herself at 3, Chor Bagh, and couldn't find it even after an exhaustive search.

'Maybe it was the weather,' Amma told her.

'Doesn't the hot climate suit my delicate, darling daughter-in-law?' Dadi had asked.

Bhai Chacha, worried by Amma's condition, decided to send her to the hills.

'The change of air will do you good. Get well and return to us soon,' he had told Didi in Baby's presence.

'The hills healed me, I stayed on,' Didi told Baby.

Who could believe such a story? Wives don't leave their husbands because they fight. Marriages don't end because of the climate, do they?

Baby asked Sita about Didi's story.

'Whatever 'Mrican mad-memsahib says,' Sita snorted.

'Tell, no.'

For the first time, ever, Sita resisted Baby's pleading.

'No.'

Baby asked Didi why Bhai Chacha never ever wrote to them; why Dadi never visited. She replied, 'Relationships are like bones – as they age, they grow brittle and snap easily.'

Mahendra Uncle came from Delhi for a visit, occasionally. But they went nowhere. Not even to Delhi, though Mahendra Uncle invited them all the time. Then, he too left. Baby saw him for the last time on her twelfth birthday. He told Didi that he had decided to accept a job in Australia as the head of a large confectionery business. It was the first time Baby saw Didi weep; weep without mopping up the tears before they spilled onto her cheeks.

Baby had shouted out, 'Let's go, let's go!' And when Didi shook her head, 'Let me go!'

Didi had come across and put a hand on her head.

'Not just yet. I won't go anywhere, Mahendra – this is my place in life. You go find yours.'

Baby's pleas to return to 3, Chor Bagh, were also rejected.

'Who for? Purush will be lying with his bottle on the sofa, Dadi will be lying on her bed with her Gita and Bhai Chacha will be lying with your Chachi. Who's going to lie next to you the way Sita does?'

Baby deeply resented Amma for taking away 3, Chor Bagh, from her. As she grew up she realized there must be more to their departure than Amma's silly story. She vowed that one day, she would return there and find out what had happened.

In the light of a dark moon, as though the sun had left behind its afterglow, she now stood on the rooftop considering the inmates of 3, Chor Bagh.

Why was the family stilled and framed in a photograph taken years ago?

It was day ten of her return to 3, Chor Bagh, and Baby had found no answer to this question. All she knew was that time did not tick by in seconds, minutes, hours or even days at 3, Chor Bagh. It progressed with a sameness that made Monday indistinguishable from Tuesday.

All day Purush occupied the sofa. At noon, he brought out a half bottle of rum and Bansi served water and sliced lemon. And hot pakoras. Purush would eat a plate of them with his afternoon rum. He skipped lunch sometimes, falling asleep as the winter sun receded from his presence. Tea was drunk out in the garden with Som Devi. Som Devi would narrate the day's events – the price of vegetables, the payment of a bill, Bansi's mendacity, Lobo Chachi's omissions. Baby noticed how her father merely listened, making the very occasional remark. He never addressed any to her. But he did watch Baby: with an unwavering, fixed stare, as though still unconvinced of her existence or presence in his home.

Bhai Chacha and Lobo Chachi always left for the bookstore immediately after breakfast and returned promptly at 7.00 p.m. each evening. Chachi had tea and sponge cake which she baked herself – chocolate, mixed fruit, vanilla. She could eat almost half a cake every day.

Bhai Chacha joined his brother for a drink. Sometimes, he brought back kebabs – seekh, boti, shammi. Cooked ones – Som Devi did not permit meat to be cooked in the house.

One evening, Lobo Chachi knocked on the door of Baby's room. Baby was lolling in a leather swivel chair that belonged to her grandfather, with a glass of brandy and a cigarette, listening inattentively to old Hindi film songs on a small Philips transistor. She was surprised to see Lobo Chachi.

'Come in – have a drink?'

As the warmth of the brandy spread through her, Lobo Chachi relaxed, put up her feet on the bed, wiggled her toes.

'So, how did Miss Lobo, the bookshop assistant, became Lobo Chachi and the only person to call Bhai Chacha by his name?'

'Ratty, you mean, child,' Lobo Chachi laughed.

Baby shuddered for Dadi: Ratan, Bhai Chacha's name had been reduced to an animal endearment.

She was the eldest of two sisters, Lobo Chachi said. Her father had worked as a librarian in the university. She was fourteen when he died, on the bus coming home. Since he had been in the university for twenty years, they took pity on his widow and gave Mrs Lobo a job as an assistant in the same library.

'By God's grace and her own hard labour, she made us a life. In the evening she would bake cakes, make caramel toffees for extra pocket money. My sister and I would home deliver.'

Miss Lobo had gone to college. After one year, she dropped out.

'I took home science, and they had cooking classes, child,' snorted Lobo Chachi. 'My mother could teach me at home. Why go to college to learn how to lay the table?'

Her sister, Clementine fell in love with a young Hindu neighbour and they ran away because his parents did not want converts in the family. Clementine was in Calcutta.

'She's changed her name to Rita and has two boys. But I know that Our God must reside in her heart because God does not leave you just because you change your name.'

Miss Lobo took over baking the cakes and caramels from her mother. She continued with the deliveries too. That was when she met Bhai Chacha. On a home delivery.

'It is the Almighty's wish that I come to this house.'

Actually, added Lobo Chachi, conscientiously, *He* had sent her to the bookshop. That was where Bhai Chacha had asked for the toffees to be delivered.

'Ratty,' Lobo Chachi said fondly, 'has a most sweet tooth and he loved our caramels. Twice a week, I would deliver caramels to him. He always made me eat one. Kind man.'

One day, she found him preoccupied, trying to manage the entire bookshop on his own. The assistant had left without warning. Seeing him harassed, Miss Lobo offered to help.

'I am good at counting, and I make very good bills.'

Before she left that evening, he offered her a job in the shop and a good salary.

Baby watched her while she spoke, this thin brown woman with sparkling teeth and scarlet lips, wearing a nylon printed sari and a lovely smile. Baby wondered whether Amma would have approved of her for Bhai Chacha.

Lobo Chachi said that after 'your Amma' had left for the hills, Bhai Chacha became very pale and slow.

'Child, there was no petrol in his tank,' Lobo Chachi explained.

He seemed alone, abandoned, and lengthened the hours he remained in the shop. He began to offer her a ride home, and would come upstairs. He would stay for a drink, even dinner.

'My mother was a most fine cook, especially when it came to sweets and meats.'

Four years after Amma had left, Bhai Chacha asked Miss Lobo to marry him.

Baby splashed more brandy into her glass and asked how her dadi and father had reacted. Lobo Chachi kissed the golden cross around her neck. 'Go, child, go,' she replied, shaking her head.

They were married in court. Her mother threw a party the same evening, 'bigger than the one she has on Christmas Day'.

Som Devi did not attend, neither did Purush. Lobo Chachi said they had danced till three in the morning. When they reached home and rang the bell, no one came to the door.

'Finally, your papa shouted from inside, "Come back tomorrow, can't you see we are sleeping?" We sat out in the porch till your mother let us in with the doodhwallah.'

She laughed a lot, Lobo Chachi. Baby liked that.

Lobo Chachi asked if she might have a little more brandy.

'Why not? I plan on having more.'

'I am the ugly Kristan, as Mummyji calls us,' she explained. 'Mummyji will not forgive me my hiccups. But,' she giggled and thrust forward her glass, 'it is a long time since I was so naughty. God forgive me.'

Curious, Baby asked why she took God's name so frequently. Did she believe in Him so sincerely?

'This is the miracle of belief: if you believe, you believe; if you don't,' she shrugged.

This miracle had eluded Baby. Didi never prayed. Sita would perform puja in the morning, the way she said Mem used to, but Didi spurned prayers saying she did not believe in rituals before plaster figures. She believed God resided in the flowers and leaves and in her heart.

'Shall I put my hands on my heart and pray?' Baby once asked Didi.

Didi had kissed her in reply.

Now Baby looked at Lobo Chachi and thought about the person Bhai Chacha must have become to choose this woman who believed in her God and His miracles, rather than settling for a wife of his mother's choice.

Putting down her glass, she asked in an abrupt change of subject: 'Tell about us, Amma and I. What have you been told about us?'

Lobo Chachi put her index finger on her lips.

'No child, no. Your Bhai Chacha gave me one golden rule: no questions. But I remember your mother too well. So fine and elegant – like a peacock. She used to come to the bookshop often and always asked how my mother was. We never spoke more than was required, but she had dignity.'

She took a sip.

'My first winter here? I suggested to Mummyji that we invite you for Diwali or for the Christmas party. She said you were none of my business. I know only what I heard pass amongst them.'

Baby sprang forward and grabbed Chachi's hand, squeezing so very hard, she heard Lobo Chachi's knuckles crunch.

'What? What?'

'That the child was born by the light of a dark moon.'

In that moment's utterance, Baby saw the white arcs on the pink toes beneath the curtain in the doorway, just before she heard the voice.

'Your God will punish you for speaking evil,' Som Devi said. 'Leave the girl.'

'The child has a right to know.'

Som Devi stood holding the curtain aside.

Lobo Chachi carefully placed the glass on the bedside table and rose. She kissed her cross and waved to Baby. Som Devi waited for her to go past and then retreated.

What had Lobo Chachi meant, wondered Baby. Had she been born on a moonless night? But so what? Who could she ask? There were no visitors to 3, Chor Bagh, and the family never seemed to go anywhere.

Oh yes, Baby remembered, there was one visitor: Dr Ganapati. He came to check Som Devi's blood pressure, give her an 'enginetion' as Bansi called it. For diabetes. Occasionally, the telephone rang in the day. Som Devi would lift the receiver and murmur. Baby never learnt who she spoke to or what she said.

Otherwise, the house Didi had left with Baby and Sita was as still as the chimes on the broken clock which hung at the end of the corridor.

One morning, over breakfast, she heard Bhai tell Som Devi that Lobo Chachi was unwell and would be staying home.

'Bhai Chacha, can I go with you to the bookshop?'

Bhai Chacha raised an eyebrow at Som Devi who glanced at Purush who was blowing the steam from his coffee mug into his face.

'Bring her back by lunch,' Som Devi ordered.

As Bhai and Baby left the dining room, she heard Purush say, 'She should feel quite at home there, shouldn't she?'

'Oh Purush, let it be!'

'She was rubbish all, she rubbished all.'

A chair stamped its feet in impatience. A door slammed in protest. Baby shuddered.

They went out into the August sunlight. Bhai raced the engine of his white Fiat. He had sold the silver-grey Oldsmobile many years earlier. It cost too much to maintain.

The bookshop was in the main marketplace. Its nameplate was in black and yellow, with a red-and-white canopy shading the front. It had large windows on both sides of a glass door, bright yellow lights inside. Cosy. Quaint. Her father was right. Baby felt immediately at home.

She roamed up and down the shelves, running fingers over the books and sniffing the fragrance of paper. She looked into Bhai's narrow, square office: it had a desk with a white steel lamp and an onyx ashtray. A large brown leather upholstered swivel chair and two upright ones opposite. He smokes, thought Baby, away from home, away from Dadi.

'Where's my uncle?' she asked the store assistant with black bullets for eyes; eyes which were aimed at her bosom. How she yearned to slap him.

'Back room,' he said, nodding towards the rear of the shop. Baby looked around and saw nothing.

'Where?' she asked in a sharp tone, thinking him deliberately misleading.

'There.' He rolled his eyes and smiled his insolence.

In the middle of one white formica-plated shelf was a brass handle. The formica parted and Bhai Chacha ducked out.

'I thought we would have some coffee and a smoke together,' Baby proposed.

In the smoky, dim office, Bhai told her about the bookstore, the kinds of books which sold best, how he tried to be modern and strike a balance 'the fine line between culture and pop culture'. She blew smoke rings in his face. But he didn't blink.

He had formed a partnership for her grandfather's publishing business because he simply couldn't manage its affairs alone. The family retained shares in the company and that brought in the bulk of their money.

'Yes, that is good because you will have the children to think of soon,' Baby commented.

Through the opacity of smoke, Bhai Chacha suddenly looked frail.

'Children?' he blinked.

'Why? Won't you and Chachi have any? Am I to be the only child in this family? The one that was fathered – what is it – by the light of a dark moon?'

She saw Bhai's eyes marble. From inside the desk drawer, he pulled out a small silver engraved box and extracted a cigarette and match box.

Slowly, as he smoked, his eyes gained focus like the lens of a camera.

Baby drummed the bridge of her nose.

'Bhai Chacha, what is the light of a dark moon?'

He rubbed his eyes in circles.

'Just talk.'

'Tell, na.'

The long strands of his hair drooped. He seemed terribly misplaced, a man who had lost himself.

Baby felt water trickle out from her right nostril and down to her lips.

Bhai didn't speak. Baby waited.

'Don't tell, then. I want to go home,' she sniffed.

He hurriedly reached for the car keys.

On the ride home, she hung her head out from the Fiat's window and let her hair race behind her face as Bhai Chacha increased the speed. They were driving at almost 60mph. Baby smiled to herself: he was in a tearing hurry to get home.

That evening, she knocked on Bhai's door in search of Lobo Chachi. When the door opened, it framed Bhai.

'Come, come,' he invited, smiling.

There was a double bed with a mosquito net, a desk and chair by the window, and two large wooden almirahs. In one, Bhai kept a collection of antique books.

'Two generations' learning,' Dadi had explained. 'They are semi-precious.' Sometimes, Som Devi had a quaint way with words.

Baby wanted to see the books. She wanted to climb into Bhai Chacha's lap as she once had, turn the pages and roll back the years with him.

Bhai brought out one of the 'semi-precious' books and placed it on the table. She turned the feather-like pages of *Hobson-Jobson*. Bhai Chacha took her hand and rubbed his thumb over her palm. She felt, instinctively, that he was tracing the lines of another hand, reviving a faded memory.

Over the next few weeks, she searched for ways to be alone with Lobo Chachi. But each time, she came up against an excuse.

Go, child, go.

Oh, I must go shell the peas, otherwise Mummyji will cluck her teeth hard at me.

No, child, I have to do an inventory of the books.

One morning, over a three-egg omelette, toast and beaten coffee, Baby asked in a casual way, 'Lobo Chachi, can I go with you to the bookstore?'

'Nahin,' replied Som Devi, her fingers nimbly drumming the thali as she cleaned the rice.

'But I want to.'

No one replied. Heads were down.

Baby rose, stamped the chair on the floor, thrice, and marched away.

Lobo Chachi said, 'May the Almighty forgive us for treating a child so.'

Baby's nostril sprang a leak.

That afternoon, Baby sneaked out of the house. She walked till the backs of her knees became painful, her ankles swollen. There were shanty shops on the roadside. She stopped: cigarette and paanwallahs, cycle-repairwallah, chaiwallah, Sharma's Generel Store, 'Sheetal Restaurant-come-Dhaba: Strict Non-Vegeterain'.

An old, gnarled tree encircled by a cement seat appeared ahead of her. Baby sat down. She needed to rest. Next to her, a woman fed her small child under the protection of her pallu. Baby instinctively raised a hand to her own breast. On the ground, in the shade of the tree, squatted five men. One sat apart, smoking a bidi. The others were playing cards and exchanging remarks, laughing.

The woman tucked her breast neatly back into her blouse. She smiled at Baby's stare.

'I keep plenty of milk for him. My girls also love him too much.'

'How many?'

'Two girls and a boy. And you?'

Baby shook her head.

'Brother-sister?'

She shook her head again, feeling small and solitary. She wished she could have nestled in the woman's arms. She wished she could have played a hand of cards with the men.

Instead, she took a cycle rickshaw home.

Lobo Chachi did not drop by her room again.

But Baby was determined to find out more about why Amma had never returned to 3, Chor Bagh, and Som Devi wasn't going to stop her.

One evening, pacing up and down the central corridor, she managed to catch Lobo Chachi entering her room alone. She darted in after her, shut the door quietly and bolted it.

'You cannot refuse me.'

'No, child. You'll get me into trouble with that scissored-face Mummyji. Leave alone.'

Baby turned away, her expression woebegone.

'Rat ... Rattan says the lights went out for your mother,' Lobo Chachi called out as Baby made to depart, 'and there was a lunar eclipse. That's why the child was born wrong. I know no more. Go then.'

Baby went to the bathroom and examined herself in the mirror. Maybe she was 'born wrong' because of Amma, she said to her reflection.

She went to Som Devi's room and found her with her knitting.

'Why did Amma leave?'

Som Devi continued her knitting in silence.

'What does it mean, Dadi,' Baby prodded, '"born wrong"?'

'Your chachi should keep her nose in her Bible. Otherwise, she will be consumed by the fires of her own Hell,' declared Dadi, as she snapped the needles. 'I am saying, it is all nonsense, moon and lights gone out. All your mother's rubbish.'

Purush's rubbish all.

'But why did we leave?'

Som Devi let her knitting needles do the talking.

Baby was late for dinner. Som Devi had eaten. Lobo Chachi looked up from her thali and smiled encouragement. Purush munched slowly. You could count an entire minute between mouthfuls. The others waited for him.

That night, Baby found it particularly maddening to watch Purush's mouth function. Chomping on lauki. What is there to masticate in the watery vegetable, Baby wondered.

She pulled out her chair with undue force.

She sat down heavily.

'Can't he eat any faster than that?'

'Likes to digest his food ... ulcers,' explained Bhai Chacha, spinning a katori.

'At this rate, it will be digested before it gets to his stomach,' Baby added.

She felt the table move. Purush was knocking his knees.

Lobo Chachi began a giggle before Som Devi's glare stifled it.

'Baby,' reproved Bhai Chacha, 'some respect for your father.'

Baby ignored him. She served herself aloo-mattar, put a spoonful in her mouth and pushed away the thali.

'Cold, all cold. Who can eat cold potatoes and marble-hard peas? Bansi!' she called out.

Bansi appeared.

'Heat this. Tastes like tatti.'

'Shall I tell you the joke about two village idiots?' Baby asked no one in particular.

'Tell, tell,' urged Lobo Chachi, 'such a long while since we had a joke in this house.'

'Two village idiots see a brown pile lying on the road. One asks the other, "What is it?" The other says, "Looks like shit." "Can't be," says the first idiot. The second idiot kneels and sniffs at it. "Smells like shit," he says. "Are you sure?" asks idiot number one. Idiot number two pokes his finger in the pile. "Tastes like shit," he says. "Isn't it a good thing we didn't walk on it?"'

With utmost care, Som Devi placed the serving spoon on a plate.

'You are late for dinner. The food is not like the sun. It cannot stay warm by itself.'

Baby banged a spoon on the thali.

'Yes, I am late, late. How many words rhyme with late? Ate, crate, date, fate, gate, mate, operate, plate, urinate, hate, hate …'

'Venerate,' added Lobo Chachi, nodding.

'Bas – enough. I'm only telling, if you do not like, you do not eat.'

Som Devi placed Bhai Chacha's thali in hers.

Baby continued to drum her thali.

'Oh, please eat, child,' requested Lobo Chachi, 'you must never go to bed hungry.'

'Child-child, she repeats all day,' complained Som Devi, 'never are we to forget about the child.'

'It is just an expression, Ma,' explained Bhai Chacha.

'I know what it is. Don't teach to me,' flashed back Som Devi. 'All day and night we have to hear "go, child, no child …" and about her "Almighty".'

Lobo Chachi stood up. Her powdered neck seemed to darken.

'Morning and evening, Mummyji sits in prayer with her Gita,' she said, the muscles in her neck seemed to contort. 'My God is not welcome in this house. I will keep Him in my heart, and my prayers, where He will not be insulted. Ratan, I refuse to sit here a moment longer. I am going.'

'Do that,' murmured Purush, but Lobo Chachi was already out of the door.

Bhai Chacha twitched the tablemat.

'Oh, Ma, why did you have to say that?'

Som Devi picked up the thalis and put them down. Then she picked them up again.

'Who are you to tell, do this, do that? Did we not have to put up with the mess you created?' She gestured towards Baby. 'Did we not have to suffer for her? Phir then.'

'Don't.' Bhai Chacha held up the palm of his hand.

'Don't eat, don't talk, don't ask questions, don't live, don't, don't, don't.'

Baby rocked back and forth on her chair with the beat of the chant.

'Drunk,' commented Purush looking at his mother, 'she sounds drunk.'

'Drunk. Don't drink too much. Drinking.'

Baby closed her eyes. Her head swayed on the waves of Honey Bee brandy.

Purush returned to the peas on his plate.

'Girls are ugly when they drink,' said Som Devi, pinching her nose.

'Girls have fathers who drink.' Baby slapped a hand on the table. 'Do you find your son ugly, Dadi?'

No reply.

'Rum is in my blood, my name's in mud... la, le-la, la, la.' Baby folded a namaste at Purush. 'Thank you, Father, dear Father, sweet Father, loving Father ...'

'Shut up! Shut up! Shut up!'

Purush raised his head and stood up simultaneously.

'You are your mother's daughter, understand? Understand? Your America-returned, fancy nightdress memsahib mother's daughter. Nothing to do with me.'

'Purush!' exclaimed Som Devi.

Bhai Chacha rose and hurried across to his brother. He placed a restraining hand on his shoulder and pressed him down. 'Don't. She is a child.'

'As if he cares,' Baby screamed, on her feet too. 'None of you cares.'

She wanted to cry. She wished her tears would spill out in drops of blood so they could see how they had wounded her.

Purush glared at her with hatred. Behind Purush's back, Bhai Chacha waved a hand up and down. She didn't know if he was telling her to sit down, or shut up. She did neither.

Instead, she marched around to where Som Devi sat.

'I've discovered your secret.'

That brought up her head.

Baby ran from the room, returned with the quarter bottle of brandy and took a swig. Bansi watched in fascination, with the serving dish in his hand.

'Want a drink, Bansi? A brandy and water with lemon? Like the sahib?'

'Shut up!'

'Shut up! Shut up! All you can say!' Baby went to where Bhai Chacha stood behind her father's chair. 'Lobo Chachi's Almighty will punish you. Punish you and punish you …'

'He already did the day He sent your Amma to us.'

Dadi rose from her chair.

'Go now to your room. I will bring you food there.'

'I know your secret about me: "the child that was born in the light of a dark moon". That's it, isn't it? Born wrong.' She nodded towards Purush. 'Why look at him – he couldn't keep his wife …'

Purush fetched the air a slap.

Baby did not move. She was panting.

'You mother's a chaudail.' Purush shoved Bhai Chacha out of the way. He bent his head into Baby's face. It gleamed with sweat. 'You know why I didn't keep your mother? Because she was already…'

'No, Purush, no,' pleaded Bhai. 'Let it go.' He stood between Purush and Baby, a shield protecting each from the other.

'You are nothing to me, understand? And one day …'

'Purush!' exclaimed Som Devi. 'No. Enough. You promised. We'll discuss it tomorrow.'

Baby had begun to cry.

'Tomorrow?'

A dull day had washed up against the grey sky. The air seeped through the slit eyes of the windowpanes, felt cool on her exposed neck. Baby tiptoed from her room, out into the garden. The mist had reached down to touch the grass. She felt the wetness against her bare feet. Running across to the mango tree, she held it with her arms. She sagged against it, shivering.

Som Devi was seated on her bed, knitting, when Baby returned to her room. A glass of milk stood on the table.

'So. You remind him of your mother,' Som Devi said without lifting her head. 'You have the same needle-like words.' Som Devi arranged her spectacles on the bridge of her nose. 'Purush says you are too much like her.'

'Drink the milk,' she said, abandoning the bed. 'Come to my room after breakfast.'

She walked out.

The dining room was empty. Through the door that led out to the back porch and the pantry, the sunlight had begun to unfold like a rolled-up carpet. Or a mystery unravelling itself, thought Baby, and asked Bansi to make her a four-egg omelette with tomatoes, onions, green chillies and grated cheese.

'No cheese,' he said.

'No cheese, then no cheese. But lots of toast.'

It was the most appetizing omelette she had ever eaten. Then or since. Oily, squishy, chilly-hot.

Som Devi sat knitting on her bed. Her fingers were as thin and grey as the needles clicking between them.

'I am only saying, you should not eat so many eggs at one time – it brings indigestion.'

'I was famished.'

Baby collapsed on the other side of the bed from her. Som Devi pulled the wool from a plastic bag.

'You want to know what happened so many years ago? I am telling you. Phir then.'

Baby was silent.

'Your mother, she has told you nothing?'

'Some silly story about the day Bhai Chacha went missing ...'

'She went mad ... bilkul pagal ... but that is only half the story. Your mother ...' Som Devi began.

The click of the needles became furious.

An hour later, Baby sat still on her bed. She heard water drip in the bathroom. Her nose trickled. She dried it on the back of her hand. She remained there, her fingers digging into her palm.

Then, all at once, she arose and hurriedly bundled her clothes into her bag. She had to leave.

She now knew what it felt like to be scarred. Not where it showed, but where it never healed. She had to get away. Far away.

She walked into the sitting room where Purush decorated the sofa. He was on his side with a folded newspaper. Eyes closed. Looking down, she saw him diminished by space and time. The tall, awesome figure of her childhood was a curled-up insect. The rhythm of his breathing said he was asleep.

Peering into Som Devi's room, Baby found her reading the Gita.

'I want to leave.'

For a moment, Som Devi appeared undecided. Then she abandoned the Gita and her stern expression, and removed a gold chain from her neck. It was thick, flat. Useful, thought Baby, to hang from a fan. Hanging seemed a good idea then. Som Devi placed the rope in her hand. She made as if to hug her granddaughter, but succeeded in hitting Baby's forehead against her mouth instead. She turned towards the bed. Baby hugged her from the back.

'Why?' Dadi whispered. Baby had no reply to give her.

She asked Bansi to fetch a rickshaw. She stood in the garden. Goodbye, mango tree.

Once she had climbed into the rickshaw, she counted out fifty rupees in ten-rupee notes and gave them to Bansi.

'You ought to be in school.'

He reached down to touch her feet and, for the first time since she had come home, a berserk sound escaped Baby. It sounded like laughter.

She sat in the scooter as it pranced down the uneven road, thinking of all that Som Devi had told her. She replayed each of her words in sickening detail and wished she could throw up the words and all they contained.

She instructed the driver to go via the main market. She would pay him extra for waiting.

'How long?'

'Five minutes.'

'Ten rupees.'

'You know how to multiply, don't you?'

She stopped the scooterwallah at the corner of the street and walked across to the bookstore. Baby stood outside. Looking in, she saw Lobo Chachi's head bent over the counter. Counting money. Bhai Chacha emerged from his office and joined Lobo Chachi. He placed a hand on her shoulder. She looked up and smiled.

Baby leaned back against the wall and breathed in deeply. Something was rising from her stomach. Dadi had been right: omelettes caused indigestion.

HILL STATION
1977

Omelettes caused indigestion. Why had she allowed Sita to persuade her to eat one this morning? Eggs never suited Didi. She burped and massaged her stomach.

Still in bed, she played football with the hot water bottle, kicking it from one foot to the other and then rolling it over. She heard the grizzle of an electric shaver and realized it was the static from the radio she had forgotten to switch off earlier. The clock's luminous dial told her it was past three in the morning. One more night without rest.

The frequency of her sleepless nights had increased ever since she had called Baby's college hostel and was told by the matron that Baby had gone home. Baby had not come to her. There was only one other place Baby would call home.

Didi had awaited, dreaded this visit to 3, Chor Bagh, certain it would be made. She knew that she was powerless to prevent it once Baby had left her for Delhi.

She reached out and turned off the radio, sat up and rubbed her cheeks vigorously.

A time will come when I will have forgotten how to sleep, she thought, yawning and stretching her arms. Oh Mem, I am so exhausted of my tiredness!

As the sunlight stole into her garden, Didi threw aside the bedclothes, wore a thick cardigan and went out into the veranda to admire her trees. The dogs struggled to their paws, half-asleep, yawning and stretching after her, duty-bound to follow. Didi walked along the stone gravel, dragging her feet. I am anchored in the past, she thought to herself, I can barely keep up with the present.

She turned at the sound of movement. The dogs had retired to the porch. Nothing stirred. But Didi felt the skin on her arms pucker and crimple as if a razor blade had grazed the sole of her foot.

Who's remembering me, she wondered

Jeff. Why had she suddenly thought of him? Perhaps because the thought of him comforted her whenever she was scared, as though the memory of his warm embrace could lessen the chill of her anxiety.

Or was it her dear cousin Mahendra in Australia? Mahendra, who was now a stamped letter that arrived dutifully every month. How many times he had entreated her to join him.

Baby will like it, and in its wide open spaces you can forget yourself, he wrote, offering to pay for their plane tickets.

Dear foolish Mahendra, who believed geography could control the mind.

The wretch. Left me alone, except for Sita, and she knows nothing. And my daughter who has left me and is right now at 3, Chor Bagh, prying into my life. She wants to confront the past, Didi told herself, when I want to avoid it. People evade taxes easily enough, so why can't I avoid this?

It began to rain. Didi wondered if Baby was sitting beneath the mango tree at 3, Chor Bagh, immovable as its trunk, and whether she would remain there until she had searched through the baggage they had left behind and picked out what she wanted.

Didi gave a heave of the shoulders and went inside, to the kitchen. She put elaichi in water, started up the gas and returned to the garden. Admired her trees, the gravel on the path, her veranda. Her home. Finally, she had one.

All because of him. If it hadn't been for him, his extraordinary generosity, she would still be living in the cramped flat Baby grew up in when they first arrived in the hill station. Didi closed her eyes and thanked him. Thank you, MC.

With the tea in a china cup and two Marie biscuits, Didi went back to her room and stared at the rain from the window. She sat perched on the sill, a bird on the edge of a perpetual expectancy.

She heard Sita take Mem's name and curse the day. A traditional morning greeting.

'Expecting someone?' Sita inquired from behind her.

'Baby.'

'Baby? Oh, but why you not say?' The crackle in Sita's voice cleared. 'I must make her favourite besan laddoos and foot-cake.'

'Fruit, fruit-cake,' Didi corrected automatically.

'Yes, foooot-cake,' repeated Sita. 'How long will she stay?'

'Not long, so don't start making anything.'

'You don't tell me what to do.' Sita came forward and snatched the empty teacup out of Didi's fingers. 'You do what you want, and I do what I want.'

'Fine,' snapped Didi. 'What I want is for you to leave me alone.'

Sita left.

'Hai hai, Mem, see how she talks to me? Where have you gone, Mem? Where have you gone and left me?'

'You know where she has gone,' shouted Didi after her. 'Want to join her?'

After her bath, Didi dusted the rooms and placed fresh flowers in the vases. Orange gladioli in one, white carnations in the other. There was a sulky silence from the kitchen. Didi found Sita seated on her green painted wicker chair, cutting her fingernails with the vegetable knife. Didi leaned against the frame of the door.

'Baby has gone to visit ... them.'

Sita dropped the knife in her lap.

'There?'

'Must be. Matron said she had gone home.'

Didi rotated the ring on her index finger, the one Mem had given her when she married Purush. 'I don't know what to do.'

Sita rose, let the knife fall to the floor.

'Oh Mem, why did we do what we did?'

'Sita, you know why.'

She must have dozed off during her vigil by the window. Suddenly, her eyes started open. An autorickshaw had drawn up in front of the gate. By the time Baby marched in, trailing a small bag, Didi was out on the veranda, her arms folded across her bust. She's a beautiful cat, Didi decided, a beautiful, lithe black cat with a crown of burnished gold. Didi felt the magnetic attraction of her daughter's presence and sorry for the man who would love her.

Didi's daughter: in a black-ribbed turtleneck sweater, tight purple corduroy jeans stuffed into black boots and a short purple jacket, her light brown hair glinting in the early sun, sparkling purple eye shadow along the eyelids, and black triangles for eyelashes. Something between a cat and a clown.

Taller than Didi by at least three inches, she stood before her mother, her face saying all that Didi did not wish to hear. Baby knocked the bridge of her nose. An old nervous gesture she had learnt from Didi.

'What in Mem's memory is that on your eyelashes so early in the day?' Didi demanded.

Without touching Didi, Baby swept past her with such force, the movement of air staggered Didi. She swayed for a moment, then placed her palms on her eyes and massaged them.

She heard Sita's clucks of pleasure and her daughter's sobs. Through the square wiring of the netted door, Didi saw Baby weep all over Sita who stood on tiptoe in an effort to gather her.

'Oh Mem, today is the worst day day of my life,' Didi proclaimed and sat down to await it.

Instinct told her she must not approach Baby until she was ready to come forward. From the sounds and smells of the next few hours, Didi knew Baby had bathed, drunk strong coffee and gone to bed. Didi sat out in the veranda, waiting.

'Got the headache?' She heard the concern in Sita's voice. 'Just like your ...'

'No.' Baby sliced off the word. 'Never like her.'

While Baby slept, Didi sat there, motionless. Between the passing cars and scooters, the fruit carts and the cyclists, her mind darted back and forth. She wished life could be rehearsed, so you knew your part before starting out. Instead, it was like a clever thief – it robbed you of time without your realizing you'd lost it. All of a sudden you searched the years and discovered they were mostly empty.

'I haven't much to show for life,' she told the bull who had chosen to peer through the bars of the gate at that very moment.

Didi resolutely pressed the past back between the pages of her memory. She would not think. She would cook. Ever since she had moved to the hills, she cooked compulsively, using Mem's old recipe book, seeking solace in the kitchen.

On these occasions, there was a keen tussle between Sita and Didi. Sita believed the kitchen belonged to her; Didi didn't care who it belonged to, she needed to use it.

'I am a worry cook. When my hands work, my mind doesn't,' she explained to Sita. 'Then I feel better.'

'Why not, instead, you visit the doctor-sahib? He will give you a tablet. It is cheaper than mushrooms.'

Sometimes Didi cooked from the memory of meals she had helped Mem cook in New York. Dishes Mem would seldom touch because she was a strict vegetarian. On these occasions, all rules of nutrition were ignored, all definitions of 'meals' flouted.

They ate hot, freshly baked brownies, made in Mem's old Bellings electric oven for breakfast; milk shakes and French fries for lunch; a thick lentil, and mutton bone soup which Didi would cook from morning to tea time with meat loaf and buttered bread and butter mushrooms for dinner. There were cakes or other bakes, vanilla ice-cream with dark chocolate sauce made from milk chocolate bars, and coffee with four tablespoons of brandy.

Sita criticized these binges, refusing to eat any of the dishes.

'Today, I will eat out,' she would announce grandly whenever Didi decided to cook.

She took money from Didi and ate at the nearest Indian dhaba.

Invariably, she had loose motions the next day.

'See what comes of eating Indian khana outside?' Didi scolded.

'See what comes of not letting me eat in my own home?' replied Sita, running between the kitchen and the toilet.

On the day Baby returned from her visit to 3, Chor Bagh, Didi knew what she wanted to cook.

A bake.

Cream butter in the pan with a wooden spoon. Add sifted white flour, allow it to gently brown, pour in the room temperature milk, mix in salt, three peppercorns, a pinch of red chilli powder and a small spoon of mustard. Turn up the flame and stir vigorously to ensure no lumps form as the milk thickens. When it protests against the spoon, add half a cup of grated processed cheese.

When the white sauce was ready, Didi diced carrots and potatoes, squared beans and shelled peas, and put them to boil in salted water; went out to the veranda for an impatient smoke; returned to strain the half-cooked vegetables, enjoying the steam on her face; and dropped them into the saucepan. A piece of butter scoured the baking dish and then the vegetables in the white sauce were poured in. Strands of cheese laced the top and she decorated it with blobs of butter. Didi felt patriotic about baked vegetables: the green, orange and white reminded her of the Indian flag. Next she would be singing the national anthem.

She pushed the dish into the oven and set the timer. Time, that invisible thief. Thirty minutes later, she inhaled deeply and smiled: nothing smelled of joy more than melting, browned cheese in a baking dish. She wanted to bury her nose in it for comfort.

First a bath.

A silk sari: orange, with purple checks. An old blouse: cream, high in the collar, long in the sleeves and nipped in at the waist. The sari pallu, she wore long. A purple shawl, a small black bindi on her forehead and a touch of L'Air du Temps under her armpits, behind her ears. She knotted her hair casually.

She was ready.

Baby was in the veranda, a plate in hand.

'Good?' inquired Didi.

Baby smeared the sauce of the bake on a slice of bread.

'I don't know which I detest more: the smell of your cooking or the scent of your perfumes.'

She got up and went into her bedroom.

The silence and bitterness between Didi and her daughter continued for days. Baby snapped each time her mother spoke. So Didi chose silence.

Consequently, they ate well but conversed extremely badly. There were hot cheese soufflés and cold cutting remarks; shrimp cocktail with sneers.

'This thing between you two is costing much money,' Sita protested to Baby one afternoon, while Didi baked an almond cake. 'She cooks as if she is still in Noo Ark and baaki you drink and smoke.'

'Don't pretend.' Baby reclined on her bed, one leg dangling off the edge.'I found out what you both hid from me all these years. At least *you* should have told me.'

Baby gave the air a swift kick.

As far as possible, Baby avoided Didi. She'd leave the house in the afternoon and return late in the evening. Didi never asked where she went.

Sita kept a close watch on Baby, running in and out of her bedroom, supplying her with food prepared by Didi as though food was a cure for whatever ailed mother and daughter.

'Hai hai, Mem, see your children! One cooks to reduce pain, the other eats to relieve it. What times are these?'

Nobody enlightened her.

'When are you going to show some interest in what is going on here?' Sita asked Didi on the fifth afternoon. Didi was snipping dead leaves off the potted flowers in the garden. 'Do you know what your daughter is doing?'

'She doesn't want me, Sita.'

'What "she want"? A mother does not supply what a child wants, she gives what she needs.'

Sita blocked Didi's view.

'She is,' Sita tipped a thumb towards her mouth, 'drinking, smoking. Like you in Noo Ark, don't I remember? Rest of the time, she is eating, eating …'

Didi pushed Sita aside. The afternoon clouds slid across her body, a pair of exploratory hands.

'And you,' continued Sita, 'are cooking.'

'Something to do, Sita.'

'Do something for your daughter. Look what she does.'

'All children do these days.'

Sita jerked Didi around.

'This is my Baby. You look after her the proper way. You make her stop. She will be a sharaabi and then who will marry her?'

'It's not drinking and smoking which get you into trouble.' Didi looked up and beyond Sita. 'It's yourself.'

'This all I do not understand. I want Baby better. It is your duty.' Sita shook Didi by the shoulders. Irritably, Didi shrugged her off.

The next morning, Didi entered Baby's bedroom to find her daughter manicuring her nails.

'You should paint them light pink. It will suit the colour of your skin.'

'Did you paint yours black to match the colour of your character?'

Baby locked herself in the bathroom.

Didi automatically began to pick up Baby's discarded clothes and tidy the bed. She held her daughter's blouse to her nose. Momentary joys bear lifelong consequences, she told herself.

In the eight days since Baby's return from her visit to 3, Chor Bagh, there had not been a moment of release from the tension.

Only Sita tried to loosen its grip on them.

'Whatever happened has happened, Baby. Let be now,' she would soothe Baby.

'Yes, but I should have known. You, and *she*, let me grow up thinking they did not care about me. All the time, it was *her*.'

Sita pressed Baby's knee.

'She always cares for you. She mourns, Baby. Each time she cooks.'

'Then she should go to Tirupati, or Haridwar, and open a restaurant. Nothing less, like I said, can cleanse her soul.'

'Don't be like that. Let be, Baby. Let Didi go her way.'

Baby pushed Sita's hand off and jumped to her feet. She tore a comb through her long light hair, pinked in her mouth and poured eau de toilette between her breasts.

'Baby,' Didi said from the bedroom doorway, 'my first concern is to protect you.'

'With your lies and secrecy?'

Baby strode past her mother and out of the house.

Didi stood knocking the wooden ladle against the bridge of her nose.

'Each time I speak, I create more trouble.'

Sita took the ladle from her and patted her gently on the hand with it.

'When you open your mouth, insects crawl out. She doesn't want your explanations. She wants the truth.'

The timer rang on the oven.

'The truth,' Didi remarked, opening the oven door, 'who knows what that is?'

'What are you doing?'

'What does it look like I am doing?'

'Packing.'

'Leaving.'

'Sita will be very upset.'

'Sita doesn't have to eat your food every day and then fit into my jeans. Like I said, my absence will do you good.'

'How so?'

'You can stop feeding your guilt.'

Baby went across to the dressing table and scooped her make-up into the bag. She took out a blue eye shadow and started applying it with thick strokes on her lids.

'What is it you know, Baby?'

Didi sat down on the bed. She could see Baby in the mirror.

Baby paused to face her mother's reflection.

'How you loved the bookshop storeroom. The storeroom of the bookshop! Remember?' She compressed her lips.

'Oh, is it still the same?'

'See? That's all that bothers you! You have no shame! None.'

Didi scratched the surface of the bedcover, picking out stray threads.

Baby flung the blue eye shadow into her bag and slammed into the toilet.

'No shame,' she called out, 'in the storeroom!'

One thread began to unravel the pattern and Didi pulled harder.

'Leaving my father on the sofa and rushing off to the bookstore. In front of everybody. And because of that we had to leave 3, Chor Bagh, and come here.'

The skein of the bedspread resembled a snake. A little like Som Devil, thought Didi with bitterness. That snake had told Baby everything Didi had hidden for so long. I named her well – *devil*. The smile on Didi's lips was so tight, it would have to be slit open with a penknife. She shook her head.

'To think people can die, a man can go missing, because of a cricket match,' she said suddenly.

Baby stared at her.

'What are you talking about? Which man? There was another man, not just Bhai Chacha?' she hissed. 'I'm going.' Baby picked up her bag. She pulled at her nose.

'Was it so important? A man? Did you have feelings for him?'

'Maybe, Baby.'

'And once you began, you just couldn't stop, could you?'

'It's like eating peanuts, Baby. Once you begin, you cannot stop.'

Baby stared at her mother, tears running black down her cheeks.

'All I've had is trouble …'

'Not true, we have had good times …'

'But you manage to ruin everything, every time.' Baby wiped her face, but the tears collected faster than she could clear them. 'Why did you give birth to me on the night of a dark moon?' she shouted.

Didi's features creased in perplexity.

'What are you talking about?'

'Lobo Chachi told me: the child was born on the night of a dark moon. It brings bad luck. That's all I am! Bad luck.'

Didi reached out and caught her daughter by the shoulders. She pushed her back on the bed. Baby fought to rise. Didi pushed her again.

'You're all wrong. This Lobo knows nothing. It's no such thing. You were born on a cloudless, beautiful, clear night. Promise.' Didi placed a hand on Baby's head. 'There was no dark moon for you, ever.'

Baby struggled to her feet.

'Oh, how do I care!' She crossed her chest with her arms, glared at Didi. 'I am going to leave. To put as much distance as I can between us. See if I don't.'

She turned and walked swiftly out, the way people do when they have no intention of returning. Sita went clattering after her.

'Don't go so soon, come soon, soon. Hai Mem, what are these times?'

Didi watched her daughter disappear through the gate. She sighed, sat down in the kitchen and began to peel potatoes.

'We did have good times, Baby. We did. We just choose to forget.'

Didi thought back to 3, Chor Bagh, and the genuine happiness she had known for a few months. With her eyes she touched the contours of Bhai's body.

3, CHOR BAGH
1960

With her eyes she touched the contours of Bhai's body. He was slight, with an inward curving bottom. He had other protrusions. Ears that stood out; a sharp, triangular nose. Everything else about him was concave. As if he had been hollowed out.

'Scarecrow,' Didi would call him.

He was a man who had not matured into masculinity. Yet, when he caught her eye across the dining table, Didi felt an itch about her navel. It's faintly ludicrous, even humiliating, she scolded herself. She was in her late twenties – married into a family which lived in the oldest part of the ancient city, to a man who may or may not have got there once but never did so again, with a child who did not belong to him – alone and pent-up with her unspent longings, scratching her belly button whenever she met a particular expression in her brother-in-law's eyes. How would she ever explain it?

She had used him. Seduced him. Wretched, helpless Bhai. The student of history who loved poetry. The teenager who led protests at the university against the British Empire but recited English verse under his breath. The nationalist who wore khadi during the day but slept in a nightsuit. The older son who dutifully ran the family publishing business while his younger brother lay on a New York sofa. The bachelor who wouldn't find a wife because his eyes clung to his sister-in-law's body.

Bhai.

Didi could never satisfactorily explain to herself why, after living in the same house for over three years, this irresistible urge had seized them. Time colluded with opportunity, her boredom with his frustration. But that did not explain why. So she blamed it on *Gone with the Wind.*

The first afternoon at the bookstore. It would have ended there, at a delicious touch-me-not tour of the bookshelves, but for Som Devi and Purush.

Didi had accompanied Bhai to the bookstore saying she wanted to pick up something to read. She had spent time amidst the mystery bookshelves in an effort to avoid the heat of Bhai's body and the adhesive of his eyes. She returned home with three James Hadley Chase and several Agatha Christie books.

Som Devi and Purush were drinking tea in the garden. Within hearing distance, Baby chased Budhoo around the mango tree with delighted squeals.

'Baby, I am only asking, does your mother think we are transferring the bookshop into the house?' smirked Som Devi, sucking in tea from a saucer.

Didi placed the books on the table in front of her mother-in-law and poured tea into a cup.

Som Devi reached for the cup of tea that Didi had poured for herself, and emptied it into her own saucer. Didi overturned the teapot, but there was only enough to fill a quarter cup.

'If she loves books so much, why doesn't she make herself useful?' remarked Purush. 'Go work in the bookstore, this America-returned memsahib?' He reached out for a boondi ka laddoo and began to munch.

Didi rose and picked up the books.

'Good idea. Maybe I will. Someone should help Bhai support his younger brother's habits.'

Som Devi powdered a laddoo between her fingers.

'And who better than his dutiful wife?' she commented, momentarily forgetting she never addressed Didi directly. 'Kyon, Purush?' She nudged her son, causing the cup to fall and the tea to spill onto his immaculate trousers and then the grass.

'About time,' sneered Didi's husband, kicking the cup towards Didi. 'She thinks she has no duties towards her husband.'

Didi stared at the divide in Purush's pants where the spilled tea had spread into a stain.

'I don't know,' added Som Devi, as she assembled the crumbled laddoo into a ball, 'what she thinks of herself, this maharani memsahib. Poor upbringing, I'm only telling,' added Som Devi, eating the laddoo crumbs. 'It is Mem who spoilt her.'

Didi experienced a violent desire to shove Som Devi's nose up her nostrils. Instead, she walked away to her room.

After lunch the next day, Didi followed Bhai out to the car.

'You can't have read those books already, Didi!' he exclaimed, wiping his hands on his kurta.

'I,' announced Didi with a small curtsy, 'am coming to help you.' Bhai's eyes and hands jerked in consternation.

'The bookshelves could do with some arrangement,' she added.

'I don't think so. Didi, Ma and Purush—'

'Are the ones who suggested it. Go ask, then,' she challenged when he remained irresolute by the car.

He returned almost immediately. She had already climbed into the backseat of the Oldsmobile.

'Dutiful, dutiful Bhai,' Didi observed. 'What did they say?'

'Good riddance to rubbish all!' he replied automatically and then compressed his mouth, stricken by his imitation of Purush.

'Driver, chalo,' Didi commanded, and the breeze carried her laughter through the open windows of the house into Som Devi's ears. Her eyes flashed open.

It was to be the first time. Opening the door, Didi followed Bhai into the storeroom where he had gone to check the stock. He was standing with his back to her and she saw a huge brown fly settle on the elongation of his neck.

'Looks like a bee,' she whispered, glancing around. 'Wait.'

She picked up a slim hardback.

'Hold still,' she ordered, and after what seemed the lengthiest pause in the history of fly-swatting, Didi brought down the book at the precise moment he turned and caught her by the hair.

Later, as she rose from the floor, she discovered the fly splayed out where they had lain.

'We have just,' she informed Bhai, who was struggling into his kurta, 'killed a fly.'

Those afternoons. Bhai sent Miss Lobo to the wholesalers, the publishers or printers, and put the 'Closed for Lunch' sign outside the shop. He read love sonnets to her from Palgrave's *Golden Treasury* and showered her with admiration the way people do rose petals on a newly-wed couple. She should have put out her hand to seal his lips. Instead, whenever she opened her mouth to speak, confess her weakness, he placed his hand on it.

'The problem with you, Bhai,' Didi once told him, avoiding his fingers, 'is that you are good. A caring man. Very boring. The only thing which saves you from being a yawn is me.'

His nostrils flared. She studied the light through the cobwebs of her hair.

'Are you sorry?'

He placed a folded arm over his eyes and stretched out.

'He's my brother.'

'He's been no husband to me, Bhai, and I've been a bad wife to him.'

'That is a matter between you.'

She pulled the shield of his arm away from his eyes.

'Oh, don't be so pompous! You lie between Purush and me. Listen,' she said as he screwed his eyes more tightly, 'you must know this: we are not a dutiful couple.'

With her fingers, she prised open his right eye, then the left.

'I did not want to marry your brother, I didn't want to marry at all. But Dada was dying …'

Didi pinched him under the chin and his eyes started open.

'You cannot imagine what it was like for a young Indian girl who had never been further than Delhi, to live in the most exciting city of the world – sparkling like champagne in the glass! Oh those bubbles! Pouf! Pouf! And then, this marriage, and I am transported back a century. From Manhattan to 3, Chor Bagh. And Purush.'

Didi stood up and went to lean against the wall.

'I was very cruel to him the first night. I hid my true feelings under my petticoat. That's what women do.' Didi fingered the books on the nearest shelf.

'We didn't manage to please each other that night.' Didi returned to stand in front of Bhai. 'Or any since. We try to do our duty, that's all.'

He put his hands on his ears.

'I don't want to know.'

'You must. Otherwise, how can I explain this.' She pointed to where the fly had been squashed by their weight.

'You're ruining everything – leave the pain of love to the poets,' Bhai begged, 'I don't want to know before and after. Just now.'

He took her hand and drew circles on her palm.

She tightened her fingers to clasp his.

He placed her hand over his eyes.

I am your blind spot and your guilty secret, Didi thought.

There was so much she wanted to say to him but could not. How the shape and feel of Purush revolted her. His sag in the sofa, in the small of her back. How that made this right in a way that was not wrong. Should she feel guilt? She would close her eyes and try out remorse for size. She had been dutiful. She had obeyed Dada and Dadi, she had pleased Mem and Father, she had tried to submit to Purush.

By dint of loyalty, she had forgiven her grandfather his stubborn attachment to tradition that had forced her into marriage. She never considered forgiving either Purush or herself. To forgive would have meant to understand, and how could she possibly understand what she had done? Who could explain any of it? Not Didi.

'Why have you not married, Bhai?' Didi asked.

They were standing on the rooftop. He was teaching Baby to fly a kite. Expertly, with his long fingers. She felt the scratches he had left on her back tingle.

'Why?' she persisted, holding her hair in the autumn wind.

'Because I wanted a wife who would please my family and recite poetry with me, yes,' he said, smacking Baby's hands which were pulling the string so hard, the kite see-sawed. Budhoo pranced around, snapping at the air.

'Oooooh,' cried out Baby. 'Up-di-doo, Bhai Thatha,' she lisped.

Didi could not resist: she went across and kissed her.

Budhoo climbed up her back and nuzzled her thighs.

'Dirty dog! Shoo.' Didi took off a chappal and threw it. Budhoo raced off after it.

'And?' Didi asked as the kite staggered down the sky to collapse near their feet.

'It was rather too much to ask for. When your proposal came, I didn't show much interest and Ma was so keen that Purush be married – she thought it would cure him of whatever ailed him.'

Bhai bent down and pinched Baby's nose. She rubbed it into his palm, then ran across to fetch a new kite. Didi took Bhai's hand.

'You read out poetry with serious passion,' she said.

'And you listen with such a rapt expression,' he replied.

That night, after dinner, after Baby had gone to bed, after all the lights in the house were extinguished, after Purush had fallen asleep on her New York sofa, Didi and Bhai stole up to the roof, by way of a wooden ladder. The sky was spotless.

'The stars are missing,' Didi observed. 'I know. I read in the paper, it's the night of a lunar eclipse. I always wanted to see the moon when it was hidden.' Didi offered her face to the sky.

'It will blind you.'

Bhai tried to shield her face with his body.

Didi pushed him aside.

'That is the solar eclipse.'

'Ma says the lunar eclipse is inauspicious. You should stay indoors.'

'I like the forbidden,' said Didi, hugging herself. 'Especially when your mother forbids it. "Ma says"! Why are all men mama's boys?'

'Well, because they are!' he replied and laughed.

Didi removed the shawl from about her shoulders, let the sari pallu fall forward, stretched her arms wide open.

'Come, feast on me!' she whispered.

'What are you doing, Didi? Are you insane? Has the eclipse already muddled your mind?' Bhai flung the shawl over Didi's body and held her as she tried to wriggle free.

'You brothers are such cowards!' She eluded him and ran to the edge of the parapet.

He followed her.

'It's not that,' he said. 'I want you safe.'

Didi sank down on the roof parapet. She held out her arms to the night.

'Come.'

And then Bhai came between her and the night. There was no light at all.

It was morning, there was still no light. The sky had darkened into a scowl and it seemed like night had fallen.

That must be the reason for her uneasiness. A thin, cool breeze blew out the curtains, but Didi felt a glue in her armpits. She hoped it would rain. Restless, she turned to find Purush fast asleep on the bed beside her. It was unusual for him to come to the bedroom. What had possessed him last night? She shuddered.

Heavy. Chilled. Didi prodded her stomach to find a familiar discomfort, a gentle bloated tenderness. Must be biological: when women were unusually excited, or agitated, their bodies responded. She had read that somewhere.

But she knew herself to be lying. She hadn't had her 'woman's holiday' as Sita called it. This was the second month in succession. Oh dear Mem, what have I done? Again?

She sat up in instant resolution.

This time, she would do things differently, she told herself. This time she would do the right thing.

Just before breakfast, Didi threw up.

'Bet India will win this one.'

Purush squared the omelette into eleven equal pieces and forked one piece into his expectant mouth. Cricket was one subject that aroused Purush. He discussed each day's play in detail with Bhai, over breakfast. Didi listened with deaf ears. She ate an apple, thinking it might settle her stomach.

It was the second test, in Kanpur. India versus Pakistan.

'I hope the match ends in a draw,' said Bhai, peeling a banana. 'Each time there is an Indo-Pak match, we have fireworks in the city.'

'Rubbish all,' exclaimed Purush. 'India must win. National pride.'

'No, Purush.' Bhai got to his feet. 'Remember last time?'

'Oh,' Purush said dismissively, accepting a segment of an orange from Som Devi. 'Only a few shops were looted.'

'Two people died, many homes were ransacked and shops gutted.'

'Oh, them.' Purush nodded and swallowed. They should have gone to Pakistan.'

Bhai flexed his jaws, his ears reddened.

'They distribute sweets for a Paki win,' added Som Devi, holding out another orange segment to Purush, 'then they should live there too.'

She offered her palm to Bhai.

'I still pray for a draw,' insisted Bhai, taking an orange segment and walking away.

'You needn't worry, Bhai,' Purush yelled out after him, 'you'll be safe – you belong to the right side.'

He removed a thread from the skin of the orange and flicked it into the air.

She was bending over to find a hairpin when she felt him in the cleft of her buttocks. She straightened and his hands pressed her back. Dutifully, she went to lie down. He followed. Neither could wait. He took her hand between unsteady fingers and squeezed her taut frame, eyes shut firm. Minutes later, he rose and automatically began to comb his hair.

'Purush!' called his mother outside the bedroom door.

He buttoned up his trousers. Didi passed him on her way to the bathroom.

'Coming, Ma, I was just about to come.'

Didi let the water wash him away. After her bath, she sat with a paper writing pad, underneath the mango tree.

She wrote to Mahendra: *We haven't met in simply a lifetime. Or is it more? Oh, how I want to see you, and the shades of green in the winter leaves of Delhi. How is Prem and my young nephew? Is he enjoying boarding school? I miss you all very much. I am making plans to visit you – yes, with Baby! I will book my train ticket and let you know by telegram when I arrive. It's been such a very, very long time. Didi loves you.*

She pasted the envelope with her tongue and then rushed to the toilet. When she emerged, Sita was by the dressing table.

'What is it?'

'Nothing.'

Didi wrote Mahendra's address on the envelope.

'I heard what I heard.'

'And what did you hear?'

'Wah-wah, wah-wah.'

Sita poked out her tongue and let her eyes bulge.

'The deaf always hear sounds in their head.'

Didi reached for a stamp from a tin box on her lap.

'See what she says?' Sita addressed the fan. 'Am I that old that my ears have ripened and rotted?'

Didi held out the envelope to her.

'Go post this, Sita. Make sure you put it into the box, properly.'

'How else should I put it? My eyes are here,' she pointed to her face, 'not there.' She indicated her feet.

'Go.'

'Hai hai, Mem, save me from this girl of yours.'

'Only death will do that.'

Sita tucked the letter into her waistband and left the room.

Didi remained in her room all day. She sat with a book, she took up her mending, she rearranged her almirah, her mind in disarray. She clutched her head in her hands, tried to hold it in stillness, but it slipped out of her control.

At lunch, Baby came to call her. Didi refused.

'Mama has headache?' asked Baby, touching her own forehead.

'Hmmmm.'

'Ek do teen, Amma's so mean ...' trilled Baby, skipping out of the room.

Fitful, Didi tossed about on her bed. A shadow crossed and the mask of Bhai's face appeared, flattened against the windowpane of the garden door.

'Not well?' he asked when she opened it.

She shook her head.

'Famous headache?'

She nodded.

'Shall I press it?'

She shook her head.

'I'll be back early in the evening. We can take Baby for a drive.'

She nodded.

He waved himself away.

A solitary tear strayed out. Didi felt tiny, lonely, with a strange buzz in her ears. For the second time in her life, she had permitted herself the luxury of an indiscretion. She blamed herself for selfishly, and single-mindedly, living on impulse.

'Now, I must do what I must for all of us.'

She drew the curtains, shut out the light and the warmth of the day. She lay there, wrapped in a quilt of remorse, imagining the shape of life to come.

It was after 7.30 p.m. when she heard Bhai join his brother for a drink in the garden.

She was in her room with Baby, who had asked her to draw the bird that went 'coo-ooo, coo-ooo' every morning in her sleep. Didi was drawing a rather ungainly, plump koel.

'You hear? Those bloody Pakis still there!' Purush exclaimed.

Didi heard glass respond to the tinkle of ice.

'There was trouble in the city,' she heard Bhai say. 'The police had to block the road to keep people apart.'

'Congress rally?'

'No. According to Miss Lobo, someone said Javed Burki had scored a century. One group of men began to chant "Burki is a bakra". This angered the young men in the masjid area, who threw stones at them. Suddenly, there was a fight in the middle of the street. Miss Lobo says fifty men. By the time I got onto the road, there was a procession: they were chanting something about the Pakistani team. They held hands and blocked the crossroads. The police had to clear them.'

'Paki pigs!'

'Purush!'

'Arre, Bhai, can't I talk in my own house? We will send them Pak-ing. Ha ha, get it? Pak-ing!' laughed Purush.

'It's just a game, Purush.'

'Don't be such a pyjama. We must win.'

There was a silence.

'And you know what's funny?' asked Bhai. 'Barki hadn't scored a century – he was not out on 73.'

'Useless laddoos. The Indian bowling. Can't they catch even one bakra?'

'You're really ...'

'Arre, Bhai, only joking, Bhai.'

It was the evening of the fifth and final day of the Test match. Didi sat outside in the veranda, reading to Baby from *Water Babies* in a distracted manner. She heard the telephone ring twice and Som Devi answer it.

'Maharaj,' Som Devi called out, 'dinner!'

When Didi went to the kitchen, she found Maharaj heating the food.

'Bhaisahib is not back,' she queried the comment. It was after eight.

'Big memsahib said to put food,' replied Maharaj.

Didi shrugged and carried the dishes to the table.

When no one talked at the dining table, Didi asked, 'Where is Bhai?'

'Baby, tell your mother she need not be so concerned about her brother-in-law,' Som Devi commanded, serving dal in a katori and placing it in front of Baby's thali. 'It is enough if she looks after you.'

Som Devi lowered her voice to Purush: 'You know, there is much hangama in the city.'

Purush carefully completed chewing and swallowed.

'Kya?'

'They,' went on Som Devi in a voice hushed with secret import, 'were sad that someone – what is his name? – did not score well in the second innings, and smashed some street lights. Our boys hit back. Bhai says Miss Lobo saw two men carried away, bilkul gone.' She shut her eyes dramatically.

As Som Devi continued with her account, an extraordinary unease seized Didi, her heart thudded loud, her forehead turned damp, hot. Even as her hands were moist and growing cold, her stomach muscles bent into nails against its lining ...

'Can't trust them,' she heard Purush say, snatching the hot phulka dangling from Som Devi's fingers. 'They should be made to live in special parts of the city and a green line drawn around the areas.'

Didi pushed back her chair, rose unsteadily.

'Baby, tell your mother she should clear the table after we have eaten.'

'Maharaj, call me when they have finished eating Muslims for dinner,' Didi called out as she left the dining room.

'Maybe she and her precious daughter should wear a burkha and go live with those bakras,' shouted Purush.

'Let be, Purush. God will get her.'

At 9.30 p.m., there was still no Bhai. Didi, drained from her peculiar experience at the dining table, had to make a considerable effort to rise from her position in the veranda outside her bedroom and proceed to the hallway. She dialled the bookstore number. It rang, reassuring Didi with its sound: Bhai must be on his way. Didi retired to her bed.

Sita's breath of elaichi wafted into her nostrils, like smelling salts.

'Get up, Didi, how you are sleeping so? Listen outside. Listen.'

Didi heard the distant sound of a hum.

'What's happening?'

She straightened out.

'Maharaj says there are big-big crowds and many policemen. He says he can hear the flames from here …'

'Nonsense.'

Didi struggled into a warm dressing gown and wrapped a shawl around her shoulders.

'Is Bhaisahib back?'

'No.'

Didi went out into the dim corridor. The door to Som Devi's room was open for a slice of light. Didi stood in the doorway and saw her mother-in-law reading the Gita by a bed lamp.

'Do you know where Bhai is?'

Som Devi continued to read.

'He must have told you something.'

Didi entered the room and advanced towards her mother-in-law. Som Devi closed the Gita with a clap.

'Nothing I need to tell you.'

'Look, there is trouble in the city. He could be stuck. We should look for him. Ask your son to go.'

'And I am only asking, where shall he go?' Som Devi rose from her bed.

'We can't just sit here!'

'And how will we go? Bhai has the car.'

Didi marched out.

'Let my son be,' warned Som Devi. 'Keep separate from him.'

Didi marched out of the house to the gate, peered down the lane, both ways. There was the hesitation of indecision and then she stepped out onto the deserted road. She heard Sita behind her. Didi quickened her steps, but in what seemed like the distance of darkness from the earth to the sky, she trudged forever. There were no streetlights, so she walked with her hands outstretched, blindly feeling her way until she arrived at the end of the lane, where it reached out to join the main road.

'No, Didi,' Sita panted behind her. 'Stop now. I am feeling scared.'

The cold hit Didi on the nose and numbed her naked toes. Sita was almost upon her. Like the hair on the small of my back, she clings to me, thought Didi irritably. She sneezed.

That was when she saw smoke. It was murky and dense in the clear of the night. Didi's thoughts went to *Gone With The Wind*: Atlanta was burning, this city was on broil.

She inched forward. There was the flicker of a light, was it a torch, a fire? She could not tell. She pierced the opacity of the night with her eyes. And fell back, clutching at her stomach.

She heard the distant words:

Pakistan! Pigs' paradise!
Hindus! Cow shit!
Go home! Get out!
We'll take you with us.

Bhai.

Didi gathered herself and rushed down the road, but Sita caught her and hung onto her waist.

'Don't be like a budhoo, Didi, we cannot … where do we wander? We must turn back. Now. There's nothing but darkness. Hai hai, Mem, make her listen to me.'

Sita held on hard. Didi went limp in her ayah's clutches. She stared ahead, her eyes bulging.

Later she would say she saw men die, later she would say she saw horrible sightings from another consciousness. Later, she would try to describe them to Bhai: they were frames, Bhai, frames unrelated, vivid, shreds of the unknown.

A hallucination?

Much, much worse.

She had known fear before but this was a feeling, visceral and profound; she was on the parting of a hairline. Was it madness?

Abruptly, as they had appeared, the images vanished, leaving her sagging in exhaustion.

She stared at the darkness and then turned towards Sita, her face wiped clean, her eyes unblinking. 'See …' She pointed before her.

Sita peered.

'There's nothing there.'

Didi looked again, jerked up straight and breathed deeply.

'Feel sick,' she managed.

'Didi, come, there's nothing only. Let's go home. It's dark …'

'And Bhai?'

Sita pulled back the hair from her face hard, until the skin wrinkled in stretch marks.

'Bhai? Is he down this road? He can look after himself. But my Baby? If something happens to us, now, on the street, who will look after Baby? Her Dadi?'

Didi's eyes narrowed.

'Or then Purushji?' added Sita, holding on tight. Didi bent forward and vomited. When it was over, she pushed Sita's hands away and stood up. She dragged herself back up the road.

When they reached the house, she went inside, teeth chattering, her hands on her stomach. 'Where's B-b-hai?' she stuttered at Som Devi's door. 'You must know. Tell me.'

'If your Didi paid half as much attention to Purush as she does to the other,' Som Devi observed from her bedroom to Sita, 'it would be more in keeping …'

Sita hobbled into Som Devi's room. She placed both her hands on her plentiful hips.

'See, Mataji, know how to speak like an elder.'

'You know nothing, Sita,' Som Devi exclaimed. 'You are completely pagal about your Didi. Didi, Didi, Didi,' she mimicked Sita, baring her teeth, 'she has struck lightning in your eyes, so you see nothing. I am saying. Just look …'

'Show me …'

'Stop it, both of you,' shrieked Didi, advancing towards Som Devi. 'Just tell me where he is or—'

'Fires in the main market,' Som Devi interrupted. 'There is looting going on, shops burning. There is curfew. They say someone threw pig's meat outside Mahal Theatre. The masjid in New Bazaar is around the corner: if one had to throw, throw there. Ulloo!' Som Devi rocked herself. 'We have no brains. But it is good: I am thinking, we are teaching them a good lesson. Phir then.'

'Lesson? And your son may be caught up in the trouble, injured? Dying?' Didi pushed Sita aside and advanced towards Som Devi. 'What kind of mother talks like this?'

'Pull out her tongue and curse the day she came into the family,' shouted Som Devi. 'What kind of wife are you—'

'Shoo, Mataji, shooo!'

'Nothing – nothing,' spat out Som Devi. 'You know nothing. My son is fine. He called in the evening. He called me, *me*.' She poked her thin chest. 'He went to drop Miss Lobo home, bas, that's all,' Som Devi added with relish, glancing at Didi. 'What's to worry, I ask?'

Didi rushed out.

'Why did you not say this earlier?' Sita demanded.

'Say?' responded Som Devi. 'I am his mother. Who are you?'

'I have Miss Lobo's contact number.' Didi began to dial.

'Didi, no,' protested Sita, 'it is too late.'

'So. She doesn't like him to stay at Miss Lobo's, that's what.' Som Devi spoke from the bedroom. 'Ask me, haven't I seen his eyes on her? And hers stuck to him like lice to hair? You think I don't know what is happening?'

Didi replaced the telephone receiver.

'Why is everyone yelling in the middle of the night?'

Purush appeared in the doorway, tousled in shirt and trousers.

'Bhai … he is missing,' replied Didi.

'And this woman,' Som Devi added, 'this dayan says he's dead.'

Purush ignored her and turned back into the hallway corridor. He approached Didi, his hand raised.

'Bhai, Bhai, Bhai. Disgusting. You are the bad spirit in our house. I am not enough for you, so you put your eyes in my brother's pockets? You …' He pushed her, vicious. She fell against the wall, hitting her head. 'Now see what you have done …'

'Done?' Didi repeated. 'Day is done, gone the sun …' She began to sing in a hoarse voice.

There was a sharp crackle and immediate darkness.

'Didi!' cried out Sita.

Didi was scratching the surface of the wall.

Afterwards, when they spoke of the night Bhai went missing, Didi hid inside herself. She knew what had happened, it was just that her mind had suffered a temporary breakdown. That was all.

What she didn't know, Sita would tell her. How the lights went out, how she had dragged Didi to her room and put her to bed. It was first light before she had fallen asleep, fitful and muttering, 'Day is done …'

In the early hours of the morning, Sita saw Som Devi seated on a stool by the phone. The maali was seated at her feet. Many, many people had died, he announced with relish, cars and shops had been burnt, police personnel were on the streets. It was being said that the army was coming. And there were dead cows and pigs everywhere.

'Mataji, people say there have never been so many birds low in the sky.'

It was then that Budhoo darted out of the front door and barked.

'Bhaisahib's car is coming! Bhaisahib's car is coming!' Sita heard Maharaj rejoice as the silver-grey Oldsmobile eased up the lane with Bhai behind its wheel.

'Maharaj, as soon as shops open, run and buy two kilos of jalebis. My son is home,' Som Devi ordered, rushing out to receive him.

Sita had run into Didi's bedroom.

'Bhaisahib is home, Didi, Bhaisahib is home.'

Didi slept on.

Over tea, at the dining table, Bhai described the night before.

'It was like after the British left and the people took to the streets against each other. A dirty yellow-grey afternoon sky. The streets pelted with stones, echoing sticks. The thumri of death, the stink of stale, lifeless blood. The smoke, rising from the corner of the eye, lingering as a reminder of what had been burnt below, a shroud covering the shame …'

'Writer,' marvelled Som Devi. 'Why you don't become writer?'

The owners of the shops in the market had thought they should close down. Bhai had said that would be a mistake. It might further incite the troublemakers. Let us behave normally, he had advised. There was a reluctant agreement: they would lock the doors but the sign would say 'Open'.

By late afternoon, Bhai could smell the hatred approach, hear it in the caws of the crows.

There was a sudden commotion as shutters climbed down around them.

'There's meat outside Mahal. They don't know if it is human, pig or cow meat,' Sohan Lal, the owner of Bharat Watch Company, told Bhai. The police want us to go home. Bhai looked across at Miss Lobo. He must see her home. He rang home and told Som Devi.

As they drove towards the city's outskirts where Miss Lobo lived, there was complete normalcy.

'We inhabit the same city but live separate lives,' Bhai told Miss Lobo. 'Tomorrow, we'll read in the newspapers about what happened here, today, as if it happened somewhere else.'

On the way home, he decided to go past the bookstore. Just to check. Two shops had been ransacked. Then he heard the din of human thunder. He thought of his lovely books. It was well past nine. Bhai decided to stay back – if anything happened, he would be there. The telephone line was dead. He sat slumped in his office chair.

He slept, he woke up, he peered outside. It was early morning. He stepped out, climbed into the Oldsmobile and drove home through the deserted streets, but the night's destructiveness had left some shops in shambles and the road littered with stones.

'Where's Didi?' Bhai asked, sucking on a piece of lemon pickle.

There was silence.

'Sleeping,' replied Som Devi. 'You know how she enjoys her beauty sleep.'

Bhai had caught Sita's eye.

After a bath, he came knocking on the outside garden door. Sita let him in.

Didi lay sprawled in complete disarray. Bhai tried to speak to her, shake her, rouse her.

'It's I ... Bhai. Bhai, Didi.'

Didi smiled. Sita told him of the night before. Bhai fetched a small white tablet. He made Didi swallow it. He stayed stroking her hair, murmuring, 'Foolish Didi, to think I would die …'

On the third day, Sita told Bhai to send for the doctor. Didi was definitely sick.

'She does not eat or speak.'

Som Devi was irritated.

'Doing,' she commented, 'drama.'

The doctor said she was fine but a little pale and unresponsive. Take rest, he advised. He prescribed a couple of tonics for strength.

'She is weak,' said the doctor.

Four days later, the telephone rang. It was Mahendra on a trunk call from Delhi. Som Devi picked up the receiver. Sita heard her.

'You know how she likes her beauty sleep. I am saying, you all spoilt her too, too much. Sita ! Sita!'

Som Devi thrust the telephone at Sita's nose.

Mahendra told Sita that he had received Didi's letter which said she was going to visit him and asked when they were coming.

Sita described Didi's 'condition', how she had been 'like this' for days. 'She sits or lies down, bilkul straight. Refuses food. No talking, only muttering nonsense.'

'What did the doctor say?'

'Take rest.'

'She needs a change.'

'Yes, yes,' agreed Sita and hailed Mem's memory.

When Mahendra came to take Didi to Delhi, Bhai was the most reluctant to let her go.

'So, take her,' disagreed Som Devi, 'take her. She is doing nothing useful here.'

And so Didi, Baby and Sita accompanied Mahendra on the night train to Delhi.

Didi sat in the garden or the veranda in Mahendra's home. It was an old-fashioned bungalow, with high ceilings, a veranda outside each room, and a large garden. In the afternoons she dozed off; at night, wrapped up in her old New York overcoat, she stared at the blackened plants, shadows of their daylight selves.

People moved around her, offering food, refreshments, love and conversation. Her smiles were mechanical; she accepted what she could swallow without feeling sick, put up her hand when she could stomach no more. Baby would approach her, put Didi's cool hand on her cheeks and say, 'Horsie, Amma, horsie.' She would place Baby on her lap and rock her, until Baby tired of the game and jumped off and away.

Didi never wanted to go out. If relatives or an old school friend came to visit, she said she had 'the headache' and slipped into her bedroom after a few minutes. If Prem suggested a shopping expedition to Chandni Chowk or CP, a matinee show, Didi simply said, 'You go. Take Baby and Sita with you.'

Sita realized Didi was sick but she couldn't make her better. She told Mahendra he must show Didi to a 'big Delhi doctor'.

Mahendra's GP made an evening house call and repeated the same advice that Didi had received at 3, Chor Bagh – take rest.

One morning, Mahendra scooped her up and put her into his black Buick. They went to Prem's lady doctor.

When they returned to the car, Mahendra's voice was elated: 'Why did you not say? Wait till I tell everyone!'

'No.'

Didi snatched and held Mahendra's wrist, hard.

'No,' she whispered.

Didi shrunk into the car seat but held fast to Mahendra's wrist.

'Purush …'

'No.' Didi's voice grated across the surface of her sore throat. 'No one.'

'Why?'

'The lights had gone out,' she whispered. 'Please, don't ask me to explain. Please do as I ask.'

Ever since the night Bhai went missing and darkness descended upon 3, Chor Bagh, Didi had been searching for the switch to her mind. The connection between her past and the future had snapped, plunging her into a black, unknown present.

Didi tried to forget the events before the Test match and the cricket riots. She sat out in the porch, her hands on her stomach. She wrestled to command her mind, to remember the good times. Jeff. Ed's loft. Bhai. The storeroom. Baby being chased around the mango tree by Budhoo.

It had been like a dream.

DELHI
1978

It had been like a dream; one whose edges had frayed with constant remembrance. When he thought of life with Baby and then without her, once she had left him for New York, life was nothing but a continuous replay of the time he had spent with her. His days were filled with the absence of her.

Kartik felt the emptiness of the space around him. Lying in bed, he would reach out and touch the void beside him; sitting out on the roof of his barsati, he would suddenly look across at the hammock, sagging without her. He had suffered, brooded, visited scenes they had created together before she departed.

Lodhi Gardens.

Chanakya Cinema.

Tib Dhabs.

Imperial Hotel on Janpath.

Once, he sat in its lobby until the manager came across and demanded to know if he was waiting for someone. When Kartik replied in the negative, he was asked to leave.

'This is not a railway platform, sir.'

They used to eat club sandwiches at the coffee shop, paid for with money she earned working as a hostess at exhibitions or an usher at film festivals. They would climb the steps to the first floor of the hotel and military march across the length of the parquet corridor, admiring the painted portraits on the walls, and invent a love life for each.

'This one has a thin moustache – he's married to a country girl. This one – she's got a long nose, she looks down on her husband but she's living it up with the munshi. And that one? He's got small, mean, pale eyes – not to be trusted. He is involved with his children's ayah – see how he looks just beyond and behind!'

They would salute each one and solemnly pass by.

Once, he had stopped her.

'I want to.'

She had leaned against the wall between an English lady and a Maharaja.

'Promise me, you'll hang me here.'

Yes, he had walked down that corridor of desire several times after Baby left him and wondered what story his portrait would have told.

'Eyes, deep set with dark circles and a lost expression – he's been left for a sahib across the many seas.'

The Def. Col. barsati became intolerable. Vacant, yet full of the memories he would prefer to leave outside the door with his chappals. No matter how hard he swept and cleaned it, dusted the shelves, tables and chair, rearranged the furniture, he could not remove Baby from it. She was like a permanent dye. He found himself unable to abandon the barsati or live with its memory of her. So he paid the rent and moved in with Ajay, returning to the barsati occasionally when he felt homesick for Baby. Ajay was appearing a second time for the exams and Kartik, for want of an alternative, joined him. He would prove himself, he would justify leaving home.

Home. The money orders from Chachaji, the food packets from Mummu continued to arrive, but they were never accompanied by an invitation home from Pitaji. Rukmini had married, Chachaji informed him in a three-line letter, but Kartik remained unforgiven.

For the next two and a half years, Kartik studied diligently. He gave school tuitions to earn more money and divert his mind from continuous study. Ajay and he failed in their second attempt to pass the UPSC exams. They decided on a third and final attempt. This time, Kartik would study with his eyes closed, reciting the chapters by heart as he turned the pages. He would lie on a bed, Ajay sat at the desk. They studied till they fell asleep, smoked till the landlord knocked on the door and demanded to know if they had started a fire inside. They discussed their future.

'You'll see, we'll be the steel frame of this country, yah,' Ajay would say, 'I'll marry Avantika …'

'And me?' Kartik inquired.

'You'll see, the moment you're in the Service, there'll be so many offers, you'll be the one doing the rejecting! Relax, yah. Forget Baby, concentrate on modern European history.'

He did not forget Baby. But he did try to concentrate on the books and notes piled up next to him. Each day took up what the days before had left behind: the monotonous routine he knew so well. Except that there was no Baby to relieve the tedium, no shared intimacies, no steam of ginger tea, no scent of her skin. Instead, there was this male thing of stale cigarette smoke, studying late and rising later, crumpled kurtas and shorts, lengthening hair and growing beards, and Saturday nights when they bought a half bottle of rum, joined a few friends, drank till not a peg was left between them, drove out to Pindi's for a late dinner of butter chicken, brain curry, makhni dal – the soft naans putty in their fingers.

Then, the moment of release: they would drive Ajay's motorcycle at a high speed down the empty, late night Rajpath avenue, screaming, 'Zeenie play my teenie-weenie' all the way up to Rashtrapati Bhavan's imposing gates and down again to India Gate.

No, there was no Baby, but there was this male thing for comfort.

Kartik's third attempt at the IAS exams was successful. He stood ninety-sixth on the list, Ajay fortieth. Ajay would make the IAS, as would their friend Abhijeet, but Kartik's future hovered between the Defence Accounts Service and the Audits and Accounts Service. He was chagrined. He had wanted to be a collector in a district, in charge of people's lives, not counting or collecting monies. He wasn't going to sit in some dingy, airless government office, next to a water cooler, filling in the number columns. That wasn't why he had left home and refused to go back. And what would Baby think? He refused both Services, despite his friends' persuasions.

A period of utmost loneliness followed. His scraggly beard, his unkempt hair, his crushed clothes, his dishevelled state. It was as if even appearances had betrayed Kartik. Where was the confident, energetic, passionate young student with tight, springy curls and excitable nostrils, who had lectured Baby on life as they sat on the university library steps? Who had spoken so cockily of death, not knowing what it meant to live through failure? His place had been taken by this creature with listless hair and hunched shoulders.

Eventually, Kartik cut his hair, shaved his beard, gave away his notes and books to other aspiring IAS hopefuls, and sat aimless, alone, waiting for something to happen. He didn't know what to do with himself. He couldn't go home. He didn't know where to start looking for a job.

Meanwhile, Ajay and Abhijeet prepared to leave for training, Prakash was going abroad on a scholarship, Vinay had taken a job as a college lecturer, Naseer had joined a foreign bank. Everyone but Kartik had plans.

They held a reunion at Ajay's before their futures took them their separate ways. Kartik bought food from Karim's near Jama Masjid, Prakash swiped a bottle of Cutty Sark scotch from his father's bar. Kartik tried hard to smile big all evening, to disguise the growing realization that he alone didn't seem to have a future to look forward to.

His friends tried to humour him, put Kartik back on track. They discussed his prospects, in the third person, with all the affection for an absentee mate.

'Just bad luck, yaar,' said Abhijeet, 'third time unlucky.'

'Yah,' agreed Ajay. 'Take Raman: mugged all of last year, didn't go home for the summer hols and ended up without his number on the list. This year, he's been running after that girl and he is number 11.'

'Can't you see the guy is suffering a maha big sense of loss, man?' remarked Naseer. 'Lay off. Let him try something completely new.'

'Yes boss,' felt Vinay, 'but he'll feel depressed for a long time, you know, respect of the self, etc.'

'I could find out at the bank,' offered Naseer. 'They're bound to be looking for more recruits.'

'Man, he's an M.A in history,' pointed out Vinay, 'what will they do with him in a bank?'

'Ask him to study past accounts?' offered Abhijeet and they all laughed.

Kartik jumped on him. They rolled on the floor, with the others clapping, until Kartik had Abhijeet in an arm twist up his back.

'Just joking, yaar,' Abhijeet croaked. 'Tell him to let go, guys. If he wants to ruin his life, what's it to me?'

It was after midnight. The others had left. Ajay and Kartik sat through the dark, smoking the ends of cigarettes, contemplating Kartik's options.

'There must be something a clever guy like you can do,' insisted Ajay, punching him on the shoulder.

'Yes, sooo.'

Kartik switched on the bathroom light, kicked up the toilet seat. He stared at the white tiles in front of him. They're as blank as my future, he thought. As he reached to flush, he noticed something in the toilet bowl. It had small black eyes and a face like a rat. It was a rat. Kartik fell back. What if it had climbed up the side, while he was ... He hurried out to tell Ajay, who simply laughed at this 'invention'. Kartik dragged him by the arm to the bathroom and they both contemplated the toilet bowl.

'Whisky,' burped Ajay, swaying.

'Not whisky,' said Kartik, holding him, 'whiskers. See?'

Ajay saw.

A large, fat, brown-grey rat with greying whiskers. Its paws bobbed up and down in a freestyle swimming stroke.

'How did he get in there?' asked Ajay.

'Does it matter?'

'Is he dead?'

'Either way, he must be pulled out or else he will get stuck in the drainpipe.'

'A shitty prospect,' smirked Ajay.

They argued over the rescue operations. How would it be done? Who would do it? Ajay backed off: he couldn't put his hand in there.

Kartik was pale – he had always been scared of rats, bats and lizards. Ajay shrugged and said they would see to it in the morning. But suppose they wanted to go at night – we can't pee on him, argued Kartik. Ajay advised him to pee on the roof. Kartik shook his head, rubbed his hands together, rolled up his sleeves and fetched the chimti from the kitchen. Ajay stood in the bedroom with his fingers in his ears. Kartik pushed the chimti into the toilet hole, fastened it around the rat's tail and pulled swiftly with his eyes averted.

When he opened them, the rat was still floating in the bowl. He repeated the exercise thrice, failing each time.

'This is ridiculous, yah.' Ajay entered the bathroom and pulled the flush.

Kartik screamed, 'You bastard!' as the bowl gurgled. The water rose, rose and up floated the rat.

'Catch it! Catch it!' yelled Ajay, retreating as the water approached the brink.

There was a swoosh and the water was sucked back in.

Kartik and Ajay peered inside. The rat's tail stuck out from inside the bowl.

'Now he's really stuck! Why did you interfere?' demanded Kartik.

'Thought it would help,' sulked Ajay

They pulled the flush again and again. Each time the water rose to the top of the bowl and the two friends retreated. But the tail did not budge.

'It's a maha fat cat rat,' Ajay observed, 'and obstinate. Let Dulari deal with it. They know how to do these things.' Dulari came in each morning to sweep and clean the rooms.

Kartik stared at him with an expression resembling dislike.

'What you did was disgusting.'

'Yah, yah and you are God on earth. I'm going to bed.'

Kartik slept the night with the rat.

Next morning, he asked the street jamadar and the sewer cleaner. Both refused. This was not part of their dharma.

'So whose job is it to put their hand in the toilet bowl?' demanded Ajay. 'Is there a special type for it?'

When Ajay explained the matter to the plumber on the telephone, he said, 'Sahib, this is no job for a plumber. Why don't you just push a stick up?'

'Excellent idea,' Ajay said to Kartik, and added that he was off to Avantika's because he had to go to the toilet.

Finally, Kartik asked Dulari. Even she refused to have anything to do with the rat.

'Great, just great.'

Kartik went to the market and returned with his purchases. He pulled on a pair of gloves, covered his face with a handkerchief upto his eyes, grasped the rat's tail, shook it to loosen its body. When that didn't work, he pushed the wire up the hump of the toilet drain. Then he poured two bottles of acid he had bought into the toilet bowl, pulled down the lid and waited five minutes before pulling the flush. A white, stinging smoke smarted his eyes, singed his nose. He peered inside the toilet bowl: the rat had disappeared.

Kartik peered worriedly into the bowl. Had the rat been flushed down or had the acid cut through its poor dead flesh and bones? Had it dissolved? Kartik felt faint, morally repulsed by his actions.

'I have given a rat his last rites,' he told everyone later.

Ajay recounted the rat story to all their friends. It became part of their lore, repeated whenever they reunited. 'Remember when Kartik gave a rat his last rites?'

Avantika was impressed. 'Chooha' she took to calling Kartik affectionately. 'What you did was very brave. That Ajay of mine could never have done it.'

'Yah, I can see that he will become a district magistrate and I will be disposing of rodents. Worse, collecting garbage.'

Kartik forgot about the incident. He went back to his Def. Col. barsati and took up a job in a private IAS tutorial class, preparing Q&A for the students. He thought he might apply for a college lecturer's position. It was a steady job and would put to use all those years of studying history. Besides, he could teach anywhere. He prepared applications, he cut out advertisements for lecturers' jobs from newspapers and wrote a glowing account of the many attributes that made him the perfect teacher. He addressed letters to the leading colleges in Delhi. But he never got around to posting them. He knew he didn't want to teach. He wanted to do, not talk. Nor did he want to be known as the guy who didn't make it to the IAS. He was waiting for a new job definition.

When his chance came, it was unexpected; something he could never have imagined.

One evening, Kartik had accompanied Ajay to pick up Avantika for a movie. While they waited for her, they sat in the living room with her father who was reading a newspaper.

'So, Kartik, my young friend, what are your plans now?' he asked politely but with absent-minded interest.

Kartik shifted uncomfortably on the sofa.

'Nothing, Uncle, sir …'

'Nothing?'

'No sir, I mean Uncle …'

'How is that possible for a well-educated young man?'

Ajay kicked Kartik on his shin.

'He's applied to colleges for a lecturer's job,' Ajay declared. 'Should be hearing from them soon.'

Avantika's father lowered the newspaper.

'Ah, that's a noble profession.'

'But I don't want to teach, sir,' blurted out Kartik, pushing aside Ajay's restraining hand, 'not at all.'

'Then why are you applying? What is it you want to do?' asked Avantika's father with a frown.

Kartik shrugged helplessly.

'I don't know,' he admitted, 'serve …'

Ajay shouted with laughter.

'In a restaurant, maybe?'

Kartik flushed with anger.

'I didn't mean that kind,' he snapped and then stopped: Avantika's father was watching him. 'I meant to serve, as in serve the nation, people ...' he trailed off feeling foolish and inarticulate.

At that moment, Avantika strolled in. Kartik had never been more pleased to see her. Her father was still staring at him as they got up to leave.

A few months later.

'Chooha,' Avantika rang him one evening. 'How would you like to be a self-employed man?'

Avantika's father was Delhi's secretary health and he was promoting citizens' self-help groups. On Avantika's advice, Kartik went to see him one morning, more out of curiosity than an overpowering desire to be a philanthropist.

'So my friend, you really want to do something? Make something of yourself and be useful to the community?'

Kartik nodded, uncertain but wishing to make the right impression.

'Well, it's like this. How would you like to help me "Keep Delhi Beautiful"?'

The plan was this: since garbage was the most visible statement of filth in the city and the source of the greatest stench, attack it first. But there was too much garbage and the collection network run by the municipal authorities was painfully slow, inadequate. The city was filthy.

The secretary health had instituted a review committee which, after a six-month study and two trips abroad, had made recommendations. The government had sanctioned the use of the 'latest' European trucks that mechanically and rapidly picked up rubbish from the dumps, and transported it within sealed containers to the main depots – this increased the speed of collection, was more efficient and minimized the smell quotient.

At the same time, the municipal staff lacked the zeal or the numbers to clean up the city. Private initiative was needed and the secretary health wanted to enlist resident welfare associations for rubbish collection. Networks had to be established that would collect garbage from house to house and deposit it at the nearby clearing dens for the trucks to pick up.

'This way we will also generate employment, Mr Kartik. And that is where people like you enter,' explained the secretary health. 'It's like this: we want the community, NGOs run by like-minded persons with a strong sense of commitment, to train and oversee the local collections. We want public self-help schemes. Very successful in Korea.'

The government would help the NGOs receive funding for the purpose. They had to form small, localized teams for the garbage collection and educate residents – why, even supervise the hydraulic truck services, if the scheme worked well. The secretary health suggested that Kartik could set up office in south Delhi and begin in posh colonies where the problem was less acute.

'Six months we try out – and then we will see what we will see. So, my friend, have you got a nose for it?' the secretary health asked.

Kartik closed his eyes. He muttered the Gayatri Mantra. He imagined garbage and thought of the rats that burrowed into it. His soul hesitated. Out of nowhere had come this offer. It was a far cry from his dreams of being an IAS officer and all he had wanted to achieve. But Baby had left him, he didn't have any immediate prospects, he didn't want to teach and how long could he live off Chachaji's money orders and the IAS tutorials? This provided him with a task - until he found a real job, of course, fitting for a man of his education. Besides, it was for just six months and if he could clean up a city, wasn't that a superior calling? Better than counting money? Kartik stood up like a new army recruit.

'Sir.'

'Excellent! Looking at you, I knew you were the man for the job.'

Eight months later, Kartik was in business.

He found office space in Jangpura on Mathura Road. It was a two-storey building with a large lawn in the front, where the women of the foundation ate their lunch under the shade of an Ashoka tree.

Kartik had decided to employ women only. Women, he argued, were cleaner than men, more scrupulous about cleanliness and easier to manage.

His first recruit was Dulari. Her sister-in-law Devi, and Devi's daughter-in-law Sushila also joined. Devi told her husband that Kartik had promised her a proper job, a regular salary; she was going to work with him.

'And what will you do with him?' sneered her husband.

'I will do what he wishes,' replied Devi, with a shrug.

'And what's that?'

'Whatever,' Devi said.

'Whatever?' he asked. 'You will touch garbage?'

'What's it to you? You don't touch me any longer,' she observed, and there was appreciative laughter from the people gathered outside their jhuggi.

When Ram Singh, who had cooked for Kartik since his barsati days in Def. Col. received a telephone call from Kartik, he told his wife to sign up. Jamuna was a reluctant draftee.

'He is doing a great thing. We must help,' Ram Singh told Jamuna.

'But I don't want to go anywhere near garbage,' she protested.

'You clean the houses of sahibs and memsahibs …'

'That is different, no? We work for them in their houses,' argued Jamuna with what seemed to her irrefutable logic.

'How different can garbage be from person to person, Jamuna? The sahib has asked me, you have to go.'

'You go then.'

'Sahib wants to give employment to women.'

'But—'

'No buts. Sahib is like Gandhiji …'

'*Hain*?'

'Didn't Gandhiji teach us to clean our own dirt? Didn't he clean?'

'Was he a Mahatma because he cleaned his own bathroom?' asked Jamuna, thinking herself very clever.

Ram Singh observed his wife with pitying superiority.

'You women know nothing.'

The day she joined the foundation, Jamuna immediately sought out Dulari for a clarification: 'What do they call a female Mahatma?'

Three months later, Miranda and Shaheen joined them. Miranda lived at the back of the small church house near the Nizamuddin main road. The church ran a kindergarten crèche for young children from the surrounding slums. Miranda did secretarial work at the crèche and in return she and her husband, a bus driver at a convent school, were allowed to live there. They had been married two years.

That year, the church authorities decided to cut back on their employees. Austerity measures, they claimed. Miranda, by virtue of being married to Srinivas, a South Indian and a Hindu, was one of the first to be asked to leave. Thus, one morning, she found herself out on the street corner. Looking for somewhere to go, she found herself before the foundation and wondered why so many women entered its premises. Thinking it to be a women's hostel, Miranda followed the women into the building and found herself in front of Kartik's office. He told her that if she liked, she could be the secretary since she knew how to type. He offered to let them live at the foundation, but her husband would have to do chowkidari at night.

Shaheen was a young widow with a three-year-old daughter. Her husband Riaz had worked as the driver at Avantika's, and Shaheen was employed as a cleaner in the house. One morning, Riaz stopped the car on the INA flyover and jumped off the side before anyone could stop him. He died on the way to hospital. Shaheen was left without a husband, a livelihood, or any idea why Riaz had committed suicide. Avantika sent her to Kartik.

That left Mrs Singh and Mrs Malhotra. Mrs Singh and Mrs Malhotra were close friends from college, wives of IAS officers who were colleagues of Avantika's father. They were into supporting good causes. They had tried reading at the Blind School, working at the drug abuse centre and teaching slum children English. The first had been tedious, the second disturbing and the third beyond their capabilities. At the secretary health's initiative, they paid Kartik a visit, liked what they saw, and decided to stay.

The other women had not liked the look of them: chiffon saris, pearls, high heels – rich to look at and perfume so strong, Devi claimed, it must be giving them a headache.

'It might give me the headache,' Mrs Singh conceded later when the women knew each other well enough to discuss intimacies, 'but it gives my husband a tool up!'

Kartik was uninterested in the women's appearances. However, he recognized the need for well-educated women who could argue and negotiate with the residents of the south Delhi colonies. Besides, the secretary health had recommended them.

And so work began at the foundation.

Kartik moved out of Def. Col. and found a one-room barsati for himself in Nizamuddin West. Ram Singh came to work for him.

He wrote to Baby at Didi's address. He had not written to her earlier, nor heard from her; he had not expected to. When she left in a taxi for Palam airport, she had waved to him from the rear window; but after staring at her receding face framed by the glass, he had turned away without returning the salute. They were, he had thought, headed in opposite directions.

His letter was one terse sentence: *I have become a collector.*

Six months later, he received an inland letter. He sat on the floor of his flat, cross-legged, reading and re-reading it, as if the contents would miraculously change each time.

We have heard from people we know in Delhi that you have begun to work in the garbage business, wrote his father without preamble. *You have made us sad. Is this why I sent you to the best missionary school? Is this why I paid for you to learn Queen's English from Chatty Madam? So you …?*

Your mother says it is all her fault. How, I know not. But I have decided. You have shamed our community, our family. Please do not write or send any token amount to Lata and Rukmini for the festivals. We cannot touch anything you have earned. People ask me: how do you have a son who does work that is meant for the scavenger class? I tell them, I have no son.

This land that I have lived on and tilled all these years, that has been in the family one hundred years, was meant to be yours, so that it would be ours for another hundred years. Not any more.

Kartik stared at the letter, this missive of exile. It had not occurred to him to consider how his family would react to his collecting garbage when he took up the secretary health's offer. He didn't stop to think that his father would find out. When he thought about the family, it was in the belief that they would be ignorant of his actions, as they had been of his life ever since his banishment. Home had been slowly erased from his future, like a bumpy old village cycle lane through the fields when the tarmac roads are laid out beside it.

He neatly folded the letter and put it in the Britannia biscuit tin along with the other letters he had received from home. He wanted to preserve what he could of his past, and the tin had become its repository.

Kartik glanced at his watch. At this time of the day, his father would be in the fields, holding his starched dhoti in one hand and stopping to sniff the fruits, the manure, rubbing them against his nose to judge their quality. Chacha would be neatly filing away the accounts in the big room, the sun from the large window highlighting the sharp tip of his nose which would be spotted with sweat beads. Chachi would be sorting out clothes and complaining to herself about the washerman's work. And Mummu? In the kitchen, chopping onions so fine they resembled translucent insect wings, tears glistening in her eyes, decades since she had cut her first one.

Mummu. How he missed her.

At the end of the first year, Avantika's father was happy enough with the experiment to grant the foundation a five-year extension.

The next few years were to be tumultuous ones. With the assault on the Golden Temple and Bhindranwale's death, everyone in Delhi thought the Punjab problem was over. Then came Mrs Gandhi's assassination.

The morning after, Kartik woke up late. He had been with his landlord Uncle Sondhi till late, discussing her death. Kartik was careful not to argue when Uncle began to rant about Mrs Gandhi's treatment of Sikhs. Wisely, he realized that this was not the time to raise questions about Bhindranwale and the Punjab insurgency.

Uncle's telephone had rung constantly that night. There had been news of violence and demonstrations in the city, of Sikhs being rounded up. Some of them were fleeing the capital. Kartik warned 'Uncle' but he had shrugged it off saying this was their home, they would not budge.

But in the morning he summoned Kartik. He was pale, he looked bewildered. He said his automobile showroom in Green Park had been vandalized; two of his mechanics had been beaten up before they could escape. The others had deserted the shop. There was a curfew in the city but his relatives and friends had been calling from different parts of Delhi with accounts of looting and attacks on Sikhs.

Kartik nodded. Earlier, from the balcony, he had heard the din of people shouting in the distance, drum beats. He had seen the smoke rise in solitary pyres.

'Partition,' said Uncle, 'just as during Partition. They're going after anyone in a turban. My showroom gone,' he added with tears in his eyes as he allowed Kartik inside and double locked the front door. Kartik saw Aunty, and her son and daughter in one of the bedrooms, throwing their belongings into suitcases.

'Gone,' Uncle Sondhi repeated as he collapsed in the chair.

'Uncle …' Kartik began, not knowing what to say. 'Why is Aunty packing?'

Uncle looked up.

'My brother called from Maharani Bagh. The houses of all Sikhs are being burnt down. There is trouble at the gurudwara. Soon it will happen here. We must leave.'

He rose hastily.

'But you will be recognized on the road!' protested Kartik. 'And where will you go?'

'My friends, the Sharmas on Pandara Road told us to come to them. They will hide us. No one would dare go to an official's house.' He headed towards his bedroom. 'We must leave.'

'You can't drive looking like that!' blurted out Kartik, pointing to his turban.

Uncle turned to him.

'Will you,' he asked, staring at Kartik, 'drive us?'

Kartik gulped. He didn't feel particularly brave. From Uncle's accounts, the situation outside was grim. His impulse was to ask Uncle to remove his turban and take his chances on the road. Then he looked into Uncle's imploring eyes.

'Of course,' he replied. 'Of course I will.'

He was rewarded with a bear hug.

'Thank you,' whispered Uncle. 'Good boy.'

It took another twenty minutes to secure the house. The phone rang thrice, and each time, Uncle replaced the receiver with a shake of his head, muttering, 'Partition ...'

Kartik helped Aunty into the car. The entire family crouched below the level of the windows, Uncle hid beside Kartik in the driver's seat as he eased the car out of the gate.

The ten-minute drive was uneventful. They could hear the hum of people but although it seemed to be approaching, the streets were deserted apart from policemen and a few white Ambassadors with official number plates. The emptiness combined with the clouds of smoke frightened Kartik: he had never seen Delhi so still before, never felt so threatened by it.

He increased the speed of the car.

When they stopped in front of the DII government flats on Pandara Road, Mr Sharma was there to greet them. Aunty and the children hugged Kartik and hurried away.

'You had better leave too,' advised Uncle. 'They will see my name on the letter box and enter.' He held out his arms to Kartik. 'Don't worry about rent for this month. If we survive this—'

'Uncle, don't talk like that.'

He felt Uncle's throat constrict against his neck as he patted him on the back. Then he climbed into the car, waved, and drove back towards Nizamuddin, scared the police would stop him. He drove slowly and with his eyes always on the road ahead of him.

Once home, Kartik went upstairs to his flat. He picked up le Carré's *The Little Drummer Girl* and his cigarettes, and locked himself inside the toilet. He sat there against the door, reading, waiting.

He must have fallen asleep because when he opened his eyes he was lying with his head resting on the wall. It was 5 p.m. by his watch. He listened carefully. Hearing nothing, he opened the door and went back into his bedroom. He turned on a switch but the light did not respond. He tried the fan, it did not move. Kartik felt scared. Supposing intruders had entered Uncle's house and were waiting for him? He went out onto the balcony and looked down. There was a solitary man standing beneath a tree. He heard the crows but otherwise there was silence. He returned inside.

Over the next few days, the smoke hovered overhead, ominous as the silence in the city. Everyone had a Sikh story to tell: of lost relatives, friends, destroyed property, of hiding a family from the sound of fury on the streets that never seemed to materialize into people. A fortnight after he had fled his home, Uncle Sondhi returned with his family.

The summer of 1986 was no worse than previous ones, but to Kartik the heat seemed particularly unbearable that year.

In the city, people were dry, hot and flinty, ready to go up in flames. Kartik could not remember a summer such as this one. The power situation had deteriorated. The chief minister promised twenty-four-hour power supply in seventy-two hours. 'Just give me a few days,' he pleaded.

The heat was leading to impassioned, hot-tempered arguments at the foundation. They argued over everything: how hot had it been last summer? When was the last time temperatures had been so high in June? Who could remember a season as hot and dry as this one? Did anyone recall a time when the relative humidity was a maximum of thirty-nine and a minimum of seven?

Each morning, Mrs Singh earnestly scrutinized and compared the temperature charts in the newspapers and the reports on the weather.

The heatwave was coming from Rajasthan's Thar desert, she read out, some 300 kilometres from Delhi.

Mrs Singh was sceptical.

'No way could heat travel so far, so fast,' she told the women at the foundation.

Her husband described it more artistically: Delhi's population, he said, was melting as in a Salvador Dali painting.

There was very little water. Even less electricity. The government reported that against a minimum demand of 2,400 MW, there was a shortage of 300 MW. The chief minister insisted that new projects within the next three years would provide the capital with 2,300 MW. But who could live in the future?

The chief minister promised only three hours of load-shedding each day for different parts of the city. Kartik called it organized suffering. The lights at the foundation certainly went out at exactly the appointed hour, but seldom returned with such accuracy.

'Now, now, it will come back,' Miranda would keep reciting. But it didn't. Sometimes all day, sometimes all night. During lunch, the women complained about their lives: clothes lay piled up, unwashed; dishes were caked with dal, dotted with dried grains of rice; the air was filled with a warm pungency of fruits, vegetables, yogurt and other rotting food. The milk curdled into paneer, butter dripped from the knife like soup (Mrs Malhotra said), water was hot as though someone had thrust it through a fire. Everything exhaled salty sweat and rancid odours.

Devi and Sushma who lived by the river said its bed was empty, muddy, cracked. They had no potable water to drink. The one pipe that had water was spurting poisonous elements because sewage was mixed with the drinking supply. And those who did get some water from the hand pumps hid it away like a secret, refusing others even a sip.

Kartik found that his body protested against the living conditions. He developed a high fever and sore throat, and had to remain in bed for a week. Then his stomach collapsed and he had to survive on lassi and khichdi for a whole week. The only positive aspect of this mess was the absence of mosquitoes. Kartik noticed that they had disappeared, vanished – pouf! It had become too hot for them; they had either died or migrated to cooler parts.

That's when the protests began. At the Boat Club, on Rajpath, large crowds gathered at a meeting organized by the Opposition.

'Some people are born with power, others have power thrust on them but here in the capital of India, most of us are deprived of power. We want power!' thundered Communist union leaders.

It became so unbearably hot that Kartik wanted to tear off his skin to cool his insides. Each day he read of new trouble in the city: village Khichripur in east Delhi was a tinderbox. Residents, unbathed, unshaved, unchanged for three days, had marched to the nearest electricity office and ransacked the premises. They bodily lifted up the technicians and flung them outside on the road. The chief engineer of the area was roughed up. The police was summoned. There was a lathi charge. Several people bled. Slogans had cut through the hot air.

'Delhi Vidyut Board hai, hai! Engineer sahib hai hai ...'

From east Delhi, right across to the west. Naraina was the next conflagration. Here, people carrying sticks and stones they'd picked up on their way went to the municipal commissioner's office. They shattered the windscreen of his Ambassador, pelted everyone in sight and stormed into his office, shoving aside his staff. They surrounded the commissioner with sticks raised high in the air: 'Maro! Maro! Beat him till the last drop of sweat drips from his body,' cried out one agitator, and action would have followed words but for the women who resisted the idea.

'How will beating him,' they asked with scorn, 'benefit us? Will it bring us electricity? Water in our taps? Take the garbage away?'

Reluctantly, spitting and fuming, the crowd withdrew.

The temperature has increased because of the people's anger, Dulari confided in Kartik one evening as they sat outside beneath a heavy sky.

'Nonsense, Dulari.'

'Oho, sahib never listens to me.'

Two weeks after he had promised to restore power to the people, the chief minister recanted. In a special radio and TV broadcast to the people of Delhi, watched by Kartik and the women, he apologized.

That unrelenting, unbearable, pitiless summer.

The secretary health summoned Kartik and other NGO heads to his office and told them that there were far too many complaints about the local garbage collection. His minister was displeased: every day he saw photographs in the newspapers of dumps overflowing with litter, surrounded by dogs and buffaloes. What were they doing to correct this picture, the secretary health wished to know.

Why doesn't he stop reading the newspaper, Kartik was tempted to reply. Instead, he launched into a lengthy explanation of the problems he faced. The secretary health laughed sympathetically.

'Arre bhai, it is the same story everywhere. What can we do? It would be best if we could all migrate to another country, but which foreign government will accept hundreds of millions of Indians?'

'What about Antarctica?' Kartik asked, cheekily.

Avantika's father leaned back and studied him without amusement. It was lunchtime; his wife had sent stuffed karelas and dry masala chicken. He was eager to eat.

He twirled the Eiffel Tower that lay imprisoned inside the paperweight on his desk.

'See, it is like this, Kartik. We are already understaffed and you know as well as I do that these karamcharis are waiting for this scheme, my scheme, to fail. The municipal commissioner was here this morning. "Sahib," he told me, "the condition of the city is like a loose stomach ... rubbish is running everywhere." Ha, ha, ha.'

Kartik did not know what was so funny.

'You must galvanise. Show more initiative.'

The secretary health considered Kartik's Adam's apple and looked at the other people seated around the table.

'You must find a way out, otherwise the consequences will be severe, for all of us. Do you understand?'

Everyone around the table nodded, rose. Kartik could smell food. One of the things he had learnt over the years was to never do business on an empty stomach.

'We will try our best, sir.'

'And better.' The secretary health rose. 'I knew I could depend upon you. Have a bite before you go? My missis is an excellent cook.'

Kartik declined and left. He drove around aimlessly for half an hour, recalled the secretary's words and wondered how the foundation would cope with the rest of the summer. There would have to be new temporary recruits, night shifts …

He drove into Khan Market. Ravenous, he parked and went straight into the sweet shop. He ordered a milkshake and two chocolate ice-cream cups.

Twenty minutes later, angry at his inability to resist ice cream when he had a bad stomach, he strolled towards Bahri Sons. He thought he might look at the latest books.

He entered to the sound of familiar laughter. Then he saw her, this tall, striking woman at the stationery counter, one hand on her hip, the other held out for her purchases. Kartik felt like a ghost of his own past, and bit his tongue to reassure himself of the present. He ducked and darted to his right, instinctively. There was a moment then, before she turned towards him, when he could have hidden behind the smell of books, from the memory of her, returned to the rest of his life. He willed himself to walk out of the bookstore, abandon her just as she had deserted him.

His body detained him. He stood immobile between the historical books and the biographies as though she had yelled 'statue' and he had frozen on the spot. Sideways, he observed her carefully, his heart thudding so loudly, he thought the man by his side looked at him because he could hear it.

Her face. The forehead broad and wide, the nose small and rounded at its tip, nostrils slim, straight in their incline, her skin taut. Different. Does time make us unrecognizable? Would he, one day, look into the mirror and see someone else in his own reflection?

She turned abruptly and before he could glance away, her eyes latched on to to his, wide and still. Eyes that remained with him long after her departure: hazel brown with tiny golden flecks in the sunlight, the colour of caramel honey inside.

Kartik peered into Baby's face, searching for clues to her sudden reappearance.

She came forward, clucking her tongue.

'Bookstores seem to be our destiny.'

He refused to reply, knowing that whatever he said would be foolish, inadequate to express his feelings which were somewhere between uncontrollable rage at her abrupt departure and irrepressible joy at her return. She held out her hand. He willed himself not to extend his own. His will triumphed.

She let her hand fall by her side.

'Well, then, I'll be seeing you.'

She walked out before his legs had regained the power of movement. Maybe I imagined her, he thought.

Five days later, he received a dinner invitation from Sukanya, an old college friend of Baby's. He knew he should refuse, resist, rededicate himself to the task of making Delhi beautiful, but it was another test he failed. He had to attend the dinner and find out why Baby had returned.

Kartik smiled himself into Sukanya's apartment. In front of him was a small sitting area with a heavy sofa in deep burgundy velvet, matching armchairs and two low-roped ones. There were chiks on the window and a door leading out onto the terrace. Sukanya has mixed up her metaphors, thought Kartik, she cannot decide whether she wants to be ethnic chic or nouveau rich.

He saw the hair first – a shaft of light, straight and blond. Next, her arms, curved in an L along the chair. She wore a black cotton sari with a narrow gold border, a sleeveless gold blouse.

He smelt the scent of her.

She stood up, turned and drew him close, as though about to dance, and bit his left ear lobe. A remembered intimacy. He wished he were a dog that could snap at her ankles or slobber over her hand.

Baby.

'Kartik.'

Bronzed, blond. Not beautiful, never that, but warm and inviting. He thought of sand beaches in the summer sun.

'So what brings you to your rotting homeland?' In that question was all the resentment, bitterness and pain Kartik had preserved inside for the day he met Baby again.

The scent of her body, mingled with the smoke from her nostrils, did strange things to him. Kartik shivered. Must be a cold coming on, he told himself.

On the sofa, next to Baby was a woman with short black hair, small, sharp features. Loose black trousers and a tight black cotton shirt, offset by a thick gold chain around her neck.

'Forgive me if I don't get up,' her lipsticked lips said, 'but as you can see, I can't.'

She lifted a trouser leg seductively to reveal more than the stretch bandage around her ankle.

Baby laughed and pulled down her companion's trousers.

'Pay no attention to her,' she said, rising as lightly as steam. 'Anu flirts in her sleep.'

She held out her hand. He saw the solitaire on her little finger, felt the heat of her. She gestured to the sofa. He sank into it and immediately felt diminished. Next to him, her golden hair, her tanned skin. He wanted to touch both, discover if she felt smooth as a hot oil massage.

'I was about to call you,' she said.

'Of course.'

'Seriously.'

'Of course.'

Annoyance narrowed her eyes.

'Who do you think invited you here?'

She sat, carefully crossing her legs, and lit a cigarette.

'Are we going to play games or have a proper conversation?'

'Uh-oh.' Anu inched one cheek and then the other off the sofa. 'Time to go.'

Kartik made to rise in remonstrance but she pressed down his shoulder. 'I know you have not come to flirt with me.' She sighed and hobbled away.

Baby tapped her nose with her knuckle. The old nervousness.

Kartik stared at the ring on her finger. She shrugged and smiled, an embarrassed smile.

'I am not married,' she said.

A look in her eyes and he reclaimed the territory of her body, like a landlord who had regained possession of his property after a lengthy interval.

Had he possessed her in his barsati strewn with books, papers, clothes, littered with cigarette butts and the evidence of occasional revelry in empty bottles of Old Monk rum? Had he?

Were people belongings, he wondered, hooking his toes around her left big toe, one afternoon after she had returned to him and lay next to him, asleep.

'Are you mine?' he whispered.

She grunted. Can you purchase human beings? By the length and width of their bodies? By the hectare or the metre? By the weight of their flesh against yours? Can you value them as a piece of jewellery?

Kartik was reminded of the time he paid a man the price of his wife. Sapna. In a pink dupatta pitted with gold discs, a nose ring as large as a curtain ring and scarlet smeared on her forehead, on her lips, and rubbed into the parting of her hair.

Sapna. With dancing eyes, red ribbons in her heavily oiled hair, red and gold bangles on her wrists, and silver anklets. Sapna, who announced her arrival with the jangle of her jewellery and left with a wave of her plaits; Sapna who cleaned the floor of his Nizamuddin flat as though it was the skin on her body.

Sapna, who had dangled from the bus, waiting for it to slow down for her to alight, waiting to rush home to her three-year-old son. The bus, stuffed with people spilling onto the step, teetered left on a sharp turn. Sapna's foot slipped and her head hit the gravel at forty kilometres per hour. The bus driver did not stop to pick up what he had so carelessly let fall.

Her husband Kamal had arrived at Kartik's a day later. In his arms was a small, dry-eyed boy, white around the nostrils.

'Sahib, give me enough to burn her properly.'

Kartik counted out the notes and gave them to Sapna's good-looking husband. Kamal lowered the child to the floor.

'Sahib, what will happen with this?' He spread out the three hundred-rupee notes.

'Isn't that enough to burn her?' Kartik asked, disliking the man's face. He didn't seem moved by the misfortune, overwhelmed by his loss, bewildered by the whimsicality of his wife's chance death.

'Arre sahib, I am left with this burden now.' He poked his son in the stomach.

'What is the going price for a dead mother nowadays? One thousand? Fifteen hundred?'

'Sahib is making fun of my situation.'

'No, really, I'd just like to know.'

The man stared at him, his body a taunt. He folded his hands in polite supplication; but his face didn't reflect the gesture.

Kartik went into his bedroom and returned a moment later. He held out five one-hundred-rupee notes. The man took them, counted them.

'Has the bus driver been arrested?'

Kamal shook his head.

'Then they'll never find him. I know some people. High up. You come back and let me know the name of the constable and which police station you went to. I'll have a word.'

The bereaved husband dipped his head in a namaste and turned away. There was passive resistance in his slack body. Kartik knew he would never visit again; he knew he couldn't get more for the accidental death of a wife.

Kartik shivered from the recollection and cuddled Baby's sleeping form. How much was Baby worth? How much of her did he own as he lay beside her? Had she been somebody else's in New York?

'Baby, do you belong to me?'

Baby sat up, a white sheet draped around her like a sari. She admired her fingers.

'You know perfectly well nobody belongs to anybody, not even to themselves. I have to go.'

He watched her dress, snatch her cigarettes and lighter. She bit his ear.

'Bye now.'

When he looked into the bathroom mirror later, he saw a triumphant smile on his mouth. She had returned to him. He had done nothing, he had not made a move, but she had returned.

'But why yaar, after the way she ditched you?' Ajay asked when he told him of the reunion at Sukanya's. 'Why are you back with her? You know what she is like.'

Yes, he knew. How she took long-term decisions in haste and lingered over daily ones. She would spend hours in Cottage Industries, trying out kurtas and saris, and leave without buying any. But she had invited him back into her life in the time it took to bite his ear. Her complete casualness exhilarated him.

'What about the hajaar women we have introduced you to? You couldn't find a single one to please you?' asked Avantika. 'Only this Baby, looking like a hijra, a freak in her blond-dyed hair and sun lotion? Only she must you bed.'

'Don't talk sex to my friend, Tikoo,' warned Ajay. 'He will think you are making a pass at him.'

'I would give him a gala time, better than that witch …'

In the days after her return from New York, Baby seldom spoke of her time there. She wanted to keep things separate. But such discretion was impossible. Lifelines crossed, occasionally. He told her of his vist to her mother, his repeated attempts at the IAS exams, the extraordinary job offer from Avantika's father, his exile from home. Then he asked what she had done in New York.

'Studied. Worked in a bookstore.'

'Yes, but what did you do there?'

'Like I said, read books.'

'No, seriously …'

'Sold them?'

'Funny.'

She told him fleetingly about Ramaji Rameshwar Rao, but not what mattered. Only that she worked at his bookstore and that he was her benefactor.

'In what way did he benefit you?'

She looked him straight in the eye without a blink.

'You really want me to describe it to you?'

'I can guess.'

'Then why ask?'

'How long are you staying?'

She took his hand.

He drew it back.

'What is it that you want?'

'I want you to make me stay.'

Kartik lit cigarettes for both of them, then rose to sit away from her.

'Is that why you have come back?'

Baby smiled. Shrugged.

'Maybe, perhaps, who knows? There's no satisfactory explanation why.'

NEW YORK
1985

There was no satisfactory explanation why. Why she had ignored Kartik's one-line letter: *I have become a collector.*

Why she had stayed on in New York for so long.

She had come to New York to get away from all of them: Didi, Chor Bagh, Kartik. They were not to be part of this new existence; her past life, she vowed to herself, must never catch up with the present. They should always maintain the distance of the years between them.

Besides, she didn't want them to see her like this: sitting behind the cashier's counter at ABC Books, waiting for Ramaji to pick her up. He owned the bookstore, one in a chain of Asian Book Company stores across USA and Canada that kept books on spirituality, cookery and self-healing. He said that most Indo–Pakis pray, fast, then eat and worry about their bodily functions. He simply made a living off the ritual cycle of subcontinental existence.

One day, almost eight months after her arrival in New York, Baby had seen a 'Help Wanted' sign outside the store and began to work there while attending private college. She didn't have any friends, and was unfriendly to those who approached her. She enjoyed her solitude, wishing for a place where she could hide and enjoy it alone. ABC Books, from the moment she had stepped in, felt comfortable, comforting.

For seven months she met few people apart from the two other girls in the store, Angelina and Jodie, and the customers. Then one Saturday, while she was seated behind the counter, reading a novel hidden within the covers of B.K.S. Iyengar's *Light on Yoga*, Ramaji Rameshwar Rao, on a random check of the store, stole up and caught her. Like a butterfly between his fingers, she fluttered nervously, then subsided as his hand closed around her

He was a large man, Ramaji. His shape reminded her of a block of granite. Swarthy, bushy eyebrows, huge hands, and a moustache that said he had once been or wished to be in the army. He was solid, Ramaji. If you banged into him, you were bruised.

He took a great liking to her. Maybe it was because when she was barefoot, she was nearly as tall as he was. He visited the bookstore frequently and escorted her back to her college dorm. She let him. She decided she preferred the company of this older man to the young ones around her, someone who would stand firm against the winds of bad luck that blew in her face. Someone who would take charge, change the course of the fate lines on her palm.

He had this ability to shape those he met, Ramaji. In the beginning, he made her his pet – he spoilt her. Every meeting, she received a special treat: a gift, dinner, a long drive. When he got to know her better, he would comb her hair, stroke her, seat her on his lap.

'You are my Goldilocks,' he would whisper into her ear.

In the beginning she enjoyed the petting. When Ramaji ran his palm from the top of her head to the tips of her toes, she would stretch and squirm. She had forgotten that pets are eventually tied up, placed on a leash and punished when they stray or disobey. When you have a master, you're no longer his pet; you become his bitch. But that was later.

Two months after they had met, he invited her to stay the weekend at his suburban home. At the end of her first year at college, when the long summer break stretched ahead of her without a destination, he suggested she move in with him. She didn't hesitate. She was pleased at the idea. She hated sharing her college dorm room with a girl from Norway. Each disliked the smell of the other. Baby found her breath meaty, stale. The Norwegian complained about the mustard oil Baby used in her hair and on her body before a bath.

Also, if she was honest, she quite liked the idea of fine living. And there he was, Ramaji, waving his green bucks in her face like the American flag. He installed her behind the black, raw silk blinds he had on all the windows of his house. She liked them at first sight, but came to detest them later because they confined her to his world. He had planted her in a pot inside his house and showered her with gifts, waiting for her to bloom.

Ramaji liked fast cars and long drives. Every morning they drove into New York down the highway, in his Porsche to eat hot sambar-vada at a small south Indian restaurant in Brooklyn. Then they went to work: he to his office, she to college and then the bookstore. Twice a week, he would pick her up late from the bookstore and they would eat out, each time at a new, expensive restaurant. The rest of the week, especially the weekends, they stayed home. Just the two of them. And Jacaranda, the housekeeper. No visitors.

He never left Baby. Even when he went out of town, the telephone would ring constantly and throughout the day.

'Just checking to make sure my little Red Riding Hood hasn't met any big bad wolves!' he would guffaw.

Over time, Baby's life was secured like a lock. Slowly, she learnt that she would not be let out any further than Ramaji wished. She could go to the bookstore but no further without him; it upset him. If she wanted to watch a movie or visit the theatre, he would drop her and pick her up once the show was over. That was his way: she lived in a luxury prison with Ramaji as the warden.

The bookstore was her parole. She stayed at Ramaji's house, but the bookstore was home. She loved the smell of paper, the rainbow colours of book covers lit up under the studio lights. It reminded her of another bookstore.

Baby hardly knew anyone in New York. Although she inhabited the city, she continued to dwell elsewhere. When old college friends in India wrote in envy of her life, she wrote back, *this is just my postal address, I am searching for a permanent one.*

Kartik would never understand why she fled, why she lived with Ramaji. Some days, neither did she. Especially after Ramaji's drinking increased and she lay pinned beneath the weight of their life together.

When did they begin to change? Maybe it was when she leaned against him for support but hated it when he imprisoned her in his arms. Maybe it was when the business telephone calls increased and hers became just another number he dialled. Or maybe it was the day she walked straight into a shower from a sleepy bed and noticed the red blotches on her back and arms in the mirror.

Ramaji didn't bruise her because of an unhappy childhood. He didn't have one. Nor was he ever out of work: he'd been employed since the age of eighteen, first in his father's cement business and then in setting up his own successful business. He drank heavily, but that simply increased his ardour. He wasn't the type of man who beat women.

Perhaps, Baby began to believe, it was a quirk in his character, rather like his comic book speech.

He hit her at random times: the morning after, when he was bathed and breakfasted, attired in a three-piece suit and a bright tie. He would slap aftershave – Old Spice, always – on his face and grab her hard by the upper arms, pinch her skin. Where it wouldn't show. A hard pinch, he said, was a reminder 'of my interest in you, my Baby Baby quite contrary'. When she asked him why, the first time, he tweaked the edges of his military moustache, buttoned his jacket, ran a brush through his thick, steel hair.

'It was just a Jack and Jill fumble-tumble, nothing else!' he replied on other occasions, in that obscure way he had.

Once, in the middle of her exercise routine, she bent to touch her toes and saw him approach. Before she could straighten up, he was on his knees, surprisingly agile for his size, and had fixed his teeth into her left thigh. She screamed.

'No, no,' he soothed, stroked her hair, breathing moist heat into her face, 'now wasn't that a dainty dish to set before the king?'

He thought he was playful as a pup but the marks remained for twenty-seven days – one short of four weeks. When they lay in bed, she winced with the weight of him. She thought of Kartik, gentle on his side, rubbing the vein in her wrist to make it rear up so he could kiss it. She began to long for him, the way she ached for sleep when it was past 3 a.m.

Baby liked to think that Ramaji's mind had developed loose hinges, like an old door opened too often. She learnt to put up with the violence because each time it happened, it hurt a little less.

It was only when new bruises developed over the old ones that Baby began to hit back. In her own way. She was clever, well read and, as Kartik could vouchsafe, pretty sharp with her tongue. She would laugh at Ramaji's hair follicles, at his curious speech pattern, at his appetite for tomato chutney and his mother's homemade pickles.

A time came when she began to dislike herself for staying on. She had turned to him for the sturdy fullness of his body, not because she cared for him. Perhaps he knew that. Perhaps they both did. And that was why she stayed. Women, she thought, gave men strange reasons for their cruelty.

With time, the violence began to leave its mark on her and she began to think of leaving him. As she contemplated a separation, she was held back by the thought of Didi and the time she had deserted 3, Chor Bagh. Baby had deeply resented her mother for that decision. But now she wondered what it had been like for her, then, to leave behind everything except Sita, a small child and a few belongings. To begin all over again.

HILL STATION
1962

To begin all over again. In a different town, a new home. It could have been worse, thought Didi.

Sita disagreed. In her opinion, their home in the hills was worse than bad, it was small and irritating, 'like a makhee,' she remarked disdainfully.

The house Didi rented had three rooms. A garden spilled onto the lane, barely large enough to contain Baby's swing and two cane chairs. The building, an old army barrack, had been constructed as a series of rooms in a straight line, connected by doors. Didi used the first to seat the students who came for 'tootion'. The room's only window opened by the Ashoka tree; Baby's swing was so close, Didi could push it from inside. The room was sparsely furnished, with the minimum of fuss, as if Didi was – perpetually – moving in or out.

Didi used her parents' furniture, but just a few pieces fit into the small space. There was a mahogany study table with a china blue-and-white lamp, two upright chairs. Two armchairs and a table between them completed the room. There were framed photographs of Mem, Father and Baby on the mantlepiece. Didi spread a Persian carpet, three by six feet, near the fireplace in winter when they lit a fire; but otherwise the fireplace was blocked by an old quilt to keep out rats, bats and the hill-station chill.

Baby's room had a queen-size bed in the middle because she liked to roll from side to side. A small table was placed by its side. A green-and-purple rug lay on the floor. There was a steel bookshelf for toys and books. A charpoy was propped against the wall. Sita slept on it at night.

The third room had once been a store. It was small and had wide cement shelves along the far wall, and a skylight instead of a window. Here, Didi slept on a single bed. There was a pedestal lamp with a red shade, a red-and-blue floral carpet where her feet first met the floor when she stepped out of the bed. And there was Sita's big black trunk with its large brass Godrej lock.

From Didi's room, a door led out to the courtyard where there was the toilet and the kitchen.

The kitchen was square, with shelves and on either side. It was an old-fashioned cooking space with a chimney in front and a washbasin in the left corner. In the middle, Didi had placed a square table that she covered with a fresh tablecloth every day. It served as a dining table and Baby's study table.

As Baby grew older, she complained about eating in the kitchen.

'Sita,' she said, 'you know where my school friends have their dining table?'

'Where?' Sita asked without interest.

'In the dining room, of course!' Baby clapped her hands. Her plaits danced, her light eyes grinned.

'So why is ours in the kitchen?' Baby asked, pulling Sita's pallu off her shoulder and exposing her bosom, which fetched her a 'Baby, don't Baby!' reproach from Sita.

'How do I know?' answered Sita. 'I know nothing around here. I do as I am told, bas.'

'If you don't know, who does?' Baby kept tugging at her sari.

'Mrican-madam, she!'

'Hain?'

'That 'Mrican-mother of yours. She says, in 'Mrica everyone eats in the kitchen.'

'Amma, why must we eat in the kitchen when we live in India?' demanded Baby of Didi.

'Because we don't have a dining room, you silly!'

In those first six months up in the hills, Didi had cooked frequently. It had been a tense time. Every evening, Baby would crawl underneath her bedclothes and refuse to emerge, demand they go back home.

'Where are Dadi and Bhai Chacha?'

'They are in their own home.'

'Why are we living in this place?'

'Because this is now our home.'

'How long will we have to live here?'

'I don't know: how long is life?'

They were new to the town, though the town was familiar to Didi. This was one of the hill stations of her childhood, when every summer Father, Mem, Mahendra and she, accompanied by Sita, would spend a month away from Delhi's heat. Didi did not wish to meet the people Mem and Father had known then, people she had visited in her childhood. She made a point of avoiding places from the past. She need not have bothered. The town had changed. Familiar people had died, shifted to the big cities. Didi didn't recognize the nameplates outside bungalows. Many were padlocked, overgrown with weeds, still with the long silence of emptiness.

The old haunts – the club, the horse riding track, the bakery – were cluttered with new faces, and the mall had been transformed into a tourist spot with gift shops, photo studios and small eateries. Loud Hindi film music blared from loudspeakers.

The town had five English-medium institutions of high repute for girls. Two were missionary boarding schools, one was a day-boarding convent, another a day convent and the last a day public school. There were government schools too, but Didi had no intention of sending Baby to one of those.

She would go to the day convent.

Didi did not know where the money would come from for her education and their daily expenses. She had already sold two of Father's carpets and put the money in a fixed deposit in Baby's name, vowing not to touch it. She didn't want to touch her jewellery, family heirlooms she wanted Baby to inherit. Mahendra sent money orders and promised to look after 'his family' but Didi not wish to live as his dependent. Bhai had pressed an envelope into her hand when they left; Didi opened it on the train to find that it contained cheques for various amounts. She had drawn money for establishing them in the house, then written to Bhai saying he should not send more till she asked for it. She never asked for it.

She seriously considered converting Baby so that her education, uniform and books would be free at the convent. And but for Sita, she may have.

'What has religion done for Mem, you or me?' Didi asked Sita.

'Kismet is kismet,' insisted Sita. 'She was born a Hindu: that was God's choice.'

'Yes, but you always said there was some "phoren" blood in Mem's family, remember? Who knows which English man or woman gave Mem's family their fair skin, their light eyes and hair? Who knows how Baby got hers?'

Sita had risen from the blouse she was ironing.

'Baby looks exactly like her father,' she declared, her eyes still in remembrance. 'Exactly,' she repeated.

Didi took Mem's name eleven times and shrugged Sita off.

'Who else should she look like? You? Now, if you let me call her Baby Mary, we can educate her for free.'

Sita held the lobes of her ears. She ran from the room and locked herself in the toilet.

There she stayed.

Didi knocked repeatedly, but Sita refused to reply.

'You cannot stay in there forever,' Didi shouted. 'Look, if you, a low caste form of life can share a bathroom with us upper-wallahs, why can't Baby become a Christian? Baby, tell this silly old woman to come out.'

'Sita, Sita, why are you in the bathroom?'

'Why do you think?' screamed Sita.

Didi and Baby kicked the door.

There was silence.

'Fine, stay then.'

Didi pulled Baby away.

Ten minutes later, there was still no sign of Sita.

Didi told Baby to learn her tables and returned to the bathroom door.

'Sita,' she hissed. 'There is no air left inside except your own gas. Come out at once.'

'I cannot,' replied Sita in a squeaky voice.

'Why not?'

'Because there are two fat-fat lizards at the top of the door. If I open it, they will fall on me.'

'Shoo them away.'

'Nowhere to shoo. You have chosen a house with such a small toilet that when I squat, my knees touch the door. Hai hai, Mem, where are you?'

'But they say it is good luck if a lizard falls on you.'

'Mar jaungi,' promised Sita. 'I will die!'

'Try, Sita.'

Sita snarled.

'They're watching me with their small-small black-black eyes. If I breathe even, they will drop on me!'

Urged by Didi to be a little braver than the lizards, which were 'one hundredth your size', Sita gently unlocked the door, eased it open, her eyes clinging to the lizards.

'That's it, that's it,' encouraged Didi.

Half of Sita was still inside the bathroom plastered to the doorway. One lizard hung down his head to leer at her.

'Eeeeeee! Sita!' squealed Baby, appearing on the scene. 'See, lizards!'

'Haieeeeeee!'

Sita darted out and clapped her hands over her ears.

'Why do you close your ears?' demanded Baby, perplexed.

'So those creatures don't fall on me,' gasped Sita, her eyes firmly closed.

The lizard's eyes never wavered, unperturbed by the commotion.

And so Didi had given up the idea of converting Baby.

A pity, she wrote to Mahendra, *because she could always have gone back to being a Hindu once she finished school.*

She's not something you pawned and can reclaim when you have paid the price, Didi, wrote back a stern Mahendra.

At night, when Didi felt particularly disheartened by her peculiar circumstances and insecure about Baby's future, she considered writing to Jeff and requesting him for the money. A few hundred dollars here and there would be nothing to him. He was kind, at least he used to be. Perhaps he would be generous to her, if for no other reason than the memory of their relationship. Didi would fall asleep determined to write to him the next morning.

But with sunrise she would realize how impossible it was to think of revisiting Jeff and her life in New York. How could she even think of applying to him? He was what she had left behind and she never thought of him as part of what lay ahead. She remembered him only with the nostalgia for the woman she had been with him and the occasional physical yearning. Also, he might ask questions she could not answer. No, Jeff must remain a photograph in the wallet of her memory.

Instead, Didi set out in search of work. The choice of profession was extremely limited.

Women of my time, in our community, were not supposed to work, remember? she complained to Mahendra in a letter. *Remember my lessons with that fat Mrs O'Hare? She taught me English history, Romantic poetry and Japanese fish farming. What can I do with that?*

She might, suggested Mahendra, take up tuitions. She was almost a BA, wasn't she?

'Yes,' agreed Sita when Didi told her. 'You used to argue with Father Sahib, in English. Children will be easy.'

Didi put up a notice at the local clubhouse, the most frequented restaurants in town, the old bakery shop and in all major schools.

Wanted: Students who wish to command the English language
The way the British ruled India.
Take lessons from America-returned outstanding teacher tutored by
English professor.
Taught in the USA for two years.

When Baby pointed out that Sita said she had never done a day's work in America, Didi snapped: 'Read your book.'

White lies, she wrote to Mahendra, *don't show up on paper.*

The response was instantaneous. Within a fortnight, Didi had over two dozen applications. Boys and girls of all ages and sizes came to have a look at the "Mrica-returned ma'am", as Sita put it. The number doubled in a month. They came accompanied by parents or ayahs and drivers. With varying degrees of proficiency in English, *ranging from the type who are learning A, B, C for the first time,* Didi wrote to Mahendra, *to those who study Shakespeare.*

Didi chose the brighter students. She had four senior students for one hour each, five days a week, and eight less accomplished students thrice a week. Weekend mornings, she taught adults, mothers of some of the students. Tuitions began at 2.30 p.m. By the time the last child left, Didi had a sore throat and eyes, and a very tired Baby ready for bed.

Weekday mornings, Didi studied *Wren & Martin* for English grammar or corrected the students' homework.

'Hai hai, Mem,' Sita would sigh, watching Didi at her books. 'Why did you marry Purush and then leave him?'

'You know why,' Mem's daughter replied.

It had begun to rain outside. Didi hoped Sita had taken the umbrella with her to Baby's school-bus stop.

Didi straightened out the pleats of her sari and her hair, cocked an ear: the doorbell was ringing. She had taken a late bath. The tuitions were still half an hour away. The bell rang again and this time it didn't stop. Didi rushed to the kitchen, grabbed the hammer from the drawer and ran to the front door.

That's how he saw her for the first time. Didi with her hair open on her shoulders, her arm held up, her hand clenched around a hammer. Even as he recoiled, she smiled and swung the hammer at the bell. Its black plastic shell broke and the white button popped back up: the ringing stopped. Didi giggled at his admiring but alarmed expression.

Then she lifted an eyebrow in inquiry.

He explained that he was a relative of Prem, Mahendra's wife.

'Oh,' she observed, 'how nice.'

'For whom?' he wanted to know.

'For all of us,' she replied hastily.

He laughed and folded his hands in greeting.

'I am M.C. Hamer – that's Hamer with one 'm'. Mahesh Chandra Hamer. Everyone calls me MC. Or Hamer. As you like it.'

She looked from him to the hammer in her hand.

'I know, I know,' he responded. 'Hamer is German. My great-grandfather adopted it when he bought out the German owner of our hotel chain, yes chain; so people would think it was still in the family.'

'I believe Hamer suits you better than MC,' Didi said after critical consideration of the man standing at her doorstep.

'Only Hamer – that's …'

'With one 'm', I know. Come in, Mr Hamer.'

By the time she sat him down in the armchair and put the water to boil for tea, Sita had returned with Baby. Baby glared at him when introduced, looked stubborn and unresponsive when asked to say 'namaste' and ran to her bedroom when he asked how old she was. Didi thought of apologizing, but that would have drawn attention to Baby's rudeness. Baby had grown up in her own way and refused to comply with how others wanted her to behave. Especially her mother. It was best to leave her alone.

As it happened, Baby did not leave them alone. She returned within minutes, still in her school uniform, the blue belt eating into her waist. She sat close to Didi. And stared at him.

Over a cup of tea, he explained he was Prem aunt's cousin, from the other side.

'We understand,' completed Baby. 'Amma does not have another side. And I have no family, because,' she glared at Didi, 'she brought me here. Sita, give me something to eat! I am hungeeee!'

They sipped tea. Crunched Nice biscuits which had crystals of sugar on top.

He told her he had lived here most of his life. Most of it, except for the years he had been to college in Calcutta and then London for management studies. He'd returned and taken charge of the family hotel: Carlton House.

'It is the biggest hotel in the area for miles around. Twenty-two rooms, yes twenty—'

'We heard the first time.' Baby rolled a crisp paratha, dipped it in yogurt and observed him over its edge. 'Why do you keep saying the same thing?'

Mr Hamer nodded and smiled at her, reaching for another biscuit. He said he had added a new wing to the hotel and modernized it. He had built an open-air restaurant which overlooked the cliff's edge. A band played at dinner. There was dancing with lights in the trees. Just like he had seen in Paris. Yes, in Paris.

Didi smiled through this recital, thinking that M.C. Hamer was a funny little man. Yes, funny. Oh god, she was already picking up his habit of repetition.

He asked for more tea, if it was not a bother. Didi told Baby to get fresh tea from the kitchen. Baby kicked at the table.

'Go.'

'No.'

'Go.'

Didi dug her nails into Baby's forearm.

'Ouch.'

'Go.'

Sullen, reluctant Baby got up and took the teapot away.

'That was clever of you. To know I wanted to speak to you in private.'

'What is it?'

'I was in Australia, Sydney, a few weeks ago and met Mahendra Bhai. He told me a little about you, because I also live here. He said he had written to me last year when you settled here. But I received no letter ... the post, you know. He asked me to assist you if I could. Yes, assist. Also, he has sent this letter for you.'

He held out a white envelope. She took it and placed it under the cushion of the sofa she was sitting upon. She would look at it later, when no one was around. There was more to it than a letter, she was sure.

'Thank you.'

'For what? I haven't helped you yet.'

'And in what way do you think you can help?'

He played with the loose metal band of his wristwatch.

'I don't know, because I am unaware of your needs.'

Baby returned with the teapot. She thrust it upon the tray so that some tea spilled from the nozzle.

He drank another cup of tea and crunched another Nice biscuit.

'You must visit my hotel …'

'Have,' said Baby.

'… as my guests. We make excellent tea.'

'Then why do you drink so much of ours?' Baby asked.

He nodded again. Smiled. Didi felt an irresistible urge to hug and spank her daughter at the same time.

'I meant we make excellent cakes, doughnuts, scones, muffins: a very English tea.'

As Baby opened her mouth, Didi pinched her, on the thigh.

'She's pinching me because of you,' Baby told him.

He nodded and smiled again.

'I must leave; return to my hotel. When will you come and have tea?'

'Sunday at four,' Didi said promptly before Baby could speak.

'I won't go,' threatened Baby, 'I won't.'

This time he merely nodded.

After he left, Didi said, 'Must you make people think badly of you, Baby?'

'I don't care. Who is he? Where's my father, where's my Bhai Chacha and Dadi? Why do we have to live here without them?'

Baby covered the tears on her face with her hands.

Didi knew better than to try and touch her – her rage erupted like an allergic rash. Instead, Didi went to the kitchen where Sita was slurping tea.

'Go to Baby, she's crying.'

It was only later, as she stared out of the window, waiting for her pupil to write five sentences with a past participle, that Didi thought of his appearance. Short, maybe an inch taller than her. Greying hair, soft and wavy. It covered his ears and reached the nape of his neck.

He had a few pockmarks on his face, small, ripe cherry lips, especially the lower one. I will suggest he grows a moustache, Didi thought, it will suit him.

Mr Hamer's eyes were black. The most extraordinary features in his face were his lashes: long, curled, each one fine and separate as though they were combed out each morning. She hadn't seen such eyelashes on a man before.

He had worn... what was it? A brown suit, pink shirt and burgundy tie, soft brown suede shoes. A coral ring on the middle finger. Neat small fingernails.

Didi went to tea that Sunday afternoon without Baby, who lay in bed claiming to have a headache.

'Got it from you,' she said from underneath the bedclothes.

Didi dressed in a tangerine orange Banaras silk sari that had a cream border and pallu. She wore no jewellery except for the ring Mem and Father had given her when she got married to Purush and small gold balis in her ears. Her hair was pinned into a bun. She carried a brown-and-gold-striped baroque leather bag that Father had bought during one of his trips to Italy.

She sat in the open-air restaurant looking at the smoke rise from the village dwellings in the valley below. Tea was served in white china teacups with a gold rim. There were thin brown-bread ham sandwiches touched with mustard, soft scones with melting butter, and rich coffee cake dusted with chocolate shavings. It was a long time since Didi had eaten such delicacies. It all tasted so good, tasted of the one time she had been completely happy: New York.

Didi's mind travelled home, to Baby lying in bed with her head covered. She felt the mustard sting her tongue. Baby would have enjoyed this tea. Is it my fault or is Baby to blame too? She munched a sandwich and mulled over the question.

Mr Hamer asked, 'What brought you to my home town?'

When she didn't reply, he began to speak. He told her that he was a widower. His wife had died five years ago from an advanced case of TB. Yes, TB. They had discovered it too late. He had one son, settled in England. Twin grandchildren. A daughter in Bangalore, with one child, a girl. He had a brother in Bombay but he visited him only during weddings or deaths. Yes, weddings or deaths. He didn't care to keep up with the rest of the world because his world was his hotel and the people who worked there. When he felt lonely, he listened to the radio.

He asked her again, 'What brought you to my hometown?'

She said she'd tell him on some other occasion when the tea was less delicious.

Over the next several months and many pots of tea, between delicate bites of thin cucumber sandwiches, Didi revealed herself in instalments – chapters from a serialized novel in a women's magazine.

Mr Hamer listened silently, courteously. He never asked direct questions about her life, but showed a gentle interest in everything she had to say, prompting her every once in a while, 'And then?'

Or, he would nod and smile, rotating his wristwatch.

Whenever she returned from the hotel, Baby would demand to see Bhai Chacha and Dadi, and refuse to speak to her. The fifth time it happened, Didi caught Baby by her plait.

'Don't be so foolish, Baby, and learn to behave.'

'First you behave, Amma. First you.'

And the same questions.

'Tell me, tell me, Amma.'

Each time, Didi would reply, 'I just had to leave.'

'But why didn't you leave me with them? '

'I couldn't leave you, Baby.'

'You always say that.'

Baby's pale eyes, the colour of liquid honey with a tiger's stripes, would snap.

'You are too young to understand,' Didi would say, and knew it to be a mistake.

'I am not too young! You just don't want to tell the truth because you are bad.'

Didi appealed to Sita for help.

'Make her understand.' She put a hand on the ayah's shoulder.

Sita turned away.

'What's to understand? My Didi wanting to be with a man, always.'

Didi pushed a strand of Sita's hair off her face and tucked it behind her ear.

'It is said,' continued the older woman, 'when a man and a woman who are not married meet, then mischief follows.'

'Mischief you, evil you and your sayings which you make up to suit the moment, you old trouble-maker. Wait and see: if I ever catch you talking to the maali alone in the garden again, or with the men at Baby's bus stop, I will look for mischief under your petticoat.'

'Hai hai, Mem, what she say, this daughter of yours?'

M.C. Hamer.

She always addressed him with the respectful 'Mr Hamer', thought of him in the third person, as if this gave them intimacy but kept them perpetually at a distance. It was odd and sometimes confusing, but try as she might, she could not bring herself to call him by his given name.

The first time he asked her to have dinner with him, Didi refused. The second time, she said, 'Why don't you come home and eat Sita's cooking? It's very tasty.'

He apologized; he hadn't meant to insult her with his invitation.

She laughed.

'Don't be ridiculous. I would love to eat at your dining table, but I think it is better if you came to mine. Let me repay some of your generosity.'

It was then that he mentioned it, five months after he had first rung her doorbell.

He said he could be even more generous, if she let him. He had plenty of everything. Yes, everything. Except company.

What exactly was he looking for?

Company. Her company.

She told him not to be silly, he already had that.

He didn't immediately repeat the request. He came to dinner one Saturday night. He brought French white wine for her and a bottle of Chivas Regal whisky for himself. She had moved the kitchen table into the living room, dressed it in a white tablecloth, put out her silver candlebras and lit two twisted red candlesticks. There were pink carnations in glass vases. So typical, it was ordinary. Didi was delighted: it had been years since she had dined like this.

They barely spoke. Lest they be overheard by Sita or Baby, who refused to come in and say hello. Baby said she would eat where she always did: in the kitchen. Didi rose to play the radio. The wine seemed to have loosened her limbs and she swayed from side to side to the music, waltzing by herself. She asked him once, 'Would you like to?'

He shook his head and smiled. 'No, you go ahead. I am a clumsy dancer.'

Didi danced. She was wearing a black south Indian silk sari with a gold temple border. A gold blouse down to her navel, with puffed sleeves, Chinese collar clasped to her chin. A black bindi on her forehead, no jewellery.

Suddenly, she saw Sita and Baby watching her from the doorway. There was a curious mix of indulgence and disapproval in Sita's eyes, and in Baby's an unguarded look of desire. Didi stopped and held out a hand to her daughter, whose eyes darted across to him. Baby retreated into the kitchen, pulling Sita after her. Didi's shoulders rose and sank in a sigh.

Over dinner, she discussed Father and Mem. Safe subjects. Her tuitions, his hotel.

Suddenly, Didi rose and rushed to the bathroom. Sita hammered on the door.

'Just like Noo Ark: drinking and then ulti – too much drink and then ulti. All that Jafferi's fault.'

Didi was too busy with her heaves to correct her pronunciation.

'This is your fault, you did this,' she heard Baby yell as she stepped out. 'You're making my mother sick. Yes, sick.'

Through the waves of nausea, Didi smiled. Baby too had picked up his absurd affectation of speech.

Baby's dislike of him intensified after that dinner. Whenever he came, and Didi ensured it was only once a month, Baby would sit in the kitchen and talk loudly about the old days, remembered stories of 3, Chor Bagh. Bhai and Purush featured frequently in these monologues. Smiling and nodding, he would listen.

'You never react to her rudeness,' Didi once said to him.

'Maybe my skin is thicker than a coconut's shell,' he replied.

Thick-skinned Mr Hamer may have been, but he remained avuncular and indulgent. Didi admired his forbearance. No one else would have put up with Baby's insolence. For that, and for his utmost generosity, Didi was baking an extra special cake for his birthday. It was three years since they had moved to the hill station. Six since she had met him.

Didi picked up the tumbler of rum. Half a glass. That's what the recipe had said: pull out the vanilla cake mixture from the oven fifteen minutes after you have placed it inside, pour in the rum mixed with sliced almonds and honey. The almonds will settle at the top, the rum and honey will soak into the sponge cake. In her haste, Didi had forgotten to add the rum to the honey and almonds.

'What will I do with it now?' she chided herself.

'Ask Mr Mahesh Chandra Hamer with one "m",' Baby suggested, behind her.

Didi shivered. Her daughter often stole into Didi's space without her realizing. Just like Som Devi, Didi thought.

Didi kept her head down and sprinkled the rum onto the cake through a tea-strainer. She thought that if she concentrated on a simple task, if she methodically and slowly went about her business, she could endure Baby.

Baby, in long schoolgirl plaits tied in light blue ribbons, wispy because Didi had refused Sita the luxury of soaking Baby's hair in mustard oil. Baby at the bus stop in her blue tunic with the dark blue plastic school belt tied so tight about the waist, it had left a permanent red welt there. Didi would anoint it with glycerine and rose water at night and tell Baby to wear the belt loose.

'But every girl wears it loose. I want to be different. Besides, it shows off my waist.'

Baby, tall for her age, slim at the waist, but the hips were already beginning to round the corners of her bones ... Lovely Baby.

Didi shook her head and returned to the task at hand: Mr Hamer's cake.

'What' inquired Baby, 'is the occasion?'

'I told you, it's his birthday and he's taking me for a drive.'

'Oh,' replied Baby, biting into a slice of bread, the butter smearing her lip and nose. Didi reached out to wipe the smudge. Baby swerved.

'Go wipe his.'

'Baby.'

'Don't.'

Serrated. Scraped out of her mouth as if by the same knife she cut the bread. Didi felt touched by this Baby, whose mouth lost its shape when she was upset, who swallowed food without munching, and who hated Mr M.C. Hamer.

It was time to leave. Too much had been said already.

'And don't go away like that.' Baby's voice was like tyres coming to a screeching halt. 'Why do you always do that when I want to say something?'

'I don't wish to argue.'

'Should've thought of that before.'

'When was before, Baby? Before I conceived you, gave you birth? Before I married Purush? Before I left his home? When should I have sat and thought it all out?'

Didi walked towards the kitchen door.

'I want,' proclaimed Baby, puffy in the face, swollen in voice, 'my father, my Bhai Chacha ...'

'Leave your chacha and father out,' advised Sita, advancing into the kitchen. 'You know nothing ...'

'Then why doesn't anybody tell me? I'm big now. I understand everything.'

Didi smiled at the thought of her daughter understanding everything.

'See? Amma, you never have an answer. Never.'

'There are no answers, Baby.' Didi held the doorknob, twisting it and absently thinking that it would fall off soon. So many things in this house needed replacing. 'It's about making do with what you chose and and what you got.'

Didi left the kitchen.

'Amma!' shouted Baby. 'Wait. Wait. When I grow up, I will do what you have done: leave you for a man, two men, three men, four …'

The birthday drive ended outside a bungalow. It was empty but for the mango trees in flower and suddenly she could smell 3, Chor Bagh again. Mr Hamer took her in and unlocked the front door. The house was furnished, clean, but stuffy in its emptiness. He told her it was waiting for an occupant and he wondered if she would like to grace it.

Didi was bewildered. Why didn't he 'grace it', as he put it, himself? It was far superior to his hotel suite.

He shook his head and walked out to sit on the top step of the veranda.

This was his wife's house, he explained. It had belonged to her family, for generations, yes, generations.

'She liked to spend the weekends here. Family and friends came to stay too. It was a house filled with the sounds of people on holiday. When she fell ill and there was no possibility of recovery, she came here.'

He pointed to the front room. Didi saw a teak-wood bed with a big headboard. A green shaded lamp on a square table. Bottles of medicines still filled with pills.

One armchair. No curtains.

'She didn't like curtains,' he said, the hint of a cry still lingering in his voice. 'She wanted the outside world to join her inner space. She died on that bed, yes, that bed. I was with her. She did not die alone.'

'We all die alone,' Didi commented dryly.

'No.' He shook his head. 'That is not true. I am always with her, even when she isn't here.'

Didi did not contradict him: she didn't want to spoil the moment.

'Why don't the children come here for a holiday?'

'Too busy. They live so far away. When they go on holiday, they prefer to visit other places. They come here only to be with me. They don't have time for an old house like this.'

'But you, *you* have plenty of time.'

'I cannot live in her house. I would be constantly reminded of her. Those weekends were most special. It was just the two of us, no telephone, no hotel, no visitors, just us. Now, there is only the hotel, no her, no family.'

Didi gazed into the shaded bedroom, up at the sunlit mango trees.

Maybe, she thought, like her, I could let the outer world fill my inner spaces.

In the car, he asked her, 'Will you?'

She replied, 'I will.'

'How could you?' shouted Baby when Didi told her.

'He's a friend,' replied Didi.

'He's *your* friend,' Baby shot back, 'nothing to me. Nothing.'

Didi considered gathering this turbulent girl into her arms. That was the only way to resist the temptation of slapping her. Baby had turned away and was striding out of the room. Didi pulled her back by her long braids, Baby screamed and her head fell against Didi's bosom. 'Ouch!' Didi strapped the wriggling girl to her. 'Be still, Baby.'

'Won't,' gulped Baby. 'You're horrid.'

'Horrid, porridge ... At least see the house.' Didi stroked her forehead.

Baby became still, alert.

'If I don't like it, I don't have to live there?'

Baby's head heaved along with Didi's sigh.

'If you really don't want to, I promise to send you to hostel.'

'No ji,' Sita interrupted. 'Hai hai, Mem! Two big strong women cannot look after one little girl? She will stay here, with us, until he comes and takes her away.'

'Who's *he*?' asked a puzzled Didi, kissing her daughter.

'A ghost,' Baby squirmed with delight. 'Bhoot.'

'I mean he who is your future,' explained Sita.

'I don't want to get married or be kissed.' Baby suddenly dropped from Didi's arms onto her haunches. 'And if I do, the man will drive up in a Mercedes, yes, a Mercedes, and take me far, far away from the two of you old women.' She turned to Didi. 'Then you can live in his house with him and Sita can press his hairy legs.'

When Baby visited the house the first time, she refused to enter it. She slouched outside in the garden, going from mango tree to mango tree and sniffing the bark.

'This one's as old as Dadi, this one is about Sita's age, this one is lean like my father, this one mean like my mother and this,' she leaned against the one nearest to the house, small compared to all the others, 'is dainty like me.'

She never said a word about the house to Didi. When the packing started, she slunk about in sullen silence. The day the truck removed all their belongings and a taxi stood outside, she climbed in without pleasure or protest.

'The mango trees remind me of home,' she confided in Sita. 'That's the reason I have agreed to live there.'

'Whatever,' replied Sita with folded hands, 'makes you happy.'

The house became Didi's refuge. It was cool, quiet, secluded. Safe. Here, in the shade of the litchi and mango trees, along the narrow gravel path from the gate to the veranda, she would stroll up and down until her legs ached. Then she would sit on the white wicker chair in the veranda and gaze at the garden.

The only person she visited was Mr Hamer, at his hotel. Baby still scowled each time she set out, but Didi ignored her.

He remained unperturbed by Baby's reactions to him, by what may have been the public speculation about him and Didi. When Didi complained to him about Baby, or narrated the tales Sita brought back from the town, he merely stroked his fading locks.

'Baby is a child and the people of the town don't matter.' And he turned the conversation elsewhere.

Didi stared at him. What was the point of talking to someone who did not listen?

But he did listen, over the fragrant steam of Earl Grey, to her stories of Purushottam and Som Devi, Mem and Father, the day Father died, the evening she saw *Gone with the Wind* with Bhai, the night Baby was born ... Didi told him everything. And in the telling, she found release, the comfort of knowing that there was one person in the world who knew the truth about everything. It was like a confessional, the hotel, and Didi always left lighter in spirit than she had arrived.

He seldom talked about his family – a letter sent, a card received, a phone call missed, an arrival expected.

'You say nothing,' she complained once. 'I lay out my life like a durree on the grass and you just sit on it!'

'I don't experience the need to talk about myself.'

'No, you just like to waste a lot of money!'

Mr Hamer liked to buy her gifts. Books. A shawl. A handbag. The sort of things he seemed to instinctively realize she would never purchase. She accepted these without demur, never offering anything in return. He said her company was enough.

'I don't have anything else.' She knocked the bridge of her nose.

The first time he slid an envelope across the table, she pushed it back.

'No.'

'This is what you need more than anything else. This is the most invisible gift. Baby need never know and you can spend some of it on her. Or save it for her marriage.'

Briefly, Didi wondered whether the difficulty she experienced in swallowing was the constriction of her circumstances. Was she the kind of woman who lived off a man?

Did she have a choice? She still took tuitions but few students were willing to pay what she demanded. Besides, the schools were offering after-class tuitions themselves and there were many more home tuition options with younger teachers. So she needed more money, but felt uncomfortable accepting it in return for nothing.

She had asked him one night, sitting in the hotel's restaurant that had long since been abandoned by its guests: 'Mr Hamer, is there something you want ... other than my company over dinner?'

He gazed out to where the hill dropped out of sight, sipping his coffee delicately. To Didi it appeared as if he were drinking in the night, filling an inner emptiness with something just as intangible.

'I suppose,' he said, placing the coffee cup on the table, 'it is difficult to understand that a man simply wishes to sit out here and listen. But why is that surprising? I am solitary; there is no one who needs me. I have more than I need, and my children don't need more. I have little conversation. You? You talk about yourself, you dance with yourself, you cook food Sita will not eat, you're different, yes, different.'

She placed the cup on the saucer.

'You're being silly.'

'You place so little value on yourself?'

'My record is poor. I feel I should give you more in return than my ... behaviour.'

He offered her a cigarette, which she accepted, and more tea, which she declined.

'I do not wish for more. I am growing old.' He held the cup to his lips and was about to take a sip. Then, he hesitated as though arrested by a thought. 'But you, I never thought ... perhaps, you ...?'

'No, no,' exclaimed Didi with a shudder. 'I have had enough. Never again.'

Never again, Didi told herself, would she permit her feelings to come in the way of her life. It had happened twice and each time others suffered the consequences.

Seated out there in the companionable silence of the night, she felt she ought to reach out to Mr Hamer despite her own reluctance, touch him in gratitude for being close enough to keep his distance from her.

But suppose he misunderstood, suppose they both learned to feel again?

No, that had ended for her. The day Bhai went missing.

DELHI
1962

The day Bhai went missing during the India–Pakistan Test match, Didi had retreated into the recesses of her mind. This withdrawal widened into an unbreachable divide between the other household members and Didi. Then, Mahendra had arrived and taken her back with him to Delhi. She spent her days in the veranda and the garden of his house. She sat out in the open, confined to the inner core of her being where no one could find her. She said she was searching for her misplaced self.

That was how Bhai found her, one morning, six weeks after she had left 3, Chor Bagh.

Didi turned as the gate creaked open and a slim shadow reached out.

'Didi,' Bhai murmured. She let her head sink as though it was too heavy to hold upright.

'Didi, I …'

'Bhai Chacha, Bhai Chacha, it's him, he's here.' Baby's tongue raced faster than her little legs could carry her down the corridor and out into Bhai's outstretched arms.

For the rest of the day, Baby monopolized Bhai, never once allowing him a moment alone with Didi or Mahendra. She insisted she would sleep with him at night.

'Otherwise you might run away like a bhoot into the dark.'

'Sita, go away,' ordered Baby in her mother's tone, 'only Bhai Chacha and Baby. Yes?'

Bhai clasped her outstretched hand.

'Yes.'

The next morning, the sun brushed aside the clouds as Baby threw off the quilt and leapt out of bed, pulling Bhai with her. He stumbled out into the veranda.

The deep sky, high, light, weightless. A white aircraft, so small in the distance you could measure it between two fingers, chalked a straight line across its blueness. A tiny white bird chased after it a moment later. Then, an abrupt commotion in the clutter of leaves and three crows emerged, in mortal dispute.

It was the perfect Delhi spring morning.

Didi sat immobile as though she had not moved since the previous night. Baby jumped onto her lap, disturbing the still arrangement of her body. Didi mechanically moved her knees for 'horsie'. Bhai sat down beside her.

'Bas,' Didi placed the child's feet on the ground. 'Amma is tired.'

'Amma always tired, Amma always has a headache. I'll ride Sita. Sita, arre o Sita ... Amma says leave all your work and play with me! Issi minute!'

She scampered into the house. Bhai chuckled.

Didi moved a hand to stretch the sari across her belly. Bhai reached out to cut through the heaviness of her silence but Didi grated her chair back.

'There's no need.'

Bhai snatched his hand and back gnawed the knuckle. 'I just wanted you to know I am here. That I've come ... to take you home. We'll take better care of you. I promise. You can do what you like. Really, Didi, Purush says it's fine with him too. I have told him that Ma read too much into your coming with me to the bookstore ... I had to reassure him,' he finished lamely.

Didi's smile was so secret, it remained hidden.

He reached out again and this time captured her hand.

'Didi? What is it? What's happened to you? Tell me.'

He squeezed her fingers so hard, her bones groaned.

'Didi, what you want is fine, just fine with me. Only, please talk. I promise nothing more will happen.'

Bhai's voice petered out like a trail that had lost its way.

A door squeaked and Mahendra emerged from the house. Bhai dropped Didi's hand.

'I was just saying,' he muttered wiping his hands on his kurta, 'it is time for Didi to come home. It's been a long while. Everyone is asking.'

Mahendra scorched Bhai with his eyes.

'Let them. She is in this state because of you and your family, understand?' He observed Didi's face. 'I will say no more, here.'

'But why is she crying?' Bhai demanded, bending to peer at Didi's face. 'Didi, I promise I won't let any harm come to you. Trust me.'

'I'd rather trust Bal Gopal with butter first,' whispered Mahendra.

Bhai crossed his toes, inclined his head towards Didi. She pulled away and in haste, rose and stepped on the grass barefoot. A crow flew over her head and she crouched, sheltering her head with her arms, crying out, 'Nahin, nahin.'

Mahendra and Bhai rushed forward. Half the skeleton of a small claw lay on the grass beside Didi. Mahendra cast it into the flowerbeds.

'You're a bad omen for her. Understand?' he told Bhai with a glare and strode away.

'Why does he dislike me so?' Bhai whispered to Didi. His thin face crumpled in anxiety.

Bhai waited, irresolute, but when Didi made no move to detain him, he got up and followed Mahendra into his study.

'Lock it.'

Bhai bolted the door. He shook in his tall reed frame, as if his body had lost all muscular control.

Mahendra looked out of the window.

'She sits out in the cold for hours doing nothing. What did you do to her?' He spun around to Bhai who had sat down opposite him.

'I don't know.' Bhai stared just beyond Mahendra's eyes, so their eyes did not have to meet. 'The night of the riots? Claimed she had seen incidents, weird images ... but nothing happened near our house that night ...'

Mahendra reached out and grasped the window frame.

'Under normal circumstances,' he said, 'we would be rejoicing. Under normal circumstances we would be celebrating Didi's good fortune. But these are not normal circumstances. Are they?'

Bhai twitched the sleeves of his kurta.

'I'm not sure I know what you mean.'

'You will understand when I tell you ...'

'What?' Bhai inquired.

With his back to Bhai, Mahendra began to speak.

'Under the circumstances,' he concluded, 'we feel Didi must not be disturbed further. So, she stays here until this is over. We want none of you here. Understand?'

He slapped the table as Bhai struggled to his feet.

'I promised her,' Mahendra added, 'I would not tell you. So be careful what you say, understand?'

Mahendra rustled the files on the desk.

'If anything happens to my sister, I will not spare any of you.'

There was a knock at the door.

'Coming!' Mahendra responded. 'Why aren't you married?' he asked abruptly.

Bhai shook his head.

Mahendra fingered his tie, tightened it and walked out of the room, leaving Bhai with a fist in his mouth.

'Behaving like he's Didi,' Mahendra muttered to himself in the corridor, 'as though they've taken a vow not to speak.'

After a few minutes, Bhai went out to the veranda. Didi's chair was vacant. He found Sita in the backyard, hanging out clothes to dry.

'Where's Didi, Sita?' Bhai wiped his face with the sleeve of his white kurta.

'Why should I tell you? You decide to visit us, and immediately you make her cry ...'

Bhai squinted and tugged at his hair.

'Where is she now, Sita?'

'In her room, lying down. And you're not to go there.'

Bhai took a step back.

'I wasn't going to enter her bedroom.'

'It's not the first time,' remarked Sita.

Bhai retreated into the shadows of the house. He didn't emerge from his room all day.

Baby came to scratch his door. Sita scolded her: 'Can you not hear ... he is sleeping?'

'Sita, don't be so silly, how can I hear him sleep?'

'Aah,' Sita replied wisely, 'that is the secret power of those who listen to what they're told.'

That evening, when Mahendra returned, Didi was still outside, in the chill. The cold was descending with all the majesty of a royal entry: slow, ponderous, rich and heavy.

Away from Delhi, Didi had longed for its winter afternoons in the sun and the nights around a bonfire. This year, she wanted to stand naked against the white of the moon at the coldest hour of the night, till she stiffened into limpness.

She didn't communicate this desire to any one. Secrecy permitted her many hours, days of morbid pleasure in solitary contemplation, thinking how best to punish herself. She should have stopped herself in the storeroom. The night Bhai went missing, she should have rushed forward into the night's darkness, ended it all there and then. But Sita had held her back and Baby tugged at her heartstrings.

Didi hugged the memories to herself.

She was thinking that the night was particularly chilly when Mahendra collapsed next to her with a cup of tea in his hand, his slurps loud and appreciative.

'Come, let's go inside, Didi, it's cold here and we must talk.'

Didi saw the steam rise into his face.

'As though,' she commented, 'the one has anything to do with the other.'

He grinned.

'Say it out here.'

'No, in private.'

Didi stretched out a hand and patted his arm.

'You think you can keep it a secret forever?'

Didi covered her face with her pallu.

'Until it's over,' her muffled voice said.

'Why?'

Didi got up and stood behind him. She began to massage his shoulders.

'You're my older brother, Mahendra,' she evaded, 'good and loyal.'

There was a footfall, then Bhai's silhouette crept into view by the light of the corridor lamp.

Mahendra shifted so that his shadow stretched like darknesss between Didi and Bhai.

'Didi,' he said, his voice suddenly loud, 'Bhai agrees with me that it is better if you stay here just now and enjoy the Delhi weather. Isn't that so, Bhai?'

Bhai emerged into the light.

'Yes, of course.'

Didi released Mahendra's shoulders, shrugged open her hair, crossed over to the rose bushes and snatched at the stems till her fingers oozed a crimson stickiness.

'I wish I was a rose bush in your garden.'

Mahendra strode across to Bhai.

'You see what you have done to her? There's no understanding her!'

He turned away and went to join Didi. 'Roses, Didi,' he said, tightening the shawl around her shoulders, 'wither away quickly.'

'Oh, I wouldn't mind …'

'Didi …' He enfolded her shoulders in his large arms.

'Don't be silly, Mahendra,' Didi whispered, 'there's Baby.'

She wiped her eyes and nose on his tie.

'Get it dry-cleaned.'

'Food!' Prem called out from behind Bhai.

As they went inside, Mahendra stalled Didi at the door. 'Promise you'll remain here, until …'

Didi recited, *It is too late to depart I must stay here with my hurt.*

Mahendra turned to Bhai and asked, 'Does that mean she will stay?'

An hour after dinner, Bhai joined Didi in the veranda once again. The overhead lamp shone on Bhai's forehead, highlighting its deepening lines. He examined his fingernails intently.

'Mahendraji is right, Didi. You ought to stay here as long as you like. I will make everything alright. I will explain it to them, Purush …'

'I don't care,' Didi rasped.

He sat down on the step near her.

'Don't care?'

'Only for Baby.'

'Yes, of course, Baby, yes.'

Didi walked away to lean against a pillar.

'Bhai?' she whispered to herself. 'You were like ... I don't want to talk about that,' she added aloud. She pulled back her hair and twisted it into a knot.

'It's decided then.' Bhai's voice was small and tight as though he held it in his fist. 'You stay here as long as you think it's necessary.'

Bhai reached out and captured her right hand.

'Let me look at your fate line,' Bhai said.

'Left for women,' replied Didi as she stuck it out.

'I always thought of you as someone who went against fate,' he observed, rubbing the lines on her palm with his thumb.

'And see where it has got her!' Sita pronounced as she came towards them with a glass of milk. She placed it on the table and disappeared.

'The storeroom was full of sunshine,' Didi murmured to Bhai suddenly.

Bhai shrugged.

If there was a moon, it had hidden behind the clouds, for it shed no light on them now. In the darkness there only remained the clicking of the beetles, and the ragged sound of human breathing.

'Rest now.'

'You too.'

'You need it more. In your condition.'

'What condition?'

She straightened up and turned on him, her elbow jerking into his solar plexus.

He looked straight at her.

'Only that Mahendraji ... says you are weak ... very weak and the doctors advise complete rest. What else?'

He tugged at her arm, drawing her close. Just then a cold wind blew them apart.

'Didi, may I ask a question?' Before she could reply, he continued, 'None of my business, so you don't have to answer... of course it is only natural ... I simply assumed ...'

Didi kept her eyes on the night.

'Didi, while we were ... I mean, you ... Purush ...?'

Bhai pushed back his sleeves, adjusted his kurta collar, opened and closed its buttons.

'Never mind.'

Didi gave his hand a perfunctory pat.

'Let me be for a while with the night.'

Bhai left the next day. Before leaving, he went to Didi's room and finding it locked, raised his hand to knock and then paused. He turned and walked away, out to Mahendra's car.

The following week saw no change in Didi's routine or behaviour. She sat in the veranda, a blanket around her knees, often knuckling her nose. She was thinking.

The days ran seamlessly into each other, but her thoughts collided as she considered her predicament. She began to realize that there was only one way ahead: whatever had to happen, must happen; but it had to be at 3, Chor Bagh, behind its closed doors. Not sitting out here in the sunlight of Mahendra's life.

It took a few days of argument to convince Mahendra. By the time she boarded the train, almost two months had passed since she had left 3, Chor Bagh.

As the taxi approached the lane that climbed straight up to the bungalow, Baby pulled down the window and flung her head out.

'I'm coming,' she hooted. 'Wait for me!'

Before the car could halt, Sita had opened the door and Baby clattered out, falling to scrape her knees as Budhoo launched himself upon the little girl.

Didi watched in dismay and disgust.

'This is what happens here. Someone always gets hurt.'

Didi's unexpected return to her husband's home created an air of puzzlement that hung from the cobwebs clinging to the corners of the ceiling, too high for Som Devi's ageing vision to detect. Everyone wondered what had prompted Didi's sudden and unexpected appearance. On his return from Delhi, Bhai had spoken of Didi as frail and sickly, and as planning to stay away indefinitely.

Now here she was, pale, frail, certainly – and completely – withdrawn, but she went about the house and her chores with ease. So what, if anything at all, was the matter with her? Som Devi, Purush, and Bhai, each had an explanation.

Som Devi believed Bhai had lied to her.

Purush believed Didi had lied to everyone.

Bhai believed Mahendra had lied to him.

Meanwhile, Budhoo snuggled at Didi's feet.

'Dadima wants to know why you not tell her,' said Roop, oiling Didi's hair with her crabbed fingers, one morning soon after her return. 'Why,' she whispered into Didi's ear, 'the secret, hain?'

'Don't knit your fingers so,' Didi replied, 'this is my hair, not wool.'

'Then ask your Sita, who thinks no end of herself, to give you a massage. Why call me?' Roop pressed Didi's temples with greasy thumbs.

'Because Sita's fingers are as fat as potatoes,' remarked Didi.

Roop took time out from her task to clap her hands in delight and emit a cackle. 'But,' she continued, returning to her task, 'why not tell of your coming, hain? I heard Bhaisahib tell Dadima, he would have come to pick you up, if only he knew.'

Didi extended her limbs and let the sun catch their extremities. She was seated under the mango tree. It was a flawless spring morning, clear and sharp.

'Everyone,' accused Roop, 'is surprised.'

'Bas,' Didi ordered, 'enough of your needle-like fingers. Knit and purl, knit and purl …'

Roop flounced off to the kitchen, to renew speculation about Didi with Maharaj.

When the inhabitants of 3, Chor Bagh, shook off their bewilderment, they began to circle Didi, trying to sniff out the truth. Each one did so individually, wanting to be alone with their discoveries.

For Purush it was the bedroom. Here, in its privacy, he was sure of what he wanted, uncertain of how to obtain it; his life alternated between the two conditions, swinging from desire to impotence. It was in this room and on that bed that he had vanquished her and failed himself. It was here, behind drawn curtains, that he had humiliated her with his intimate demands and she belittled him by her passive acquiescence.

The day of her return, listening to the commotion of her arrival, he had shakily sought refuge in Bhai's toilet. He smoked, listening for the return of normalcy. Then he resumed his sentinel place on the sofa, remaining there like he did every other day. At the dining table, he kept his head firmly bent over his thali, although his knees hesitated beneath. He heard the tinkle of her glass bangles, her murmured instructions to Baby, smelt her perfume, but he refused to look up.

At night, he drank a little more than usual, alone in the green glow of a table lamp.

'Go to sleep,' Som Devi had advised, noticing his upright silhouette on the sofa as she passed by, 'don't let her keep you from your bed.'

When he had creaked down beside her, she was hissing sleep through her teeth. When he stretched awake next morning, she was missing. From the sofa, he saw her seated beneath the mango tree with her back to him. Later, shaking out the folded newspaper, he saw her rise and bend over the flowerbeds. His legs leaped up before him: he would approach her, touch her shoulder in the familiar gesture, press himself against her, yes ...

Something about Didi's motionless back discouraged him, defied his approach. Purush felt weak in his urgency, frightened by the memory of past failures.

How he hated what she did to him.

The nights were the most torturous: when loathing and desire mingled, pinned him down to the sofa. He refused dinner, lay stretched out in the darkness of the room, the rising cigarette smoke being the only thing that signalled his presence. At some point, a blanket descended upon him and he felt the peace of the night in its folds. Ma. She always woke up in the middle of the night and walked around the house to make sure its doors were locked firm against intruders. Purush drew her love around him, and vowed that the next day he would go out and buy her a few magazines – she liked reading the knitting recipes.

On the third morning after Didi's return, Som Devi stood behind the sofa, sipping her morning cup of coffee. The prematurely grey day was overcast, bleak and heavy. Purush stared intently into a small mirror and snipped at the fine strands of hair on his ears. Som Devi stared straight ahead. Out on the lawn, wrapped in a shawl, Didi sat reading to Baby who was sprawled upon her lap. Budhoo lay at her feet, snapping at flies.

'So,' Som Devi remarked, 'I should have known from the start.'

She balanced her cup on Purush's head.

'I was think ...'

Purush scrutinized a strand of hair between the scissor blades.

'You know ...'

Purush snapped the mirror shut.

'Why,' Som Devi drained her coffee, 'she never told us.'

'She never tells us anything, so what's new?' he observed, pulling his right ear.

'True, but considering the circumstances,' Som Devi compressed her lips, 'she should have. Especially you, her husband.'

She walked across to the door leading out into the garden and leaned against its frame, contemplating her daughter-in-law.

'She cannot hide it any longer.'

He jerked up his head.

'Hmm,' Som Devi paused, tapping the frame.

Purush studied Didi.

'You,' Som Devi turned back to her son, 'were such a handsome boy.' She approached him and patted Purush's head. 'Fair, light-eyed, sharp features, right body type. Will this one be like you, then?'

Som Devi waited, her hand in his hair. He did not respond. She gave it a gentle ruffle and walked back into the house.

Purush felt damp on his forehead, under his armpits and between his legs.

He watched her from his sofa. She sat unruffled by the breeze that rustled the long strands of her hair and toyed with her sari. He noticed the embroidery of her petticoat, the egg-curve of her ankles and the silver anklets clasped around them. He waited for the petticoat to rise and reveal her calves, waited for her to turn and meet his frantic gaze, but he held his breath in vain. The petticoat remained caught between her legs and Didi sat with her eyes fixed on the flowerbeds.

Purush could not summon the resolve to speak to Didi, and he saw her refuse conversation with others. She turned away from Som Devi, held up her hand when Sita opened her mouth and shook her head when Bhai approached her.

'Tell your mother we know why she doesn't speak to anyone,' Som Devi remarked to Baby at dinner when Bhai's repeated queries about how she felt elicited no response from Didi. 'She is eating her words to swell her belly … like so!' Som Devi rounded the air with her fingers. She tittered.

Purush didn't join them for dinner, despite Som Devi's repeated maternal entreaties. As soon as she retreated, he pulled out the bottle of rum from beneath the sofa and took a few swift gulps, shook his head as the alcohol travelled through his body and gasped.

He lay stretched straight out on the bed, sweating gently, when Didi entered their bedroom.

The crickets played in the background.

She stood before the dressing table, combing her hair in slow, luxurious strokes. He counted to forty-seven before rising to stand behind her, his eyes glazed. Stiffly, he thrust himself forward and seized her by the shoulders. She swayed back and then stumbled forward as she reached out to grasp the mirror with both hands. He pulled at her.

'Now,' he muttered. 'Here. Like this …'

'No.'

'No?' He clamped the bands of his arms around her chest. 'I will.' He pulled her again.

She resisted.

'I,' he jutted into her, 'have the right.'

'Never this.'

'This and everything else, too!'

'Where did that ever get you?'

A breathless wind gasped through the leaves of the trees.

His hands slid down the slope of her stomach. Her muscles retracted.

There was a momentary lull outside, heightening the clamour of the crickets' song.

'You entertain others,' he said, staring at her belly, 'and refuse me?'

'I …'

He pushed her, and she fell against the mirror. He strode away, circling the room as though searching for an escape.

'I will have my way, you wait and see. I will tell Ma … and Bhai, tomorrow. Yes, I shall … You think you can get away with this, again?'

She walked across to the bed, sat down and knuckled the bridge of her nose.

'Stop it!' He slapped away her hand. 'I hate it when you do that.'

She tucked her hands under her thighs.

The breeze and the crickets had fallen silent.

'I don't think,' she said, exhaling slowly, 'you need tell any one. What will it say about you, if you do?' Didi lay on the bed carefully, like a freshly ironed garment. 'You'll just make a fool of yourself. Better to pretend. Spare,' Didi said, turning her head to look into his beaded face, 'yourself.'

He pressed a fist into his stomach.

The crickets resumed their clatter.

She folded her hands over her heart, closed her eyes.

'Whose?'

He came to stand over her.

'You,' he shook, 'rubbish dump.'

Licking his lips, he strode across to the side table and poured himself three successive glasses of water, which he swallowed in huge, hurried mouthfuls. 'Showing everyone your shame.' He returned to the side of the bed.

'That first night, if you had let me get there, things would have been different. But you,' he dabbed his handkerchief on his mouth, 'you never gave me a chance.'

She smoothed a hand over her hair.

'We have tried many, many times since,' she said. 'A man should be able to … All you ever do is lie limp on the sofa.'

He put a hand to his cheek, slapped by the contempt in her voice. He crossed over to the door leading into the garden, opened it a fraction and retched for breath.

'Your grandfather came with the proposal. And this is how you treat me.'

He went to the table for another glass of water.

'Why?' He banged the glass down. 'What have I done to you?'

At that, she opened her eyes, wide.

'Done?' she responded. 'Exactly. Nothing, you've done nothing. Whatever I did has been before and after you. But you … nothing. Ever since that first night …'

He wound his index finger around the edge of his kurta.

'Each time you come to me, it's the same story. You say my grandfather made the proposal. But did you, did anyone here tell him you didn't have a job, would never have a job, and could never get the job done?'

'That's your doing,' he blurted out.

She turned towards him.

'You lie there all day on the sofa, as if you have no limbs. You let your brother work for the entire family. You drink and eat your kebabs and pakoras like you're some sort of maharaja. You can do nothing, nothing.'

'Bas.' He put out a hand. 'You betray your husband, you flaunt it in my face, make me look like a gadha, a complete fool. What are you?' He thought he had shouted, but all that emerged was a hoarse squeak.

'I begged them,' she whispered, 'begged them not to get us married. I wept at my father's feet and pleaded with him, but he said he could not disobey his father. And with Dada dying …' She stopped. 'Who listens to a woman or her wishes?'

'I'll …'

'You'll what?' she asked and began to cry.

The door shuddered from the force of his departure.

The wind resumed its restless journey through the trees.

The crickets held their chorus line.

In the sitting room, Purush drank the remnants of the rum in the bottle, neat. His eyes fluttered, a sniffle escaped his nose.

Later, much later, when he had slumped into slumber, something soft and warm covered him. He curled up, reached out.

'Stay, Ma …'

The fingers withdrew.

Purush thought he recognised the tinkle of glass bangles, the smell of her perfume.

Som Devi preferred the delayed approach. She displayed no hurry in cornering her prey. She watched her sons – Purush's agitation, Bhai's solicitous consideration of his sister-in-law – and she prayed for their souls. She observed Didi's stillness in the garden and Purush's on his sofa. She blamed Didi for turning him against himself.

'Like a moorthi,' she confided to Bhai, 'she has carved him into one of those statues in the temples,'

'Ma,' replied Bhai, 'they may both be to blame.'

No use speaking to him, Som Devi realized. She should never have agreed to Didi accompanying Bhai to the bookstore last summer. But she had done so, and by the time she trained her shrewd eyes upon her elder son and her daughter-in-law, and penetrated their secret, Bhai had gone missing and Didi had begun her 'drama', as Som Devi called it, of being ill.

When the doctor who had come to examine her ordered complete bed rest and peace for Didi, Som Devi remonstrated, 'What could happen to her? *Hatti-katti*, she is hale and hearty.'

'Ma,' Bhai protested, 'the doctor thinks she has had a nervous breakdown.'

'Breakdown? Is she your father's Oldsmobile that she has had a breakdown?'

When Mahendra rang to say he would come and take Didi to Delhi, Som Devi agreed with alacrity. It was best to separate Didi from Bhai, and perhaps Baby too. She said as much to Mahendra when he arrived at 3, Chor Bagh.

Mahendra nodded. After meeting Didi, he told Som Devi that Didi wanted to take Baby with her.

At the dinner table that night, Som Devi tried again.

'Baby, tell your mother that her condition is not healthy for a little girl. Poor thing.' She gave Baby a kind look. 'What,' she added, looking innocently at Bhai, 'do you think? Is it not in the interest of the child that she be spared the sight of her mother like this, in the middle of her ... what did you call it ... downpour?'

'Breakdown, Ma.' Bhai's fingers of food approached his mouth several times and then returned to the thali. 'I think we ought to leave the decision to Didi.'

'But she, you said the doctor says, is having a nervous disease ...'

'Not disease, Ma, breakdown.'

'Yes, but I am only asking,' Som Devi spooned more vegetable into his plate and then her own, 'is she good for the child?'

'Who cares about the child? Let them both go.' Purush chewed hard.

'I must say,' Mahendra spoke up, 'I find your attitudes offensive. The way you are discussing my sister. If you will excuse me, I will go and sit with Didi.'

'Bloody rubbish all,' munched Purush. 'Who is he?'

'He is your brother-in-law,' Bhai spoke up, 'and deserves a little civility.'

'Don't teach me manners, or else I will have to teach you ...'

'Just try ...'

'You think I don't know ...' Purush half rose.

'Eat your food, the two of you, and stop arguing,' interrupted Som Devi. 'Baby, stop sucking your fingers. Have more.'

Five minutes later, Didi, shrouded in a white silk sari with tiny blue butis, her hair in a plait, appeared at the dining table. She stood behind her daughter's chair, ran a hand over her head.

'Come,' she said, 'you're going with me.'

And she had left with Baby. Only to return when she decided to. Som Devi felt the injustice of it all. But her love for Baby prevented her from saying too much in reproach.

Baby was what saved Som Devi.

'See, see how weak my Baby is,' Som Devi remarked the first day of their return to 3, Chor Bagh. 'You have become so thin, I can't see you.'

'Then play hide and seek, Dadi!' laughed the little girl.

'Little red pepper,' said Som Devi with affection. 'Chal, come here and tell your Dadi what you want to eat.'

Som Devi would sit out in the sun with Baby, kneading oil into Baby's body the way she used to after she was born. Then, there were the afternoons of hide and seek: she sought and Baby hid, mostly behind the mango tree or in the folds of the thick velvet curtains in the bedrooms. Som Devi knew exactly where to look because Budhoo showed her the way with a series of yelps; but she made a huge fuss, deliberately searching in the wrong places until Baby, unable to contain her triumphant excitement any longer, came rushing out.

'Dadi, you're so slow,' she'd clap her hands.

In the evenings, Baby would sit with Som Devi on her bed and comb her long, thinning black-grey hair while Som Devi read the Bhagvad Gita. On a few occasions, she would creep into the little girl's bed at night. These were a special treat for the child.

Baby clutched at her grandmother's waning breasts.

'Say no Dadi, say,' she implored.

'Which?' asked Som Devi, drawing the child's warmth into her chilled bones.

'The one about the girl with blood …'

'Dhat!' scolded Som Devi, 'always, only blood …'

'Say Dadi, say.'

Som Devi needed no further persuasion.

'Once, there was this poor young girl, whose papa and mama had gone to visit the gods. They say the good are always taken up first into heaven. I know this to be true. Only look at my mother, your par-dadi and your dada? Both young and full of life, taken away …'

'The young girl, Dadi …' prompted Baby, chewing the edge of Som Devi's sari.

'I'm telling. Where was I? Yes, so the little girl was left with her chacha and chachi who were loving. Like your Bhai Chacha loves you? Just the same. He's been a very good chacha, I must say, even if he is my own son, always taking you for a ride in the car, buying you toys, bringing books back from the bookstore …'

'Dadi …' Baby nuzzled Som Devi's stomach.

'I'm telling. Yes, the little girl was happy, like you are happy to be back here, no? I must say, I don't know why your mother took you and stayed away so long. Two months and not one word. And as for that Mahendra Mama of yours? I must say, why didn't he ring us? What is it?' she asked as Baby bit her on her breast.

'I'm telling, I'm telling. One day, at the school, the girl found a big piece of white paper, very big … at her feet …'

'But how did it get there, Dadi?'

'Get there? Why, maybe a bird flew it in on its wings, perhaps the wind carried it on its breath, maybe the gods or the devil sent it. Or maybe it was the work of those creatures which roam day and night but cannot be seen by the light of the sun or moon …'

'Oooh,' Baby clung to Som Devi's thin frame, 'how are they to look at, Dadi?'

'How should I know?'

Baby slapped Som Devi's thigh.

'Of course you must know, Dadi. You are telling the story.'

Som Devi laughed.

'You know what was written on the paper?'

'"Careful – when you are alone, we will catch you!"'

'So. Then …'

'Then,' sat up Baby, 'then … another letter dropped at her feet …'

'Five times …'

'Last time you said three …' remonstrated Baby.

'What's the difference? The girl began to have bad dreams.'

Baby placed her head on Som Devi's bony thighs.

'For two days, the little girl did not attend school. She was very frightened. The day she went back to school, she was seated at her desk and was reading an English poem aloud. She liked poetry. Like your chacha; he is fond of poetry, English verse. Did you know? He loved to recite it as a child and won prizes. He had such a lovely voice. Even now, he always reads late into the night.

'So. Last summer, he tried to teach your mother how to read poetry. She was lying about in the house, doing nothing. "Ma," he said, "I will occupy her idle mind." He took her to the bookstore, he asked my permission, of course, and made her read there. "Education, Ma," he said, "is important for the Indian woman of free India." But your mother, what did she do in return?'

'Hai hai, Mem, what does Mataji say about our Didi with me lying here?'

Sita rose from the floor, a fat figure in white, her face obscured by the darkness. Baby screamed.

'Dadi, see, one of those creatures!'

'Oho, I forgot she was here,' sighed Som Devi. 'Anyway, I am saying only right. We know how she returned her gratitude, how she behaved the night when Bhai did not return. I have never thought of such a thing.'

'What do you want to say, Dadi Membsahib? Say clearly.'

'Those who know what I am talking about, know what I am talking about.'

In the dark, the hidden expressions of the two women were tense with dislike.

'Then?' asked Baby.

'Then, this Sita makes me forget where I was ...'

'In my Baby's bed,' replied Sita, asking forgiveness from Mem for the impertinence.

'Shhh, Sita, you sleep or go to Amma's room,' ordered Baby.

'Amma's room? Even her husband is not welcome there,' remarked Som Devi.

In a flash, Sita stepped forward.

'You say any more about my Didi—'

'What is left to say? Can I not see with my eyes?'

Baby put a finger on her grandmother's lips.

'Tell story.'

Som Devi glared at the darkness that hid Sita.

Baby pinched Som Devi on the arm.

'The little girl, Dadi, was reading poetry when she looked down ...'

'And screamed!' continued Som Devi. 'There on the floor, what was lying?'

Baby clapped her hands.

'Blood ... fat drops of blood!'

'Oooh.'

'She screamed, and all the other girls screamed too ...'

'Eeeeeeh,' essayed Baby, 'like that?'

'One thing,' called out Sita, 'you can never get is any sleep in this house.'

'Chacha and Chachi were called and the little girl told the entire story, weeping. On the fourth day she went to school and in the English class, she found drops of blood by her desk. She was white by now, like your nails which need cutting in the morning. So long they have grown, you will draw blood ...'

'Blood,' repeated Baby with evident pleasure, 'khooooon.'

'I don't know why your mother and your great Sita do not look after you. Every Sunday morning, oil hair, cut nails ...'

'Blood, Dadi ...'

'I'm telling. Two nights later, the little girl woke up and switched on the light to go to the bathroom. The window was open. She shouted. What was it?'

'Blood,' said Baby, helpfully.

'So. In a circle like this chain,' Som Devi pulled out the gold one around her neck. 'Chacha and Chachi came running. Who had done this wickedness?'

'Any doubt?' said Sita in a muffled voice, 'It is the Chachi and Chacha. They don't want to keep the girl …'

'Sita, you are spoiling the story,' complained Baby.

'And you are spoiling my sleep,' retorted Sita, 'but who cares about that?'

'Dadi …'

'I'm telling. Next night, the police surrounded the house. When you wait, the hands of the clock seem to be sleeping. Ask me. I, too, have waited outside doors, waited and watched what happens in this house behind darkness. They think I don't know, but I know everything … Did I not see my son standing outside her room? Did I not see when they went up to the roof? And then when she was at his window? I know it all. But I say nothing.'

'This story will never end,' complained Baby.

'I'm ending. It was very late when the girl stood in the darkness by the bed. The policeman outside switched on his torch. The girl had scissors in her hand and was poking it into her finger.'

'Khoooon,' whispered Baby.

'Phir then. Dripping. Her eyes were bilkul open, not blinking. The police called Chacha. He shook her gently. "Beti, beti why did you do this?" The girl replied, "I am calling my parents, they will smell my blood and take me away." So. Her eyes were locked firm as my Godrej locks. Then she lay down and fell asleep. Next morning, she did not remember one thing.'

'Then?' asked Baby.

'They say the spirits of her mother and father had entered her.'

'Will they take her away? Will they stay inside her forever and ever?'

'I don't know, but I hope they will. Every child needs a papa and a mama. Like you … Now,' Som Devi tightened the sheet and quilt around Baby, 'the end tomorrow.'

Dutifully, Baby placed her head upon Dadi's lap.

'Amma always tells to the end,' she complained. 'Always.'

'Arre, your amma, what to say of her!' Som Devi patted Baby on the head in a rhythmic beat. 'Does what she likes.' She thumped Baby on the head.

'What?' asked a sleepy Baby.

'This time? I will see how she does what she wants. Phir then.'

Som Devi fell silent and so did the room. Sita took Mem's name in silence. She feared for Didi.

While Som Devi watched and waited, Bhai was losing weight.

'Thinning,' his mother told the dining table, 'slim as a spinach leaf. Eat more.'

Bhai ate more but appeared to shrink further. His long hair dangled aimlessly about his pinched face, often hiding it from view. His cotton trousers began to slip down the straight line of his stomach till Som Devi gave him a pair of black braces that belonged to his father.

'If only,' she added, 'they could hold up your spirit too. What is the matter, Bhai? You should be the happiest member of this house, seeing how fond you are of your Didi and Baby. Their return should give you much joy.'

'I am happy, Ma. I am. Now, I must leave for work.'

During Didi's absence from 3, Chor Bagh, Bhai had found himself in the wrong place whichever way he turned. If he was with Purush, he suffered from the knowledge that he had been with his wife; when he encountered Som Devi's needle eyes, he felt the sharpness of her rebuke and turned away in embarrassment. Mahendra had filled him with shame, and just thinking of Didi confronted him with a choice between desire and renunciation.

When he first saw Didi alight from the taxi, Bhai had felt joy and apprehension. He had wanted her to return, but now that she was here, he had no idea how to behave. He had given his word to Mahendra that he would not speak of Didi's condition, but he hated the secrecy.

He wondered, he brooded, he chased his worst fears round the circles of his cluttered mind: whose baby was Didi carrying? If it was not his, that meant Didi ... and Purush ... But how could Didi have been with both? And how was he ever going to ask her?

At dinner, he would glance at Didi and picture the sunlight in the storeroom of the bookshop. Then, he would turn to his brother and imagine the darkness of their bedroom. He felt sorry for all of them. He began to hope, believe that the child might redeem them all. Didi would not return to the bookstore after the child. He would not ask it of her. That was over. It was over the night he went missing. His sole aim now was to establish the paternity of the child; then, everyone could return to their prearranged lives.

Didi, however, did not permit him any intimacy. Whenever he sought her out, in the garden, in the kitchen courtyard, she simply shook her head.

'Not now,' he heard her murmur, 'not now.'

He sought out Baby instead, just as his mother did, but his motives were less pure. He thought he might have a word with Didi by being a good chacha to her daughter. He enjoyed Baby, but part of her charm for him was her mother. With Baby on his lap, he could sit next to Didi in the garden; with Baby around his shoulders, he could walk into her bedroom and sit on the bed where she lay. He could even converse with her.

Baby hung her head out during the drive and wouldn't listen to me.

Baby wants to go to the movies.

Baby ate too much strawberry ice-cream.

Baby has scratched her cheeks on the rose bush.

Baby, Baby, Baby.

Didi responded to these sallies, but never followed up the conversation when he led it astray.

One day, he walked into her room with Baby seated on his shoulders and said, 'Didi, I was telling Baby, the next time we go shopping we might buy you some material for new blouses, you know ...'

'Sita has let out the old ones.'

She pressed her fingers to her temples.

'Something wrong? Shall I get you something?'
Didi turned away.
'I've got a headache.'
'Shall I call the doctor and ask?'
'About a headache? You'll sound ridiculous.'
Offended, Bhai reluctantly put Baby down. He hurried out of the room and collided with Som Devi, stepping on her toes.
'Oh Ma, why do you stand in the middle of the corridor, doing nothing?'
Som Devi rubbed her toes against the back of her calf.
'Don't talk to me like that. With her, your tongue runs soft as silk.'
It was a cloudless full-moon night. Bhai knocked on Didi's door, which was shut as often as it was open since her return from Delhi. Each time Som Devi opened it, Didi closed it or asked Sita to do so.
'Who is it?'
'Chachoo, Chachoo!'
The door swung open and he found Baby scrambling up his legs. He picked her up, smoothed back her golden hair, gazed deeply into her light eyes. He entered the room.
'I've always wondered exactly whom she resembles. Ma claims she looks like her when she was a child, but I don't know how she can be so sure when there are no photographs of her childhood.'
Didi was seated at the dressing table, filing her nails. Sita was folding her sari. Bhai walked across to the dressing table and admired the picture Baby and he made behind Didi in the mirror.
'A little like Chacha.' He chucked Baby's chin. 'Hmm? Didi, what do you say? Maybe the child will grow up to look like me?'
Didi continued to file her nails.
'What do you think?' he asked.
Didi blew on her nails and admired them.
'About what?'
'The child,' he repeated, slowly, deliberately. 'Don't you think there might be a resemblance?'
'I don't know,' she replied, without glancing up at him.

He placed Baby on the floor.

'It's a full moon tonight, have you noticed?'

Didi rose.

'Sita,' she called out, 'Baby's milk.'

'And yours, ji,' added Sita, waddling out. Bhai stood close to Didi, near enough to touch her without allowing his breath to reach her nape.

'What?'

He sighed.

'Let's go up to the roof and look at the moon.'

'Baby will like that.'

Bhai retreated in dismay. He was baffled. He thought back to when she had arrived as a bride, the glint of her distant smiles in the kitchen garden, the elegant sway of her hair, her bold stares and frank words. She had always looked a person in the eye. It was he who blinked first. She had a faint, coquettish archness during the months before that summer in the storeroom; beckoning but restrained. He could never forget the flush of her skin, the sudden, bubbling release of her breath and the gouge of her nails on the small of his back.

Now, in company, Didi treated Bhai with a casual politeness and when they were alone, she deliberately withheld herself from him. He didn't know how to reach her, regain the confidence of her eyes.

It was a solitary, chilling time.

Purush wished Didi would disappear forever.

Som Devi wished Didi would go away, leaving Baby behind.

Bhai wished Didi's baby would look like him.

The inhabitants of 3, Chor Bagh, kept their heads down and ghosted past each other, so as not to attract attention. The long corridor hummed with pigeons nesting in the half-open skylight. Baby rattled her tricycle up and down its emptiness with squeals of pleasure, and Budhoo panted after her.

'Shut up!' Purush would yell out. 'Who said she could cycle down my corridor?'

It was nearly Holi.

The sun shone bright and hot, the days remained virtually still, with a clear light blue sky. The midday temperature rose to twenty-nine degrees centigrade. Then suddenly one morning, the sky was grey, blustery and a light shower splattered the windows. At night, a heavy shower fell. The rain intensified and a cold shiver ran through the city.

Forty-eight hours before Holi, on a pale morning, the inhabitants of 3, Chor Bagh, were being oiled. Bhai stood out in the kitchen garden where the sun was strongest, rubbing mustard oil into his hair.

In her room, Som Devi was just about done with massaging almond oil into her face and neck after a warm bath. She did this each morning, every winter, and claimed it kept her free of wrinkles. Her face may have aged, loosened, but it was unlined. When she smiled, there was a hint of a fold, but never a crease.

Beside her on the bed, Baby lay naked on a towel, kicking the air.

'Dadi, tell a story, na.'

'Na, na,' clucked Som Devi, 'this is no time for stories. This is time for you to have a proper massage. Look at your knees and elbows, like tree bark. That mother of yours and Sita, what do they do all day? Just sit out in the sun. No wonder you are so dry and growing dark …'

'No,' shouted Baby, 'I'm not …'

Som Devi lifted a silver bowl and poured hot mustard oil onto Baby's belly.

'Heeeeeeeh,' giggled the little girl.

'Chup! Your father will set angry if he hears you …'

'Always angry …'

'No, don't say that. My boy is sweet by nature. It's your mother … Now, turn on your back so I can massage your laddoos.'

'Baby wants to eat laddoos, Baby wants to …' crooned the child.

'Shhh, later.'

Purush was seated by the window in Bhai's room, his legs knee deep in a bucket of warm salt water. He was hoping the water would ease the ache in his varicose veins.

From where he sat, Purush could see Didi in the shade of the mango tree.

Roop was combing Didi's hair, Sita massaging her feet.

'Didi memsahib has so much hair, it will take me the entire morning to comb it,' he heard Roop complain.

'What other work have you?' Sita replied.

'Bloody American mem,' muttered Purush and stamped his feet so hard, Budhoo, lying near him, started up with a yelp.

It was then that Purush's chair rocked.

Som Devi noticed the lamps sway.

Bhai felt the ground shudder.

Didi clutched her stomach.

Baby, Roopvati and Sita were far too busy talking to notice.

But Budhoo bayed as he never had before.

For a few seconds, the earth lost control of itself.

From the kitchen garden, Bhai rushed into the dining room through Didi's bedroom and out into the front lawn.

'Didi! Didi!'

The scream was so timorous, Purush jammed both index fingers into his ears and Som Devi started up from her bed. Both of them closed their eyes.

The next morning, Som Devi marched into the dining room, vowing she would never again believe a word in the newspapers. Not one word about the earthquake in the morning paper – how was it possible? Bhai, rising from his breakfast, said he was very surprised. He had definitely seen the veranda pillars move.

Head down, Purush sipped a cup of coffee.

'Purush?'

Som Devi placed a banana on his plate.

Purush returned the banana to the fruit bowl. Som Devi put the banana back on his plate.

Purush said his chair had rattled like dice. He glared at the banana.

'Didi,' asked Bhai, pushing his chair back in place, 'didn't you feel anything?'

Her stomach, she replied, had vibrated. Now would he mind passing her a banana?

Purush's head snapped up, he grabbed the banana on his plate and threw it into the empty space between Bhai and Didi.

Som Devi shook her head. Purush glared at Bhai who clutched the table and dropped his head.

After breakfast, Som Devi rang up Saxenaji, her provision storeman. There was no reply.

Holiday, she told herself, closed, of course.

She went into the sitting room, where Purush was lighting a cigarette.

'Didn't you hear about the earthquake on the radio?'

Purush said he had heard nothing.

'But that means nothing, Ma. All India Radio only tells you what happens in Delhi.'

Midday brought the maali into the picture, and an impatient Som Devi pounced on him.

'What damage has there been to the city?'

'From what,' asked the puzzled maali.

'From the earthquake, what else?'

The maali asked, 'The one when the old Naaz Cinema was half broken and the high court building ...?'

Som Devi twitched her nose, causing her spectacles to jump up and down.

'Talking to you is useless; you are even more stupid than Budhoo. Go, pick up each and every leaf in the garden. I will come and check.'

Maali shrugged and said it was wrong to compare a man to a dog and insult him for telling the truth.

'Ja, ja,' dismissed Som Devi, 'You're a big one for the truth.'

In the kitchen there was much discussion.

'All I remember is Bhaisahib flying through the air towards Didi Memsahib,' Roop told Maharaj. 'He looked so frightened, I thought Badi Memsahib had passed on or what.'

'Maybe,' speculated Sita, 'the earthquake was only in 3, Chor Bagh.'

'Possibly,' came Roop's prompt answer. 'The earth does move every time you walk.'

No one ever found out the truth about the earthquake. But the damage had been done, however invisibly: it would be a long time before Purush looked at his brother or talked to him and when he did, he would hold one knee to prevent it from knocking against the other.

Som Devi stared at her sons, sadly.

'So …' she sighed.

Holi morning. In the distance, drums and dholaks beat in unison along with the sound of singing. At 3, Chor Bagh, there was silence and commotion. Silence in the drawing room; silence from Didi's bedroom, where the door remained closed and the curtains drawn.

On the other side of the house, Som Devi was plastering oil on Baby who was yelling, 'Holi-boli-doli!'

From the kitchen, the aroma of sweetened ghee wafted through the entire house as Maharaj cooked for the festival: gujiyas and jalebis. Roop and Sita squatted in the kitchen veranda, sharing out the colours: vermilion, parrot green, primrose yellow. Baby came outside with a steel water-gun filled with water and sprayed it inside her mouth. Sita shouted at her not to – 'Don't know where that water came from' – and Som Devi told her to stop that noise, her son 'and your memsahib' were still asleep. At this point, Bhai emerged from the shadows, his long locks scraped behind his ears, wearing a crumpled kurta and rumpled pyjamas. In the brightness of the day, he appeared thinner than ever.

'Aise, you look like a beggar on the street. I am saying, what has happened to you, Bhai?'

Bhai touched Som Devi's cheek.

'Let's play Holi, Ma.'

Within half an hour, the garden would fill up with squeals and shouts, yells and yelps and helpless giggles.

'Bachao, bachao!' Baby's pleas went unheeded as Bhai and Sita picked her up, swung her about and deposited her in the aluminium bath tub full of deep red water.

'Khoon, Dadi, khoon,' she whooped as she took the plunge.

Then it was the turn of Dadi and Bhai, who voluntarily and obediently climbed into the tub so that Baby could pour mugs of water on them. Budhoo barked and ran around the tub, wagging his tail in violent appeal.

'Budhoo wants to play Holi?' inquired Baby. 'Budhoo will play Holi,' and she scooped him up awkwardly and helped him into the tub. There was a loud, piercing protest as Budhoo splashed water on Som Devi. She retreated to one side of the tub, but Budhoo caught the dripping pallu of her sari in his teeth.

'Hey bhagvan, where are you?' Som Devi tugged at her sari and tried to climb out. 'Baby, how could you?'

Baby danced around the tub and clapped.

'Chhi-chhi,' Sita's voice called out from a distance. 'You'll all need a bath in Ganga water now.'

'Quiet!' snapped Som Devi, wrenching her pallu from Budhoo's jaws.

'Where's Sita gone?' inquired Bhai. 'Get Sita, Baby.'

Baby took off with Budhoo and Roop in pursuit. Sita was nowhere to be found. The maali joined the hunt, but their efforts were futile.

'Amma's room,' Baby suggested, and burst into Didi's room. There was no Sita, only Didi by the bed. Baby raced away with Budhoo, Roop hobbling valiantly behind her, one fist full of red colour.

'I am coming, Sita,' she warned. 'I am coming.'

There was a clatter on the ladder leading up to the roof.

'Roof, Baby, roof!' Bhai shouted, pointing. 'Look, there's Sita!'

Baby's war cries brought Didi out of her room in a pink chikan sari, her hair flung open behind her. Bhai felt her look straight at him; the soles of his feet burned. He thought back to previous year's Holi when she had played and danced with him, holding his hand. She had eaten a bhang laddoo and fallen asleep in the sun of the lawn. He stepped forward and touched green powder to her cheeks.

'Shagun,' he whispered, 'for good luck.'

She took some colour from his hand and rubbed it hard into his cheeks. He smiled. At that moment, Som Devi came around the corner of the front porch, squeezing water from her sodden sari, muttering to herself. She almost collided with Purush stepping out of Bhai's bathroom. He clutched something small in his left hand and in the right, a bucket.

Bhai fell back.

Purush approached Didi. As he neared, he raised the bucket and flung the contents at her. Blue water slew off Bhai's shoulder as he ducked for cover, but hit Didi in her face, on her arms, neck and chest. Dropping the empty brass bucket, Purush yanked Didi by her arm. She fell against him obediently and he opened the box in his other hand, rubbed his fingers in it and then on her cheeks and forehead, again and again. It was boot polish.

'Now you're black and blue like the dayan you are.'

He backed away down the veranda, into the garden, and spat on the grass.

'A very happy Holi,' he proclaimed with a crooked, lopsided smile. 'Ma, where is your granddaughter? Let me play Holi with her, too.'

'No.' Som Devi held up her right hand, stood before him. 'Not that.'

Purush laughed.

'Of course not. That,' he flung the box of boot polish into the air, 'was for her.'

Didi stood outside her room, holding her lower lip with her upper teeth as if to steady herself, her face the colour of night.

'Just like Kali Ma,' Som Devi observed with a giggle.

'Ma, please,' gulped Bhai. He shifted the weight of his body from one foot to the other, betraying his indecision.

Som Devi tightened her eyes, pursed her mouth, pale in her translucent skin. 'We know why you speak on her behalf; don't make me say more.'

Bhai's body caved in a little.

'Your own brother ...' added Som Devi.

'I know,' Bhai whispered, his chin receding into his neck. 'I know.'

Didi had returned to her room and bolted the door behind her. A few hours after Purush had blackened his wife's face, she unbolted the door to Sita's persistent knocks. She was still dressed in the pink chikan sari, her hair open, her face mottled with the polish. She smelt damp. Sita led her into the bathroom, stripped off her clothes, made her sit on a stool and began to clean her. She took the scrub and scoured Didi's face and arms, her body. But the stain remained firmly engrained in the pores of her skin.

'Let it be. It will disappear with time.'

Sita reached for a towel and wrapped it around Didi's hair and wrung it out.

'I don't want them to see you like this.'

'Everyone should see me as I am.'

At dinner, Didi ate nothing, choosing to feed Baby instead. Som Devi, Purush and Bhai could not take their eyes off her face.

At night, Didi sat near the door of the veranda, gazing out at the mango tree.

Sita offered her a warm glass of milk.

Didi pushed it aside.

'No.'

She sat there knuckling her nose.

HILL STATION
1986

She sat there knuckling her nose. Whenever she felt the past creeping up behind her to ambush the present, she knuckled the bridge of her nose until there was a purple stain down the middle. She had been thinking of that visit to Mahendra's when Bhai came to take her back to 3, Chor Bagh, and how Purush had smeared the polish on her face that Holi day. She could still feel the black cling to her, like paint to a wall.

'Sita,' she called out, 'come and do your duty – always lying about like a carpet.'

Minutes later, Didi was stretched out on her bed, with Sita muttering to herself by her side.

Didi felt her calves like stone as Sita kneaded them. She flinched, held the sides of the bed. Sita dipped the tip of her fingers in mustard oil and then set to work. Didi thought of Mem. I used to massage her poor arthritic legs. So did Sita. Now Sita is pressing mine. Something wobbled her stomach – a piece of the past she had not digested or evacuated. Didi sniffled. Then she giggled.

'Exercise your fingers the way you do your tongue, Sita,' she ordered. 'My legs are not musical instruments, this soft touch of yours only tickles.'

Sita mercilessly knuckled around Didi's knees. She was in no mood to trade words with Didi today. She was annoyed. It had been three weeks since Baby had returned home from New York, and she wanted to know why Baby drank and smoked so much. Especially after the telephone calls from that man. 'Just let me see that man,' she told Didi, 'just let me see him.'

'See?' Didi asked.

'Yes, I want to see what he looks like.'

'See what he looks like?' repeated Didi. 'Is he the Taj Mahal?'

Sita returned to the kitchen and collapsed on the folding chair that Didi had bought for her. She reached for the vegetable knife and began to clean her nails.

'He did something to our Baby. We should know who he is,' she declared as Didi joined her.

'Some fat lala type,' speculated Didi.

Didi did not ask Baby too many questions about her life in New York. She feared that in return, Baby would want to know about 3, Chor Bagh. As for that 'stinky man' she had heard on the telephone, why, the mere idea of him was sufficient to create a film of revulsion in Didi's mouth.

One afternoon, Didi, urged on by Sita to 'behave more like a conscientious mother', went through Baby's belongings in the suitcases under her bed. Baby had gone for a long walk and Didi summoned Sita into her room. Among the clothes and cosmetics they found a photo album with photographs of Kartik, Sita, Didi, a few American girls, and one of a dark man. Didi studied him, his starched, military moustache, small, entrenched eyes, his swarthy skin and bulky body, and concluded that he was the 'stinky man'. She found him ludicrous.

Sita had scrutinized the photo with the magnifiying glass she used to thread needles.

'Bit,' she said, observing the pores of his skin, 'too black.'

Colour was primary to Sita's judgement of people.

Didi wondered at Baby's preference. Kartik was lean and clean, with thin features drawn by a freshly sharpened pencil. This man was broad everywhere, as though someone had slapped him together with a thick paintbrush. Didi shuddered at the thought of his touch. Didi never mentioned Ramaji to her daughter, that winter of her return. Not that Baby gave her much of a chance. She slept late into the morning, went for long walks in the afternoon and joined her mother in the veranda just before dinner. There was small talk or no talk. Baby made a few phone calls, received some. Didi resisted the temptation to listen in on the calls from the extension; so she did not know who Baby spoke to, nor what about. Eavesdropping when she could, she heard Baby's fierce whispers.

I can't.

I won't.

Oh yes, you will.

One evening, after the parrots had long since fallen silent in the high trees and the sun had left behind a pink glow that covered the sky like the gentle light of a lamp shade, Didi and Baby sat in the veranda. Baby was drinking. It was her second large peg. Didi stared at her daughter, stretched out her toes, wiggled them.

'You're drinking too much too fast, you'll be sick soon.'

Baby ignored her. They sat in silence. Finally, after Didi had tried to initiate a conversation several times and Baby had responded with clinks of her glass, Didi shrugged and called out for Sita. Dinner. Baby said she didn't want any. Didi got up to go inside.

'You should not drink any more.'

'Maybe I would stop drinking if you would stop pestering me all the time. I am the one who should pester you. What really happened, Amma? Why did we leave Dadi and 3, Chor Bagh? Why won't you tell me?'

'Your grandmother must have.'

'It's your turn. I want you, my mother, to tell me. Why did you do it? Why did you ruin our lives? What was so terrible about my father that you had to leave? What?' Baby took a long sip of her drink, 'What?' And when Didi did not reply, she shouted, 'I am not leaving until you tell me; so you'd best sharpen your memory!'

When Sita appeared in her bedroom later, Didi was lying on her back, staring at the ceiling.

'Hot coffee, black, when the time comes.'

'I know, no need to tell me what to do.'

Didi lay awake, listening to the sounds of her daughter: a match struck, an ice cube flung against crystal, a splash. She sighed and crept deeper into the bedclothes. She thought of Baby and what she must do with her. A grown woman could not live at home with her mother and an ayah. What about her plans, her future? What about money? The longer Baby sat idle, the more she thought about the past and nagged Didi about the parts she felt had been erased. And drank.

'Perversity.' Didi tightened the quilt about her. 'Pure perversity.' To come here and harass her mother about 3, Chor Bagh, when it was years behind them.

Didi heard the smoky cough of another cigarette, the clink of ice. It was past one. Then, the sound she had been waiting for. She rose slowly, groped and pushed her feet into her slippers, shuffled along the passageway.

Baby was slung across the toilet seat. As Didi approached, she noticed a thin line of blood stagger drunkenly across the white of the bowl. Without turning, Baby clutched at Didi's nightdress.

'Make it stop, Amma,' she sobbed, 'make it stop at once.'

Didi pressed her hands.

'Just give it time. It will stop.'

For the next three days, Baby could not swallow without wincing, or speak without pain even in short, halting phrases. Her throat was rough as a nail file. She ate ice cream for breakfast, lunch and dinner. 'You'll grow very fat this way,' warned Didi.

Baby shrugged and jammed another spoon of chocolate ice-cream into her mouth.

'Who,' she gulped, 'cares?'

The women spent the days in the veranda, each lost to the other. Conversation was spare, erratic and pursued only when necessary. Baby would stare at the gate, as if she could will it open by just looking. Didi observed the stillness of her intent.

Once she said, 'Do you want him to come?'

Baby shook her head vigorously.

'If he dares, I will break his nose.'

'I didn't mean him …'

Baby bit a fingernail.

'If he wants.'

'You must know what *you* want.'

'I,' sighed Baby, stretching out in the chair, 'want to be still. To stay put in one place.'

Didi arched her feet. Stillness had numbed them. Exercise, Baby always told her, so here, this was exercise. She closed her eyes. Baby, who knew so well who she did not want but could not admit to wanting Kartik.

I knew what I wanted and took it, Didi told herself. I have that to remember life by.

She belched.

These days, she experienced constant acidity and uncontrollable bouts of burping and hiccups. She would search for the trapped air all over — between her shoulder blades, in the small of her back, under her armpits — arching her body to aid its release.

Sita sniffed at her efforts. Baby shook her head in disbelief.

'Air,' Didi informed them, 'travels everywhere. Haven't you noticed?'

'No!' they cried in unison.

Alone, Didi went through unsettled times. In bed, she changed sides, positions, massaged her aching knee with one foot, opened and closed her eyes, curled up and stretched out. She dozed fitfully, but without relaxation. At the first twitter of sunrise, she rose, irritable, heavy in the stomach and head, and slightly giddy.

'Must be my BP, shooting for the stars.'

She proceeded to the bathroom and found a cigarette. Lighting up, she examined her face in the mirror.

'You look like a sad woman who hasn't been forgiven.'

She blew smoke at her own reflection and considered what she should do: how to help Baby. It came to her after the fourth puff; an idea so simple, she wondered why she had needed tobacco to think of it. Hurrying back into the bedroom, she pulled out her telephone book from under a heap of papers on the night table and rustled through its pages. Surely it was here? But her search was fruitless. She stamped her foot in annoyance. Where was it, then?

Sita walked in. Placing a cup of tea on the table, she see-sawed across to the stool near the window and sat down. There was a loud slurp as she drank tea from a steel glass.

'What are you doing?'

'What do you think?'

'Looking for an address?'

'Telephone number.'

'You haven't called anyone in years, except for the "hotel sahib", and his number you know better than your own.'

Didi ran her finger down the pages.

'So whose number?'

'Kartik's.'

Didi shut the diary and thumped it against the edge of the table.

'Not there?'

Didi turned to Sita who sat sucking in the hot tea, her mouth and eyes round.

'No, Sita, not there.'

Sita stood up and waddled out of the room.

She reappeared five minutes later, her arms behind her back.

'I might be a fool, but I never forget a thing. Here.' She brought out a wall calendar.

Didi admired it from the distance between them.

'Very nice.' She took a sip of tea. 'But what would I want with a calendar which is years out of date?'

'Now who is the fool,' gloated Sita. 'I store the calendars for Gods' pictures. And this calendar,' she waved, 'is of the year Kartik came here. And there,' she tapped the top left hand corner, 'is his address and telephone number. In his own hand.'

Didi clapped.

'Clever, very clever.' She snatched the calendar from Sita's fingers. 'Except,' she added, examining it, 'he may have changed houses since.'

'Give it back, then,' retorted Sita and snatched at the calendar.

'But maybe,' said Didi, yanking it back, 'we can try, hain?'

'First,' puffed Sita, holding on, 'you say sorry.'

The two women tugged in war.

'What,' asked Baby appearing in the doorway, 'are the two of you doing?'

That night, when everyone had retired to their rooms, Didi pulled out the calendar from under her pillow. She had taken the precaution of closing her door and the window. She dialled trunk booking, and then put the phone down before the operator answered. She paced the narrow expanse between her bed and the basin in the bathroom, an unlit cigarette in her hand.

If she got Kartik, what was she to do with him?

She had asked if Baby wanted Kartik to come. 'If he wants,' Baby had replied.

Didi reminded herself: her child was stubborn and that often made her incapable of action. Maybe I can do this for her ... Maybe he will come and take her away. That would be the best of all.

Still, she hesitated. Didi glanced at the clock. Nine-thirty.

She dialled the number. There was a loud ring.

'I must see you in the morning.' Didi spoke in a tone that said this was the end rather than the beginning of the conversation.

'I'm always free.'

The foam of cold coffee settled on the tip of her nose like a fly. She flicked it with her tongue.

'This is sublime,' Didi sighed, stretching out her legs. In the distance, there was complete silence, as if the village below the hill was still asleep. It was an abnormally warm morning with the hiss of the heat in the ears.

'I love sitting out here, in the sunlight, as though there's nothing else in life. It's the second best thing to the veranda of your house, looking at the mangoes ripen before my eyes.'

Mr Hamer crossed a leg.

'Your house.'

'It's your house, you lent it to me.'

He coughed.

'I have no house,' he insisted. 'Only a hotel room.'

She reached out to straighten his tie, brush a few crumbs off the lapels of his blazer.

'I can't understand how you cannot remember the most important moments of life and recall silly, trivial things like I like cold coffee.'

He turned away. Didi irritably bit into a ham sandwich. How could he forget that her house belonged to him? She sighed.

'I suppose there's nothing you really want to remember.'

Didi carefully removed the fat that clung to the ham and bit into the sandwich once more. She glanced at him, saw him stare sightlessly in front. Nowadays, it took Mr Hamer time to bring his mind back into focus. The first time she needed his advice, and he was in no condition to give it.

'I am worried. Baby drinks too much, smokes even more, and keeps herself a secret from me. Why is she here, what does she want and why is her hair blond? She had such lovely light brown hair. And,' added Didi with a shake of her head, 'how she pursues me: what happened at Chor Bagh, why don't I keep in touch with the family, what was wrong between Purush and me? On and on she goes, like a toy train around the same track, until her battery runs out. She keeps asking me about the light of a dark moon. I don't know what she is talking about. Says Lobo Chachi told her about it, so it must mean something. Why did this Lobo Chachi have to give her such ideas? Suppose I reveal a little, you don't know Baby – her mind is like a calculator. She will add and put the numbers together. Ooooh,' she ran a hand through her short hair in exasperation.

'Be calm,' Mr Hamer advised, his eyes staring into the distance.

Didi glowered, wanting to throw her china teacup at his head.

'But why is she so determined to know now? She's lived long enough without knowing everything, and who knows everything anyway? Look at me, I know nothing, understand less.'

Didi went on to mention the 'stinky man', Baby lying around at home ... Should she? What if? But what if she didn't? Suppose? And then what? So many questions dependent on each one's answer for a resolution.

She waited, practising patience. He sipped his gin and tonic, threw peanuts into his mouth. She snatched at another sandwich and munched furiously.

All of a sudden.

'You are standing there.' He pointed to the parapet of the veranda that gave on to the edge of the hill. 'Poised, yes, poised.'

Didi searched his face.

'I wonder how much you understand of what you say.'

Didi went home. The ham sandwiches, the cold coffee, his obtuse opinions had emboldened her. Enough to propel her straight into her bedroom, to close the door and window and dial trunk booking. When the call came through, it rang ceaselessly.

'No reply, madam,' said the operator.

'Please keep trying.'

They tried every hour upon the hour. There was no reply.

The next afternoon, Didi was in bed for an afternoon siesta when Sita arrived with a glass of milk.

'It makes me vomit. Every time I give into your entreaties and drink milk, I throw up. Take it away.' Sita seldom listened to what Didi said – less and less, as they grew old together. She did as she pleased and it pleased her to look after Didi the best she knew how. She saw how little Didi ate and felt she had to force feed her.

'I remember at 3, Chor Bagh – always standing there like a waiter with this steel glass of milk. Thhu!' Didi pretended to spit.

Sita replied, 'You did not feel ulti because of milk. We both know that.' And Sita stuck her stomach out and waddled forward.

Didi kicked at the bedclothes.

'We don't need you to demonstrate. What if Baby saw you?'

Sita stopped and sank down on her steel folding bed that had been opened out for an afternoon nap.

'As if,' she panted, swinging her feet up, 'as if she doesn't know what you were up to. Did she not visit them and did she not leave us after that? What you think that Som Devi told her? The Ramayana? Even I'm not so stupid.'

Didi reached for the dark glasses on the bedside table and wore them. Then she lay back in the bed.

'What you are is very talkative. Now let me sleep.'

'That's what you never do.'

'I have too much to remember. And then there's Baby, always asking questions. Oh, why doesn't that Kartik come and take her away?'

Didi rose with sudden purpose and reached for the telephone. She rang trunk booking and gave the number. 'Urgent,' she commanded the operator.

The number came through half an hour later. Didi took the precaution of locking her room. Then she picked up the receiver and asked for Kartik. A hoarse male voice informed her that Kartik had moved away several years earlier. Didi was about to slam down the receiver in frustration when the man gave her the new telephone number. Didi blew kisses into the receiver. She redialled trunk booking and gave the new number.

'Coming and going? What do you mean your sahib keeps coming and going? How you servants speak nowadays, such cheekiness!'

'No memsahib, truly. Sahib is gone. On leave. Out of estation,' a man's voice explained. 'My woman works in his office, so I am knowing everything about sahib.'

'Big one to know everything,' muttered Didi. 'When will he return?'

'That he did not tell …'

'But I thought you knew everything about your sahib?' retorted Didi in triumph.

'He will be returning … soon,'

Didi replaced the telephone receiver on its cradle.

Half an hour later, an Ambassador drove up the gravel path, and fifteen minutes later Didi was seated in the veranda of the hotel.

'Here I am, again.' She paused and wiped her forehead with her sari pallu. 'What shall I do? Shall I give her money and send her away?'

'I can lend you money.'

'That's sweet.' She patted his hand impatiently. 'But not right now. I have enough.'

She rose in agitation and went across to lean by the parapet.

'They're cooking goat.' She sniffed. 'I can always tell what kind of meat is cooking by its smell.' She turned back to him. 'Shall I tell her? About Jeff? Purush?' Didi shuddered. 'As,' she added with a sigh, 'fate would have it, in that family they are all fair – except Bhai – and have such light eyes. That's why Som Devi was always convinced that Baby looked like her.' Didi returned to her cup of tea. 'Baby is a chameleon: when she sat next to her Dadi, she acquired her looks; but when I close my eyes and place her next to Jeff, she has his eyes, nose …' She collapsed in the chair. 'Oh, it's all giving me a headache.'

'Too much chocolate cake.' He nodded towards the slice on her plate.

For the second time that afternoon, Didi was displeased with him.

'Hold, Didi, yes, hold.'

'Hold what?'

Upon her return home, Didi found Baby in the kitchen with Sita. Baby was cooking.

'What's this concoction?' asked Didi, sniffing. 'Smells odd.'
'Like you,' grumbled Sita, 'cooking animals.'
Baby raised the ladle to her nose.
'It's meat soup. Why don't you go make the beds, Sita?'
'Just like your mother!' retorted Sita, slapping Baby's buttock.
Didi pushed her towards the door.
'Go ask the maali about his second wife.'
Didi returned to the kitchen table and sat on its edge, resolute.
'Care to tell me what your plans are?'
Baby did not turn around.
'Want me to leave?'

Yes, thought Didi to herself, that would be helpful. Instead, she said, 'No, stay as long as you like. But I do think you're too young to hide away in the hills. So long as you have something to look forward to. That's important.'

Baby turned towards her mother.

'What did you look forward to? I mean, in your marriage, and after that? Bhai Chacha? What did you plan to do with my father?'

Didi met Baby's eyes steadily with her own. She saw the stripes in Baby's turn dark, like a wasp's wings, even as she felt the sting of her words.

'I never had any ambition. But I don't want you to be like m—'
Baby turned back to her soup.
'Not to worry. I won't be. I have plans.'
'Is Kartik part of these plans?'
'Maybe.' Baby slurped her soup. 'Delicious.'
'Baby?'
'Maybe and maybe not. It's up to him.'

DELHI
1986

It's up to him. She had done what she could. She had returned, she had her plans, she'd invited him to join her. What more could she possibly do?

She was ready. But she did not want to hurry. Everything she had done before had been hurried. This time she was going to take it slow. Real slow.

Before she left for Didi's, Baby had sought out Kartik after that accidental meeting at Bahri Sons, invited him to her friend Sukanya's. It had been so natural to bite the lobe of his ear … There was no line between right and wrong that she felt she had to cross. Kartik and she had been, they were. That was all. Yes, she had gone to New York, but she had never really left him. Space multiplied by time does not equal separation.

Baby enjoyed their reunion. There was something brazen but seductive about sleeping with this man whom she had rejected. There was punishment and pleasure here: punishment in his constant looks of reproach for leaving him when she should have stayed, pleasure in the physical conquest of his moral reluctance to be with a woman who had abandoned him. It was irresistible.

Baby didn't resist.

Those afternoons on the rooftop of Kartik's Nizamuddin flat: sunlight on high, the leaves of the tree arching over, the shadow of the parapet walls closing in on them from the sides as the sun dipped and dimmed, the spicy steam of ginger tea in their face, Baby with her head on Kartik's thigh as he worked his files. It reminded her of his Def. Col. barsati, of Amma's body in the early years, and Sita's bosom.

That season of infinite comfort, she began to realize how little she missed Ramaji's overwhelming presence which had been so important to her in New York. The bruises on her body must have had something to do with it. And Kartik. When she caught the warmth of his breath as it passed by her, she wanted to capture it and hold onto it.

As Kartik became more involved in the garbage business that summer of the power cuts, Baby set about securing the future. After all, she told herself, they couldn't be collecting other people's rubbish all their lives.

Also, she had some of her own 'rubbish all' to deal with. Like a few answers from Amma – 3, Chor Bagh, Purush …

Baby had devoted a great deal of time thinking of the man who was her father while she was in New York. The last time she had seen him, he was fast asleep on the New York sofa, a rum bottle resting on the floor beside him.

In New York she was as far away from the truth as she was from Purush geographically, physically. He had begun to recede from her horizon. He no longer had the power to bruise. That Ramaji did.

With Didi, Baby was locked in a largely imaginary battle, imaginary because Amma did not retaliate or acknowledge that they were at war. She simply did what she wanted to and left the consequences to themselves. Baby wanted the fight to stop. She wanted to live by her own actions, not her mother's.

For that, she had to make things happen. That was why she had returned from New York, that was why she had made a phone call to the past. Several phone calls over several months.

Then she had travelled out of Delhi. She took a taxi from the airport to the main shopping centre. She admired the awnings, blue and white striped, and the midnight blue door with tinted glass. The tinkle as she pushed open the door announced her arrival. The young assistant behind the cash counter transfered his eyes to her. She was sure he had a small plastic comb in his back pocket; young shop assistants were all alike. She walked past him towards the office, stopping on the way to check whether or not the handle on a particular shelf was still there. It was.

The storeroom.

She walked past and entered the office.

He was seated behind the desk as though he hadn't stirred since she last saw him. A few weedy grey hairs crossed the round of his scalp and a toothbrush bristle curved around his ears. He mopped his wet face: he seemed to have sweated off kilos and suddenly Baby glimpsed the young man she had once known in the loose folds of his clothes. He had begun to resemble his mother. Dadi.

'I must say you look very ... fine, Baby.' Bhai Chacha came around the desk to admire her blonde hair.

Baby shook her head.

'You've lost weight. You look more like Dadi now. How is she?'

'Well, looking forward to meeting you.'

'I have very little time, Bhai Chacha. The flight leaves in three hours. I will come again.'

Bhai Chacha looked crestfallen.

'Of course you will.' He reached inside the desk drawer. 'I have it ready.'

'Any problems?'

'We – your Dadi and I, Lobo Chachi – are pleased to help. It is as it should be.'

'And him?'

He scratched his bald head.

'Purush?'

'Yes?'

'I have taken the liberty of deciding. I am the older brother. He has his share. We are taking nothing away from him. You must be given what is yours. Ma wants it. She will handle him. So my assent is enough.'

Baby opened the envelope he offered her and rifled through the papers inside, reading them carefully.

'It's alright, then, Baby?'

He cocked his head to one side in entreaty. Poor, dear Bhai Chacha, thought Baby, always so earnest, always trying to do what is right.

'Thank you, Bhai Chacha.'

'You're sure you won't,' he asked hesitantly, 'come home? Your Dadi has cooked kheer for you …'

'I have to get back. But I wish you and Lobo Chachi well. Hug Dadi for me.'

He strummed Baby's shoulder.

'Some other time, then.'

She nodded. At least they were thinking of another time.

'Baby?'

She turned.

'You look more and more like your mother.'

He spoke in a clear voice with a gaze as straight as the truth. Baby understood that this was his way of saying he hadn't forgotten. Didi. Amma.

She admired the deed papers which made her the legal owner of the family bookshop brand, giving her franchise rights to start up her own bookshop with the family name and a share in the store's profits. She tapped the envelope on the bridge of her nose and inhaled the smell of books. As she approached the taxi, Baby recalled another time in this very bookshop and other times in other bookshops. Where her story began, where it travelled, where it had returned. There was a neat circularity to this which she didn't like or believe in. Words are just letters arranged to mean something, even if the meaning eludes you, she thought, wondering what meaning, if any, her story had.

Back in Delhi, Baby studied the calendar and chose Thursday, an auspicious day. She dressed with utmost care: a sage green chikan work kurta, a tight white churidar to show off her long legs, and a matching green chikan dupatta. She plaited her hair like Amma used to for her, and flung it behind her. She decided to wear no make-up, no jewellery. She wanted to be totally unlike the woman she had been in New York.

She hired a taxi and drove to the foundation, where she asked the driver to wait for twenty minutes.

'Time waiting twenty per cent.'

'Of what?'

'Entire bill.'

'You're joking?'

Baby thrust out a hip, flung back her body and stared hard into Sardarji's eyes.

'That's the rate, madamji. Twenty per cent. Otherwise I go?'

She climbed the steps. A policeman showed her the way in. Baby wondered what was going on. Kartik had said nothing to her about the trouble at the foundation.

The door was wide open. She marched straight in without a knock. Kartik was standing by the window, a cigarette between his long fingers. She went across and took it from him. A long drag and she blew out the smoke. He retreated automatically and she aimed her rounded mouth beyond his shoulder.

He looked intently at her. Clenched his hands. His eyes sparkled. Always so intense. Not, observed Baby, in a good mood. Not particularly pleased to see her, either.

'Why do you look like you are in deep trouble? Are you, or is this your normal expression in office?'

Their conversations had always been a series of unfinished sentences. Now he ignored her.

'I have come here with a,' that made him look at her, 'proposal. A good one.'

He narrowed his eyes. Oh dear, sighed Baby.

'I own a bookstore in New York. A big one. Don't ask how. I want to start up the same type here. It will be a bookstore, a music shop, a coffee bar. We can improve on the idea as we go along. I have acquired our family bookshop brand name, I have enough money to buy the first property in Delhi. Now, all I need is a partner.'

He did not stir.

'A fifty-fifty partner.' Baby tried to make her voice conversational, inviting. 'Do you know anyone who would want to be my partner?'

He looked away.

'Well, in case you do, I know you know where to find me.'

She crushed the cigarette and waited. Still no response.

Her legs were slugs as she took the slow walk down the stairs and out into the waiting taxi, twenty per cent waiting. Clearly, her old magic wasn't working. Not with the Sardarji and, it seemed for all the passion of their reunion, not with Kartik either. She must have changed.

In the Ambassador, Baby thought about Kartik. He had not changed; there was still that excitability about him that she remembered from those evenings in the university, the tension in his body that had always tightened his curls. That spring had not been fully uncoiled yet. If anything, he was like a dart waiting to shoot forward.

She stopped in Defence Colony market and rang him.

'How about dinner tonight? Your place,' she added. 'I'll buy the booze; you cook the food.'

'I'm busy, do what you want' was his acceptance speech.

That evening, on the way to Nizamuddin, she stopped at a 'Forin liquor store' in Jangpura. There were two men behind the counter but no customer other than Baby. As they saw her approach, they stopped their conversation. She asked for a bottle of Honey Bee brandy.

'Phul?' said the man sitting on a stool and swinging his legs.

'Full.'

'None.'

Then why ask, you bastard, thought Baby as she wiped her forehead with her palm.

'Half then.'

'None.'

She studied the bristles of the man's bulldog moustache.

'What size do you have?'

Without looking through the shelves, the man replied, nasty, insinuating, 'What size you want?'

'Quarter?'

The other attendant was buttoning his shirt, staring at Baby. He grinned.

'Quarter, yes, but no Honey Bee.' His big eyes were a taunt.

'Give me two quarters then.'

'Two quarters are …' he paused and elbowed his companion, 'big enough?'

Their eyes were upon her. This must be how they penetrated women. With the lance of their wanton, sneering eyes. Sita used to tell Baby, the trick is to never meet their eyes with yours. But Baby knew different. She had learnt a thing or two in Delhi. One was how to deal with men. She lifted one eyebrow.

'Are you going to serve me?'

'See, first you asked for a full, but two quarters are only half,' replied the man on the stool. He turned to the other man. 'Did I say anything wrong?'

'Not a thing,' replied the other, one hand scratching his oily hair, the other hovering above the zip of his trousers.

Baby took out the wallet from her pocket.

'Give me two, and only two, quarters.'

He jumped down and searched the shelves. Her eyes accompanied him. She saw half bottles of Honey Bee.

'There are half bottles – there,' Baby pointed out.

The man grinned and then picked out a half bottle. He slammed it down on the counter without bothering to wipe the dust off it.

'Thirty-seven rupees,' said the other attendant.

She placed a hundred rupee note on the counter.

'No change,' he said without checking the drawer desk. He didn't touch the note.

'I don't have any change either,' she replied.

He shrugged.

The other attendant came and placed his hands upon the counter.

'Buy more, or,' he leered, 'take nothing.' His teeth were tiny, dainty, his gums large and very pink.

'Give me two halves more, then, and keep the change.'

He placed the bottles in front of her.

'Put them in a packet.'

'No packet.'

Baby breathed out slowly. She knew there were packets, just as there had been half bottles of brandy, and change in the drawer. She would have liked to twist their eyeballs so that they remained permanently cocked.

Instead, she put away her wallet. Then she reached up and tore open the front of her shirt to her bust, then scratched her chest with two index finger nails. Very sharp. The red welts stood out clearly on her pale skin. She scratched her stomach and arms, until blood oozed to the surface.

'I am going to the police station,' Baby announced. The two men had stiffened to attention. 'I will tell them how you assaulted me. Tried to rape me. And I shall give them this address.'

Their faces turned blotchy like inked blotting paper.

She buttoned up, picked up the bottles and turned away: bastards, bastards, bastards, she cursed to herself; but walked away in slow motion. Behind her, she could hear the shop attendants argue with one another.

When she arrived at Kartik's she was still in a combative mood, and he still seemed in a coil. Maybe that was why they fought over nothing.

It was a stupid argument. An old magazine cover lining his cupboard shelf which Baby had decided to change, just as she used to rearrange his cupboard when he was preparing for the IAS exams. The magazine cover had a picture of the Golden Temple, barricaded, and Indian army soldiers crossed with rifles, Bhindranwale's dead head in the upper right corner.

She was about to throw it away when Kartik snatched it from her and put it in the Britannia biscuit box along with the letters from his family.

He was outraged by the Indian soldiers entering the temple. Baby was cool, indifferent.

'Aren't you getting too het up about nothing?' she yawned. 'Full of moral indignation at something that has nothing to do with you.'

'The army entered and desecrated a temple,' Kartik hissed back, 'killed people who had been declared terrorists by the very prime minister – your wonderful Indira Gandhi of the Emergency – who had encouraged their previous activities. Yesterday, the Sikhs were the most successful and hardworking Indians. Today, they're Khalistani terrorists we crack jokes about: what is the national bird of Punjab? Tandoori Chicken.'

Baby smiled at that, a forced conciliatory smile. She was trying to forget how to fight.

'Do you have any idea what this is doing to the India we took pride in?' he shouted.

'What's so terrible, after all?' she said, folding his shirts. 'Mrs G. could not have let Bhindranwale hide inside the Golden Temple forever. He had to be removed. If that single act can cleanse the atmosphere, what's bad about it?'

'She attacked a religion when she ordered troops into the temple,' answered Kartik, intense, 'erected barriers in our minds we're not able to dismantle. Now every Sikh you see is a militant. Today, it's the Sikhs, tomorrow Parsis, Jains, Muslims. And you say everything will return to normal now that Bhindranwale is dead? Well, you're wrong: it will lead to more hatred.'

'Because people like you, bleeding liberal hearts like yours, will not let it alone. You will not let us forget.' Baby commented over her shoulder.

'Have you forgotten your past? Why should we? That's history. Otherwise, why write it, why study it?'

'You take everything too seriously. Millions die in this country every year of malnutrition, disease, poverty and neglect. What difference does this make, then?'

She waved at Kartik, casually.

'You have just cultivated a guilty conscience. As if the Sikh problem is the only one we face.'

With that, she flung herself down on the small couch, admired her nail polish.

'I am bored out of my bra with all these – Punjab, Assam … da-da-da …Who cares? Give me electricity and clean water and phones which function.'

'Because people like you think the way you do, this country is rotting,' he shouted, jumping up. 'Your ignorant indifference will lead us to disaster.'

'That's why people like me went away; so we don't have to fossilize along with our monuments.'

'Stay away, then.'

'Is that what you want?'

'Since when did you care about that?'

'Oh, go garland yourself,' she said flippantly.

Dinner was silent. She had forgotten that he took these matters personally. Still, she didn't want to fight.

He helped himself to a breast of chicken, pushed the dish towards her. Baby felt her neck flush.

'Don't shove things at me. Have some manners.'

'Manners? You're telling me about manners? Did you have any when you left me? Just walked up and left? Apologize.'

He sprang up from his chair and twisted her right arm behind her back.

She forked a chicken leg and bit into it.

'Go on.' He inched her arm up further. She remained silent.

Then he released her arm, kicked her chair with a mean, hard thrust of the foot. She fell, her forehead hitting the mosaic floor. She saw him cross over to the large, old wooden-framed mirror hanging near the table, stare into his stretched features, and then shatter his face into many little, splintered pieces.

On his haunches, he admired the shrapnels of glass in his hand. The blood was smeared ketchup on finger chips.

Baby rose unsteadily to her feet, clutching her side. The left corner of her forehead thudded with pain.

'Looks too red to be real,' she said, approaching Kartik. 'Shall I lick? Taste the madness in you?'

She lowered her mouth to his knuckles.

'Karela,' she observed, 'your blood tastes of bitter gourd.'

She went into the kitchen, took out ice from the freezer knotted it into a handkerchief and pressed it against her forehead.

'Come here,' she commanded.

He came across to where she stood by the kitchen sink. Baby examined the wounds, then held his hand under the running cold water. She observed his expression, wild, glazed with a violent frustration as he looked at his bloodied hand.

It was a bad time to talk about the bookstore, or partnership, Baby realized, Kartik wasn't himself. He was on the verge of something.

DELHI
1986

He was on the verge of something. It felt like a precipice. He had done what he had to do and if, in return, he had to take a tumble, so be it.

He reached one hand into his pocket, hiding the fingers that scratched his thigh. He had been scratching it since he left home, a few hours earlier.

Home. Who knew when they would allow him to go home? He hoped it would be soon. The Nizamuddin police station was pleasant as police stations go, but he would much rather not stay there. It was a small, almost quaint old structure hidden partially from view by the enveloping trees on Mathura Road, just short of the roundabout with the blue dome. Kartik studied the dome. The ancient tiles, cracked by centuries of heat and dust, were peeling like the shell of a boiled egg. Opposite the police station, there was Kataria nursery, one of the oldest in New Delhi, and a little way ahead, Nizamuddin's Tomb, obscured by tall neem trees and a string of small, squat shops – cycle repair, cement, barber, travel agency and a fruit juice vendor. Kartik scratched the sole of his left foot with his big right toenail. A blister had formed – yellow, bulbuous, squishy. That was what happened when you were dragged out of your home in your rubber chappals. Kartik threw off the offending chappals and squatted on the floor, the tape of his pyjamas hanging between his legs.

'Sexy, chooha, a little long, but definitely the mark of a man,' observed an amused voice.

'Tell me,' he wiggled his toes, 'why it is, Avantika, that whatever you say sounds like you mean something else?'

'That's my appeal.' She pinched his cheek.

'Where is that husband of yours? Why is it taking him so long to arrange everything?'

'You are not maha big on gratitude.' Avantika slapped his shoulder with a swing of her black patent leather handbag. 'Ek toh, you have an

IAS officer helping you out. Think of the millions of ordinary Indians who don't have such friends.'

'You, Avantika,' Kartik said, momentarily diverted, 'never think of the millions of ordinary Indians.'

'Well, you know what I mean. You'd be in Tihar Jail with the rest of them. Why did you have to hit that man so hard and threaten him?'

'Because he was poking it right into my face and breathing heavily. I might have caught his germs.'

Ajay appeared in the doorway. Kartik stood up. There were just two police constables leaning on their lathis, but Kartik felt as if he was surrounded by men in khaki. He couldn't breathe.

'Let's get out of here.'

Ajay restrained him with a hand on his arm.

'Not so fast, yaar. They're claiming you hit him so hard, he's got a critical head injury.'

'I hit as hard as I could, but it was he who went and banged his head against the wall, repeatedly, till it was bloodied. I told the police that. Now I wish I had damaged his brain, permanently, bast—'

'Do you mind? This is the police station!'

Kartik jumped the two steps and strode up and down the sandy driveway. Ajay disappeared inside and it was ten minutes before he emerged.

'They will let you go for now. I've managed to keep everything off the records. But,' Ajay wiped his nose with a handkerchief, 'if that guy doesn't make a full recovery, you could be in big trouble.'

Kartik's bleary, red eyes widened in outrage.

'He's the one who should be in trouble. He, not me.' Kartik poked a finger into his chest. 'What's wrong with this country? I try to rescue a woman and the police arrive at my door, drag me out of bed before I can even pee …'

'Not now, please,' urged Ajay, turning Kartik away towards the gate.

'And they keep me here for over,' he looked at his watch, 'four hours, while that bastard,' Kartik kicked at a stray dog that lay in his way, 'is going to press charges against me!'

The dog yelped, rose in haste and hobbled away.

They had reached the car, a white Ambassador. It was Avantika's father's official car. Ajay sat in front with the driver while Avantika and Kartik occupied the backseat.

Avantika reached into her purse and pulled out a bottle of eau de cologne. She sprayed Kartik and herself.

'You stink, Chooha, not at all pleasant early in the morning.'

'Who asked you to come?' Kartik furiously wiped his face and arms. 'You could have stayed at home—'

'Shut up,' Ajay interrupted, angrily, 'and listen to me: you have caused enough trouble for one morning. They say it's because of you that Miranda was assaulted! So don't give Tikoo a lecture. She came to hold your bloody stupid hand which you couldn't control with that man.'

Kartik sank back and massaged his forehead. 'Sorry. You're right. I didn't mean to …' He touched Avantika's arm apologetically. 'Thanks … I'm just tired …'

'Relax, yaar. Can it. Don't turn yourself into a martyr.'

'I must get away from here, it's becoming too much …'

'A good idea,' agreed Ajay, without turning. 'Let things settle. Where will you go?'

Kartik ran a hand over his face. He peered out of the window. 'Haven't a clue.'

'Well, let's go home and have a morning drink. I could do with a large one. And tell us: what on earth happened? That night?'

That night. It had come upon them unexpectedly, though it had been coming a long time, and Kartik, had he not been distracted by Baby, ought to have anticipated it.

His foundation's collection schemes had made a difference. Local newspaper pages carried regular updates on the progress of the local self-help schemes. 'How green is our Delhi' claimed one, alongside a photograph of the health minister garlanding members of the first local citizens collection team which the foundation had set up in Nizamuddin East.

Delhi began to notice the difference. So did Kartik. When he stood on the rooftop of the foundation and inhaled deeply, the air smelt only faintly rancid. He thumped his chest, pleased. He was not the only one. Avantika's father, who made weekly rounds to check on the foundation's work, was equally satisfied with what he found. Community schemes did make a difference; he had said it all along. Now if only the contract karamcharis would cooperate.

In the beginning, they had remained silent, unable to understand the full import of what the secretary health had initiated. The first year slipped by. Into the second year, discontent surfaced. Here, there, not enough to cause trouble, but enough to draw attention to itself. The truckers and contractors who used to collect the garbage found themselves shifted from the New Delhi area to the densely populated lower income areas, east, west, where they had to work much harder. Their pay was increased but that didn't assuage their feelings of insecurity. They had been sidelined. The foundation and others like it had taken over – with the Delhi government's blessings.

The men were furious. If NGOs and local community groups took over, what would they do? They met the secretary health. For all his persuasiveness, he failed to impress them. He promised them an increase in wages; the workers were subdued for a while. However, the continuing success of the local garbage collection soon saw a small shamiana erected outside the foundation's building, and a white banner proclaim the presence of the disaffected truckwallahs, the contractors and their workers. A banner read in red lettering: 'Karamchari Cleaners' Onion'.

Each day, a few men gathered in the shamiana and raised slogans.

Kartik ignored them. They were lazy, indolent, insolent. Kartik, with the Delhi government backing him, and international funding, had procured new garbage pick-up trucks. So had others like him. The trucks were more efficient. But they required qualified personnel. People with technical abilities replaced the karamcharis. This led to lay-offs in semi-skilled staff and more truckwallahs found themselves in the shamiana. The secretary health offered them compensation. There were takers, but a significant number wanted more than compensation. They wanted jobs. So the numbers in the shamiana increased.

The men did not merely raise slogans. In their frustration, they began to hurl abuse at the foundation workers and those who visited its office.

'Sir,' Miranda told Kartik one afternoon when she saw Sushila run up the foundation's steps chased by harsh words, 'those men are beginning to insult us women.'

'Just walk away, don't get into an argument,' advised Kartik. 'Men get excited if you women pay them attention.'

'It's not that, sir, we say nothing; but one day, our husbands might hear about this, and then?'

'Then what?' Kartik said, picking up the telephone. 'Control your men, Miranda. Isn't that what women do?'

'Sir!' Miranda laughed. 'Sir has never wanted to be controlled?'

'Can't find a woman who can!'

Everything remained under control, until that summer of the heatwave. Then, Delhi was on the boil: relentless power cuts, water shortages, anger. It seemed there was more garbage than ever before. Its rancid smell hung over the city. The secretary health asked Kartik to redouble efforts. Although he did not threaten to reconsider the foundation's contract, he put the NGOs on indefinite notice. Kartik began to receive reports of contractors who had been previously laid off being seen working in many of the foundation's colonies.

Kartik found it difficult to cope. More alarming stories followed: these contractors were bringing in workers from the neighbouring states at very cheap rates, picking up garbage from other areas and dumping it in the foundation's circles at night. Next morning, they would complain to the authorities about the foundation's inefficiency. Kartik complained to the secretary health.

'If your foundation cannot do the job, then I must permit others to complete it,' came the secretary's reprimand.

The contractors asked to be paid more for lifting more garbage than they were originally contracted to lift. The foundation held a meeting.

'I think,' advised Dulari, 'that we should stop this rubbish work.'

Everyone nodded in agreement. Kartik rocked in his chair. 'Any better ideas?'

'Hire a private detective and find out what these goondas are up to. Catch them in the act?' Mrs Singh joked.

'Yes,' agreed the women and clapped.

'You're serious?' Mrs Singh clutched the emerald pendant fastened to her throat.

Kartik stood up.

'What do you say, Dulari?'

'Yes, why not, but sahib never listens to me, na!'

And she laughed along with the rest of them.

The name was Eagle Private Detectives, 36, Devika Towers, Nehru Place, Telephone Number 6215690. The Yellow Pages said they undertook 'all matter of secret work'.

'But this is the first time, ever, in my entire twenty-six years in the business,' guffawed Colonel Pritam Singh Choudary, Retd., when he visited the foundation's office and Kartik explained the assignment, 'that we are posting men at garbage dumps!'

The first week yielded no discoveries. Into the third week, one extremely humid afternoon, Colonel Choudhary walked into Kartik's office, the sweat streaking down his face, his arms, and the front of his shirt. Kartik thought he had never seen a sweatier human being.

'Then, just like in the films,' Miranda later reported to the rest of the team, 'he threw down a thick brown envelope on sir's desk. "See," he pointed to it, "here's the proof. We caught them with their fingers in the dirt."'

Kartik sent the reports with the photographs to the secretary health. The next afternoon, Miranda informed Kartik that there was a man to see him. She said 'a man' as though he was some other form of life. She added that she'd told him that Kartik was busy, but he had given her such a look, she had been alarmed. Also, she remembered him as one of the men from the shamiana. He was amongst those who harassed Shaheen and Sushila with long whistles.

A few minutes went by before a man in betel-nut brown skin, slicked back black hair and a moustache that covered his mouth, stepped in. Kartik instantly recognized him from Colonel Pritam Singh Choudhary's photograph.

'The sahib,' he stated and stood tapping the chair, 'the sahib did a very wrong thing. You have taken away our contract. Your lies to the secretary have snatched away our jobs.'

He sat down in front of Kartik without invitation.

'No lies. You were caught by the detectives piling up more rubbish in our areas. Then you make more money by carrying away the same garbage. You also reported us for inefficiency to the authorities and we were put on three months' notice. You're trying to get rid of the foundation.'

The man lit a beedi, its smoke sneaked out of his nostrils like a serpent.

'We could have worked this out between us. But the sahib went to the authorities and now we have lost our contract and our jobs.'

'You did wrong.'

'Wrong?' The man sprang forward, and Kartik noticed that the whites of his eyes were yellow. Liverish, probably drinks too much, he suspected. 'What's wrong in trying to earn money? Four months we have sat in the sun until we are dark as our futures, dry as our wallets. You make us jobless. We are already poor, doing filthy work. Here,' he rose and came around to Kartik, 'smell this.'

He held out his arm under Kartik's evasive nose.

'Smell my skin. We are truckwallahs who transport garbage. It's a dirty job, and now you want to take away even that from us?'

'What's your name?' asked Kartik.

'Arre, what will you do knowing my name?'

The man rose, extinguished the beedi between two fingers and returned it to the conical pack that he slipped into his shirt pocket. He withdrew a comb from the back pocket of his trousers and ran his thumb along its teeth. Kartik noticed his long, shapely fingers with large, well-shaped nails. He could have been a musician.

The man said, looking straight at Kartik, 'This will not be good for you. Unless,' he ran the comb ever so slowly over his fingers, 'you take back the complaint.'

Kartik's nose itched, his ears sang. He took a deep breath and sank back.

'I cannot change anything,' he proclaimed. 'You should not have played dirty.'

The man snapped a tooth of the comb, slipped the comb into his pocket, and deposited the broken tooth on Kartik's desk.

'But I am in a dirty business, no? The sahib is taking a big riks, big riks. I will,' he promised, 'make you regret this day.'

'Chal, chal,' called out Miranda from the doorway, 'you're a big one with your threats to sir. Let's see the size of your …'

'Miranda!' Kartik rose in warning. 'Don't talk like that to a man like him.'

'Seen many his size before, will see many bigger, after. Leave now, or I will call the police.'

The man held Kartik's eyes steadily and then turned away. He brushed past Miranda without looking at her. Kartik came around the table and looked out of the window. The man was descending the foundation stairs two at a time.

'You mustn't talk like that, Miranda, you don't know his type of men. Be careful.'

There was no reply.

The next morning, there was the usual commotion outside. Kartik walked across to the window that looked out onto the shamiana. He sighed and wondered at fate. Just when the foundation was going through its worst period, Baby had returned to him. He chastised himself for his weakness. This was no time for blighted love. He had to focus on the problem at hand. The foundation was under siege; the secretary health was expecting more from him; the women were exhausted and the garbage was piling up.

Kartik concentrated on the garbage. He planned more efficient routes for the collection. He increased recruitment. The foundation women began to work two shifts. They often returned late in the evening, the smell of the day's work clinging to them like their sweaty clothes.

Kartik insisted they bathe in water boiled with neem leaves and wash their hands in Dettol water. It was a habit all the women, except Mrs Singh and Mrs Malhotra, had acquired. They scrubbed their bodies with the plastic scrubbers that Ram Singh used to clean utensils and sniffed each other for confirmation. Kartik was outraged by their reddened skins when they emerged from their baths.

'If we don't remove this smell, sahib, our husbands will not come near us,' explained Sushila. 'Sahib doesn't know what these men are like.'

'Forget the men,' countered her mother-in-law, Devi. 'I can't stand my own stink!'

It was Friday night. Eight p.m. Sushila, Devi and Shaheen were still out. Kartik had ordered food from the dhaba and told Miranda to keep it ready: the minute the women returned, they would eat.

'First they'll bathe. The water is ready.'

Kartik returned to the papers on his desk. He heard a noise downstairs and rubbed his stomach. He hoped the women would bathe quickly: he was ravenous. When he glanced at his watch next, it was almost nine. He was ready for dinner.

Downstairs, the neon tubes spread their metallic light across the reception area. I will change these lights, Kartik vowed, they make me feel like I am living inside an empty aluminium tin. He switched them off. The rush of water into a bucket made him head towards the bathrooms. He tried to turn off the tap, but it circled loosely between his fingers. He must tell Miranda to send for the plumber tomorrow.

He returned to the empty reception hall, stood in the dark, gazing out of the window at the street where cars eased up in front of a red light.

Red lights look the same to me, anywhere. I could be in Bombay, Calcutta, maybe even Baby's New York.

A pant and a titter. Low voices from the kitchen. The women gossiping. Kartik decided to creep up and listen in. He removed his Kolhapuri chappals that squeaked in their newness and tiptoed forward.

Then he stopped, rocked back on his heels.

The voice grew louder.

Kartik leaned back against the wall and inched sideways along it. What was going on?

'That's it,' a man's voice said. 'Bilkul perfect. Hold it right there.'

'Good enough,' added another male voice, slurping at his words, 'to lick.'

Kartik heard sniggers.

Where were the women, he wondered.

'You,' continued the first voice, 'listen and you listen good: don't ever make fun of me again, hain? When you see me, you keep your eyes down. Understood?'

Kartik recognized the voice. 'Otherwise,' threatened a third voice, 'we'll have to teach you another lesson.'

More titters.

'Don't,' added the first voice, 'run like melting ghee to that sahib of yours and sneak on us, because then you will force me to take this cross of yours and dangle it from somewhere else. Your Lord won't like that, hain, will He?'

'Ghee? We can spread it out and eat …'

The aroma of hot food reached Kartik's nostrils.

How dare they eat his food?

A whimper.

'That's good, good.'

Kartik's fingernails scraped the wall paint, his toes clenched. He tiptoed back to the reception hall, searching for Ramesh outside. No sign. He hurried back.

'Folding hands? That day in your sahib's office, you were like Jhansi ki rani, hain? What's my size, you asked? I'll show you. Nahin, better, I'll just measure it here in front of you.' There was a sneer in the voice. 'What do you say, bhai log? One foot, hain?'

'Naaa …'

'More than one foot?'

Muffled merriment.

'Chalo, so now you know. But,' there was a pause, 'don't worry, I am too big for you. I'll leave you to your sahib.'

Laughter.

'Let him taste.'

'Let him eat.'

Stifled guffaws.

'Eat, eat, eat …'

Kartik felt the sweat drip from his armpit. He stepped forward. Automatically, the huddle opened.

Miranda stood in a yellow blouse, the sari tied around her thighs. Her hair, stomach and legs were covered in brown meat curry and thick yellow dal. One of the men held a piece of roti to her suppressed lips.

All that Kartik recalled later was that he had stepped forward and snatched the piece of roti out of the man's hand, grabbed him by the back of his head and as the startled man's mouth opened, shoved the roti inside, then swung him around and hit him hard in the face. He elbowed someone behind him. His hair was pulled, he was kicked on the shin. He shook the man with such force that the piece of roti came flying out from between his lips and hit Kartik in the left eye.

Kartik punched the man in the back. Arms imprisoned his legs. He held the man and tried to squeeze his neck but he was pushed against him from behind. Both of them fell against the motionless Miranda, who went sprawling backwards and hit her head against the kitchen closet. The man crumpled to the floor with Kartik on top of him. Suddenly, Kartik felt the tip of a shoe in his right ear.

'Maaro, maaro!' he heard the first voice command. 'Hit him so he never forgets. Afterwards, we'll throw them both out with the garbage.'

Someone was holding him down hard with the heel of his boot in the small of his back. Kartik could barely breathe but he still clutched the man below him by the head, pressing it hard against the floor. Then he was being dragged by his feet. His eyes passed by dusty, worn out black shoes and black trouser bottoms as he skidded along the floor.

'At some point,' he told Ajay later, 'the women and Ramesh arrived. Three of the men managed to escape. The fourth was left behind. I caught him from under the armpits and the next thing I knew, he began to bang his head against the wall, again and again, screaming, "Bachao, bachao." I tried stopping him but he was beyond control.'

By the time Ramesh and Kartik had restrained him, there was blood everywhere, a red patch, like a squashed ripe tomato dripping down the wall, and the man's bloodied face. The man ran, skidding on his own blood and though Shaheen chased him, he raced out of the gate and across to the other side of the street. He had disappeared into the darkness.

The women escorted the cowering Miranda to the bathroom and bathed her in the same neem water that she had kept ready for them. The red welts on her arms, legs and stomach were anointed with antiseptic cream. The doctor was summoned. Shaheen and Sushila dressed her in a fresh cotton sari. Devi offered to stay the night, but Miranda shook her head. Ramesh held her hand tight.

The doctor gave her an injection, dressed her wounds, prescribed medication and recommended she be sent to Safdarjang Hospital next day for her burns.

Kartik called the Nizamuddin police station and half an hour later, a constable and sub-inspector arrived on a white motorcycle. They examined the kitchen, they noted the bloodied wall and floor. They questioned everyone. They asked Kartik if he wished to file a complaint. Kartik's nose dribbled.

Yes, he wanted to file a complaint. He knew the men, he would recognize them, he would kill them ...

'Control yourself, sahib,' the policemen counselled, 'anger may get you into trouble.'

The official procedure continued for twenty minutes. The policemen wanted to meet Miranda but Ramesh refused.

'No, no more men tonight,' he said firmly.

'It will strengthen the case,' argued the policemen.

'No,' Kartik said, 'she's had enough.'

'Of course, if we had seen her as you say you saw her, dressed in ... what was it ... meat curry and dal, that would have been best. You should not have tampered with the evidence.'

Kartik noticed them exchange a smirk of amused scepticism and made allowances for their incredulity. Who could believe that a woman could be draped in her own dinner?

'The flies would have sat on her' was all he said.

The policemen nodded and said they would return the next day with a senior officer.

'Instead,' Kartik informed Ajay, 'instead, one day later, they come knocking on my door at five in the bloody morning and before I had a chance to ...'

'Yes, yes,' soothed Ajay hurriedly, 'we have heard that already.'

'... and those men are roaming around free. Honestly, we live in a Hindi film. Except,' he reminded himself, 'for Miranda.'

The night the men dressed Miranda in her dinner, Kartik had remained at the foundation. He lay on the sofa. Each time he dozed, he saw the copper vessel his mother cooked dal in, being emptied over Miranda's head by the man with the comb. He rose with a pain behind his eyes and went down to check on Miranda. She was lying on the cot, her eyes half open, the neon light throwing a grey shadow over her. He wanted to reach out, comfort her, but resisted. She would be embarrassed by his touch, might even flinch at it.

In office, next day, he paced up and down in a rage. He could do nothing for Miranda. The men were still at large. He called Colonel Choudhary and asked for full-time guards at the foundation. He gave him a description of the men who had assaulted Miranda and asked him to find them.

Kartik could not forgive himself. He ought to have walked straight into the kitchen instead of waiting outside. What had he waited for?

He summoned Ramesh and Miranda into his office. She appeared in Shaheen's burkha. When Kartik raised an eyebrow, Ramesh shrugged.

'She feels the need to hide herself.'

All Kartik saw were Miranda's dulled eyes. He vowed to make the men suffer. He gave Ramesh money. 'Go visit her family,' he ordered. 'You need to get away,' he added.

Miranda remained withdrawn inside the burkha.

'Okay,' Ramesh said.

'And Miranda,' he added as she turned away, 'I am so sorry. Last night. I should have stopped it, only I didn't realize.'

He saw her shudder and felt his throat constrict.

'I told you not to speak to that man that day? You see how they are?'

Ramesh grasped Kartik's shoulder. 'She did right, sahib,' he said. 'We face these bullies all the time. If we don't reply, they will cut out our tongues and eat them. Then we will never be able to speak.'

'And what happened to her – what about that? Next time—'

'I want to go,' interrupted Miranda in a whisper, 'home.'

Ramesh took her hand and led her out.

Kartik banged his fist into his palm, strode across to the window and glared down into the shamiana. Hungrily, angrily, his eyes scanned the men and to his surprise, he found what he was looking for. The moustache, the brown comb peeking out of his bottom. He had come. He had the gall to come to the foundation, calm as a still night, the morning after he had stripped a woman of her dignity. Kartik felt his stomach clench into a fist. He sped down the stairs, rushed out and grabbed the man by his shirt. He shook him, pummelled, shoved him, grabbed the comb out of his trouser pocket and scratched the man's face until it was lined with blood.

'Save,' the man panted, 'me.'

'I'll eat you for dinner,' Kartik screamed, 'brain curry in blood gravy. With plenty of green chillies to make you palatable.'

Kartik massaged his stomach, breathed in and out, rhythmically, to ease his tension. He hadn't moved from the window. He knew it would be a mistake. If he assaulted the man in front of the crowd, they would beat him up.

He called the women for a meeting. He wanted to know what they thought should be done. They shrugged, they hung their heads, they did not reply. They were sullen, sleepless, scared.

'What if it's one of us next time, sahib?' asked Shaheen.

Kartik said he'd asked Colonel Choudhary for full-time security.

Devi raised her head.

'When a man decides to teach us a lesson, nothing will stop him. We know.'

The others nodded.

'Ram Singh is always most gentle,' Jamuna disagreed, loyal to her husband.

Mrs Singh was keen to take Miranda's case to the press.

'It's too much,' she complained, 'these goondas waiting out there to attack us ... with our own food. We must cover ourselves with press protection.'

'Might create more trouble,' observed Mrs Malhotra.

Kartik agreed. He didn't want a tamasha.

'I told sahib to stay out of this rubbish business,' Dulari spoke up, 'but sahib never listens—'

'Can't you ever say anything new?' snapped Devi. 'Always the same story, like you're reciting a mantra. It's irritating.'

'So what should I do, if you are irritated? Go relieve yourself. I will say what I want to say ...'

'Please, let's not fight,' implored Shaheen, 'as if we don't have enough problems without you oldies pulling out each other's hair.'

Devi turned, lunged forward.

'Will pull out yours.'

'Stop,' commanded Mrs Singh in a compelling voice. Everyone fell back. It was the first time she had spoken so. 'This is silly. Why are we fighting? Let's carry on as though nothing happened.'

The bustling stopped. The women shrugged, jostled each other and then filed out. Kartik was left wondering what he ought to do. He couldn't think. He went home, tried to ring Baby, received no reply and slept fourteen hours.

The next morning, the police had come and taken him to the police station. After Ajay secured his release, Kartik returned to the office. It was a late afternoon. The sun wore a dazed expression as if exhausted by the heat it had generated during the day. The sky was hazy, covered in a polythene film wrapped around it to preserve the moment. It was an uneasy, uncomfortable weather. He tried Baby again. Still no reply.

Kartik heard the steps on the stairs.

Opening his eyes, he saw his man standing in front of him. Kartik pursed his lips.

The man approached the table.

'So the sahib has got himself into trouble, hain?' he observed, the comb in his hand, the left thumb scraping its teeth. 'I told the sahib it would not be good for him.'

Kartik remained still. He must be careful, cunning.

'The sahib should not lose his temper so. Our man is in hospital, very serious, hain …'

'That's because he banged his head against the wall …' began Kartik, unable to stop himself.

The man tapped his foot.

'No, the sahib hit him. We saw. He also told to the police.'

Kartik got to his feet very slowly.

'He lies.'

'What proof?'

'There were people present. They saw that I hit him only once.'

'What did I say!'

'Once,' repeated Kartik.

The man nodded.

'He went mad,' continued Kartik, 'banging his head, we couldn't stop him.'

'He says you hit him again and again.'

'He lies,' Kartik spoke, his voice soft.

'But the sahib admits to hitting him? Who will believe that a man would hurt himself like that, hain?' The man took his comb and ran it through his luxuriant moustache.

They stood facing each other, neither backing away.

'I have told the police that he did it.'

'Yes, but the sahib is the one they took to the police station?'

'I have filed a complaint against you and your chamchas.'

The man slicked the comb through his oiled hair and slipped it back into his pocket. He caressed his teeth with his tongue, appeared to find something between two of them and slowly ran his thumbnail through the crevice. Kartik recalled a recurring nightmare in which he clenched his teeth so hard, they broke one by one, and fell headlong down his throat and he could do nothing to stop them. He hoped it would happen to the man.

The man examined the result of his labours and flicked his thumb and index finger in the direction of Kartik, who instinctively backed away. 'Doctor sahib says his condition is critical.'

Kartik came around the table and poked a finger in the man's chest.

'I will take what you did to Miranda higher up. You just wait and see if I don't.'

The man watched Kartik's finger.

'Again, the sahib, I advise him to be careful. That Christian girl is just one woman, you have others.'

Kartik stamped on his foot.

The man stumbled, fell. He held his foot, massaged his toes, flexed them and then rose, adjusting his trousers which were slipping off his flat hips.

'You are too angry,' he smiled. 'If I were to tell the police, they will make keema of the sahib.'

He tucked his brown shirt into his black trousers.

'But you go ahead and complain. The sahib can go to the chief minister, the prime minister, even the president. I am not scared. Who saw anything? Your women? They should be careful before they speak, hain?'

He turned and walked out. Kartik remained standing where he was. He waited for the footfall on the stairs, the tick-tock of shoes on the granite. Then he threw himself on the couch and covered his eyes. He was being tricked. He was being framed and he had lost his temper once too often. What was the matter with him? The pressure was turning his head into a cooker and any moment now, he'd blow everthing. He must get way, he counselled himself, collect himself before he lost control again.

He sat late into the evening. He slept the night on the sofa and dreamt that Baby was dressed in dal. In the morning he rang up Sukanya's to speak to Baby. Sukanya said she wasn't there. She'd gone to see her mother.

Then he spoke to Mrs Malhotra and Mrs Singh. 'I think I need a break. I'm not thinking clearly. I need to get out of town, otherwise I don't know what I might do. Will the two of you be able to run the show? Also, it might be better if I am not around for a while with the police on my case. Ajay agrees. I might inflame things more.' He nodded towards the window. 'Why do you never buy your own?' he snapped as Mrs Malhotra reached for his packet of cigarettes.

'I,' replied Mrs Malhotra, puffing, 'don't like to smoke.'

Kartik frowned.

'Can you manage?' he asked.

The two women eyed each other.

'Shouldn't be a problem,' said Mrs Singh, 'as long as she does not blow smoke in their faces.'

'Don't be ridiculous, those fucker-sisters—'

'You mean, sister-fuckers, sister …' corrected Mrs Singh.

'What's the difference?' asked Mrs Malhotra, blowing smoke in her face.

The same night Kartik caught the train out of Delhi.

When the train arrived at its final stop, it was early morning. Kartik's bogey stopped just short of the A.G. Wheeler Booksellers stall. He swung his bag onto his back and jumped off. Past the tea vendor, the bread pakora pyramid cart, the juice and biscuit stall, straight into the sunlight, towards the white station building. He turned right, offered his ticket to the collector in his black coat, black tie and untucked white shirt. People everywhere, and a faint stale odour as you passed them. Kartik was jostled, pushed, and fell against a coolie who was approaching him from the opposite direction. Kartik hurried past him and down the steps.

Scooter?
Where you want to go?
Rickshaw?
Thirty rupees only.
I'll take you cheaper.
Taxi?
Private?
How much you want to pay?
They were like leeches, waiting to feed off him.
Where?
Where?
Where?
He stopped, arms akimbo.
'Home.'

The scooterwallah rattled away, trailing fumes. Kartik ran his fingers through his dishevelled hair and over his crumpled clothes. With his other hand, he thrust open the gate. It moaned like the loose strings of an old sitar. He felt reassured: the hinges had been rusty throughout his childhood. Pitaji used to call it his private 'alarum system' because it alerted the household to entries and departures. I will oil it before I leave, Kartik promised himself.

He strutted in, trying to create an impression of self-confidence even though he felt slightly lightheaded. A ribbon of pansies, bright purple and yellow, lined the pathway. Beyond it, the thick grass of the garden, soft and springy. Bougainvillea bushes were in full bloom, pink, flaming orange, overarching the porch of the house. How beautiful it looked, better than his memory of it.

Automatically, he skirted the empty front veranda and decided to sneak in through the back, the way he had as a child. Turning the corner of the house, Kartik saw the sunlight warm on a cluster of potted plants, green with envy of each other's bloom. It was such a cheerful sight.

Lata's voice strolled out of the kitchen and she behind it, carrying a tray of tea. At the other end of the veranda, partially in the shade, Kartik saw his mother seated in a long garden chair, a light shawl on her lap. He walked up to her and waited, willing himself to be still.

His mother opened her eyes.

'Arre Kartik, kab aye?'

'Just now, on the train, Mummu.'

When Pitaji came in from the fields, Kartik was seated inside with the rest of the family. He rose and went across to touch his feet. Pitaji sat down, reached for a cup of tea and sipped, making a sound like a whistle from a faraway train. He stared at his son.

'So,' he eventually spoke, 'have you got a proper job or are you …?' he trailed off in embarrassment.

Kartik suppressed a smile.

'Yes, Pitaji.'

'Yes what?'

Kartik shook his head and reached for his mother's hand. It was chilled.

Pitaji got up and left.

In the days that followed, Kartik spent most of his time by his mother's side. When she slept in the afternoon, he slept. This was the first time since he had begun work at the foundation that he was on holiday, and each day he felt more tired than on the day before.

In the evenings, the family would gather in his parents' bedroom – Chachaji and Chachiji, Lata and her husband Vishnu, and Tarkesh's wife Soni who was visiting while her husband was on a business trip to Calcutta. Lata's daughter had been sent to a girls' boarding school. 'She must go to college like you, Dada,' Lata explained.

They sat on Mummu's bed, spread themselves out like an eiderdown on Pitaji's, and spoke in gentle voices and soft tones so as not to 'excite' Kartik's mother, explained Chachiji with a kind smile. Even the laughter escaped them in small hisses. They discussed, gossiped, recounted tales of everything and everyone … the cycle of births, weddings, anniversaries and deaths. One topic alone remained untouched: Kartik's life in Delhi. That was treacherous ground, fraught with unknown potholes.

Pitaji never joined these sessions. He sat by himself in the big room, smoking his hookah and reading the morning newspaper.

Later, after dinner, Kartik strolled in the garden with Chachaji, and listened to details of the family business. Chachaji said Kartik's cousins had sold English Ice Queen – no one wanted homemade ice-cream any longer.

'It's all your fault,' Chachaji admonished Kartik. 'If you had married Rukmini, like you were ordered to, we would have come to Delhi and got those auto-machines you told your father about. As it was, your Pitaji refused to let anyone visit Delhi or mention those machines.'

Two ice-cream parlours were still in operation in the nearby town, and the old restaurant, Tirupati, had added new fast food to the menu. 'You must come with me and eat the keema dosa,' recommended Chachaji, 'it is too good.'

Chachaji's sons were more interested in the transport business.

'They say all the money is there. They hardly come home. They are always travelling to Calcutta and the east.'

The mango orchards had expanded. The fruit was in such abundance that Lata and Vishnu had begun a small jams and pickle business.

'Too good,' exclaimed Chachaji.

However, it was the land that remained the mainstay of the family. Vishnu had introduced new techniques – 'all the way from Punjab' – so the crops of wheat, rice and bajra were plentiful and the yield exceptionally high. Chachaji said Pitaji was very pleased with the new techniques and praised Lata's husband 'no end'.

During the day, Kartik would recount to his mother tales from his years away from home: the failed IAS exams, Baby's departure and reappearance, Didi, the garbage collection scheme. His mother would listen with eyes half closed. Occasionally, he felt the protest flutter through her body and she tensed, but he held her hand firm till it subsided.

Once she asked, 'Kartik?'

'Hmm.'

'Kartik, you enjoy what you do?'

'Hmm.'

She had looked at him then.

'Don't you think you could have found something else?'

'It happened, Mummu, I didn't plan it.'

Kartik tried to explain, but his mother's eyes, deep inside their sockets, withdrew from the conversation.

Another time.

'Won't you marry, Kartik?'

'I hope to, Mummu.'

'This ... that Baby?'

'I hope so, Mummu.'

She turned away and he arranged the bed sheet about her shoulders. 'Kartik?'

'Hmm?'

'Try to do it before I go.'

Kartik felt himself close to tears. He swallowed, inarticulate with grief, remorse. His mother, as he had suspected all along, was not well. She was frail, she had low blood pressure, a very poor haemoglobin count, and a host of little ailments which kept her in bed.

She was on a variety of medicines and tonics, and often dozed off in the middle of a conversation. Lata told Kartik not to be deceived: their mother was healthier than her frail looks indicated.

'And Rukmini?' asked Kartik, dropping his chin.

'You can look at me when you speak her name, Dada. It is okay.'

Rukmini, married and settled in Ranchi, was busy raising three children. Kartik pretended shock.

Lata smacked his hand.

'Dada, it doesn't take all that long to have babies.'

He wanted to chase her around the room the way he used to when they were young, but he felt foolish in his sentimentality.

Kartik rejoiced in his homecoming, in this land. He kicked stray stones in the fields, wanting to kick himself. He had missed his family in all those empty spaces of their absence from his city life. He had been selfish. Never thought how his actions would affect his family. Whenever he had thought of home, it was in the manner of a man turning the pages of an old album and running his hand over the pictures to remove the dust, aching to relive the moments they had captured.

But he had lost the way home.

And there was the foundation.

And then, there was Baby.

And there was his cowardice. He had not been able to summon the courage to face Pitaji or Mummu. He knew he was a disappointment to them. Every move he made seemed to take him away from his family, until all thought of returning to them was but a chimera, trembling on the roads of hot summer months.

It had taken the attack on Miranda to show him the way back. When he told Mrs Singh and Mrs Malhotra he wanted to go away, it was Didi he had planned to visit. Instead, at New Delhi railway station, he found himself impulsively buying a ticket for the train home.

He thanked that impulse. He was glad to be here and they were pleased to see him. Even Pitaji had a curious strangled expression in his eyes when he looked at his son. Kartik realized he had made a terrible error of judgement: he should never have taken his father so seriously, held steadfast to the spirit of Pitaji's letter. At the time he wrote it, Pitaji may have meant every word. But now he appeared grateful, even pleased to see him, never once mentioning previous events. Maybe he had been waiting for Kartik to make the first move.

One night, seeing his father seated alone in the big room, he went to sit beside him.

'May I?' he asked.

For an instant, his father clutched the hookah tightly, then passed it to his son. As it went from the older hand with the strained veins to the younger one with the protruding knuckles, their fingers made fleeting contact. It was the first time Pitaji had touched Kartik since his visit to Delhi with Rukmini.

Kartik puffed and began to cough. Awkwardly, his father thumped him on the back.

'Not like that. You city wallahs only know how to smoke cigarettes. Oh yes,' Pitaji added as Kartik shook his head in denial, 'I have smelt the smoke on your clothes. See, you must draw like this, breath in-out, out-in.' He sucked at the hookah, puffing his thinning cheeks. 'That's the way to enjoy.'

Kartik reached out and put a tentative hand on his shoulder.

'Thank you, Pitaji.'

'For what?'

His father offered him the hookah, studied his wriggling toes.

'Your mother, she grows weaker every day. Don't you find it so?'

Kartik inhaled deeply.

'You ought to have taken care, Pitaji,' he spluttered. 'All those years while I was growing up, Mummu was sick for days at a time. The doctor told you she was too weak, she could not bear any more children …'

'She didn't,' whispered Pitaji.

Pitaji wrung his hands. Kartik saw genuine sadness in the hump of his father's posture and felt a sharp pain, a mixture of outrage and pity, clutch at his heart. He sat on his haunches in front of his father. Pitaji instantly straightened up.

'If you had been an obedient son, we could have had grandchildren by now,' Pitaji whispered. 'Why did I educate you? So you could leave us? You would have tilled this land, brought the benefit of your education to the fields. We would have done well. Instead, you and your cousins have scattered like seeds at sowing time and are growing roots away from us. We will never be together again. Never. A family which puts down roots together grows strong together, that is why we have been here a hundred years …'

He rose and strode across to the oak almirah, took out a bottle of Red Label whisky. He poured it into two steel glasses and offered one to Kartik. They knocked the glasses back and shook their heads like wet dogs.

'Aaah,' burped Pitaji.

'Aaah,' responded Kartik.

'One more for sleep?' suggested Pitaji.

'Why not?'

Pitaji wiped his mouth on his handkerchief and said softly, 'You still do that rubbish job?'

Kartik smiled. He sensed that between them, silence was the best peacemaker. He sat down on the throne chair which still dominated the big room, ran his hands over its fine, old wooden arms, then thrust them into the open lion mouths carved into their edges.

'Pitaji, I told you I wanted to join government service. But I didn't get through the exams the first time. Or the second …' He noticed his father's eyes retreat. 'What I am trying to say is that things just happen, there's not always a logical reason for them.'

'Now you say collecting garbage is your destiny? I can never,' insisted Pitaji, 'accept that.'

'Whatever you wish, Pitaji,' Kartik agreed, suddenly tired of the conversation. 'I am sorry. Let's keep what is, not pine for what is not.'

Pitaji crossed over to the hookah and took a few hurried puffs.

'I know a lotus grows in dirty waters, but you have shamed the family …'

'I am so far away now, Pitaji, no stigma attaches to you. It has been many years now.'

Pitaji placed his glass on the table, with utmost care.

'You blame me?'

'I don't blame you. I chose to do what I wanted, you did what you must. We are even, fifty-fifty.'

Pitaji sighed.

'You say I must accept. But have I not accepted?'

Kartik rose and went across to him. He pressed his shoulder. Pitaji remained still, but his nostrils flared in response.

'Yes, Pitaji, you have been most generous.'

Pitaji's head sank.

'Why didn't you come earlier?' he asked in a whisper. 'Why did you wait for so long?'

Kartik reached down to touch his father's feet and Pitaji's hand hovered over his head. He smiled.

'Your Mummu,' sighed the older man, 'needs me now. She likes me pressing her legs at night, you know?'

Kartik nodded.

'Yes, and speak to her,' he added, 'of the old times.'

He paused, and walked towards the door, turning slightly just before he stepped out. 'Achcha, then …'

Something in his tone told Kartik he had been forgiven.

Standing by a window, Kartik felt the cool monsoon air clear against his skin. If only he could take it with him to Delhi. He gazed upon the house. The people inside it had changed little, but their living conditions had improved considerably. There were two large refrigerators now and a colour TV was the centrepiece in the big room. Lata had a two-in-one. The bedrooms had attached bathrooms. On the first floor, a new suite had been constructed for Lata's family, and spare bedrooms for when the boys came home. There was a new Mahendra jeep parked in the shed, taken out when the children went on a drive or the family went to the big town. And a bright red tractor. Kartik was grateful to Vishnu for the changes he had introduced and felt slightly envious of him. What had he done for his family?

The opportunity came a few days later. He was in the kitchen veranda listening to old Hindi film songs on Lata's two-in-one when he heard her call out for Chachiji. She called out again and with more urgency, but her voice did not penetrate Chachiji's afternoon slumber. Lata called out once more, and Kartik followed the direction of her voice. He found her in their parents' bedroom where she was trying to lift their mother from her bed. Kartik reached out to assist but his mother cried, 'No, not him!' and jerked away.

Lata placed a cautioning hand on his wrist.

'Mummu, how does it matter?'

'No,' she insisted, pulling into herself.

'What is it?' Kartik asked, astonished and a little hurt.

Lata stepped back.

'She cannot always control herself ... but she doesn't want you to touch her.'

Kartik rembered the occasion when, as a child, he had eaten too many mangoes and was unable to control himself. It was Mummu who had rescued him from his humiliation. He squared his shoulders and before Lata or his mother could react, he picked up Mummu and carried her into the bathroom. She moaned as he placed her gently on the plastic chair and waved him away with a flutter of her fingers.

Back in the bedroom, he stripped the bed of its sheets, rolled them up and dropped them on the floor in a puddle. He took the rubber sheet below and went into the bathroom to squeals of protest from both women.

'Don't look,' said Lata.

'I am looking, I am looking,' he teased.

'No!' he heard his mother plead.

He returned to the room with the rubber sheet, dried it with a towel and replaced it on the mattress. There were fresh white sheets in the cupboard. Kartik made up his mother's bed, slowly, carefully, tucking in the corners of the sheet firmly, smoothing out even the smallest hint of a crease as he tightened its ends. He fluffed out the pillows in their new cases and opened the coverlet at the bottom of the bed. Turning around, he saw the talcum powder lying on the dressing table and went across to fetch it. He sprinkled powder in the air and a little on the sheets.

'Fresh as a bathed baby,' Kartik congratulated himself.

He knocked on the bathroom door.

Lata had bathed and dressed his mother. He knelt down beside her and snatching the towel from Lata's shoulder, he began to wipe his mother's feet.

'Oh no,' she murmured faintly, 'stop him, stop him.'

'Sshhh,' whispered Kartik.

The next moment his mother was in his arms and he was carrying her back to her bed.

'There! Fifteen minutes and you're as good as new.'

His mother seemed to crawl into her skin.

Lata placed a finger on her lips and gestured to him to follow her out.

That evening, the doctor had to be summoned. He examined Kartik's mother and said that her agitation was due to a sudden rise in her blood pressure. 'Nothing to worry. Just rest, bas.'

'What else does she do all day?' muttered Kartik to Lata. 'Can't he prescribe something stronger than "rest"?'

They were seated outside in the front lawn.

'She was crying. That's why the pressure is up,' explained Lata, peeling the cucumbers that lay in her lap.

Kartik reached across and popped some pieces into his mouth. They were crunchy. He reached for more, but Lata slapped at his hand. He caught hers and twisted it, she laughed.

'Why was she crying? Was she in pain?'

'Not the kind you mean.'

'What other kind is there?'

'Dada, please, don't act stupid.' Lata snapped. 'She's upset.'

'Why?'

'Oh, Dada! She didn't want you to touch her,' said Lata, 'but you insisted.'

'Yes, so?'

'You are her son.'

'And you her daughter.'

Lata crunched a cucumber.

'It's different. See, these are her beliefs, we must not try to change her now, what's the point? And,' she continued in a practical voice, 'you see what happens if you try?'

Kartik rose and paced on the grass, which sprang up in response to his footfall. It was a still, humid evening and mosquitoes hovered over his head in a drunken merry-go-round.

'It's ridiculous,' he observed, bending to wrench out a fistful of grass. 'I have supervized the cleaning of garbage dumps in Delhi, been with the poor, the sick, all kinds of people in all kinds of places. And I cannot pick up my own mother when she is ill and needs help?' He scratched his nose with a green blade.

'She cannot accept it. Can't you understand?'

'Absurd!' raged Kartik, kicking at the air.

'Here,' shouted Lata and threw a piece of cucumber towards him.

'Don't waste food, Lata, people don't get to eat in this land of ours …' She threw another one at him.

'Dada, please!' She smiled and then straightened her mouth. 'Leave your big city ideas at … India Gate. Here, you must abide—'

'And you must change,' implored Kartik, kneeling beside his sister. 'We cannot abide by the past forever. You see that, don't you?'

Lata hid the thali behind her back and got up.

'I have sent your niece to school, haven't I? When she is older, I will send her to Delhi, to college, like you. Then you can lecture her, Mr Batty Chatty!'

Kartik hugged his sister.

He went into his parents' room before dinner. He found his mother sitting up, her lips quivering to the words of her mantra. He reached out and patted her hand. It trembled.

After dinner, they sat in the big room. Pitaji, Chachaji, Vishnu and Kartik. Pitaji took out the whisky and poured out four glasses.

Mummu was asleep. Pitaji pulled on the hookah and passed it down the line. There was a communal silence, one that made Kartik feel glad for this togetherness. He stretched out his legs and arched his body. He wanted a proper smoke with a cigarette, but decided to wait until later. Let the moment linger as long as possible. He felt his father's eyes on him.

'I am thinking, Kartik …'

'Pitaji …'

'Why don't I send your mother and Lata to Delhi with you? Hmm?'

Kartik saw Chachaji and Vishnu turn to study him.

'The doctor says a change will do her good. And that way, she can be with you and you can show her to the big doctors, the specialists. The best opinion in the country. You take her to All India, make sure she has nothing serious. What do you say? Good idea, na?'

Everyone agreed: taking Kartik's mother to the All India Institute of Medical Sciences was a good idea.

Chachaji thrust the hookah into his hand.

'Excellent idea. Your Chachiji can go too. She is very close to your mother.' He glanced at Kartik.

'It will change your mother's mood, lift her spirits,' continued Pitaji, swallowing his whisky. 'Tomorrow, I can can buy tickets …'

Kartik stood up. He stretched and yawned.

'We'll talk in the morning, Pitaji. I'm going to sleep now.'

'Smoke that cigarette, you mean.'

Kartik bent to touch his feet. He touched Chachaji's on the way out.

In bed, Kartik switched positions restlessly. He couldn't find sleep anywhere: in the Gayatri Mantra, in thoughts of his mother, in counting numbers backwards … in the realization that his father had reclaimed him totally, otherwise he would never have suggested that his mother accompany him back to Delhi. Nothing worked. He climbed out of bed and went to stand outside his parents' bedroom door. Once, he thought he heard a gentle moan. He went back to his room. He thought of his life in Delhi: his small flat, the garbage collection, the karamchari strike, a man in hospital because of him, the police on his case, the promise of Baby …

Early the next morning, he followed his father to the fields.

'Pitaji … I don't think Mummu … should visit me … at least not just yet.'

His father blinked.

'Why not?'

Pitaji walked on, Kartik behind him.

'What I do,' continued Kartik, swallowing, 'she will be most awkward with it, with my life. You know it. Besides, with the rains, my work will increase. I will have very little time.'

His father stared at him.

'I have responsibilities right now, Pitaji …'

'None towards your own mother?'

Kartik took a deep breath. 'My sense of responsibility tells me

Mummu will be most unhappy if she goes with me right now. I will go to All India, find out about the doctors and you can bring her to Delhi a little later. Stay at the South-Ex guest house. Staying with me will not …'

Pitaji put out a hand.

'Bas. I understand. If you can't, then you can't.'

'Pitaji …'

They had reached the gate. Pitaji opened it and the hinges wailed in protest. He passed through the gate and then turned to his son.

'Well, keep coming and going …'

Kartik knew he had been dismissed.

The next evening, despite Mummu and Lata's protests, Kartik left home. At the railway station, his father stood on the platform, waving him out of sight.

In the morning, he had arrived outside the familiar gate, rung the bell, then thrust it aside and walked in.

Didi was seated in the veranda, drinking tea in mechanical sips. She looked up.

'About time,' she remarked, and disappeared inside the house.

'Baby,' she called out. 'See who has come.'

Sita stood in the doorway, her eyes circular, nodding her head in encouragement.

He heard Baby's voice: 'Like I said, you old women get excited about the stupidest things.'

He saw her step out into the corridor.

'See,' coaxed Sita. 'See, see.'

'A, B, C, D …' Baby shouted. She opened the netted door, thrust out one hip and called out: 'Yes?'

Kartik studied her. There was a question that had been troubling him ever since they had met again, one that he was always on the verge of asking, but never quite got around to.

'Why,' he blurted out, flinging down his bag, 'why have you got yellow hair?'

NEW YORK
1985

Yellow hair. She dyed it herself. It shone like gold. It made her unusual, so unlike herself that if she met herself, she may have walked by. Anonymity. After what Ramaji did to her, she didn't want be the woman he had known.

It happened the night she had cooked an Indian dinner and Amma's sooji halwa. Ramaji was late. Baby had placed all the dishes on the trolley so that the minute he arrived, she could heat up the food and roll out the trolley onto the patio where they would eat by the shimmering lake to the left of his house.

Baby was hungry and alone. It was a solitude she often filled with music. Anything to break the monotony of her own breathing and the sound of her footsteps as she walked through the house, cleaning and rearranging. She had developed a yen for shifting the furniture. It made the rooms look different; it was like living a new life. It also occupied time, space. The maid, Jacaranda, complained about bumping into something where she least expected it.

Baby knew Ramaji was in office. She didn't expect him to call. He no longer checked on her as he used to in the first flush of his infatuation with her. His schedule was erratic: time and place depended on his business. Baby never knew where he might be, and when he might return. In contrast, Baby led a routine existence. Every evening she would return from the bookstore by 5 p.m. Her shift ended at 4.15 p.m. Yusuf would come in at 4 p.m. and stay till nine. He was studying at New York University. Film Studies. He'd come all the way from Lahore.

'What's the point of studying films?' Baby once asked him.

'Because there's nothing better I like doing than watching them.'

'What will you do with a degree in films back in Pakistan?'

'Who said I am going back?'

So many of them who came and didn't go back. Like Baby herself.

It was 8 p.m. by her watch. Still no message from Ramaji. He usually called when he was very late. She liked it when he was late.

The later he came, the less he drank. The fewer drinks he had, the less he tried to fool around with her. The less he fooled around, the less they grew apart.

She felt uneasy. She had come out of a long bath, with lavender salts soaking into her skin. She had creamed and oiled herself, listened to music. She wore a white sleeveless blouse and a grey-and-black candy stripe georgette sari studded with silver sequins in front where the pleats folded and where the pallu fell. She wore diamond tops in her ears – Ramaji had given them to her early in their relationship when he expressed his feelings in gifts, not bruises – and sparkling purple mascara on her eye lashes. That was another thing she liked to do: dress up, wear make-up.

Ramaji used to tease her.

'Photo, photo on the wall, is my Baby the fairest of them all?'

Baby paid no attention. He said she admired herself too much. She replied there was no one else to admire her.

Only Kartik had done that.

Kartik.

She regretted him more each day. Regretted walking away. Regretted not returning to him. But she had been caught up in a private world of her own redemption.

She pressed a pimple between two fingers and let the blood dry on them. These pimples, she felt, lent character to her face. Her otherwise flawless complexion had the unnatural sheen of plastic like in women's magazines.

She was listening to Hari Prasad Chaurasia on the flute. It was 9.43 p.m. Morning for Amma. Baby imagined her sitting by her bed, drinking tea. On impulse, she reached across for the telephone and dialled her number, swinging gently to the rhythm of the music.

'Yes?'

'Amma?'

'What's happened, Baby?'

'What can happen to a beautiful young girl like me? What about you?'

Amma didn't reply. She disliked questions.

'Amma ...'

'I am the same as I was yesterday, and yesterday I was the same as I was on Tuesday.'

'There's never any talking to you.'

'Then why are you talking to me?'

'Call Sita, please.'

Baby heard Sita ask Amma to leave the room. She wanted to have a 'pivate' word with her Baby. If there had to be an Amma, if there had to be a Baby, thank god there was a Sita. She was the constant between them.

There was Amma's voice in the background.

'She is saying,' informed Sita, 'not to waste her child's money on silly conversations with silly Sita.'

Baby laughed, Sita stormed and then there was a click, but not before Sita had told her to eat garlic every day, and lots of yoghurt.

'Apply also to face and arms and hair,' Sita recommended, 'very cooling.'

'The garlic?' Baby asked.

'Hai hai, Mem, why have you gone and left me with these children of yours? Yoghurt,' she explained, 'yoghurt.'

Baby wanted to say that here on the east coast of the United States of America, we don't need cooling, but Sita had already disconnected the call.

At 10 p.m. Baby considered eating on her own, and decided against it. It would only bedevil Ramaji further.

She sank back into the white cushions of the sofa and shook her legs from side to side in an effort to shake off a lingering unease. Maybe it was the bird she had seen that morning.

It had alighted on the branch of an oak tree in the garden. She was out there gathering morning dew flowers for the vases: flame roses, pink ones, green heather.

Something cool fell in the parting of her hair. Instinctively, she glanced up and the bird peered down at her like an old woman over her reading glasses. She was grey and brown, with a hint of a yellow plume beneath closed wings.

As soon as Baby moved away, the bird flew off. Within seconds, however, she had returned to occupy exactly the same perch. Baby shielded her eyes with the flowers and watched the bird go to and fro between the branch and the open sky in a relay race of her own. She seemed unable to decide which she preferred: freedom or security. Finally, she settled for the branch and Baby saw the small chest pump hard and rapidly. Then she began to shake her head, firmly, insistently.

Without warning, she suddenly swooped down, turned and flew straight towards the trunk of the oak tree.

'No, no,' Baby cried out.

The bird carried on heedless. Her head collided with the trunk and she collapsed on the grass below.

Baby waited for her to rise and fly away. Nothing stirred. Baby stepped across to the tree, crushing the flowers to her body. She found the bird amongst the strewn leaves, still, lifeless.

Baby bit into a rose petal. It tasted as bitter as it smelt sweet.

She, too, wanted to bang her head against the tree trunk.

There was a rush of wind at the door. Hurried little steps followed by heavy, long strides. A square head with crisp grey curls and the curves of a bushy moustache appeared around the door. Ramaji. Smiling.

Baby headed for the kitchen.

Jacaranda had already lit the stove and placed the pans on the burners.

'You go now, Jacaranda, I will take the food out on the trolley.'

'I can help.'

'No, no, it is very late. I can manage.'

Baby allowed the food to burble and bubble and spit till the steam rose to her face. Then, carefully filling each container, she wheeled the trolley through the drawing room to the door leading out into the patio.

'Wait, my sweet,' said Ramaji, 'let me have my Scotch.'

Baby applied the brakes on the trolley and went to switch off the buzz of the music system. Chaurasia had long since ceased to flute.

When she turned, Ramaji was sunk deep into the sofa's feathered lightness, his legs wide apart, the grey flannel trousers climbing up in tight creases. His blue blazer with its gold medallion buttons had been flung aside to reveal the white shirt stretched against his body in protest, its buttons straining to contain him. He preferred to wear transparent shirts, netted vests so the curls of his black hair were visible. He lay sprawled there, his fingers alternately reaching inside his shirt to scratch the area around his navel, and sharpen the edges of his moustache. He opened his mouth in a hole so large, Baby thought he would swallow the mouth of the glass.

He took a long sip of his drink.

'All in silver and black. You are like the moon spread out on the lake.' He poured himself another drink, added three cubes of ice.

'Beauty and the beast,' he said. He scratched himself and sank back. 'This beauty,' he thumped his chest, 'that beast!' He toasted her.

He laughed then. With such gusto, she could see right up to the back of his throat. She was repulsed by him. People were supposed to grow on you, but Ramaji and she had long since outgrown each other.

'Dinner, I am starving.'

He rose and put out his hand in invitation. Baby stared at the thick lifelines on his palm – healthy and wealthy.

She walked away to the trolley.

'Wait, I am still having my Scotch.'

Baby opened the door and stepped out onto the patio. In her silver high heels, she clattered down the stone steps that went all the way to the edge of the lake. She sat on the bottom-most step, her arms clasped around her knees, the pallu of the sari wound around her neck, her arms naked.

'I thought I asked you to wait?' Ramaji appeared in the open doorway.

Baby did not offer a reply.

'Here, then, have your dinner, my little beast.'

Baby turned to see him push the trolley like a pram down the steps. He took a sip from his glass and followed the trolley as it bumped along.

Even as she watched, his fingers slid off the trolley and it hurtled down the remaining steps. The lids of the containers flew into the air, and the dal and the vegetables slashed her across the face. The trolley collided with her, oversetting the remaining food on her arms and body.

The searing pain of something simmering on her skin. The constant desire to tear off the bandages and scratch her face off.

The doctors said they had to rearrange her face a little. Like I did the furniture, Baby grimaced to herself. When they had removed the bandgages and she looked into the mirror, she saw someone she knew but did not immediately recognize. She was no longer the Baby anyone had known, although there were no major scars left behind by the burns. The skin was just a little tighter, as though it had shrunk, become too small for her features.

She was in hospital for six weeks during which time she saw no one apart from Ramaji. Behind her bandages, she thought ceaselessly of the trolley falling on her. Had he deliberately released it, given it a little shove in the right direction? Or did he simply stumble after three large, quick drinks? Amma and Kartik said things just happened. Baby had never agreed. Up until now. Maybe this did just happen. Maybe not. Suddenly, Baby was scared of them together. That's when she knew she had to leave him.

This time she would choose who she wanted to be. She didn't want to be Purush's daughter – dispense with her. She didn't want to be Amma's resentful child – discard her. She didn't want to be the woman who had left Kartik – dismiss her. Most of all, she didn't want to be Ramaji Rameshwar Rao's Little Red Riding Hood or his 'beast'. She was the one Baby had to peel off first.

But she had things to do before she could leave him. First, she dyed her hair blonde. It drew the attention away from her altered features. Second, she asked Ramaji for the bookstore. He said it was hers already. No, she told him firmly, in my name. Legally. Otherwise, she might have to file a case against him for her injury. Three days later, the title deeds to the bookstore were in Baby's hand.

'My Little Red Riding Hood, this is my gift to you, and I know it will make us hickory-dickory dock again.'

How Baby hated nursery rhymes.

The day she left Ramaji, she carried out her Louis Vuitton suitcases into the New York sunlight and climbed into a taxi. As the plane took off, she felt she was travelling back in time, returning to everything and everyone she had left behind.

'Madam,' a male voice interrupted her reverie, 'would you like a glass of beer?'

HILL STATION
1986

'Would you like a glass of beer?' demanded Kartik, swallowing hard. 'Listening makes me very thirsty.'

Didi and Baby were seated at the table in the veranda while Kartik strolled in the veranda and Sita scraped potatoes on the steps.

Under the slant of her eyelids, Didi watched Baby and Kartik and crossed her fingers under the table. There was an opening here, she could see, the way the sky revealed itself when the clouds part after a monsoon shower. Baby was gentler, less combative, and the droop to Kartik's mouth had lifted at the corners.

'So, how about it?' Kartik asked again.

Didi accepted a glass and smiled graciously at Kartik. She took a large sip and turned away from the picture of Kartik holding a glass to Baby's lips and she spraying him with the bottle. Didi's mind stopped, clicked: from the film roll of the past, she saw a photograph of herself spraying Jeff with champagne. Jeff ...

A snatch of conversation brought her back to her surroundings.

'... a police report. I honestly think you should have filed it as protection. See what has happened to me. After what he did to you, that man needs watching,' said Kartik.

Baby fingered the rim of the glass he held out.

'It is better to keep it hanging over Ramaji's head.'

Didi massaged both temples.

'I am sure he did it on purpose,' she remarked.

'Why?' Baby was immediately watchful.

'Because I never liked his photo,' Didi replied tartly. 'Never. Ask Sita. Sita, Sita!' she yelled.

'Aaeeeey,' called back Sita.

'Don't yell, Amma, please,' Baby complained. 'You're all so loud in India.'

Didi ignored her.

'Sita, didn't I tell you that man of Baby's in New York was a stinky fellow?'

'Amma!'

'Yes.' Sita wagged the sharp chopping knife in the air like it was Ramaji. 'Stinky fellow.'

The colour stole into Baby's cheeks.

'Why do you talk like that about someone you don't know?'

Didi felt a warning nerve tug in her head. She ignored it.

'Well, I was right, wasn't I?'

'But that is not the point. Why don't you leave my life alone?'

Didi pressed her forehead, breathed out slowly.

'Your life is a part of my life. It's difficult to separate the two the way you want to. I have hardly interfered. How could I? You aren't here. But how you came to choose to live with that man, allowed him to treat you badly … I can't understand it.'

Baby stood up, let her hair fall loose. Kartik stood behind her. She leaned back against him as if he were a wall, one foot balanced on his calf.

'We all make mistakes.' She glared at her mother.

'That,' Didi reached for her beer, 'I know.'

Baby slapped Didi's glass off the table.

'Hai hai, Mem, take me where you are so I do not have to watch these two.'

Sita waddled indoors and returned with a broom. Baby snatched it out of her hand and gathered the glass shards.

'Always horrid,' she complained on her haunches. 'Leave it,' she told Sita, 'I will pick up the pieces. She makes me so hot in the head …'

Baby stormed into the house, slamming the door behind her. Kartik took a step forward, stopped, reproached Didi with his eyes.

Didi inclined her head. Kartik went inside.

Moments later, Baby strode out, her face dripping water, her hands twining her hair into a bun slung low on her neck. She was grinding her teeth.

'I am trying, but you like to make me feel small.'

'No.' Didi reached for the half full beer bottle on the table and shook it till the foam rose to its mouth. 'I like nothing. You asked a question,' she blew on the foam, 'and I told you what I thought.'

Baby jutted out her thinned lower lip, then retrenched it. She sat down next to her mother and hid her face in her hands. They sat in angry silence.

After a brief moment, she took her mother's fingers in her hand and began to press them, one by one.

'Shall we talk about Chor Bagh, then?' she said quietly. 'Shall I tell him about that?' She shifted her gaze to Kartik. 'Shall we tell him what you thought of your husband, and your brother-in-law?'

'Let her be,' Sita intervened, pulling at Baby's shoulder. 'Getting after her like this.'

Baby shrugged off Sita. She glared at Didi.

'Whose life has she not touched? My father's, Bhai Chacha's, mine. Bhai Chacha,' she said in the small, mean voice of a child. 'Tell us about Bhai Chacha, Amma, and why we had to leave the only home I really loved. Tell us about the storeroom.'

Didi felt her blood run cold. Her daughter still pressed her fingers with the full force of her thumbs. Didi winced but tried a smile.

'Kartik,' she cleared her throat, 'would you mind taking Baby away?'

'Forever?' he asked, cheerfully.

Baby pressed Didi's middle finger painfully hard.

'I won't be led away. I won't.'

'Okay, you won't.'

'No, I won't.

'You've said that already.'

'And I will say it a hundred times again if it pleases me.'

Didi bent forward and felt her stomach roll. She needed a cigarette.

'Baby, let's stop now.'

'Stop? Why didn't you stop, Amma? Why?' Baby released Didi's hand and placed both her palms on the glass top of the table. She stretched out her fingers. 'Shall I tell you why? Sometimes one cannot stop, sometimes you keep doing something even when you know it's wrong. I know.'

'Stop,' Didi repeated, sinking back.

Baby lifted her hands and admired their imprint on the glass, 'Tell us, then, what made you not stop your little …?'

Didi burst into tears.

Later, while a quarter moon stood still on a calm sky, Baby entered Didi's room. Her mother lay with her hands near her heart, her eyes open, inert. She did not blink.

'Amma.' Baby shook her. 'Amma.'

Didi closed her eyes.

Baby went across to the window, perched on its ledge, swinging a leg. With her right index finger she traced her name in the dust on the windowpane.

'I shouldn't have said all that.'

'It had to come out,' Didi turned on her side.

'I came here to move on from the past. And I thought I was doing quite well. Lying in a hospital bed gives you plenty of time to think, and I thought, what's the point of all this between us? It seemed simple then, between the white sheets: what I had lived had so far been about you. Now, it was up to me to do something with myself. That's why I returned – to find Kartik and to change things between us. But I still need to know what happened at Chor Bagh and you won't tell.'

'Let it lie low and it will bury itself. Are you,' Didi switched sides, 'are you going to continue with Kartik?'

'If he wants.'

'He never stopped, Baby.'

Baby shuddered.

'Don't ... I ought to have stopped out there ...'

'You said yourself, one can't always stop ...'

Baby stood over her mother. In the dark, and from a height, Didi was diminutive. She reminded Baby of the bird who flew so thoughtlessly into the oak tree.

'Why did you ...?'

'Just.'

'Amma ... that is no answer.'

'There is no answer.' Didi felt her body tighten. 'I was unhappy, he was there, it was autumn ... It happened.'

Baby sat down on the bed next to Didi and turned over her hands, thumbed the fingers. Then she held them tight, in a hurtful grip.

They sat like that, Didi and Baby, long into the night. Didi spoke of 3, Chor Bagh, described Baby's childhood to her. As histories went, it was deliberately selective. She had always wondered what had been said to the girl on her solitary visit to 3, Chor Bagh, after Kartik had failed the UPSC exams, the visit that had brought Baby back to her, bursting with rage.

In the intervening years, while Baby was in New York, in all the telephone conversations across the continents, they had never spoken of the past or of her visit to 3, Chor Bagh. Baby lived in the present, the continuous present, refusing to discuss anything but the immediate.

Didi had fretted over what Baby knew of the past, what she had learnt, what she had concluded or misconstrued. But asking had been forbidden. Until this visit. Everything Didi wished to avoid was abruptly, without notice, wrenched back into focus.

Now, Didi used a comb with wide teeth to untangle the knots of her past – she left the most painful ones alone. Like your tongue, some things had to remain inside your mouth.

Didi spoke and Baby listened. At some stage, she went to sit on the window ledge, swinging her legs, tying and untying her hair, withholding her gaze from her mother.

Didi described her journey from New York, omitting any mention of Jeff, to an arranged marriage at 3, Chor Bagh, and the deaths of Father and Mem that had left her alone with Baby. She tried to explain the failure with Purush, blamed herself for the inability to adjust, for failing in marriage, without mentioning Purush's failure in bed. And there was Bhai's shadow hovering constantly, protectively, on the fringes of her existence.

'I was young and passionate like you are. The only person I could hug was you and you hated being held for long. You would sit on my lap, horsie-horsie and then jump and run away with Budhoo.'

Didi avoided emotion, blandishments as she spoke briefly of the bookstore. Bhai had lent fleeting romance to his younger brother's discontented wife. That summer was inevitable and so commonplace, Didi said, sometimes she wished she could disown it. She didn't blame Bhai or herself too much. It happened and it ended, as such relations must, sadly.

'The night your Bhai Chacha went missing, there was a buzz in my head. I was wild with panic. I can't explain it but I was seized by a dreadful fear that Mem's gods had trapped me. I thought he had died in the cricket riots because of me.

'I saw terrible images in the shadows. My mind collapsed, I felt it crumble. For a long while, I could not control my thoughts, concentrate. I would be sitting outside, reading to you and suddenly, I'd feel hot, there was this flash before my eyes ... The nights were the worst.

'How could I have stayed there, Baby? In a house where there was so much ... I don't know what words to use ... bad feeling? A sense of continuous dread at what might happen? My presence in that house brought out the worst in all of us. All that had happened ... It had to end and Som Devi ended it. Let me tell you, my departure released all of us – Purush, Bhai and me – from the awkward situation we had placed ourselves in. You were hurt, but the person who suffered most was your Dadi. Losing you.'

Baby was shrugging back tears.

'Baby, no ... She took the decision to let you go when she asked me to leave. She knew the price. And she never called us back. She was a proud soul.'

'You hated each other.'

'I disliked her. She disliked what I did to those she loved.'

'You shouldn't have. Purush was awful, don't I know,' Baby wiped her nose, 'how awful? But you and Bhai Chacha ... this man Hamer ...'

Didi struggled into a sitting position, pushed herself off the bed and stood up. Her fingers latched onto to her daughter's shoulders.

'I will say this to you, Baby. Bhai was wrong, but only because he was the wrong man. Whereas, Mr Hamer, he has been a good friend, the best. That's all. Then, now, forever. Nothing more. After Chor Bagh, I was finished with all that. Don't you see? I could never forget what it had done to us.'

'If only you had exercised control, Amma, Dadi would not have thrown you out.'

Didi nodded.

Baby rose and held her mother's fingers.

'You're not exercising them like I told you, five times a day, in out, out in ...' She bent them backwards and forward.

Didi nodded again.

Baby went towards the door.

'What you did is something I can't forget.' She looked back at her mother.

'Forget? I have trouble forgetting it myself, but,' Didi got up and touched her cheek so gently, Baby felt only the heat of her fingers, 'perhaps you could learn to be a little kinder about the past?'

Baby smiled and knuckled her nose.

Didi turned away.

'Amma?'

'Hmm.'

'You know what I think?'

Didi shook her head.

'We all deserve to try again.'

She left without waiting for Didi's reply.

Didi sighed, climbed back onto her bed. So Baby had been spared. Som Devi had told her only the little truths.

She lay awake, comforted by what remained of the night. In the morning she called the hotel for a car.

Mr Hamer was seated outside in the garden, an unopened newspaper lying on his lap, half asleep. He opened his eyes to greet her. She sat down next to him. 'Did you know that,' Didi asked as though in the middle of a conversation, 'little truths lead to bigger lies?'

3, CHOR BAGH
1962

Little truths lead to bigger lies. Growing bigger all the while. Her stomach was a small, tight protrusion. Not visibly bloated, she had been able to disguise herself beneath the sari tied deliberately high.

Little truths and bigger lies meant only one thing: trouble. Trouble in the form of Som Devi. Didi had not fooled her even for a moment. She knew from the way Som Devi stared at her. She knew. Everything.

'More than even I do,' Didi said.

'Do what?' came the voice from the foot of her bed.

'Why is it that you are never here when I want you and always here when I wish you were far away?'

Sita struggled up to a sitting position, her hair tumbling open from the loose knot and cascading about her round face.

'Didi, I want peace,' she complained. 'Afternoon is the only time I get it. Mem never disturbed me in the afternoons.'

Didi raised her head from the book she was reading.

'Mem, Mem, Mem, that's all you say.'

The door swung open and Baby appeared with Budhoo behind her, his head, ears and tail drooping.

'Sita, say something else,' Baby ordered. 'All the time Nani's name only.'

Sita pulled her down next to her into the pile of mending clothes.

'You too? Go to sleep,' she ordered, patting the space next to her.

Budhoo collapsed by her side, in obedience.

'Oh no,' Sita pushed him away, 'not you! You are not sharing my bed.'

'No male ever does,' observed Didi.

Baby clapped as if she appreciated what Didi had said.

'Just because you have—'

'Shut,' Didi interrupted firmly, 'up.'

'Aaayeee,' squealed Sita, wiggling and straightening up.

Didi raised her head once more.

'Now what?'

'This Budhoo is poking me ... in ...!' protested Sita, smacking at Budhoo's snout which was venturing between her legs.

Baby giggled.

'Stop it, stop it ...' Sita pushed the dog.

'Budhoo, come here.' The voice emerged from a pair of feet in the doorway, behind the drawn curtain. 'This minute.'

Budhoo turned with his tail in the air and shuffled towards the figure, sniffed the toes dutifully, and sauntered off.

'Even a dog is not welcome in this room,' Som Devi remarked. 'Come, Baby, I will show you how to make samosas and tell you a story about the three ghosts who lived inside your grandfather's briefcase.'

Baby jumped up and ran to her grandmother, colliding with her.

'Khoon! Let's go, Dadi. Amma and Sita are too boring.'

'You stay with your Dadi, Baby, always, achcha?'

'A-cha!' Baby imitated her grandmother's enunciation. 'Tata Amma, tata Sita ...' Her voice trailed away with her footsteps.

Didi and Sita were left to each other.

'That one is going to give you a lot of trouble.' Sita nodded towards the door.

'Yes,' agreed Didi, 'but which one?'

Didi tried to relieve the strain of her anxiety with a yawn. However, each time she opened her mouth, her jaws locked and a small gasp squeaked out. She breathed deeply a few times and then rose. From the almirah, she took out an old pair of winter socks and wore them on her hands. Then she sat by the dressing table and mechanically wiped each item between her socked hands. She found it comforting.

She was perspiring. It was another balmy summer afternoon.

Didi placed the last perfume bottle on the glass top and stared up at the ceiling fan that creaked above her head. Ever since she had come to 3, Chor Bagh, it had been whirring at the same tired speed.

'Grown old,' she told it, 'trying to cool our tempers, our passions.'

Who would give her trouble? Before her return to 3, Chor Bagh, she had calculated the odds and decided they fell in favour of concealment. Who would reveal her condition? Not Purush. Any disclosure of her pregnancy would be an admission of his failure. Not Bhai – it would be an admission of his own involvement. That left Som Devi. Didi was unsure of her mother-in-law. She was cool, sharp, and she knew. However, that was not the source of her power: her real strength lay in her closeness to Baby and knowing that the child was Didi's one weakness. To protect Baby, Didi would go far, very far.

What did Som Devi have in mind? How did she plan to deal with Didi? So far, she had remained aloof. Why did she wait silently at the edges of Didi's existence, watching but never revealing herself entirely? Why didn't she come out into the open and confront her daughter-in-law with what she knew?

'No wonder she tells such good stories to Baby,' Didi complained aloud. 'She's ghostly.'

'Huh?' Sita stirred.

'Go to sleep,' Didi murmured.

She brooded, wondering when Som Devi would strike. As for Baby, she had said nothing. She hadn't questioned the trip to Delhi, the abrupt return. Once in a while, she complained that Amma rested too much, 'always has the headache', and she laughed about Amma's stomach. 'Dadi says Amma is fat because she is eating for two-two!'

Didi listened in silence to Som Devi's snide remarks and humoured Baby.

Curiously, Som Devi hadn't said a word to Baby, either. Didi wondered why. 'We are both playing blind,' Didi said aloud, rising awkwardly and pacing the floor, 'gambling on unseen cards, uncertain of the other's hand.'

Didi's pains began one afternoon. She was strolling in the lawn with Baby, teaching her a nursery rhyme when she felt the discomfort. She recognized the feeling and rushed inside. Baby trailed her, reciting,
Humpty sat on a fwall ...
Dumpty had a big all ...
'Great, Baby, Humpty-Dumpty had a great fall,' Didi corrected automatically from behind the bathroom door.
'Gweat fall ...'
'Grrrr, Baby, grrr ...'
'Like Budhoo?'
'Exactly like Budhoo.'
Didi emerged from the bathroom, took Baby by the hand and sat on the bed.
'Then?'
Baby pursed her mouth in concentration: '*All the kingmen and all the horses ...* Go horsie, horsie!'
Didi pulled her daughter close and kissed her on both cheeks.
'Six years old and so smart? Learnt it in one day! C.V. Raman ... you will be great one day.'
'C.V., T.B., pee-pee ...' sang out the girl.
'Very musical too,' added Didi. 'You tell Bhai Chacha to take you for ice cream tonight.' Didi smoothed down her frock. 'Listen, Baby, I am going to lie down because I am feeling very tired.'
'Ek do teen ...' chanted Baby.
'... and not too well.'
'Amma's so mean.'
'Until I send for you, I want you to stay with Dadi. Understand?'
Baby nodded. Didi hugged her.
'Promise?'
'Plomise.'
'Go now and send Sita.'
Baby ran out of the room.

'Seeee-ta, Seeta …'

A few minutes later, Sita entered with a steel glass.

'Not now, Sita.'

'Then when, I ask? You've eaten nothing …'

'Not,' Didi pointed at her stomach and cramped her fingers, 'now.'

'Oh,' exclaimed Sita in surprise.

'Oh?'

Didi nodded.

'Oh,' Sita concluded in a knowing voice and bolted the door behind her.

'I have spoken to Roop. She knows what to do.' She drew the curtains on the garden door.

'No, open them and the bedroom door, just now,' panted Didi, 'otherwise that woman will arrive.'

'She will in any case.'

'Yes, but we must try and avoid it until … Let's be as quiet as we can.'

Approximately an hour later, Som Devi stopped outside Didi's bedroom door. She thought she heard Didi and Sita talking in undertones. She placed one foot on the other and wiggled her toes. Sita noticed the shadow beneath the door and pinched Didi, who looked around.

'Sita,' she said in a strained, but loud voice, 'go get that milk, now, my headache is better. And Sita?'

'What it is?'

'Warm it well.'

'Hai hai, Mem, as if I give cold milk!'

She moved towards the corridor.

Som Devi's toes returned to their chappals in haste, and her feet moved to one side. As Sita went out, Som Devi inspected her.

'Is something the matter?'

'You know my Didi.' Sita was conspiratorial. 'Always too stubborn.'

Som Devi was not interested in Didi's character. She turned away, then halted.

'If she doesn't want cold milk, why doesn't she blow on it? Her tongue is hot enough to light a fire!'

Didi stuffed the bed sheet inside her mouth and breathed out heavily through her nose.

That night she did not join the dinner party.

When Bhai inquired why, Baby tapped her head.

'Your mother has gone mental?' asked Purush, hopefully.

The little girl's lips trembled.

'Leave her alone,' Som Devi said. 'She's just a child, what does she know?'

'I know,' announced Baby with a defiant stare. 'Amma has the headache.'

'Always the headache,' Purush sneered. 'Why don't they open it up and take out whatever is in there?'

Som Devi saw Bhai pale, but he did not speak.

They ate. Each one seemed unusually hungry, so the meal was lengthier and quieter than normal. As Baby rose, she poked out her stomach and marched forward to her grandmother.

'Like Amma,' she boasted.

One glance at Purush's face and Bhai spoke up.

'Let's go for a drive, Baby?'

'Yes!' She jumped up and down.

'Ma, will you come too?'

Som Devi smiled at her granddaughter.

'Why not? And maybe if this,' she patted her stomach, 'is smaller by the end, we can stop and have softees at D.Vinter?'

'Already empty.' Baby sucked in her stomach. 'See?'

She ran out of the dining room and into her mother's bedroom. It was in darkness save for a lamp.

'Amma, Baby go for softee.'

Didi did not reply.

'Amma …' Sita stepped out of the bathroom. She held a wrung-out towel in her hands.

'Go eat ice cream; leave Amma alone.'

Baby bent over her mother, placed a hand on her forehead. 'Chhi,' she withdrew it, 'all wet-wet.'

Didi caught her hand and wiped it with her pallu.

'Water, Baby ... just water. Go for your drive.'

Baby skipped out.

They returned some forty minutes later to find Sita seated in the porch. She caught hold of the girl's hand the moment she alighted from the Oldsmobile.

'It's time for bed,' she said and guided Baby into the bedroom. When Baby had fallen asleep, Sita crept back into Didi's room.

Didi's pains had increased. She moaned softly. Sita wiped her brow, her arms and face with perfumed water. Neither spoke. There was nothing to say. Eventually the pace picked up. Didi held the head of the bed, arched her back. She had made Sita bind her feet with a sari to the bed, raised and bent her knees so that she was in the correct position. She knew what must be done since she had consulted Prem's lady doctor in Delhi, on how best to go about the process of childbirth at home. Unlike Baby's time, when she had thrashed about agitatedly, Didi was controlled and focussed. But then a pain so severe shot through her body, she howled. Sita stuffed the sheet into her mouth.

Agitated barks and a scratch at the bedroom door announced Budhoo.

'Let him in,' gasped Didi.

'No! He's not clean,' disagreed Sita.

'Let him come, his barks ...' Another pain ravaged her. 'Mem, Mem,' she sobbed.

Half in tears herself, Sita wiped Didi's face and held her fast.

'I'll ask Bhaisahib to call a doctor ...'

'Na-na, na-na,' Didi consoled her. 'Very soon now.'

Within minutes there was a third stab of pain. Didi opened her mouth. Sita put her hand in, stifling the scream. Blood oozed where Didi's teeth had clamped down.

'Mem, oh Mem,' Didi whimpered, 'forgive me, Sita.'

Sita sucked the back of her hand, then massaged Didi's neck and shoulders.

Didi jolted up once again and Budhoo, seated by the veranda door, let out a series of long, wolfish howls that bounced off the walls into the night.

'Sita, Roop ...'

Sita stepped out into the dimly lit corridor and listened for wakeful sounds. Hearing none, she proceeded into the dining room where Roop slept on a string cot. Roop understood Sita's gentle tap. In the last two months, she had enjoyed an excellent view of Didi's small but growing belly while she stood behind her chair and oiled her hair.

'Whenever,' she had prophesied, scrambling the thick hair with bent fingers, 'this one can happen whenever.'

'I know,' replied Didi, 'you be ready when I call.'

'I am always ready, from morning to night. No problem. I have given birth to I don't know how many children. Just cut like so,' she boasted.

So when Sita's tap came in the middle of that humid night, Roop rose, automatically.

'Quick,' Sita whispered. 'Didi's pain is bigger than the room. Soon it will spread to the entire house.'

'Don't know what hurry he is in,' complained Roop, adjusting her sari, 'to enter this world just when we are ready to leave it.'

Minutes later, Roop was pressing down on Didi's compact stomach.

It was not Didi's pained cries or Budhoo's agitated barks at imagined intruders that disturbed Som Devi. She was accustomed to the restless darkness as Purush snored loudly, and Baby muttered in her sleep. No, it wasn't the sounds of the night that alerted Som Devi. It was the scent.

As she turned onto her left side, the freshness of lemons wafted into her nostrils and she imagined herself in the kitchen garden amongst the lemon trees or putting lemons to pickle in the veranda. The scent persisted and Som Devi lifted her eyelids. She sniffed the air. Why was that dayan – she knew it was Didi – using so much perfume at ...

Som Devi consulted her bedside clock … past one? Som Devi got out of bed, reached for her spectacles, hung them around her ears and crept out, barefoot.

Inside Didi's room, Roop was feeling Didi's stomach.

'What have you got in there?' she heaved. 'A pebble?'

Didi breathed in deeply and eased out to a count of twenty, nineteen, eighteen …

'Such a baby I have never seen.' Roop peered between Didi's legs.

'You haven't seen,' Didi gasped, 'this one yet, either.'

Roop applied her hands to the upper end of her belly. No one heard the knock at the door.

Didi had no sense of herself, only of the pain. She concentrated on it, thinking that if she held it in the middle of her forehead, she could contain its intensity.

Fingers circled her navel, a voice beckoned.

'Come, come, beta, come look into Roop's toothless mouth,' said Roop.

There was an insistent knocking in Didi's left ear.

'Come in,' she invited in a hoarse undertone.

'He's still inside,' explained Sita, holding Didi firmly down.

'There,' coaxed Roop, 'there.' Didi felt the world rotate in her stomach. She gathered herself into one big heave. In the blackout that followed, she saw shadows gather above her and reach down for her.

Then, she thought she heard the knocking again. And a voice.

'What's going on? Why is this door locked?'

Roop started.

'Hey bhagvan, big memsahib! She will have me for this. Whip me. Coming here without telling her. Quick, Sita, I have to go.'

There was hectic activity at the foot of the bed.

'A boy, a boy.' Roop's tone was gloating, 'I knew it!'

'Me too,' murmured Didi.

Another demanding knock.

'Clean him properly with warm soft hands and water, Sita,' Roop ordered. 'Then wash Didiji and throw all that comes out into a packet. The big memsahib will make chutney of me. Rest later.'

She dropped her sari, rushed to the toilet, hurried out wiping her hands and face, and disappeared through the door leading into the corridor.

Didi lay flattened by her exertions. She had to rise, tidy up … but first she wanted to hear a very special sound. Ah, there it was.

'Thank you, Mem.'

'I will clean and bring him.' Sita turned away.

'Hurry.'

Didi closed her swollen eyelids. She drifted from sensation to sensation, misplaced her sense of time. Water echoed down a drain, the pungency of wet earth attacked the air. Was it raining? Didi stirred restlessly and thought something white flashed across the veranda door.

Som Devi. Waiting for me, while I lie in wait for her, thought Didi.

The white sari stood out like a beacon of light in the darkness.

From the corner of her left eye, Didi noticed Sita's bulk appear near the dressing table. She had swaddled the child in her pallu that was tucked in around her midriff. Her face was drawn, her eyes dilated, glazed by her efforts. Didi felt liquid with sympathy and love: poor Sita, she was beyond exhaustion.

Suddenly she saw Som Devi's face pressed against the glass pane of the door. Didi almost howled out in fright.

Sita recoiled. Her hands waved from side to side in urgent and frantic denial.

'What,' Didi struggled to sit up, 'do you want?' she shouted out.

'What,' Som Devi replied, 'have you got?'

'That's mine.'

'Mine too …' challenged Som Devi.

'Mine first …'

Didi stared into what she judged were her mother-in-law's eyes, defiance in her own tired ones. Som Devi met the stare, impervious.

They exchanged the pitiless glare of persons who never have and never can like one another.

Som Devi retreated into the darkness.

Didi slid down the bed.

Sita collapsed upon the dressing room stool. The lines about her mouth deepened. She looked as though she was ready to cry.

'Bring him,' Didi called out in hoarse voice. 'Let me hold him ... see him.'

Sita remained motionless but for the heaviness of her breathing.

'Did you not hear, Sita? Come. Later, you can rest ... all day tomorrow.'

'Tomorrow?' Sita mopped her face with her sari, held it there. 'Who has seen tomorrow?'

Her knees rocked the bundle in her lap.

Didi lifted herself with difficulty.

'Bring,' she snapped, arms wide open.

Sita dragged herself up. She held the child so gently, she could have been lifting the air. Didi gazed down at the bundle. She drew in her breath and clutched at Sita's hand.

'Oh, Mem ...' she began, then took a deep breath and touched the tip of the baby's nose with her index finger. 'How tight this silly Sita has bundled you,' she whispered. 'Silly-billy, doesn't know a thing about babies. Let me loosen you up. What were you thinking, Sita, swaddling him so tight the poor thing can hardly breathe?'

Some time later, Sita sat on the floor at the foot of Didi's bed. She had cleaned Didi with warm salt water, creamed her, and dressed her in a pink nightdress with white lace around the neck and armholes. Now, Sita rested her head upon the mattress. Didi sat on the bed with the child on her lap. Her hair spilled out of the black ribbon that tried to restrain the strands.

'This is God's gift.' Sita folded her hands.

'Yes, Mem's gods,' Didi's voice was hoarse, 'have their own way of rewarding us for our actions.'

Sita bent her head low so that she could peer out of the veranda door.

'You know, there's no moon.' When she received no reply, she added, 'Did you hear? I said there is no moon.'

Didi stared at her toes.

'Does the moon shine when it rains?' she asked absentmindedly.

Sita straightened and tightened her hair into a bun.

'Som Deviji will be arriving soon.'

'Your grandmother,' Didi explained in a baby voice to the child. 'I call her Som Dev-il.'

Sita stood on her knees to study the child. Then a glance at Didi's face brought her to her feet. She took Didi's hands in both of hers.

'Didi!' Sita said softly. She held her head in the pleats of her crumpled sari. They remained, thus, a photograph from the album of birth. Eventually, Didi raised her eyes to Sita's face.

'Is there,' asked Didi, 'any milk?'

Sita nodded, went towards the bedroom door, listened at it carefully, slid open the latch and stared into the corridor. She crept out.

'Sita,' Didi hissed after her.

'What it is?'

'Bring phenyl with you.'

Sita frowned.

'What?'

'Phe-nyl. To clean up the mess.'

Sita disappeared. Didi was seated at the dressing table when she returned. She was staring at her reflection. Seeing Sita, she reached down for her comb and began to hurry it through her hair.

'Put the phenyl in the bathroom and bring the milk here.'

Sita did as she was told. She looked around.

'Where's the little sahib?'

'On my lap.'

'I'll take him, you drink the milk.'

'The milk,' said Didi, still brushing, 'is not for me.'

Sita picked up the infant.

'Hai hai, Mem, you feed him. It is your duty as the mother.'

Didi laughed. It came out as a cry.

'Give him the milk, Sita,' she ordered.

Sita brought a teaspoon and together with Didi held a spoon of milk to the child's lips. It dribbled down his cheeks.

'Look at him: face of ...'

'Yes.'

They gave him another spoon. It spilled again.

'Achcha,' Sita crooned, 'already stubborn?'

'Too hot,' Didi observed. She picked up the glass of milk and went into the bathroom.

She returned stirring the milk with the spoon. Her face was pale, the lips tight.

'Aha,' Sita purred, lifting the child. 'Wait, little one, I will give you milk and you will be silent. This Didi of mine knows nothing.'

Didi shivered.

'It's cold in here.'

Sita had sat down crossed-legged on the floor with the child; Didi was on the stool beside her.

'Here,' she said, holding out the glass to Sita.

Sita let fall a few drops on her palm. She bent to taste and immediately jerked up her head. Didi's hands were icy on her cheeks. Sita shook her head. Didi nodded. As Sita dropped her head, Didi lifted it tenderly and held it firm.

'Yes.'

'No.'

Sita locked her eyes with Didi's. Neither blinked.

At dawn, a knock stirred the women in the bedroom. Sita opened the door and stood aside. Didi was seated on a white wicker chair in front of the door to the veranda, staring at the mango tree. She was twisting and tightening the thick braid of her hair. She turned to see Som Devi at the threshold.

'You had best come in.'

Som Devi walked in, slowly.

'I am sorry,' Didi spoke with great gentleness, 'I am so sorry.'

Som Devi stiffened, her eyes darted about.

The whites of Didi's eyes were lined in red.

'I am sorry.'

Didi rubbed her palms into her eyes.

'Where is he? I want to see him,' Som Devi demanded.

Didi inclined her head towards the bed, wondering how Som Devi knew it was a boy.

Som Devi hurried across and peered down. A pillow case lay in the middle of the mattress.

Som Devi lifted the pillow case and held it close. As she felt the child against her cheek, her glasses tumbled down the length of her nose and her breath staggered out of her. She stared down.

'Hey bhagvan, a boy! But …'

'Yes,' agreed Didi, without turning.

Som Devi made a clucking sound inside her mouth. Then she turned the baby over and shook him gently and then again with greater force.

'Nothing.'

Didi made a soft, unintelligible sound.

'Speak up. Don't squeak like a mouse at me.'

'I said,' Didi spoke evenly, 'he didn't want to be … Just as well, there are too many things one has to bear. Like the night Bhai went missing …'

'What is all this nonsense at a time like now?'

The spit collected at the corners of Som Devi's mouth. She rose with the child, throwing a glance at Didi's bent head.

'This happened because of you. You've eaten my sons alive … driven them apart, and now this,' she turned to the pillow case, 'this little baby boy.' Som Devi began to cry.

'Would it have been all right if it was a girl?' snapped Didi. 'Would that have made it better?'

Som Devi appeared unable to speak. She placed the pillow case on the bed, turned away and clutched the arms of the wicker chair, staring before her sightlessly, her tears dribbling to the edge of her jaw.

'You are the ruin of all the men in this family,' she said in a hoarse voice. 'As long as you are here, no man can live in peace.'

Sita spoke up.

'Leave my Didi be.'

'Quiet, you,' ordered Som Devi, drying her face with her pallu, 'surrounding her like her petticoat.'

The tears started in Sita's eyes and fell in shuddering drops. In one swift movement, Didi stood up and embraced her. She led her to the bed and sat her down, held Sita's head to her stomach.

Som Devi stared from Sita to the bed in outrage. Her nostrils were virtually closed by the pincer of her spectacles. Always pale, she was now grey, translucent as tracing paper; her face was pale and drawn. She sniffed and wiped her nose on her sari.

'This boy ... we cannot ... I mean ...' She squared her shoulders, but her voice faltered. 'A stillborn. It's too much. Look at him ... Everyone will know. He looks exactly like ... And then what will happen? This family will be in ruins, for nothing. Alive, I would have seen it through, there's always family resemblance. But this ... is not worth the truth.' She looked across at Didi. 'I knew it would turn out badly. I prayed each night. But not for this ...' She walked swiftly across to the bathroom. When she emerged, it was with a purposeful air. 'Quickly,' she commanded Sita, 'get me a rickshaw. I will take him to the riverside.'

Didi took a deep breath.

'No, it must be here.'

A little later, the window curtains were thrust aside.

'It rained during the night,' Som Devi observed, 'but we can manage.'

'A bonfire in the rains?' Didi mumbled. 'It's like the light of a missing moon. Is it possible?'

'Let us bury him.'

Som Devi pushed the spectacles up her nose and moved towards the door. She halted, irresolute.

'A son ...'

'Why don't you go and see if Baby is all right?' Didi advised.

Som Devi stood her ground.

'No,' she said, 'I am staying here. I must see for myself. No more mischief.'

It was not yet 7 a.m.

★

Baby was tired. She had been lying next to her mother for what seemed like hours. Didi had her arms about her daughter and each time Baby tried to wriggle free, the clasp tightened. Didi was not asleep.

'Why are we still in bed?' Baby demanded. 'Soon it will be lunch.'

'Stay.'

'But why me?' Baby squirmed. 'You have the headache, you rest na, Amma …'

'I wish to rest with you.'

'But I want to go.'

Didi pulled Baby close.

'The time for that will come.'

A wet patch spread across the pillow beneath Didi's cheek.

'Tell me a story,' pleaded Baby.

Then she looked up to inspect Didi's face.

'Why are you crying, Amma?'

Didi pulled Baby closer.

'Stay a while.'

He entered impetuously. He didn't knock or alert the room with a cough. He rushed in and addressed the white bundle on the chair.

'Didi …'

Bhai's drawn face wore an expression that was crumpled and untidy. His long hair sloped into his eyes, his kurta hung open to reveal the lean ribcage. He had thrust his hands into his kurta pockets, tight, as though clinging to them for support.

'Didi …'

Didi's throat felt scraped and parched. She didn't wish to speak; it would hurt if she did.

'Tell me, Didi, tell me, what happened? Ma is sitting in a trance with her Gita.'

He put a hand on her shoulder but she flinched and he immediately withdrew it.

'It happened … like everything else. Perhaps it was meant to be after what had already happened,' she rasped out, all the while mending a tear in Baby's frock.

Bhai banged his hand against the wall and leaned against it.

'There's no talking to you,' he lamented, 'ever since the cricket match—'

'Don't,' she ordered.

She challenged Bhai with her eyes. He walked up to her and took possession of her hand, stilling its motion. She did not immediately withdraw it.

'Was it a boy …?' he began, tentative.

Her eyes were steady on his.

'Your family is all alike. A boy, a girl, a hijra … would it make any difference?'

Bhai shook his head, closed his eyes, then forced out the words: 'Who…se?'

Didi made to laugh but it ended as a hiccup. 'Will it matter?'

He opened his shy eyes directly into hers, engorged with sadness.

'I suppose …' he wiped his face on the arm of his kurta, 'not.'

'Then you may claim him. If,' Didi got up with the frock in her hands, 'there is anything to claim.'

She went behind the curtain and sat by the dressing table. She switched on a light and bent her head over the frock. Her needlework was a series of swift jabs.

Bhai set the curtain aside. 'But how could he just die?' Bhai demanded. 'Babies don't, do they?'

For the second time, she forbade him with her expression.

He noticed the desolate wasteland of her face, took her hand and patted it, repeatedly. They remained thus, for a few minutes, perhaps a few more.

Eventually, 'It is bad luck,' he remarked, 'that's all. Remember that night of the lunar eclipse?'

'The night of the dark moon,' Didi corrected.

Bhai shook her shoulder.

'I told you we should not be out on the roof.'

Her hand clawed Baby's dress, her entire body rigid.

'It makes no sense,' he added, sinking down to sit against the wall. 'How can a baby ... Tell me, Didi.'

She averted her gaze to a point beyond his shoulder, her eyes vacant, waiting for an expression to occupy them.

'What do you want to hear?' she spoke clearly. 'He was missing a breath? Two toes were not there? His back had a hump, like a child carrying a school bag? He looked ...' she stopped herself. 'It was always going to be difficult but like this, he had no ... chance,' she said, in a voice so harsh, his head sagged with grief.

'Does,' she focussed her eyes on him, 'that make more sense?'

When he lifted his face to hers, there was such desolation in his eyes, it might have stolen the expression in hers. He reached out to touch her forehead.

'You are not well. At all. In fact, you are very sick. Poor Didi. You need sleep and rest.'

He crossed over to the door of the veranda and drew the curtains.

In the evening, he knocked and entered carrying a wicker basket. In the dark, he heard Sita singing a hymn: '*Raghupati Raghava Raja Ram, patita pavana Sita Ram ...*' to the accompaniment of the overhead fan. A light perfume hung in the air as though it didn't know where else to go.

Bhai approached the bed.

'Fruits and nuts are good for you. They give strength. They say, after birth you should eat these ...'

'What about after death?'

'Shhh, Didi.' Sita interrupted her singing and switched on the lamp by the dressing room table. Its orange shade lit up the room like early morning light.

'Here,' said Bhai, holding out a fistful of nuts. 'We will feed you properly. You'll have complete peace and quiet. Ma and Sita will look after Baby. In a few weeks, you will feel better ...'

The doorway curtain fluttered and Purush marched in. His face wore a smile that widened into nastiness.

'So you think you'll hide your ... your shameful behaviour in here?' He stamped the floor with his right foot. 'Well, you're wrong. I won't let you. I am going to call the police and we will have a complete investigation. Where have you hidden it?'

There was the sound of laughter. Didi's. Her eyes had travelled back in time and wore the same look of distraction that they had the night Bhai went missing.

'No,' Bhai grabbed Purush's hands. 'Please.'

Purush pushed Bhai aside and confronted Didi.

'I know. I heard Roop and Sita and then Ma. Where is it?'

'He,' muttered Didi automatically, to herself.

Bhai stood before Purush.

'Purush, believe me, there is nothing. Nothing for you to worry about.'

Bhai turned to Sita, who stood clutching the bed rails.

'Ask Sita. Ask Roop.'

'Rubbish all,' shouted Purush, 'they will lie for her. You will too, though I am your brother. You let him,' he turned to Didi, 'get there, didn't you?'

Bhai shuddered.

'No, Purush, don't do this to yourse ...' he trailed off.

Purush wiped his face on his shirtsleeve.

'Ma, she will tell the truth. She is not like you all, she'll not lie to me ...' He strode towards the bedroom doorway.

'I am here, Purush.' Som Devi's voice emerged from behind the curtain. 'I have been listening.'

She stepped inside, a thin, wizened woman with hollow spaces where her features should have been.

Purush reached out and embraced her. 'Ma, you tell them. We will get her now ...'

Som Devi clasped him to her, patted his back.

'See? I told you!' His voice flung the triumphant words back into the room.

Som Devi released Purush and walked across to the bed to sit facing Didi's back. Impetuously, Bhai joined her.

'Ma …!' Purush began.

She held up her hand. She looked around the room, then picked up the pillow where Purush had flung it on the bed, stared at it and placed it on her lap, rocking it.

'Ma, come …' Purush returned to her side.

Ignoring him, Som Devi aimed her eyes between Didi's shoulder blades, narrowed her eyes.

'She? What can she do?'

Purush stared at his mother and then followed her gaze. Som Devi hugged the pillow to herself.

'She can do nothing, nothing.'

'I don't understand …' began Purush.

'What's there to understand?'

'What are you talking about, Ma?' Purush asked irritably.

Som Devi snapped at him with her eyes.

'She cannot,' Som Devi's voice was strained with the effort, 'mother the boys of this house. Her womb is not fit to be a home.'

Didi's did not flinch, or in any way respond to Som Devi's words. Purush sank down on the bed, beside Som Devi. She set aside the pillow and stroked her son's fine hair. Bhai came to them, his hand extended.

'Let it be, Purush, let it be,' Bhai said.

Bhai's hands fell as Purush raised his crumpled face to Som Devi's. She eased the sullen lines around his mouth, held his head firm in her hands. 'Let it be.'

He remained still for a moment, then thrust her away and got up and left the room.

Som Devi said, 'She must not stay.'

Bhai whirled around to face his mother.

'Ma …'

'She goes. She's been a curse since the day she came.'

'Ma, later. She has a right to be here …'

'No right.' Som Devi stood up. 'No claim.'

'Ma …'

'You,' Som Devi hissed, her voice a tight coil, 'stay out of this.'

Bhai straightened his hair and shoulders. 'She's too weak and frail—'

'Will she die too?' Som Devi snorted.

'Don't.' His fingers crawled across the netting of the door.

Sita spoke: 'Mataji, Baby …'

Som Devi faltered, her face hidden from the others.

'I wish …' her voice was barely audible, 'but such a one as this,' she looked at Didi, 'is poison for the men.'

'Ma, no,' insisted Bhai, opening the net door and approaching his mother. 'We are a family.'

Som Devi held out her hand to halt Bhai.

'Maybe, maybe not. Who knows anything with her? See…What hasn't she done: one brother lies on the sofa, useless, the other stands in front of me like a pyjama without a string, whimpering.' Her voice went rigid. 'And the boy …' she clenched her teeth on her upper lip.

'You are right,' Didi said in a soft voice. 'There is bad blood. Between us.' She stood up and slung her hair into a bun.

'She,' insisted Didi, 'is right. This blood here won't mix. Things have happened which one cannot take back. There are recollections that cling to the walls of this house and, in the dark, rise like nightmares that don't let you sleep. We cannot live with them.'

'What are you saying?' Bhai demanded. 'You can't just leave!'

'Why not?'

'But how?'

'Simple, pack her bags and go. Nothing else here belongs to her,' called out Som Devi.

'Sita,' implored Bhai.

'Hai hai, Mem.' Sita went to stand behind Didi. 'Think of Baby, Didi. She loves her Dadi, Bhai Chacha, this is her home …'

'Her greatest kindness, I am saying, would be to leave Baby to our care. You,' Som Devi remarked to Sita, 'hear how she speaks? She is like a mad monkey.'

'Baby,' Didi insisted, 'is mine.'

'Ours.'

'Mine.'

'My son's.'

'Who? Purush?' Didi's laugh was incredulous. 'Maybe, maybe not, who,' she added with steely gentleness, 'knows anything with him?'

Som Devi raised her hands to her ears.

As she walked away, the evening glow lit up the rain into glass shavings.

Bhai remained, one foot on either side of the threshold.

When Purush learnt of Som Devi's decision, he asked Maharaj to buy him a bottle of Old Monk rum, a kilo of meat for a spicy curry ('Make sure you get a few good bones with marrow') and his favorite kaju barfi as 'sweet dish'.

'Rubbish all, she's rubbish all and I am glad there will be no more of her kind in this house. But Ma, why did you not let the police take her away? You know she did something to …'

'And let her expose my family? She will tell all kinds of stories.'

Purush's hand crept down to the zip of his trouser.

'Phir then, Purush, you are not thinking.'

She patted his hand and retreated into her room. Her forehead was creased with concern. She rose twice. Once, to look in on Baby who was fast asleep in her room, the other to check on her younger son.

He placed his arms around her. 'Ma, we will be well rid. Well rid. Now, we will be a family once again.'

If, during the subsequent weeks, Som Devi did not always agree with Purush and sometimes regretted her decision, she never changed it or expressed a different opinion. At no stage did she succumb to Sita's or Bhai's persuasions. They only served to make her more steadfast in her resolve.

'She's bad for you' was her constant warning to her elder son.

'We could all start over?'

'No.'

Every morning and evening, Som Devi prayed for the salvation of her sons, prayed for her loss of Baby. Her sadness deepened into grief and in the long afternoon hours and the fretful nights, she brooded:

how could she keep Baby? She found no answers in the darkness of her room. But she knew one thing for certain: she could not expose the mother to the child.

Had Didi touched her feet and asked her forgiveness, if she had taken Purush by the hand and led him back into their bedroom, Som Devi may have relented. But there was no chance of either: she had seen her own determination in Didi's eyes.

And there was the boy. What she had seen, she could not accept. It had to be hidden. It would have torn her family apart. Exposed Bhai to Purush, set brother against brother. So she had done what was necessary – quietly laid the secret to rest and demanded Didi's departure. In her loneliest moments, in her solitary pain, Som Devi prayed for the ultimate sentence of life: death. She wished Didi would die. Just die. It was evil for a woman who read the Gita twice a day to entertain such thoughts but in Didi's case, Som Devi had crossed the boundaries of morality. There had been a trangression in the family. It would be best if she died. But since she did not, she had to leave.

'But I wonder,' she asked herself, 'which of us has won!'

In those weeks, Didi maintained a calm exterior and remained in her room. She sat inside on the wicker chair by the veranda door, knuckling the bridge of her nose almost absent-mindedly, until a sore developed and bled. Sita bandaged it. Deprived of its solace, Didi dug out the skin beneath the nails of her index fingers, ripped at the skin until it was tender and lacerated.

'Hai hai, Mem, see how she hurts herself,' Sita would exclaim, applying turmeric and salt to the wounds. 'Stop it, Didi, stop it.'

But Didi didn't stop.

Every evening, Mahendra rang from Delhi and she spoke to him for nearly half an hour. Otherwise, she spoke as sparingly as she ate and was grateful for the emptiness of her room. She didn't want human companionship other than Baby's and Sita's. Bhai's she accepted without emotion.

When Baby asked why she did not come to meals or sit beneath the mango tree, she said, 'They give me the headache.'

That was sufficient to make Baby roll her eyes and prevent any further inquiries. When Baby asked why she was packing, Didi told her that Mahendra Uncle had taken a house in the hills for them. They were going on a holiday.

'Is Dadi coming too?'

'Dadi is too old for holidays.'

'Too old!' retorted Som Devi when Baby reported the conversation. 'Next time we will leave her and you and I will go on a holiday.'

She had tears in her voice.

Bhai could not hide his distress. It stalked the house with him as he proceeded from one bedroom to the other trying to bring compromise to 3, Chor Bagh. It clung to him with the sweat of his brow. Each troubled soul in the house turned away from him: Purush, Som Devi and Didi. They all agreed: Didi must go.

In the evenings, he took to drinking with Purush, who observed that 'she was rubbish all and we brothers can do without her' before passing him the rum bottle and returning to his inner world with a sneering smirk.

In the afternoons, Bhai read Didi poetry, verses which, previously, they had recited together. She in turn spoke only of the hill station.

'Don't you care?' he once blurted out, in frustration and pain.

She did not pretend to misunderstand him.

'It's over. It was over long ago. That night,' she stopped and turned away.

He held himself up by gripping the table but later, he stood under the shower, allowing the water to wash away his desperation. Each day saw unhappiness gnaw into him so that by the time Didi was ready to leave, he needed an entire new wardrobe.

'It is a good thing she is going soon,' commented Som Devi, 'otherwise, there will be nothing left of you.'

He gave Didi money and cheques, told her to write him for more. She told him not to worry, Mahendra would help her and she could look after herself. Bhai offered to accompany her, help move her into her new home. She replied it was unnecessary. Mahendra would be there. She would manage.

'I'll come and visit you, once you've settled in.'

She shook her head.

'It's over.'

'Didi, Didi, it's never over for families. We are family, families belong, they become one, no matter what. We have ties which are elastic, they stretch,' he widened his arms, 'beyond geography. Think of Baby, Didi. I can visit and bring her home for holidays. Ma will be so pleased.'

Didi picked at her fingers.

'Sita, where is my cuticle cutter?'

She left one morning with four trunks, three suitcases, two holdalls, the two easy chairs of the New York sofa, Baby and Sita. She bid farewell to the mango tree, running her hands over it fondly, sinking down at its trunk. She grabbed a fistful of the earth, held it to her nose, then let it fall.

'Bye-bye Budhoo, bye-bye mango tree, bye-bye Dadi.' Baby hugged each one by turns. 'See you after our holiday. Soooon.'

Budhoo wagged his tail high and barked in protest at being held so tight. Som Devi crushed Baby to her for a moment, then shouted at Budhoo to stop that noise. She turned away from Didi.

On the sofa, Purush lit a cigarette. His knees shook, ever so slightly.

The mango tree remained unmoved. Aloof.

At the railway station, outside the compartment that was to take Didi away, Bhai stood, dangling arms which could not detain her. As the train stirred and jolted into departure, he raised his hands to the window railing as it slipped out of his reach. He didn't try to hold on.

From the station he drove to the bookstore, wandered about its silent pages, climbed upto the storeroom flooded with sunlight. He tied a knot in his kurta: he must remember to ask his mother for thick curtains to block the sun. It was so bright, it hurt the eyes.

HILL STATION
1986

'It was so bright, it hurt the eyes.'
    Didi turned away from the memory.

'The sun, that morning we buried him. It lit up the early morning – how it glowed.' She picked at her cuticle. 'We stood there – Sita, Som Devi and I. When it was over, Som Devi turned to me and said, "You must go." I replied, said "yes".'

Mr Hamer shook his head in seeming comprehension.

Didi sucked at a pinprick of blood on her finger.

'What?' he asked, his eyes vacant.

'He was weak and frail. And,' she tapped the table with her knuckles, 'one toe on his left foot,' she paused, 'was missing. He had a hump as though he had crouched the entire nine months inside me … to hide my secret. There was something so unnatural about him.' She placed the cup on the saucer. 'His eyes were so still, unblinking.'

She blinked rapidly.

'He was dark; he had long, thin black hair; his eyes were, for all their stillness,' she swallowed hard, 'just like his father's.' She kicked at the gravel below her feet.

This was the second time since that night that she described the birth and death of her son. Before Mahendra left for Australia, she had told him and sworn him to secrecy. She had spoken to Baby about 3, Chor Bagh, without mentioning the child, but this afternoon, she felt the need to relieve her conscience.

As was his wont, Mr Hamer listened in complete silence.

Then he said in a distant voice, 'You did what you thought was right. Yes, right.'

'You don't even know what you are saying. Your mind lives somewhere else. But, in this case, you are right: there was never any other choice.' She swallowed.

'I understand.'

'I don't think you do. I had meant to go to Delhi and… have it … have the child removed.' Her hands went instinctively to her stomach. 'No one would have known anything and I would have returned, stopped working at the bookstore, got the best I could ... for Baby. But then Bhai went missing and I lost control ... all because of a cricket match.'

'I said I understand ...'

'What's to understand?' she asked, picking up a teacup. 'I never understand anything.' Suddenly she laughed. 'It was the only thing Som Devi and I ever agreed on. Well, where would it have ended? What would he have grown up to be?' She stopped, saw his faraway look. 'A constant memory of everything that was wrong... with all of us. If it had been only him, I would have gone on. But there was Baby to think of. She would have known soon enough, Purush would have made sure of that. Could she have lived with the knowledge forever? I don't know, but I couldn't allow there to be a permanent blight on her life. No, I couldn't bear to see it, Nor,' she added, 'could Som Devi. It had to end there.'

She sat back.

'I don't know what she knew, and how much she guessed. We never discussed it. She simply accepted what she saw. But she never told Baby the whole truth and I am grateful for that.'

Didi stirred the tea aimlessly.

'In the end, we both won,' she added, knuckling her nose. 'We both lost.'

'You feel bad?'

'Even when I am not feeling it. I lost my sleep permit that night.'

Ever since she had come to live in the hills, she had become afraid of sleep because it was accompanied by recurring nightmares of the night the boy had been born and died, and what she had done.

'We had to leave. What kind of life would we have had there?'

She got up and stretched.

'He was my punishment ... and everyone's salvation.'

'His was a life, yes, life.'

She patted his outstretched hand.

'Sometimes, you have to make a human sacrifice of the living.'

That night, she lay alone with the remains of the night and the enormity of what she had done: the little she had revealed to Baby, all that she had withheld. Talk of the old days made her feel unaccountably afraid. More than anything, she was scared of Baby's continuing presence and how, without meaning to, she might betray herself.

'Oh Mem, Mem, what did I do?'

She felt a cool hand on her cheek. Baby's. She refused to reply.

'Amma, don't pretend to be sleeping when I know you are awake.'

'How do you know?'

Baby's hand remained on her cheek.

'Because your breathing is all wrong, no rhythm to it. Anyway, listen, there is something important that I have been meaning to tell you. I've been waiting for a special moment to tell you … when you were ready to hear it. Now, that Kartik is here and well …' Baby told her of her visit to Bhai Chacha, the deeds to the family bookstore, the bookstore in New York and her future business ambitions.

Didi listened, first in incomprehension, then in admiration at Baby's enterprise and finally, in increasing horror at what she had done.

'It's all clear with Dadi and Chacha and Lobo Chachi. You don't have to worry.'

'Worry?' replied Didi. 'Of course I am worried. I am amazed. And horrified. Purush …' Didi felt a sharp pain in her left arm.

'Bhai Chacha said Dadi would take care of him. Besides, he's got his share. This is mine. Rightfully. I am only taking what is mine. They have never given me anything. All these years. So I asked for this and got it. There.'

Before Didi could reply, Baby had got up and left. Didi leapt out of bed and shook her fists at the ceiling. What had Baby gone and done? For the rest of the morning, she could not keep still. She paced up and down, she rearranged her cupboard, she went to the kitchen and began to make mayonnaise but in her rattled state, it curdled and she threw it away. What she knew of Purush told her he would not like this deed business. Not at all. He would react. But what could he do?

Something that would harm Didi or Baby, that much she knew and feared. Oh dear, why had Baby revisited 3, Chor Bagh?

The next few days, she stayed in bed despite Kartik's attempts to entice her out of her room. She rested on one side, then the other, taking Mem's name, wishing Kartik would leave and take Baby with him. She felt a constant pain on the right side of her chest, parallel to her heart, and thought it must be a sympathetic pain.

'Why don't you come outside and play cards with us?' Kartik stood at the window one afternoon. 'Sita says you are great at cards. Let's see if you can beat your daughter. Come, no?'

Didi considered the fact that Kartik never addressed her by any name. He doesn't know what he should call me. All my life I have been Didi, I have no other identity.

'Let her be,' Baby ordered from behind him. 'Why are you so keen on her company? Mine not enough for you?'

Didi smiled at the coquetry in her daughter's voice. This girl, no, woman, with her startling new face, her long, lush body, her deep voice, could be irresistible. Poor Kartik.

'Stop it, Baby, you're asking for trouble.'

'What kind did you have in mind?'

'Baby! Your mother.'

'You think she doesn't know about flirting?'

'Is that what we're doing?'

'What do you think?'

'I don't know. With you, anything is possible. One moment you flirt, the next you've booked yourself on the first flight out.'

Didi felt her stomach muscles tense.

Baby replied in a cheerless voice, 'I deserve that.'

'The least.'

'You're very resentful.'

'Extremely.'

'Then why are you here?'

'Because …'

'Because?'

'Look, what began as the grand passion of my youth has turned into a trite love story about a stupid, weak, besotted man who can't get over …'

'You want to?'

'Ssshh, what will your mother think?'

'If you knew my mother, you'd know that at this moment she is lying crossed like a pair of scissors, hoping I don't mess up again. Amma?' She laughed out loudly.

'Baby!'

'You do want to?'

Didi heard a chair shift.

'It's not good enough, Baby.'

Didi crossed her legs like a pair of scissors.

'Sorry,' she heard Baby say, 'I ought to have been a long time since. Should never have let you go into the UPSC building alone. Should have held your hand.'

'Ought to have.'

'But, like I said, think of it this way: if I had, if we had married, you would have sat for the exams again, maybe made the IAS, maybe not, maybe wound up in the railways or accounts.'

'As I did.'

'And I would have been this disgruntled wife and mother, growing pregnant in the hips, resenting you.'

'But we would have tried.'

'And you would never, never have,' Baby sounded triumphant, 'had the opportunity to collect garbage!'

'Baby!'

'Like I said, I am trying. I have said sorry, but you remain unmoved.'

'I am not …'

'Hai hai, Mem, will you come down and see, just see, what your granddaughter is doing in front of the birds and the mango trees and the maali's boy sitting up there in the branches, sucking the mango as if it belonged to him?'

★

'It feels to me,' Sita observed as she cut Didi's toenails later, 'that this new yellow hair she has brought with her has changed our Baby. Bilkul different she is behaving. Even to you.'

'Thank you.' Didi's tone was sardonic.

'What's there? Everybody knows you and she could never agree, never since we left Chor Bagh.'

'I was there, remember, Sita?'

'Yes, but you are forgetting all the time.' Sita eased back the skin from the big toe and snipped at the edges.

'See, how she is giving him a lot of attention? As her Dadi used to say,' she grabbed Didi's middle toe, 'she is making big-big eyes at him.'

'Poor Kartik.'

'Why so? My Baby is the most beautiful baby in the world. Which man would not want to be looked at the way she looks at him? Just like Madhubala and Dilip Kumar in *Mughal-E-Azam*. Aha, kya film that was.'

Didi pulled her left foot away and pushed the right one into Sita's face.

'No need to push them so close,' complained Sita. 'My eyes are still good. And who could miss your toes, like the fat chilli pakoras you like to eat?'

Didi tapped the tip of Sita's nose with her big toe. Sita squealed and almost fell backwards.

'I hope,' Didi said, 'you're right. Baby must settle down. She's growing up.'

Sita rubbed her nose.

'Something you should do too.'

'I wish Baby would settle down soon,' interrupted Didi, 'so that I may die in peace and send you to make their lives hell!'

'I pray for that day too!'

Didi kicked away Sita's fingers.

'I am glad we agree. Now, go and make us some tea. It is past seven.'

'Always complaining …'

Didi stretched out on the bed and tried to touch her toes.

Her fingers reached down just below her knees. She made a few more unsuccessful attempts, then swung her legs off the bed, struggling with her breath.

'Bloody growing old,' she panted.

'Amma.' Baby walked into the room. 'Kartik wants to know why you have hung our photograph – the one of him and me – in the toilet. Like I said, are you trying,' she nudged Sita and collapsed next to her mother, 'trying to tell him something?'

She arched a look at the doorway.

Didi hiccupped.

'What is it?' Baby asked more softly, seeing Didi's face. 'I've never seen you look like this before.'

'I,' announced Didi, wiping her face on Baby's pallu and rising from the bed, panting, 'am going to the toilet.'

Baby rose with her and placed her chin on Sita's plump shoulder.

'Why is it, Sita, that those I am closest to have this thing about waste matter?'

At Sita's insistence, Didi sat at the breakfast table next morning watching Baby and Kartik eat. She noticed Baby and Kartik exchange a glance and felt herself break out into a delicate sweat. Was that how she had looked at Jeff or Bhai when her feelings were about to erupt and lead her into temptation?

'I was thinking we,' ventured Baby between mouthfuls, 'might go to the hotel this evening.'

Her voice was as carelessly studied as a discard in a game of poker. She did not look at her mother. Didi thrust a rusk into the tepid coffee with equal deliberation, her fingers on the verge of a tremble. Baby had never suggested a visit to the hotel before. In all these years.

'Why not?' Didi replied. 'As it happens, I am free this evening. We might have cocktails in the garden. Kartik, have you ever had a martini?'

'I've read about it in detective novels. The thin, clever women sit smoking at the bar and sip dry martinis with their legs crossed.'

Didi and Baby gazed at each other in astonishment, then began to laugh.

★

Didi dressed with all the attentiveness of someone draping a sari for the first time. Each movement was an exaggerated motion. She picked out a chocolate-coloured blouse with the puffs peaking at the shoulder with long, narrowing sleeves ending just above the elbow, while the V dipped between her breasts. Then it was the turn of the sari. It was brown as her blouse, with thin golden threads crossing to form small squares, each of which held a turquoise flower. It was one of the few saris that she had chosen for herself with Mem just before her wedding.

She pleated and re-pleated the folds until each one fell neatly behind the other. She wore its pallu to her waist, pinning the left corner into the blouse for it to fall open like a sheet. In each earlobe, she pierced the smallest gold cross earrings, a present on her twenty-second birthday. On her middle finger, the wedding solitaire with emeralds lay trapped in thickening arthritis.

'I will always be,' Didi thought, twisting it around to no avail, 'Purush's wife.'

All that remained was the perfume. Didi admired her collection inside the cupboard.

'I would choose Opium if I were wearing what you are,' Baby purred, rustling into the room, 'musky, heavy, sensual.'

Didi reached out for the bottles of Caleche and Opium. She held the latter over her shoulder.

'In that case, *you* should wear it.'

She sprayed the Caleche behind her ears.

She turned to see her daughter in a simple silk patola sari of white and blue. She had petit pois size pearls, Didi's, in her ears and a single string of pearls around her neck. She wore no make-up and her hair glanced off the back of her neck in a loose bun. Didi felt a sweat start up.

Baby held out her wrists as though offering to be handcuffed. Didi took the bottle from her and dabbed Opium on her pulse, at the base of her throat, behind the ears. Baby pulled Didi tentatively close, just enough for their perfumes to mingle.

'I am trying, Amma. To be kinder.'

'I know.'

Didi swallowed the saliva of tears that had collected in her mouth. She took a deep breath.

'Baby?'

'Amma?'

'Baby, those papers ... of the bookstore, give them to me. You don't need them to start a new life – that's what you want, don't you? You already have a store in New York from stin ... Ramaji.' Didi shuddered delicately. 'I have a little something. We can do this on our own. Let's not poach on the past. Let that be theirs.'

Baby's face was reddening as Didi spoke.

'Let go, Baby, it's the only way forward. Otherwise, it will always follow you.'

Baby knuckled the bridge of her nose.

'Like a pebble in the shoe?'

Didi nodded.

'What will you do with them?'

'Burn them,' replied Didi promptly.

'Rubbish all!' replied Baby and both women broke into laughter.

When the mirth gave way to smiles, Baby wiped her eyes with the pallu of Didi's sari and used it to wipe Didi's face too.

'I don't know ...' she began when the telephone rang and she ran out into the corridor, preferring to take the call there.

Didi swore. The moment was lost; Baby would never give her the papers now.

Five minutes later, the scent of Opium wafted towards her. 'Amma, hurry up, Amma,' Baby shouted from the doorway.

'What's the hurry? It's only a drink.'

'Drink?' repeated Baby behind her. 'In that case ...'

As Didi shut her purse, she saw Baby extend her hand, with the papers. Didi snatched at the papers as Baby let go.

'This,' observed Baby as Didi took the papers, 'must be the first time I have done something you wanted without putting up a fight. I must have changed.'

'Thank you, Baby.'

'For what?' Baby arched her eyebrows in a simultaneous gesture of playful challenge. Poor Kartik, thought Didi.
'For trusting me?'
'A first!'
'Yes.'
'Yes.'
'Baby?'
'Amma?'
'Do you think you could stop admiring each other and let me do that for you?' Kartik said from outside the window.

He screwed up his face.
'You don't like it?' Didi asked.
Kartik placed the cocktail glass on the table and shook his head.
'Too bitter.' They were at the hotel, drinking martinis.
Baby extracted two cigarettes from Kartik's packet of Wills. She held one between her teeth and inserted the other between his lips. With a slim silver lighter she lit her own, flaring her nostrils for the expulsion of air. She reached across and offered the cigarette in her mouth to him. 'Do you …?'
He sucked in, the cigarette tip surged orange.
'I remember everything. It's you who have …'
'… misplaced memories,' she completed the sentence.
'Come,' Didi urged Mr Hamer and stood up, impatiently shaking out her sari, clutching a fluted glass in her hand. 'You and I will walk across to the edge of the wall and look down into the evening fires below while these children do heavy breathing exercises.'
He rose with awkward politeness.
They stood at the parapet. She sniffed at the smoky air.
'Dal,' she said, 'is cooking. Heavenly smell.'
He gave his head a wag.
'Do you understand what I am saying?' she said.
'You are worried?'
'Always.'
'Just tell the truth, yes, the truth.'

'Which truth and to whom?'

She leaned over the parapet and wrapped the shawl more tightly around her shoulders.

'You cannot spend years with a lie and then offer it as a truth. And now there's this bookstore thing with Baby that I have to settle.'

Didi leaned back, held out her arms. With unaccustomed effort but with perfect grace, Mr Hamer lifted her and deposited her on the parapet's wedge. She chafed her hands.

Looking across, Didi saw Kartik and Baby smoking into each other's faces.

'Did you ever wonder what you were meant to do?'

He smiled.

'I remember, as a young girl, being seated on a horse and led up the hills with a huge softee ice-cream spilling out of my hand,' Didi said. 'My hair and fingers were sticky on my face. Mem was furious with Father for buying it. Here, in this very hill station. Now, I am drinking a dry martini, some of which spilled when you lifted me off. My fingers are sticky, and I am feeling very much as I did then. Time has trapped me in a warp. Do you feel your age?' She shook his shoulder, afraid he was in a reverie of his own.

'I haven't been to your house for a long time,' he mused. 'The last time I came, you danced. Baby was hiding, yes, hiding, in the kitchen doorway, watching, longing to join you, and you tried to make me dance. You saw Baby and invited her in, but she ran away. You drank too much. I think you were sick?'

He raised his glass to her, and took a sip of whisky.

She drained hers and placed it upon the wall.

'You live with memories as much as I do; only differently.' She fingered the pearls in her necklace.

He cleared his throat.

Didi swung her legs furiously.

'Tell me,' she held her legs to silence their commotion, 'did you never want to die?'

His eyes registered no comprehension.

'I have a long life, a few twists here and there.' She showed her hand to him. 'Oh, what's the point of talking to you!' She slapped at the parapet. 'You stare at the sky and see nothing.'

She knew she was being unfair: there were private snapshots in the depths of his eyes that only he could admire. She patted his arm and let her fingers rest near his wrist.

He cocked his head in sudden alertness.

'I see Baby is here with her friend?'

'So now you are in the present? Yes, Baby. Silly Baby … If,' she patted his open palm, 'the purpose of life is to learn from one's mistakes, then one must be given time to put the learning into practice. But by the time my chance came, there were too many mistakes and too little time to unlearn …'

She gazed across to her daughter.

'Now Baby has a chance. With Kartik. But I don't want my past to catch up with her future, which is exactly what she is intent on doing with this bookstore business. I thought I had left it behind me when I left Chor Bagh, but it turns up in front of me all the time. I worry about Purush; I can't believe he will let this go by.'

Mr Hamer pulled the skin on the back of her hand and it rose, flimsy as an excuse.

'My advice to you, yes, advice: Baby will be fine. Yes, fine,' he suddenly exclaimed, and offered his arm to her. 'It's late. Come and visit me soon.'

From a distance, Baby and Kartik watched Hamer lift Didi off her perch on the parapet.

'He's rather sweet.'

'Too sweet.'

'I like her style. The drape of her sari, her bearing. A cultivated lady. If I had been a young man when she was a young woman …'

Baby slapped her hand across his eyes.

'Like I said, what does she have to make you react like that?'

'You're Miss Envy.'

'No, confused.'

Kartik removed her hand from his face, and together they watched the older couple approach, Didi in the lead.

'I envy them the years they have had with each other.'

Baby pinched the skin on her arm.

'I plan,' she said, 'to stay a long time.'

'How long would that be?' Kartik asked, assisting Mr Hamer into a seat.

'As long as it takes to start my own book chain, as long as it takes wrinkles to develop on my new skin and make me look like my mother.'

'That you can't. Anyway, I like you the way you are.'

'You're rather sweet.'

'Too sweet.'

'Why,' exclaimed Didi, 'don't the two of you go back to Delhi and carry on this coochi-coo there? At my age, I find it revolt—'

'In Delhi,' Baby said, 'he has his garbage and his women …'

'And I like it here …' protested Kartik, but Didi was already marching away.

At home, alone in her bed, Didi arrived at a decision. Next morning, she picked up the receiver.

Later, she informed Sita that she would be going away and would be back in a day.

'I have some business' was all she revealed.

'Since when?' demanded Sita.

'Sita, please let your fingers do the talking. When you speak, you sound foolish.'

Sita asked where she was going but Didi refused to reveal anything. Sita offered to accompany her but Didi was determined to travel alone. She wanted to keep this meeting between two people.

'Three,' she told Sita, 'is always one too many. And anyway, you look after Baby. Say I have gone away on something to do with Mr Hamer. Bas.'

'But where are you really going?'

'Ssssh.' Didi placed a finger on her lips.

'Pah,' replied her faithful ayah. 'Go. See if I care.'

When Didi informed Baby she was going away, Baby arched the eyebrow she was in the middle of plucking.

'Revisiting the past? You can't resist it any more than I can,' Baby observed. 'Except I am more honest.' Seeing Didi ready to remonstrate, she added softly, 'Go, go, let go of the past, Amma.'

Three days later, Didi climbed onto the night train. In the early morning of her arrival, the streets were deserted save for a few vehicles. She took a cycle rickshaw into the city and ordered it to stop in the main shopping centre. She didn't recognize it – its shape and size may have remained the same but the exteriors were different: new shops with new names confronted her. There were only three shops that she remembered well: Tulsi Paan Bhandar at the corner, National Sweet House near Gulistan Cinema, and the bookstore.

Didi approached the bookstore, her feet dragging. The store had green and yellow striped awnings and a brown wooden shutter with the 'Closed' sign in red and white plastic. She peeped through the slits of the shutter, saw rows upon rows of shelves with colourful books. She breathed in the smell of them from memory.

Moving on, she walked till she reached Kwality's restaurant and sat on the steps outside. When it opened, she chose a seat by the tinted window and ate a heavy breakfast of omelette, toast and marmalade, canned orange juice and coffee. Lots of coffee. She wanted to smoke but decided against a public announcement of her presence. Instead, she read the newspaper that she had purchased at the railway station and sat with it till the clock struck the time of her appointment. She went out and clambered onto a rickshaw.

'Chor Bagh. Kothiwallah.'

She alighted at the corner of the side road that led to the house at the end of the lane. It was had been many years since she had stood at the same spot with Sita on the night of the cricket riots, and she could still see ...

She started up the lane.

Outside 3, Chor Bagh, she halted. The gate was wide open. That was the sign for her to enter. She went in, and instead of proceeding towards the front porch, turned left. She climbed the two steps and entered the bedroom through the open door.

The door leading out to the corridor was bolted. On the bed, Som Devi sat with her legs outstretched, reading the Gita with her fingers. Didi noticed how small she had become. In profile, she drew a straight line. The swell of her bosom had shrunk. Her once thick hair was reduced to a bun the size of a golf ball. There was a translucence about her as though you might look right through her and see nothing.

The house was noiseless. Didi had difficulty breathing, taken aback by the loudness of the silence, the absence of Budhoo's barks.

Som Devi put down her book, took off her spectacles and sniffed.

'You might have changed the perfume. It tells everyone you are here. Not,' she added, sitting up at the edge of the bed, 'that there is anyone here. Still, I will have to Flit the room and use phenyl when you go.'

Didi paled with a momentary sickness: phenyl. She reached inside her purse.

'These are yours.' She approached Som Devi and dropped the envelope into her lap.

Som Devi kept her head down.

'We gave them to Baby.'

'No need. Let it remain, here, with the family.'

Som Devi picked up the envelope and held it out without raising her head.

'It is hers … her share.'

Didi kept her hands behind her back and said in a gentle voice, 'Let it remain with the family.'

'Speak up, one of my ears is bad enough without you speaking like a shy bride.'

With that, she rose in slow motion and went across to the mantlepiece and looked at the photographs. There was one of Som Devi's husband, another of her two sons and a third of Som Devi with Baby and Budhoo.

'Who are you to come between us?'

Didi wiped her upper lip with the pallu of her sari before pulling it across her chest.

'She is starting a new life. I want her to start without any of this.' She paused. 'Let us not hang around her as a reminder of what passed between us. And the book ... the store will fade into a memory.'

Som Devi drew a finger over Baby's figure in the photograph.

'Can any of us forget?'

Didi took a resolute step forward.

'I have come to return ... no, to restore the family to what it was before.'

'Before what?'

Didi's fingers trembled. To still them, she pressed them into her back.

'You must take these back,' she insisted.

'Wasn't Baby born in this house?'

Didi drew a deep breath.

'Baby was very fair as a child,' said Didi, 'with light honey eyes, long limbs, light,' she stopped, her fingers clenching into fists, 'such light hair as if the sun had dyed it just ...'

'... like her father's.' Som Devi turned her head and stared straight at Didi. 'Bilkul same to same. I don't doubt it.'

'That's why you must keep those.' Didi nodded at the envelope.

'I brought up Baby,' Som Devi replied, as though she had not heard Didi, clutching the edge of the mantlepiece and looking into the empty fireplace, 'when you were too busy making eyes at ...' She held up a hand as Didi began to speak. 'I oiled her, I bathed her, fed her, told her stories at night, played with her ... when you were away at the bookstore, doing your mischief. And in any case,' she raised her head and looked at Didi, 'my husband always said she looked just like me.'

'And what do you say?'

'Me? I say if you can bear the name of my family, why not your daughter? Blood isn't the only thing that makes families.' She kept her head very still. 'There's upbringing too.'

For a minute, there was silence. Didi leaned back against the wall.

'You knew.'

'Did you take me for a fool?'

Som Devi went to sit on the bed.

'Even as a little boy, Purush could never keep up his strength. I gave him tonics, juices, ayurvedic cures, took him to see many doctors, even to Vaishno Devi. Nothing worked. When you married, I thought maybe you would right him. A big strong woman. But you? You had already done what you had to before, and he became worse. Nothing there. Poor Purush, never a man.' She reached for her silver paan holder, picked out a piece of supari and put it in her mouth.

Didi crossed her chest with her arms as if holding onto herself.

'And there was Bhai, with his books and all that poetry nonsense. He never even looked at a girl. I showed him so many photographs, but nothing. Till he made big-big eyes at you. All wrong. Is it,' she turned back to Didi, 'wrong to want a grandchild? And Baby was such a beautiful child, I thought Purush wouldn't mind too much; I would look after him.'

Didi looked up.

'I found out too late about you and Bhai. Still, I thought, this time it will truly be a child of this family. Can you understand that?' Som Devi regarded the photographs. 'I prayed for a boy. One to carry on our name for one more generation.' She clasped her hands in prayer. 'I was greedy.'

Didi thought of the morning when Som Devi had entered her room and looked into the face of her grandson.

'We both did wrong, and the child ... born dead,' added Som Devi. She walked towards Didi. 'This story could never end happily. For Purush, or you,' Som Devi said as she picked up the envelope from the bed. 'Phir then Bhai and Baby still had a chance.'

She held it out to Didi.

'Purush?' inquired Didi, not moving.

Som Devi smiled almost wistfully.

'He doesn't know. At least,' she added, 'I have not told him, nor will Bhai and that … that wife of his. They are on Baby's side. I will deal with Purush.'

Didi took the outstretched envelope.

'You and I have too many secrets, little lies we tried to make into big truths,' she said, placing the envelope in her bag.

Som Devi stood aside as Didi stepped out into the veranda. She replied, 'Let it remain the only relationship between us.'

When Didi returned home, she summoned Baby to her room and closed the door behind her. She removed the bookstore deed papers from under her pillow and held them out to Baby. Baby looked at them and then at her mother.

'You're sure you want me to have them?'

'She … your grandmother … wants you to have them.'

'Oh, so …'

'Precisely. Now make the most of your inheritance.'

Baby took the swath of papers and brushed Didi's right cheek with them.

'Thank you.'

The days ahead were lazy and peaceful. It was winter and the season was still in beauty: the trees stood motionless against a cloudless, uneventful sky. The dogs slept on the steps, Kartik sat with Baby, speaking in such undertones, their words barely left their mouths. Even Sita's normal bustle had given way to a gentle amble.

Didi spent more time by herself, in her room, reading, listening to the radio. She wanted to stay out of Baby's way, let Baby and Kartik sort themselves out. She prayed to Mem that the phone would ring and Kartik would be called back to his foundation.

'About time he did some work.'

Sometimes, thought Didi, I wish I could control destiny.

'Not so hard,' she complained to Sita who pressed her legs. 'Your fingers have become like a steel ice-pick, they're biting into my skin.'

Sita ignored her.

It was an afternoon after a heavy meal: meat curry, rice, potatoes and ginger peas. Dessert was by Didi: her famous sooji ka halwa in orange juice with a splash of brandy. Baby had refused to eat it saying it still made her sick.

It was the ideal afternoon for a long sleep. Sita was looking forward to her warm bed.

'Thank you, Mem, thank you for being here with me,' Didi rambled on, directing Sita's hands to her thighs. 'Punch, punch. Thank you. Now, go away.'

Sita gave Didi's thigh a final slap.

'Day or night, never happy.' She put aside the curtain and peered outside, massaging her arms with oily hands. 'Hai hai, Mem.'

'Now what are they doing?'

Didi slid the petticoat down her thighs.

'Walking up and down.'

'Talking?'

'What else? You think a man and a woman walk up and down together in silence?'

Didi gave a pretend cackle. Then, abruptly, she got up, threw her pillow to the end of the bed and reversed her position. This way, she could see the driveway where they walked. Spy.

Baby held her head high; he stooped with hands behind his back. They did not appear to be conversing.

Didi closed her eyes and prayed hard.

The next day was Sunday. Didi scowled at the sun, at the breakfast table where she pushed away every dish on offer, at Baby who asked her to cheer up.

'Stop being such bad weather on a beautful day.'

'It's gorgeous. Now if only you would smile, it would be perfect,' flattered Kartik.

Didi frowned at her daughter, bestowed the full range of her teeth on Kartik and stalked out. Baby caught up with her in the corridor.

'Amma, are you sick? When did you see the doctor last? I told you ...'

'Nothing wrong but my mood.' Didi brushed past her daughter.

Baby placed delicate, tentative hands on Didi's shoulders to restrain her. Didi stopped, reached up and patted Baby's fingers absentmindedly.

'Cheer-beer,' she sighed, seeing Baby's paling face. 'Let's go to the hotel this evening and give Kartik a taste of that bitter medicine again. A martini always cheers me up.'

It was past eight o'clock when they returned. Sita, hunched on the veranda steps with a dog beside her – one front paw slung over the other, his tongue steely in the light of the neon bulb – demanded to know what had taken them so long and ordered them to wash their hands immediately. She was making puris for dinner and they had to be eaten 'hot-hot'.

Didi said she was not eating 'hot-hot' anything after the delicious ham sandwiches at the hotel.

'Pig,' sniffed Sita, 'ulti-making.'

'Ulti-making you.'

Baby told them to cease this talk of sickness. If Amma did not want to eat, then let her go to bed with a glass of warm milk. That would put her to sleep. 'Especially after three stiff martinis.'

'Hai hai, Mem, like in New York?'

Kartik, entering the conversation behind them, looked around in wonder.

Didi raised her finger at Kartik.

'Tell me, Kartik, did you hate the martinis?'

Pulling out his tongue, Kartik wiped it on his kurta sleeve.

'Tastes thhu, but the high is as tall as the Himalayas.'

'Mount Everest, here I come, ha ha.'

'Amma, bas.'

'One thing more, Kartik.'

'Huh?'

'You still wish to be with her?'

'I suppose …'

'Can you tell me why, after three martinis, very dry, with olives and crushed cucumber?'

'Like I said, Amma, you won't understand,' Baby interjected.

'Sure I will, sure I will. Wasn't I the one who waltzed with a crystal glass full of champagne on my head and a man in my arms at the Waldorf Astoria?'

'Stop, Amma, if you twirl like that, you will fall.'

'Kartik, tell Baby to mind her own business. We are waltzing.'

'Sita, coffee. Amma has had too much to drink.'

'Say Kartik, say: do you crave my daughter like a pregnant woman does a lemon pickle?'

'Amma …'

'Have you ever cared enough, Mrs …'

'Mrs? Who are you talking to? Call me Didi.'

'Call her Amma and be done.'

'Have you ever cared that much? Amma?'

'Cared? I could have danced all night, I couldn't care less tonight.'

'Amma, you'll trip him!'

'Young man, your dancing is a-trocious! Stamping on my toes, twisting my ankles. Here, Baby, take him away and teach him how to dance, the way I taught you.'

'Yes, Amma, as soon as I've helped you into bed.'

'Bed, bed, I never went to bed, not for all the—'

'Drink this water and, like I said, lie down. Stay there. Promise?'

'Baby?'

'Mmmm?'

'I blesh … you … both.'

'You don't believe in the gods, Amma.'

'True. Sho when I die, no mumbo-jumbo. Just light me up and lesh me go.'

'Yes, Amma.'

'Promise.'

'God promise. Now be still.'

The next morning, Kartik woke up with a thick envelope of bile on his tongue. His body was wrapped in a turgid, exhausted slumber from which his brain was unable to rouse itself completely. He held his hurting head and wondered why the martini hangover had sapped him of all strength.

Outside the window, the sunlight came through the foliage of the trees in thin stripes of light; the air smelt of burning ochre leaves. In the bath, Kartik splashed mugs of hot water on himself with complete abandon. He soaped himself twice. He scrubbed his skin with his nails till red welts stood out in protest.

'I could have danced all night, I couldn't care less tonight …' he sang, hoping to divert his attention from his throbbing temples. Through the smoky foam of soap and shampoo and hazy head, he thought of Didi dancing crookedly with him the previous night. Poor dancer, she had called him, but it was she who had tripped over his feet after three martinis, very dry.

Later, once Didi had gone to bed, he had joined Baby in her room. They confided in each other as they had done every night since he had arrived here. She spoke of Ramaji Rameshwar Rao, he of his foundation and his home and the night Miranda was dressed in her dinner.

They sipped brandy. Baby had kissed him on the chin once. Otherwise, she merely held his hand. When she had risen and stretched, her short blouse had crawled up the slope of her breasts, revealing the white lace of her bra and the expanse of her stomach covered in fine light brown hair. Kartik's face had been level with her navel and he reached out his tongue. Her arms fell, her hands clamped around his head. Kartik had breathed out very slowly and felt the pressure on his temples ease. He went to bed with the taste of her.

Now, in a light blue kurta and a sweater, his short curls swept back off his face, he went into the kitchen and made himself black coffee. Sipping from the mug, he walked down the corridor and saw Baby sprawled asleep. He went across to Didi's bedroom and through a gap in the door he saw her lying with her hands on her heart, her head inclined to the left. He smiled and shook his head. Then suddenly, on an impulse, he went back to the kitchen and emerged a few moments later with a tray.

'Good morning, good morning, chaiwallah, chai, chaiwallah chai,' he droned like the tea boys at railway stations, and stood outside Didi's door. When there was no response, he opened the door with his foot and entered the room. Sita was snoring on her bed. Placing the tray on the table, he repeated: 'Chaiwallah, chai, chaiwallah chai.'

Didi groaned, complained of exhaustion and her famous headache, and refused to stir. Sita grumbled that it was Didi's fault she was up late. She got off the side of her bed and still muttering '… never lets me sleep, never lets me do anything …' she rolled up her bedding and carried it out of the room.

Kartik and Baby sat without speaking in the hiss of the downpour that ensued. Kartik watched a fly cling to the sweetness of the empty teacup, then topple inside. Instantly, he remembered an afternoon, long ago in his Defence Colony barsati, when another fly had died in his coffee cup. Baby is here with me, so much lies between us, joining and separating us, and there are these flies that have learnt nothing from their ancestors, he thought, irritably rubbing his lips.

Time passed them by in raindrops. The dogs lay on the steps with their paws in the air.

All of a sudden, a jeep drew up outside the gate. It drove in without invitation and halted before them. The dogs rose, startled, and barked in challenge.

'Mrs …?' inquired a mustachioed man in a grey safari suit, climbing the steps with his eyes on a register. He turned to Kartik.

'Good morning. Forgive the interruption,' he folded his hands, 'but our business is urgent.'

'What is it?' demanded Baby as she stood up behind Kartik.

'Mr Kartik?'

Kartik stepped forward.

'That's me.'

'Sir. We are from the Crime Branch, Delhi. Gopal Gun, the man you assaulted …?'

'Huh?'

'He did not survive.'

Kartik reached for Baby's hand.

'Please make it convenient to come with us immediately.'
There was a wail from behind them.
'Hai hai, Mem!'

DELHI
1986

'Hai, hai, Mem.'
Gun's death had led the police to Didi's home. Kartik had yelled at the Crime Branch officer, shoving his face right into the officer's face so that it left a smudge on his spectacles. He refused to go quietly, enraged at the injustice, until the police said that the Miranda case was still open and being 'actively pursued'.

Baby squeezed his hand and told him to go, she would follow. If she had a future, she said to herself as Kartik reluctantly sat in the jeep, it was not in escape. It was not in the puzzles of the past, and it was certainly not in Ramaji Rameshwar Rao's house on the edge of a lake. It lay in the feel of another person's warm, rough hand holding hers.

Baby rang Ajay and explained everything to him. He said in a very superior way that Kartik would be questioned and held as a 'mere formality'.

'How long is a formality?'

'Who knows? He may have to go to jail, but he won't stay there long. Think of it as a weekend retreat, yaar. We will get him off either in a couple of hours or a few days max.'

'I'll be there.'

When Baby told Didi she was going, she merely nodded.

'Go' was all she said.

But before she went, Baby had to make one visit – to the man she had hated since she first met him. Baby went to bid farewell to Mr Hamer. He appeared more surprised by her decision to leave for Delhi than by her solitary visit to him.

'We could have had lunch and talked of the old times.'

He had mistaken her for Amma, realized Baby. His memory had lost its elasticity: it could stretch no further than the present.

As Baby turned away, she felt the warmth of his hand upon her shoulder.

'I would be very,' Mr Hamer said in his courtly fashion, 'happy if you came to live in the cottage. It is yours, yes, yours. Please, don't let it become lonely, like me, yes me, M.C. Hamer.'

In the presence of his generosity and forgetfulness, Baby was silent.

She arrived in Delhi on a blustery afternoon with a silver grey sky. She drove straight to the foundation. Men were gathered under the multi-coloured shamiana, and slogans could be heard. She swept past them with an arrogant glare.

She went up the stairs to Kartik's office. It was empty. She picked up the telephone and rang the long remembered number. There was no response. She got up and sat on the edge of the desk and lit a cigarette.

Two women walked in. They eyed her speculatively.

'Trouble, trouble,' observed Mrs Malhotra, 'soil and bubble ...'

'Boil,' corrected Mrs Singh, 'it is boil and bubble.'

'Same thing,' Mrs Malhotra threw at her.

'It's not.'

'Achcha, not in front of her.'

Baby asked if she could sit there for a while.

'Kartik knows?' Mrs Singh asked.

Baby nodded.

'I've come to do what I can for Kartik.'

Then, said Mrs Singh, 'a hatti-katti like you' was welcome. They could do with a strong girl. The three women laughed.

Mrs Malhotra considered Baby.

'So, you are Kartik's special.'

Baby had to laugh.

'Yes.'

'Bit too fair, if you ask me.'

Baby inclined her head.

Mrs Singh said she would make some tea. The two women left the room.

Baby redialled 3, Chor Bagh.

Someone picked up the receiver, but there was no answer.

'Hallo, hallo?' she yelled. Silence.

'Hallo! Hallo?'

There was some laboured breathing.

'Hallo? Can you hear me?'

'Who is it?'

Baby instantly recognized Purushottam's voice.

'Who's speaking?'

'I am calling from Delhi. Can I speak with Bhai Chacha?'

'He is not here.'

'Please give him a message?'

'Oh, what is it?'

'Just tell him, it's Baby.'

There was the sound of laughter, harsh, almost triumphant.

'Rubbish all! Baby? Didn't you leave us long ago?'

Baby decided to ignore this, pretend not to understand him.

There was more heaving.

'Please tell Bhai Chacha.'

'Oh, yes, your famous Bhai Chacha. He will want to know, won't he? Of course I will tell him. But don't be surprised if he doesn't want to meet the "American memsahib's baby". That,' he lowered his voice, 'Lobo? Seems he got there with her at last. Finally, we will have a child in this family. You understand?'

Baby sat with her elbows on the table.

'Listen, Purushottam,' she licked her lips, 'I am delighted for Bhai Chacha and if he should ever come to Delhi, he must get in touch.'

'He never goes anywhere. Like me. We stay with our own.'

Click went the receiver.

Baby smiled and lit another cigarette, glad she had made the phone call: maybe one day Bhai Chacha would come with Lobo Chachi and their child. Maybe they might just be a family.

It was possible.

She had changed. Amma had become gentler. And Purush and she had conducted a conversation for the first time in her entire life.

Baby laughed.

'Rubbish all.'

HILL STATION
1987

'Rubbish all.'

It was dark. The sun had still to make itself known to the day. Didi lay upon her bed, gasping for breath as though she had been on the run forever. The previous week had been too much for her. She felt the overwhelming sense of the moment so acutely, she couldn't breathe. Sita returned from the bathroom with the medicine tin.

'Get me some warm milk,' Didi rasped.

'First time I hear you asking for milk,' grumbled Sita, leaving the room.

She returned within a few minutes, carrying a steel glass of milk that she placed on the table. Didi lay back and told herself to relax. Everything was better than it had been before Baby's return from New York. She had settled the past with Som Devi, the future had looked after itself with Baby and Kartik's reunion. The present was the perfect moment, balanced just so between the past and the future. She held on to it, knowing she would never recapture it. Now, if only the pain near her heart would go away.

'Your milk is growing cold.'

Didi sat up. She reached out for a bottle of tablets on the bedside table.

'Tell me again, why did we do what we did?' she asked, dropping a few tablets into her palm.

'That Mataji was right: you are mad.'

'Sita, this is a wonderful moment. Don't spoil it with your cheek. Also, I don't feel upto listening to your nonsense. It hurts, right there,' she thumped her chest.

'My time will come before yours; why you are complaining?'

'No, you're like a tree – old but sturdy. You will live for Baby and her children.'

'Oh no, she has Kartik and I am not bringing up any more children. You and Baby, enough.'

'Everyone needs a Sita.'

'Don't butter me.'

Didi burped.

'And don't say ulti, or I'll go.'

'Go, go, all of us have to go.'

Sita got up and left the room.

Didi dozed off. When she awoke and gazed outside the window, the first light of day had begun to illumine the garden. Unable to resist, she slipped on her chappals and hurried outside to sit in the wicker chair. She heard Sita behind her.

'These trees bear little fruit. I want you to plant a mango tree for me there,' she pointed to a sunlit corner in the orchard, 'and make sure you make a good chutney, like I have taught you, not that mess you make.'

'Hai hai, Mem, how long must I suffer her?' said Sita from the doorway.

'You know what?'

'What?'

'You and I have a long way to go. We will meet in the next life and if you are very lucky, I will be your ayah.'

'You? You are not fit to be an ayah.'

'Or you a memsahib. Good then, massage my legs. That is your curse for seven lives.'

Sita began to stroke Didi's thigh with a gentle hand. Didi opened her mouth for a huge yawn, rubbed her eyes. The two women remained thus. The two dogs slumbered, with occasional dismissive twitches.

Sita began to hum to herself. Didi smiled, recognizing the tune.

It spells the thrill of first-nighting ... she sang.

Dreamers with empty hands,
They sigh for exotic lands,

It's autumn in New York,
It's good to live it again.
'Always Noo Ark with you,' observed Sita.
Didi sighed.

'Who would have thought then, we would both end up here together, in a small town, with two pye-dogs for male companions! That we would do all the things we did ... ah!' she squealed as Sita pinched her thigh. 'Yes, it's been a life.'

'Ssshhh, you're always talking ... you and Baby, never just looking at the beautiful morning.'

They subsided once more into the silence of the scene. For a long time, neither spoke or moved.

Finally, one of the dogs yawned, rose, shook off his stupor and yowled. Sita sighed, nudged Didi.

'Tell me the story of Sita's pholly, once again, Didi, tell, na ...'

Her request was met by silence.

'Didi?'

Still no response.

Sita glanced back: Didi's eyes were closed, her face in calm repose, her head to one side. She rose and peered into Didi's face.

'Didi?' She shook her by the shoulder, anxious.

As she did so, she heard a raucous sound and fell back.

In the warmth of that winter morning, Didi was snoring.

Acknowledgements

With gratitude to everyone at 33-B Friends Colony East. To my brother Ishwari for always watching over me and bullying me into writing a novel; to my sister-in-law Divya and my niece Aditi who have always believed in me and supported me in all I do; to my brother Kanti; to my nephews, Shiva and Rudra and my niece Gayatri for always being there for me. To 'Aunty' Sheila Prasad for her love, her home and my first PC.

This book would not have been possible without the invaluable contributions and criticism of my 'editor' friends and hard taskmasters, Shaila Misra and Padmini Mongia, whose advice I mostly followed. Many thanks to Maneesha Dube for a very careful reading of the book. I would also like to thank my friends Ayesha Kagal, Sameera Jain and Sanghamitra Singh, as well as my cousin Indu Liberhan for vetting the book for errors.

I am grateful to Nandini Mehta, Renuka Chatterjee and Sanjeev Saith for believing in the book right at the start. My thanks to Namrata Bhatter for designing such a lovely cover.

To my friend Naresh Sawhney and Alex, my wonderful dog, both of whom I miss.

To all my family and all my friends who have been like family, especially Ranee Sahaney, Divya Puri, Purnima Bhalla, Ira and Uday Bhasker, Kishwar Desai and Gopika Nath.

I would like to thank Shekhar Gupta for his longstanding support and Akhila Sivadas for hers.

Last but not the least, to the entire team at HarperCollins India, especially to Prema Govindan for her painstaking proofing of the manuscript and for teaching me arithmetic and, finally, to my editor, V.K. Karthika for her unfailing good sense and good humour. She has kept the faith.

APRADHINI
women without men

TRANSLATED BY
Ira Pande

A SEARING COLLECTION OF LIFE-STORIES FROM THE HEART OF INDIA

The earth-eating Muggi, groomed by her brother-in-law, cons fourteen men into marrying her and runs off with their money, but falls in love with the fifteenth and eagerly awaits the day she will be released from prison so that she can return to him.

The intimidating Vaishnavi pushes a buffalo, her cruel mother-in-law and husband over the edge of a ravine and spends the rest of her life punishing herself, wandering from place to place, homeless and penniless.

In this collection of sketches of ordinary women with extraordinary pasts, we read of women whose lives have been changed because of men, women who now survive on the fringes of society – or outside it.

Compassionate without ever straying into sentimentality, Shivani's histories of the formidable women whose lives she chronicled strike a chord in our hearts even today, forty years after they were first written. A few of her short stories, inspired by these women, also form part of this brilliant translation from the Hindi by her daughter and award-winning translator Ira Pande.

STEALING KARMA
Aneesha Capur

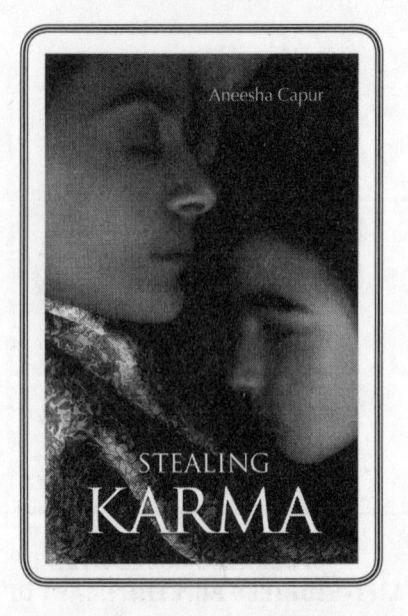

'You keep your trust in me,' Wairimu said.
*'No harm will come to this baby who is
of your womb and of my land.'*

Brought up in a convent in India and married to a man who has made Nairobi his home, Mira knows no life beyond the walls of her bungalow, until the phone rings one day and a voice informs her that her husband has died.

In the midst of an attempted military coup, Mira is left without any income and with a young child to support. Her response is to withdraw into herself, and it is left to Wairimu, their African housekeeper, to bring up Shanti. While Mira searches for memories from pasts that are not quite hers, Shanti struggles to make sense of her mother's seeming indifference as she rapidly approaches adulthood.

Set against the vast landscape of modern Africa, Aneesha Capur's debut novel is a beautifully crafted tale of a mother and daughter coming to terms with their history even as they grapple with their precarious present.

Witness
the Night

Kishwar Desai

WINNER of the
2010 COSTA FIRST NOVEL AWARD

Durga. A fourteen-year-old girl, found all alone in a sprawling house in Punjab. Silent, terrified, and the sole suspect in the mass murder of thirteen members of her family.

Simran. A whisky-swigging, chain-smoking social worker from Delhi. She is Durga's sole hope, for Simran is the only one who believes that she may be more a victim than a suspect.

As Simran tries to unravel the mystery of what really happened that night of the multiple murders, she comes in close and often uncomfortable contact with Jullundur and its people, from Durga's enigmatic tutor Harpreet and his disfigured wife to the picture-perfect high-society Amrinder and her superintendent husband Ramnath. The prejudices she encounters are deep-seated and the secrets manifold. And Simran knows she cannot rest until she has uncovered the whole truth.

A chilling first novel that gets to the heart of tradition-bound India.